Storm Damage

A Sonny Marshall Thriller

Terry R. Bacon

ISBN: 979-8-9880748-6-1 (ebook)

ISBN: 979-8-9880748-7-8 (paperback)

ISBN: 979-8-9880748-8-5(hardback)

Cover design by: Nick Castle

Printed in the United States of America

To learn more about Sonny, visit www.sonnymarshall.com or www.terryrbacon.com

Writing a book is a solitary activity, but you need many supporters to keep you on track, ensure that the result is engaging, and keep you from committing the kinds of errors that make you look like an amateur. I have been blessed to be surrounded by a wonderful team of supporters.

First, Debra is remarkable both as my life's companion and as an excellent proofreader and critic. She is first to highlight mistakes and tell me what is exciting, boring, or simply too common an expression. Linda is one of the best proofreaders I've ever had. She is thorough and persnickity in the best possible way, and she's a good friend. Thanks to my many other readers, including Chris, Kim, Wilson, Kim (yes, another one—and a great friend), Fritz, and others who have been kind enough to read the draft and offer comments, suggestions, and, occasionally, praise. They improved this novel through their patience, perseverance, and friendly persuasion.

There is no good and evil, there is only power and those too weak to seek it.   —Lord Voldemort

Destroy the seed of evil, or it will grow up to your ruin.   —Aesop

The belief in a supernatural source of evil is not necessary; men alone are quite capable of every wickedness.   —Joseph Conrad

Perhaps evil isn't a cosmological riddle, only just selfish human behavior, and this behavior the result of conscious, accountable choice.   —Joyce Carol Oates

Never trust a chef who won't eat his own cooking.   —Sonny Marshall

Dark Ain't Deep Enough

Le'Andra Kimani

You can't hide from me, baby
Can't slip my mind
You ain't find no cover, honey,
After bein' unkind.

You won't see me comin, uh-uh
Ain't nowhere to go.
Dark ain't deep enough, darlin'
You can't slip me, no.

Seen both sides of you, baby,
Seen that sleight of hand.
Heard all your lies, tellin'
'Bout a promised land.

Said you'd always love me
From your head down to your toe
Dark ain't deep enough, darlin'
You can't slip me, no.

Caught you double-crossin'
Sliding into the night.
Sayin' you're sorry, honey,
Don't make nothing right.

Someday soon goan' find you.
It don't matter where you go.
Dark ain't deep enough, darlin'
You can't slip me, no.

No, you can't slip me, no.
Can't slip me, no.
Can't slip me, no.

Contents

Prologue

An ocher haze covered Sacramento like a shroud, smoke from a wildfire in the Mendocino National Forest north of the city. The smoke had thickened overnight, black specks suspended in the air like pepper. Bob Duggins coughed when he opened his garage door and stored his golf clubs in the trunk of his Toyota Mirai. His chest tightened, a reminder of the childhood asthma he thought he'd outgrown. Inside his car, it didn't smell like he was downwind of a campfire, so he took a deep breath. Despite the air quality alert, Bob was determined to make it a good day. Before meeting his buddies for eighteen holes, he stopped at the Old Town Roasting Company, his favorite coffee shop, and ordered coffee and a pastry. While he waited for his order, he took a call from his wife and assured her he'd be home by four. Then he enjoyed the steaming cup of a dark roast blend and a creamy raspberry Danish with fruit so thick and sweet it felt like a sugar bomb had exploded in his mouth. The oozing jam was the perfect complement to the soft crunch of the pastry.

The head rush came when he left the coffee shop. He held out his arms to steady himself as a pressure wave swept through his head and settled in his teeth. He admonished himself for indulging in the Danish. Too much of a carb load, he decided, but it would pass when he was on the links. Traffic was heavier than suited him as he turned onto the Capital City Freeway and drove west toward the Castle Oaks Golf Course in the town of Ione. He couldn't tell if the haze was thicker toward Ione, but the farther he drove, the denser the air seemed. His face felt warm, and he swooned momentarily, shaking his head to clear the clutter. His eyes had developed a slow burn, and he rubbed them to get the sting out. He turned on the radio but couldn't find a station he liked. Then, a driver in the right lane ahead honked his horn, a blistering shriek that pierced Bob's ears like an arrow. Another shriek, and Bob floored his accelerator to surge ahead of the idiot. He had to punch his brakes to keep from slamming into a blue van in front of him, and he clenched the steering wheel in white-knuckled annoyance.

"Keep outta my way," he yelled at the blue van. Feeling the juice, he yelled again at no one in particular. No one could hear him, but he smiled at his sudden bravado. Bob was the president of a branch of the Bank of America. He was usually a quiet man, reserved and patient, taking care not to offend customers or upset employees, no matter what mistakes they made.   As blood surged through his head this morning, though, he felt bolder, uncompromising. "Assholes," he muttered. All of them. Everyone in his way. Everyone on this road. He rolled down his window to get some air, but the acrid fumes blowing in made him start hacking, so he cranked it up again. "Assholes," he repeated, grinning as though he'd just discovered the word and liked the sound of it. He whipped his head around to see if anyone was crowding him. Then he rolled his window back down, sticking his left arm out, waving other vehicles away. That motion made him swerve to the right, and he nearly clipped a red car in the lane beside him.

"Asshole" he screamed at the driver, an old bald guy with bulging eyes and a mouth frozen in surprise. Bob pounded the wheel and then gave the driver the finger. He watched in his mirror as the red car slowed and turned off at the next intersection. Bob laughed hysterically, bouncing in his seat and slapping the steering wheel. "Don't fuck with me," he screamed into the wind streaming through his window.

Then a jacked-up Chevy with chrome tailpipes pulled up on Bob's left, driven by some chunky Hispanic dickhead with long black hair and a mustache, the kind of guy Bob realized he hated. The guy's windows were open, and he was blasting godawful rap music at full volume. "Turn that shit off," Bob screamed at him. The arrogant prick gave Bob the finger and roared ahead, his stinking tailpipes coughing up pollution. Bob's brain boiled, his ears burning, his eyes spitting fire like roadside flares. He jerked his Mirai into the left lane and followed as the guy pulled onto Folsom and then drove into the parking lot at the Folsom Boulevard Flea Market. As he watched the dickhead park his car and open his door, Bob reached into his glove compartment and pulled out his Kimber Rapide 1911, the Cadillac of 45s. Bob was a banker and worried about being kidnapped and held for ransom. That had happened to another bank president in Los Angeles two years before, so Bob kept the loaded weapon and two extra clips of ammo in his car. He'd taken shooting lessons and was comfortable with the automatic, although he hoped he'd never have to use it. Today, the gun felt solid in his hand. Like an extension of his arm, an extension of himself, an implement of his will.

He opened his door and stepped out, shoved the two extra clips into his front pocket, and fumed at the dickhead from the Chevy strolling carefree through the crowd. "Don't walk away from me, you piece of shit," Bob yelled. The guy turned, a superior smirk on his face, and Bob aimed and squeezed the trigger. His hand snapped up with the boom of the shot, and a red rosette appeared on the guy's abdomen. Bob fired again, and people nearby screamed and stampeded away. The guy stumbled toward Bob, another rosette blooming on his upper chest, twin tides of red staining his white shirt. His mouth snapped open and shut, and then his legs turned to mush, and he plunged forward, smacking the concrete like a bat hitting a ball.

Bob's head was on fire. The screams were deafening, a wall of noise so loud it gushed like Niagara Falls through his ears, and people were running, slamming into each other, some knocked to the ground, clawing the pavement in frenzied escape. Hatred surged through Bob like red-hot lava, and he fired again, striking a woman carrying a limp child, then again into a mass of people huddled in a used book stall, their uncomprehending faces frozen in terror. Then Bob was swept forward into the maelstrom as though being sucked into a jet engine. He plunged through clothing stalls, around tables strewn with antiques, past taco places, burrito stands, and tents filled with people ducking behind racks of t-shirts. Passing a mannequin in a wedding dress, he gleefully splintered its head and fired randomly at people running pell-mell through the passage ahead. He fired the last bullet in his clip at a clump of people hiding under a counter topped with western boots, tossed away the empty clip, and rammed in a full one. Thick smoke washed over him from a fire that had started in a food stall where a barbeque had overturned. He ducked away from the smoke and flames, spied people stuffing themselves under a food truck, and started toward them. Then a large man lurched in front of him, blocking his way, a black man waving a handgun. He yelled something Bob couldn't hear, and Bob shot the bastard in the face and picked up the man's chrome revolver when he tumbled backward onto the pavement.

With spittle dripping from his mouth and eyes full of rage, Bob plunged deeper into the flea market, under tents with striped awnings, past fruit markets, picnic tables, and an adobe pizza oven. Some people sought refuge under cloth skirts covering tables piled with goods. Bob fired the revolver through the skirts, heard muffled cries, and saw panicked people scrambling beyond the tables, toppling racks of greeting cards and careening into merchandise that exploded like fireworks. Then, above the din of screams and cries, he heard distant sirens growing louder. Let the cops come, he seethed. He'd kill as many as he could. He crawled underneath a long green counter decked with colorful bucket hats and baseball caps, sliding into the darkness beside a Hispanic girl with weepy eyes and a trembling mouth. He pointed his Kimber at her forehead and warned her to keep her fucking mouth shut. Then, as a searing headache torched his soul, he lay in ambush, cocksure and angry as hell.

The detective sergeant was a quarter of a mile away investigating a lead in the Campus Commons residential area when she heard the radio call about shots fired in the Folsom Boulevard Flea Market. Dispatch reported multiple casualties, adding that 911 callers could still hear shots fired. It was a Code 3 situation, and all units in the area were ordered to respond. She hurried to her car, opened the trunk, and fumbled with her body armor, willing herself to calm down. After strapping on her vest, she sped across the American River toward Folsom. When she arrived, one patrol car blocked the exit to the parking lot while others drove inside. She parked behind the patrol cars and observed a half-dozen uniformed officers putting on their body armor while panicked civilians rushed out of the market. Ahead of her, she saw two bodies lying in smears of red on the pavement.

Two years ago, the protocol would have been for patrol officers to secure the scene and wait for SWAT to arrive and assume tactical command. Now, after lessons learned from Parkland, Uvalde, and scores of other mass shootings throughout the country, the first officers on the scene no longer waited. The situation was dynamic and ongoing as long as the shooter was active, and a market like this was a target-rich environment. On weekends, thousands of people shopped at Folsom Boulevard's 450 stalls. The market covered a large area, its passages like clogged arteries between buildings, tents, and vehicles. The fluff and clutter of merchandise offered perfect cover and concealment for a gunman more determined to murder than escape. The overwhelming characteristic of any active shooter situation is panic; the sergeant felt it herself. A dozen thoughts blitzed through her mind, and she read fearful uncertainty in the faces of her fellow officers. The highest-ranking patrolman was a corporal, which made her the ranking officer on the scene, so she assumed command. She reminded them that their priority was to neutralize the shooter and then to protect their own lives and the lives of people near the shooter. They should not stop for victims but should radio where victims are located.

They had gathered at the southern entrance to the market. A single, long passage bisected the market from there to the northern boundary. To the left of the central passage were four long green buildings housing hundreds of vendor stalls; on the right, tall electrical towers stood like sentries over a hundred more tented stalls and food trucks. She directed the corporal to take two officers and advance into the buildings on the left while she and two others searched to the right of the central passage. In the noise, chaos, and confusion, a flood of terrified people rushed out of the flea market. Some ran for their cars; others ran past the officers, ducked behind vehicles, or streamed toward Folsom. The entrance to the market was now a bottleneck. No vehicles could leave—a criticism later leveled at the police—but the entrance had to be clear for arriving police, SWAT, EMTs, and firefighters.

As she raced past the first rank of tented stalls, she heard more shots somewhere in the pandemonium ahead. Dozens of frightened people huddled in the stalls around her. When they saw her wearing body armor with her gun drawn, some cowered in place; others slinked past her toward the parking lot. She yelled, "Did anyone see the shooter?" Most kept fleeing, but one man barked that it was a white guy with short red hair. She radioed that description to her fellow officers, and one radioed back that a witness said the suspect was middle-aged and wore a yellow-striped shirt. After that, the squawking on the radio was nearly constant, and she reminded everyone to keep it to essential communication.

Flames from an overturned barbeque had sparked a fire that roared through a clothing stall. Smoke now billowed over an area thirty yards ahead, and she saw flames shooting up over some tents. The heat had created its own microclimate, black smoke swirling in cyclic clouds over the electrical towers, the fluttering air lifting ash and embers. She darted forward, scanning as rapidly as caution allowed, and saw patches of blood splatter, overturned tables poking out of stalls, a collapsed tent partially covering a body, and a riot of goods strewn as though savaged by a tornado. Ten yards ahead, a cluster of people rushed across the pathway, away from the fire. They scurried, hunched over, a father sheltering three children. Two shots pursued them, and the father stumbled, dropping one shoulder, but remained upright. The shooter had to be to the left beyond the fleeing family, so the sergeant ran another fifteen feet, kneeling beside a food truck where a victim lay prone by the front tire, a hole punched through his shirt, surrounded by a pool of blood. She felt for a pulse and, finding none, radioed the location.

Amid the bedlam of screaming and shouting, she heard the sound of the fire itself, bellowing as it raced through clothing stalls and magazine racks. A muted series of pops punctuated the roar of the fire as superheated bottles and cans exploded. She thought they might be gunshots but then saw a bottle explode and could tell the difference between that sound and gunfire. The corporal leading the officers on the left side radioed that they had cleared two buildings and not found the shooter but that the shooting seemed to have stopped. She radioed for the advancing officers to proceed with caution. A lull in the shooting could mean that he was reloading, had run out of easy targets, or had committed suicide. The radio squawked again, and she learned that SWAT was now on the scene and was moving toward her. Following them were EMTs and firefighters. Then a staccato series of shots ahead to her left told her that the gunman hadn't killed himself. She burst from her position beside the food truck and ran toward a stall packed with toys and children's clothing. A green counter lay ahead, topped with colorful hats.

The first slug hit her squarely in the chest, stunning her and knocking her backward. The impact drove her off her feet, but she was still upright when the second slug caught her in the ribs and spun her in a quarter circle. The pain was so blistering she could think of nothing but to get out of the line of fire, hit the deck, and hope she was out of sight. She felt like she'd lost control of the situation and didn't know if she still held her weapon. Then a third slug struck her in the left thigh and yanked that leg out from under her. She collapsed onto her back just feet from the toy stall, which had now burst into flames. Her thigh stung and convulsed like it was trying to shake off a demon. She had the presence of mind to cover the sticky wound with her hand, but blood still pulsed between her fingers.

Through the roar of the fire, she heard someone shout, "Officer down, officer down!" Seconds later, two people in black armor rushed past her, and she heard a burst of gunfire and men screaming. Burning canvas whipped overhead, and she felt the tremor of collapsing stalls beside her. She knew the flames were closer because her shoes felt like they were roasting her feet. She wanted to crawl away but couldn't move. The sky grew dimmer, heavy smoke smothering her like a thick blanket on a hot night. Then someone grabbed her arm, and she felt herself being dragged until everything she saw, heard, and felt was eclipsed by darkness.

Gravity

I was staring down the barrel of a Polymer 80 automatic. I knew it was a P80 because of its distinctive rachet assembly on the barrel's undercarriage. This one was a dull gray with a black grip. The guy holding it was a mid-twenties black man with lips as thin and cruel as a paper cut. He had squat eyebrows that didn't reach the outsides of his eyes and a thin, bisected mustache that didn't connect under the tip of his nose. He looked like his face was assembled from mismatched parts—a Mr. Potato Head of the criminal kind.

"Fucka you?" he mumbled, as in "Who the fuck are you?"

The Storm Lake Blues Band was playing that night at Dylan's in North Beach. I'd parked near The Stinking Rose restaurant on Columbus. I was walking toward Dylan's carrying my saxophone case when I saw a Middle America couple half a block ahead step hesitantly into an alley. They looked too uncomfortable in North Beach at twilight to be locals, and walking into an alley was totally not tourist behavior. As I approached the alley, I saw them standing still deeper in the alley, facing the opposite brick wall. The woman had grayish-brown hair combed back in a ponytail and wore white slacks with a dark green sweater. Her husband wore a blue windbreaker and jeans. He had a sharp nose and a smooth pate except for a skullcap of dark hair on the back of his head. His right arm was extended toward someone I couldn't yet see.

When I reached the alley, I slowed down. The air was still and smelled like burnt umber. A quick glimpse told me they were facing one other man. Pretending I hadn't noticed him, I raised my free hand, stepped toward the couple, and chirped, "Hi Larry. Susan. I thought we were going to meet—"

Feigning surprise, I stopped abruptly when I saw the black guy. "What's going on? What—"

The mugger waved me into the alley. I took three tentative steps toward him, set down my sax case, and edged between him and the couple. He pointed the P80 at me.

"Fucka you?" he mumbled.

"I'm, uh, just meeting my, uh, friends." He had Larry's wallet in his hand. He shoved it into the left pocket of a greasy black bomber jacket.

"Gimme you wallet," he said, waving the fingers of his left hand toward me.

The alley was brick on all three sides. One closed door a dozen feet away led into the building behind the mugger. The alley was empty except for a stack of boxes along the back wall. That was good news. The line of fire was clear to the right, and the mugger was right-handed. He wasn't hesitant or nervous. He'd done this before, and the P80 was steady in his hand. Then he dipped the barrel slightly and said, "Fuckin' deaf?"

I turned my butt so he could see my back pocket. Then, carefully, with just my right thumb and index finger, I reached in for my wallet and handed it to him. That move should have communicated that I wasn't an average mark, but he didn't react except to add my wallet to his pocket.

"Waz in that?" he said, waving the P80's barrel toward my sax case.

I looked down at the case and then back at the P80. He had his finger on the trigger, not along the trigger guard, which is the safe way to hold a handgun. He could squeeze the trigger with minimal effort. My death could even be a mistake. A little twitch. That was bad news. And if this skank killed me, he wouldn't give a damn about the life he took. His only thought would be getting away with it. In my urban dictionary, that's the definition of evil.

I probably couldn't disarm him without the handgun discharging. His finger's on the trigger—fact of life. I didn't need to rehearse my moves. I'd practiced the gun-in-your-face defense five hundred times on a Krav Maga mat, but shit happens, and my mouth turned metallic as I considered what could go south in the next few minutes. I needed him to be off guard, and playing the cowardly lion from *The Wizard of Oz* is usually a good strategy with guys who think a gun makes them king.

"A saxophone," I said. It was a Yamaha YAS 62. I'd had it for four months. "Look, take my money, okay, no problem, but I'm a musician. I'm playing tonight. I need that," I said, circling to my left so the tourists were no longer behind me.

"Waz it worth?" he said, following me with his weapon while I pleaded.

"It cost me four grand, but—"

"My four gran now," he said, grinning at his good fortune. In his mind, he was already high on angel powder or meth or whatever flipped his switch.

While he congratulated himself, I ducked at light speed and launched both hands up toward the automatic, my thumbs interlaced. As I twisted the barrel toward the back of the alley, the gun fired with a resounding boom, the bullet striking the brick wall above me and ricocheting into the dead space deep in the alley. Simultaneously, I planted my right foot and kicked him in the groin with my left. As he doubled over, I wrenched the gun away, held it with my left hand, and pulled sharply down on his thumb with my right hand. His hyperextended thumb snapped, and he raised his head and howled. I took the rest of the fight out of him by jamming the palm of my right hand into his chin in an uppercut that drove his head back into the wall behind him. I didn't hit him hard enough to kill him, but he instantly had a mother of a migraine. He sank into the brick, the entirety of his world now focused on three points of pain.

I set the P80 on the pavement and stepped on it with my left foot. Then I turned to Larry and said, "Call 911." I gave him our location and told them to hang tight. His wife wanted to get the wallets from the mugger's jacket, but I told her to wait for the police. In less than a minute, a black and white screeched to a stop outside the alley, and two uniforms jumped out. I knew the senior cop. Jerry Worcester, a brother with pointed ears, short black hair smooth as an eight ball, and a luminous smile, teeth whiter than piano keys.

He flashed that smile when he recognized me. "Sonny Marshall. I'll be damned. You fightin' crime again?"

"Somebody's got to do it," I said. "Can't depend on the cops."

"Show some respect," he replied in mock offense. Then he turned to his partner, a younger Latino with maybe a year on the job. "Hector, you know Sonny Marshall?" Hector didn't. "Man's a crime-fighting legend." He was referring to an incident last year when Kat Hastings and I recovered two missing girls and hundreds of other children who'd been kidnapped by people who wanted to create a master race.

"Just a musician," I said.

Jerry flashed that smile again, and the corners of his eyes crinkled. "So what do we have here, Mr. Sax Man?" I told Jerry and Hector what happened and learned that the tourists were Robert and Denise Bauer from Madison, Wisconsin. Jerry bent and turned the mugger's head to get a good look. "Well, if it ain't Da'Mar Franklin. Da'Mar, what's your sorry ass doin' out of jail?"

Da'Mar's waxy skin was coated in misery, and he had nothing to say.

"Here's his piece," I said, lifting my left foot. Jerry took a plastic evidence bag from his back pocket and used it to pick up the P80 by the barrel. He removed the clip without touching the grip and examined the gun as he sealed the bag.

"No serial number," he noted.

"I didn't think so," I said. The Polymer 80 is a kit gun and is illegal in California unless it is registered and has a serial number. Da'Mar's was a ghost gun. Possessing it is a felony, along with criminal threatening, armed robbery, and unlawful discharge of a firearm. Da'Mar was in serious shit, and his thumb was broken. He wouldn't be using a handgun for a while. I told Jerry he'd stuffed our wallets in his left jacket pocket. Jerry removed them and took photos of the wallets, me, Da'Mar Franklin, and the Bauers. Then he handed back our wallets. I showed him where the bullet took a chunk out of the brick wall and then ricocheted into the back of the alley.

"How'd he get a shot off?" Jerry said. "You losin' your touch?"

"His finger was on the trigger. Couldn't avoid it. But I sent the bullet out of harm's way."

"Lucky."

"Skill."

Jerry surveyed the alley and nodded. "Confined space. Yeah. But we don't like citizens firing weapons in our fair city," he said, shaking a finger at Da'Mar. Then he turned to me. "You playin' tonight?"

"Dylan's."

"All right, brother. Hector's takin' all this down. He'll type up a statement, and we'll see what these fine folks, the Bauers, have to say. We'll catch you later to sign the statement. Go play some blues."

I thanked him and then gave my card to the Bauers. I told them where to find Dylan's if they wanted good food and music. "Tell Josette you're friends of mine. Show her my card, and she'll comp you a drink." They were still shaken by what happened, but they thanked me, and I picked up my sax and left the alley. An ambulance pulled up as I turned toward Dylan's and kept walking.

I didn't spend much time dwelling on Da'Mar Franklin, but I wondered what unfortunate circumstances led him to that alley in North Beach. His was a familiar slog through tenement hallways, crack houses, and rehab clinics, and when his life story was written, it would appear in case files and murder books. Ripping off tourists to feed your addiction is not a redemptive vocation, and it has a short half-life. Trouble would be ground into Franklin's soul like dogshit beneath a shoe heel, but he has choices. We always have choices.

Dylan's is an intimate jazz and blues club with a small, half-circle stage surrounded by tables and booths along the back walls. Bathed in red light, the club feels warm and exotic. Josette Lyons, the owner, serves overpriced tapas and gourmet cocktails, craft beers, and expensive wine. She prefers soft music and doesn't have a dance floor. She wants people to linger, have a mellow evening—and spend money, which they do. Some patrons claim a table through all four sets, ending the night with their eyes closed, heads drifting, fingers still tapping to the beat. Josette has taxis lined up outside when the doors close.

I was the last band member in the green room behind the stage. K.C. Vaughn, our keyboardist, sat on a bench in the corner, playing air riffs with his eyes closed. The lime slice in a glass of clear liquid beside him told me he was drinking Bombay Sapphire and tonic. Garth Wyman, our drummer, gave me a high five when I entered, and I told him about the incident in the alley while I took out my sax and limbered up by fingering the keys. Garth co-owned Wyman Brothers Motors in Oakland, the top motorcycle chop shop in the Bay Area, and he and a ragtag army of bikers helped Kat and me rescue those children in New Mexico. Garth and I were close before that, but now we were brothers in arms, having forged the bond you can only get when you've faced conflict with someone. Soldiers who've fought beside each other in combat get it. So do first responders who've been in life-or-death situations together. Trauma bonding happens when you've crawled through hell with somebody and know what they'd sacrifice to save you. In our band, that's how it is with Garth and me.

Eric Young, our guitarist, sat on a sofa on the other side of the room, cradling his Gibson L5. The L5 is a classic. Wes Montgomery played an L5. So did jazz great Pat Martino before he switched to a Benedetto. Eric's L5 was an archtop hollow acoustic that produces a soft, resonant tone like orchestral strings, or as Eric was fond of saying, "mellow as a cello." He polished the finish with a soft cloth while tuning the strings with his ear. If he had a child, he wouldn't treat it better than he treated that instrument.

Eric looked more like a jazz musician than the rest of the band. He had sleepy chestnut eyes, a wispy mustache and goatee, and short black hair behind a broad, mahogany forehead. Triangular gold earrings hung from his earlobes, and he had an other-worldly air of insouciance like even the Second Coming wouldn't raise his pulse. But tonight, he was more glassy-eyed than usual. Eric snorted coke. He didn't have a monopoly on vices, but Eric's addiction was escalating. We'd just completed a three-month tour. Thirty-two cities, eighty-eight performances, repetitive interviews and media events, and way too many bus rides, hotel rooms, coin laundries, and album signings. Compounding that misery was fast food, loneliness, and the monotony of playing the same setlist night after night. To the uninitiated, touring with a band seems glamorous. It's not. The pace pounds your life to sludge unless you're like Taylor Swift and have an army of handlers doing everything for you.

Eric's refuge was cocaine. Not that I'm an angel. I scored too much oxy on the tour. A head-on with a drunk a dozen years ago wiped out my Harley and left me with a knee the surgeons have never gotten right. Without oxy, the pain latches onto you like a conjoined twin. I tell myself I'm handling it, but when you talk to yourself in a cracked mirror, you don't know which side of your face to believe.

But if I was still standing on two feet, Eric was slipping deeper into the quicksand. Our bass-playing band leader, Xavier McQueen, sat beside him, speaking quietly into his ear. Eric nodded by moving his head in a slow circle, but I doubt anything the X-man said penetrated Eric's cool. He looked as dazed as the day we returned to San Francisco on our final bus drive. Still, Eric has always been a consummate performer when we step on stage. He pulls it together like a sad comedian smiling when he approaches the mic.

We were well known in the Bay Area, and when we walked on stage, we caught some applause from a nearly full house. The wait staff was busy, sliding between tables. The tapas on their trays were a crayon box of colors and smelled like lavender and orange blossoms. Delicious food, warm red light, cozy atmosphere. Lovers of every stripe easing into each other. A mellow scene. Good way to be on a Saturday night. I saw Josette by the door surveying the crowd. She was in her happy place. We complemented the mood with a breezy slow piece called "The Art of Deep," one of the tracks on *Storm Damage*, the album we're releasing next month. When we started playing, I had no worries about Eric. He was hitting clean notes, choking his strings without buzzing, and totally in tempo. Grooving.

I saw the Bauers arrive during our third number. They showed Josette my card, and she nodded at me as she led them to the last available table. They were dressed like Fourth of July revelers at a Mexican Day-of-the-Dead party—not simpatico with the North Beach regulars around them. But, hey, it's San Francisco, where non-conformity rules. I checked in with them during our second break, and they said Dylan's was pricey but nice and thanked me for the free drinks and rescuing them in the alley. When I returned to the stage, I noticed Eric sitting at a back table with his husband, Jaycee Washington. Eric had parked his head against the wall and closed his eyes. He had a faraway smile like he was tripping in Neverland, and I glanced at Jaycee. He shrugged as if to say, "I don't know."

Eric was the last one back on stage. He fumbled with his guitar strap as he pulled it over his head. The X-man brought up a stool for him, and Eric regarded it as if he didn't understand its function. Then he sank onto it and smiled at the crowd. We started our third set with "The Opposite of Gravity," another new song on Storm Damage. Since composing it on the road, we'd played it a hundred times, but Eric began drifting after a four-bar bridge in the middle of the number. The rest of us knew instantly that he was out of sync, and Garth started laying back, shifting the tempo to match what Eric was playing during a guitar solo. Most audience members wouldn't have known what was happening, but K.C. gave me a "What the hell?" look, and we matched Garth's slower beat. Xavier's brow was knitted in annoyance, and he missed a few notes as he tried to match the fluctuating tempo. We might have fooled the audience if Eric hadn't kept zoning out, his fingers stumbling into different keys and then playing a riff from a different song. The song was hopelessly muddled by then, and the audience knew it. Eric stopped playing, slumped forward, and began sliding off the stool. His mouth was curled up in a beatific smile like a drunken jack-o'-lantern. When I caught him, he felt like a rumpled suit that fell off its hanger.

Xavier told the paramedics who responded that Eric had a cocaine addiction. Jaycee confirmed what we suspected—they'd been at a party before arriving at the club, and Eric had snorted coke and taken some other pill. Jaycee didn't know what. The medics gave him naloxone, although that doesn't treat a coke overdose, because he was showing symptoms they hadn't seen before. After the ambulance took him away, we returned to the stage. Xavier told the audience that Eric had been sick, which may have fooled one or two people in the room, but these battle-hardened San Franciscans knew a drug overdose when they saw one.

Most bands have songs in their repertoire that they can play if one instrument is missing. Somebody might be sick, break a string or a reed, or need the bathroom. So we resumed by playing songs that did not require a guitar. But we had a set-and-a-half left to play. When we ran out of rehearsed numbers, we started improvising, which is my favorite way to perform anyway. One of us would start a new song by soloing from somewhere deep in his imagination. That solo established the key, the tempo, and the mood. Garth usually came in next, creating a beat that matched the tempo and deepened the tone of the piece. After eight bars or so, when a chord sequence had been laid down, the X-Man would create a bass line to match the mood. Then K.C. and I would make a statement by soloing or providing a counterpoint as the song developed. Some improvs meandered like an old river; in others, we discovered a melody and found ways to play off each other to explore variations of the melody that always rewound their way to the root chord. We could sense when the song had fulfilled its potential and was ready for closure, like sensing that an orgasm was about to happen, and we would stop in a way that felt organic and aesthetically right. This is why they say that good music is better than sex—and lasts longer. Some improvised songs are so good you wish you'd recorded them; some are memorable enough that we recreate them and record them later.

I can't say we didn't miss Eric. The band felt incomplete without him and his guitar. But I watched the audience after we resumed, and they were feeling fine: eyes closed, heads bobbing, fingers tapping the beat, lazy smiles, lips pursed on wine glasses, taking slow sips, the lights dimmed, the staff laying back, and Josette purring. You know when an audience is chillaxilating, and an owner is happy.

We were nearing the end of the fourth set when the door opened, and Jerry Worcester popped in, still in uniform. I thought he was bringing the statement about the alley incident for me to sign. He crooked a finger at me and beckoned me to the door. I caught the X-Man's eye when we finished that song and canted my head toward the cop. He understood, and I left the stage and wound my way to Jerry.

"Hey, man. What's happening?"

"Got a call from dispatch," Jerry said. "They knew I'd seen you earlier and said you needed to call Lieutenant Fisher."

Paul Fisher was the police lieutenant in charge of homicide in San Francisco. He and I were old friends and had helped each other. I couldn't imagine why he'd want me to call after midnight.

"They said it was urgent," Jerry added.

I nodded, grabbed my phone from the green room, and saw two messages from Paul. I walked outside, where it was quieter to return the call.

"You must be playing tonight," Paul said when he answered. "I left messages as soon as I heard."

"Yeah, we're at Dylan's. What's up?"

"Kat Hastings has been shot."

Kat

Paul didn't know much more, just that she'd been shot during an active shooter situation at a flea market. She'd been taken to the UC Davis Medical Center in Sacramento and was in surgery. As I rushed to my car, I felt like I was standing on a precipice overlooking the ocean hundreds of feet below and was falling forward. The air had been knocked out of me, and my arms were windmilling backward as I fought for balance.

Sacramento is usually a two-hour drive from downtown San Francisco. When I reached my car, I had to drive through the city to I-80 and then cross the Oakland Bay Bridge. Traffic beyond the bridge was a slog because even past midnight, the road was clogged with semis carrying loads from the Oakland docks into the heartland. They looked like a herd of steel behemoths lumbering along, sliding into and out of lanes as they passed one another. When traffic thinned past Oakland, I caught a rabbit and made better time. A rabbit drives ten to fifteen miles an hour above the speed limit. You get on the rabbit's tail and follow him, running hot when he's hot, slowing when he slows, and punching your brakes when he does. Your rabbit will hit the radar before you do, and the cops will nail him while you're slowing to the speed limit. That strategy usually works when you need to make time. In just over an hour, I came within thirty miles of Sacramento without my rabbit being pulled over.

Katrina Hastings was a detective sergeant in the Sacramento PD. I met her on the Erin Hightower case. Erin was kidnapped when she was five years old and not seen again until seven years later when my good friend David Fetchenheir spotted her in a convenience store in Wyoming. Kat was the missing person detective responsible for the Hightower kidnapping, but the case had gone cold. I helped Kat crack a pedophile ring before she and

I tracked Erin to a compound in New Mexico, where we rescued Erin and hundreds of other kidnapped children from people who believed they could save humanity by creating a superintelligent master race that would rule through a geniocracy.

I was rebounding from a failed relationship, and Kat and I became lovers when our life-or-death struggle with Erin's kidnappers drove us into an intimacy we might not have developed otherwise. I've wondered since if our affair was born in a crucible or out of convenience. Whatever its genesis, I was drawn as much to her passion for justice as to the loveliness in her soul and the beauty behind her badge. I didn't know if my life with her would be measured in feet or miles, but I loved her spark and loopy smile and wanted to be with her whenever our insane schedules allowed.

During the drive, I called her cell phone repeatedly, doubting she would answer, but I couldn't think who else to call. I worried about Eric and thought about calling Xavier or Garth, but it was the middle of the night. I had oxy in my glove compartment and felt the urge to dry-swallow two. I was ragged and anxious, and my mouth was dry. The closer I came to Sacramento, the hazier the air became. It smelled like a burnt wick. The oxy would have calmed me, but I didn't want to become drowsy, and it felt right to be anxious. Two of the people I was closest to had gone down, one violently, and I didn't know if she was recovering or dying. I felt like a derelict scarecrow in a hurricane, whipped and shredded, pieces of me sailing into the darkness.

The UC Davis Med Center is a sprawling, modern complex that looks like it was assembled from LEGOs. Outside the Emergency entrance, I saw three Sacramento PD black and whites and two UC Davis Police SUVs among the civilian vehicles crowding the parking lot. Inside, I saw the usual mix of the ill or injured and sleep-deprived relatives waiting to be called back, pain, misery, and annoyance blurring their faces. A half-dozen cops in uniform were huddled near the reception desk, drinking coffee or on their phones. Some off-duty cops or plainclothes detectives, including Kat's partner, Keith Lau, mingled with them. When he saw me, Lau raised his chin and started toward me. He had a square face with pudgy cheeks like a bulldog and short black hair that tumbled over his forehead. His brow was permanently knitted, making him look like a spelling bee contestant who'd just been asked to spell appoggiatura.

"She's going to be okay," he said as he rushed up, his hands held out in reassurance.

"Where is she?"

"ICU," he said. "They have her sedated."

"What the hell happened?"

"Mass shooting this morning," Keith said. "Folsom Flea Market. You didn't hear about it?"

I shook my head.

"Seven dead. All civilians. Thirteen injured. Three critical. Katrina was the first to reach the shooter. She took two forty-five slugs in her vest and one in her leg."

I winced and felt heat flush through my ears. "How bad?"

"They're saying, I mean, thank God she was armored. The vest saved her. The forty-fives hit her point blank. One bruised her sternum. Pretty bad, I guess. The other broke a rib and cracked three more. The one in her thigh was a through and through. No major vessel or nerve damage."

I'd been wearing a bulletproof vest in New Mexico when I chased a guy who was using Kat as a human shield. My vest was hit twice with nine-millimeter slugs, but they were fired from a distance and didn't pack the punch of a forty-five at close range. It hurt like hell when I took two smaller slugs in my vest. A .45-caliber round is larger than a nine mil and has about thirty percent more kinetic energy. The forty-fives that hit Kat's armor must have felt like a pile driver.

"Food stall caught fire. She had some smoke inhalation but no burns," Keith said. "A patrol officer pulled her away from the flames. One SWAT officer was also hit. In the arm. May lose it."

I was tired, and my knee hurt. I felt itchy because I hadn't taken any oxy, and I had a witch's brew of emotions flooding my head—relieved that Kat was alive, concerned about her injuries, sorry about the SWAT cop, puzzled about Eric overdosing, and pissed at the son of a bitch who shot Kat. I asked what Keith could tell me about the shooter.

He pulled a small blue spiral-bound notebook from his back pocket and flipped it open. "Robert Duggins," he read. "Caucasian. Fifty-two. No priors. Weapon was a Kimber Rapide." He gave me a puzzled look. "He also had a Smith and Wesson thirty-eight. He had a DROS on the Kimber but none on the thirty-eight."

A DROS is a Dealer's Record of Sale. That would be on file with the state if he'd purchased the thirty-eight in California. If he'd brought that weapon in from another state, he'd be considered a personal firearm importer and should have reported it. I asked Keith if Duggins had a CCW. That's a Carry Concealed Weapon license, which is required if you transport a firearm in a car.

He shook his head and then looked back at his notebook. "Guy was a bank president, Sonny. Nothing in his background indicates violence. Speeding ticket when he was thirty.

Nothing since. Clean as a baby's conscience. But wits say he followed a Hispanic guy, Alberto Flores, into the Flea Market and shot him twice. Not sure if he knew the victim. Then Duggins ran into the market, shooting at everybody. Apparently at random. Wits say he looked enraged. Red hair, beet red face. He looked like his head was on fire."

I thanked Keith with a fist bump. After he left, I found the ICU where Kat had been taken and approached the nurse's station. With its jumble of phones, blinking monitors, stacks of medical records, and cups half-filled with lukewarm coffee, it was a study in organization eroding to chaos. The wall clock behind the desk said it was 2:39. The charge nurse was a mid-life brunette who, when she saw me, pasted a smile over a look of perpetual annoyance.

"Busy night," I said, trying for empathy.

"Can I help you?" The smile vanished. She wasn't buying it.

"How is Katrina Hastings doing?"

"Are you family, sir?"

"I'm—"

"Yes, he's family," came a voice behind me. I turned. It was David Hastings, Kat's ex.

"Who is he?" the nurse asked David.

"Her brother," David replied. The nurse asked for my ID, and I handed her my driver's license. She wrote my name in a folder on her desk and returned my ID.

"She's sleeping," the nurse said. "In serious but stable condition."

David pointed to a set of chairs along the wall opposite the station, and I saw Kat's 12-year-old daughter, Sara, asleep across three chairs. She lay with a jacket under her head. I walked with David back to where he'd been sitting.

"Sorry about the 'brother' thing," David said. "Nurse Ratched thinks HIPAA is one of the Ten Commandments. She won't tell you anything unless you're family and ex-husband barely made the cut when I arrived. I doubt she'd okay boyfriend."

"Thanks for vouching for me." When Kat told me how David had cheated on her, I'd developed a bad attitude about him, but as I'd gotten to know David since Kat and I had been dating, I decided he wasn't such a bad guy. He was the manager of a Sherwin-Williams franchise and wanted a safe, predictable life. Marriage to a police detective was more drama than he could stomach. When David got the call about Kat, he picked up Sara at a friend's house and rushed to the hospital. They'd been there since mid-afternoon, but Sara wouldn't leave until she knew her mom was okay, and she'd fallen asleep after dinner in the hospital cafeteria. David didn't want to wake her until someone else could stay with Kat. I told him I would, and he nudged Sara.

She rolled over and yawned into a hand. Opening her eyes, she looked at David and said, "What?" Then, stifling another yawn, "How's mom?"

"She's resting," David told her.

Sara saw me and grinned. "Oh, hi, Sonny." She sat up and stretched. I'd spent a lot of time with Kat and Sara, and Sara loved music, so I was a hit with her even though I hadn't memorized the lyrics to Olivia Rodrigo's song "Vampire" and didn't know Billie Eilish personally. When she shuffled over to me, we hugged each other. I told her I was sorry about her mom but knew she'd be okay.

"Yeah, I know," Sara said. "She's tough."

"Darn straight," I said. "I'll see you later." She nodded, and she and David left. I returned to the nurse's station and said I wanted to go to Kat's room. The nurse finished writing something and parked the pencil above her right ear.

"A36," she said, pointing down the hall and turning away. *Great bedside manner*, I thought. *The graveyard shift suits her.*

Kat lay with her head elevated on those narrow hospital beds with the railings up on both sides. She wore an oxygen mask and had an IV drip in her left arm. A white blanket was pulled up to her waist, but I could see that her left leg was larger than her right. Bandages. There were ice packs over her hospital gown on her chest and the right side of her ribcage. The monitors behind her showed her vital signs, and I could hear the soft sound of a machine pumping oxygen. Her head was tilted to the right. I walked to that side of the bed and grasped her hand. She felt warm but didn't move. After a few moments, I sank into a padded chair near the window and laid my head back. A few minutes later, a young nurse entered, checked her vitals, removed the ice packs, and pulled up her blanket.

I gazed at Kat, remembering how she'd saved my life in New Mexico when she killed a guard who was about to shoot me. Then we'd escaped through a utility tunnel and barely survived a painful dash through the desert in a raging storm. Those memories were seared in my brain. As I watched over Kat, I began drifting, thinking about our time together in New Mexico and afterward. Darkness fell, and images of her flickered through my closed eyes like frames from an old movie shimmering on the screen in a musty theater.

I awoke to a shrill tone and a crowded room, startled by the frenetic energy in front of me. Three people huddled around Kat's bed. A tall nurse looked up from Kat and read the monitors: "BP 88 over 50. Pulse 128 and rising. Oxygen 92."

I heard a man say, "She's bleeding." They'd pulled her hospital gown open, and he was probing her right side with his fingers.

The tall nurse leaned over Kat's head and said, "Can you tell me your name?" Kat opened her eyes but didn't respond. "What is your name?" the nurse said louder. Kat gazed at her but didn't answer. "Do you know where you are?"

While that nurse tried to get Kat to respond, the doctor said, "Let's do the FAST scan." A younger Asian nurse smeared a clear gel on Kat's right side and stomach and passed a probe over those areas while she and the doctor examined the screen on a small portable machine. I learned later that FAST stands for "focused assessment with sonography in trauma." It's a rapid bedside ultrasound examination.

'Right," the doctor said. "Her liver laceration is unstable. I want six units of blood in the OR and open up her IV. We need to get her to surgery now."

I rose from the chair but stayed back and watched as the Asian nurse set aside the FAST scan unit, removed the nasal cannula from Kat's nose, and put a non-rebreather mask over her nose. Then she turned a knob on her IV and moved the IV fluid bottle to an attachment on her bed.

A male nurse hurried into the room as the doctor rushed out. The three nurses busied themselves around her bed, detaching some tubes, attaching others to the bed frame, and wheeling the bed toward the door. A few minutes after they took Kat away, the male nurse returned and began straightening up. He was a young, prematurely balding man with a ghost of a mustache above his lip and thin, almost transparent eyebrows.

"What happened?" I asked him.

"She's bleeding internally," he said. "You're her brother, right?"

I nodded.

"The broken rib lacerated her liver. Those injuries usually heal themselves, but she wasn't so lucky. They'll operate to repair the laceration." He wheeled a chrome IV stand back toward the wall and approached me. He had a white towel folded over one arm.

He pursed his lips as he studied the towel, carefully lining up the folds along one side. "I don't want to scare you. I'm sure she'll be okay," he said. Then he looked at me. "But you might want to call your parents. The changes to her vitals indicated she was going into shock."

I felt the blood drain from my face. "How long will she be in surgery?"

"Depends on what they find. Probably three to four hours. You need anything?"

I shook my head, and he left. I sank back into the chair. Dawn eased into the window behind me and cast a diffuse glow on the sterile wall opposite. The clock above the TV read seven-thirty.

Market Street

I was running strong down a trail between a forest on my right and a river on my left. The trail was worn and rutted, with ragged grass along its sides defining the path. Although the air smelled parched—all the moisture sucked from it—I was breathing easily, counting my strides, almost gliding over the landscape. I ran with the river, matching its meandering pace, following a twisted log as it surfaced, dove beneath the waves, and reappeared like it was coming up for air. I followed the swimmer until we reached a fork in the stream, and it chose left while my path veered right.

Ahead, I could see a trail merging with mine, and I saw another runner, a woman with a long ponytail, flopping behind her from right to left in a windshield-wiper pattern as she ran. When our paths became one, I was thirty yards behind her. My pace was faster than hers, and I worried I would startle her if I came up behind too quickly, so I yelled, "On your left," as I drew near. Despite my warning, she turned to me with an ashen face and put out a hand to warn me off. Then she smiled when she recognized me. It was my older sister, Aileen. She took my hand when I came up beside her, and we ran together like a synchronized swimming duo.

Her eyes reflected the gleaming sun, bright with purpose and radiant as the morning. She ran steadily, and I suddenly found myself struggling to keep up. I felt warm and unzipped my jacket. My T-shirt was dark and damp. Sweat trickled from my temples onto my cheeks, and as I wiped it off, I noticed a pink glow through the trees with wisps of white rising like a vapor. It might have been dawn's reflected light or a distant fire. In minutes, it grew redder, and then I noticed a red patch on Aileen's leg.

She wore loose-fitting black shorts, and as we ran, I saw more blood spotting her legs. When Aileen was seventeen and I was twelve, she was raped during a home invasion. I found her tied to a bed with blood between her legs and attacked her assailant, but I couldn't stop what had happened to her. The rapist threw me over a banister and broke my legs. Now, I watched in horror as the blood on her legs grew into a steady stream, flowing as powerfully as the river we ran along. I pulled on her arm to stop us and laid her on the ground, but I couldn't do anything to staunch the flow of blood. My hands were soon caked with red, and the blood seemed to flow from my fingers.

Then a sheet of smoke was thrown over us, and I began coughing. It felt like a vise was crushing my chest. Flames flickered through the trees, and I heard the roar of the approaching fire. Smoke billowed from a wall of flames that now consumed the forest, balls of contagion bursting outward like black cotton candy exploding from a giant cannon. I heard a racking cough and saw Kat sprawled beside me. Her face was scrunched like a prune. Black mucus had clotted in her nostrils. I tried to pull it out so she could breathe, but more mucus flowed, forming an oily sludge that filled her mouth and covered her chin. She stopped breathing and—

—I jerked awake, cold and sweaty, my hands clutching the sides of the chair. I was alone in a bare room with white antiseptic walls. Kat's hospital room. Sacramento. She'd been shot, I remembered, flashing back to the night drive on the interstate, seeing her lying on the bed, an oxygen tube in her nose, before a medical team descended and whisked her away.

I returned to the nurse's station and saw a half-dozen people behind the counter—the morning shift. The nurse I spoke to had large brown teddy bear eyes and tendrils of gray-black hair hanging from the bun on the back of her head. She had dimples and pretty teeth and told me Kat was in the recovery room. The surgery had gone well, she said, and my sister would be returned to her room in an hour or two. I closed my eyes and laid my head on the counter, and she touched my shoulder and asked if I was okay. I said yes, just relieved and in need of coffee.

I confessed that Kat was not my sister, and she smiled and said, "I know. I looked you up when I saw your name. I remembered reading about you and her. We'll just let it be our secret." She touched my hand and directed me to the cafeteria, where I ate an orange and had a large coffee in a paper cup. It was bitter and hot and jolted me awake. My phone said it was just after noon. I returned to Kat's room, sat in the chair, and checked my phone. A message from David Hastings said they'd be back this afternoon, along with

Kat's parents. Sara was up much of the night and needed her sleep. I also had a message from Garth asking me to call him.

"Hey, brother," I said when he picked up.

"How is she?"

"Rough night. She was back in surgery this morning for internal bleeding."

"Shit, man. She okay?"

"They said the surgery went well. I'm in her room. She's not back yet. What's happening with Eric?"

"Dunno, bro. They took him to Zuckerberg last night." Zuckerberg San Francisco General Hospital and Trauma Center was the city's major treatment center for drug overdoses. "I was just there. Wouldn't let me see him, but Xavier said he's still tripping."

"Christ. Twelve hours later?"

"What they say. Saw Jaycee Washington in the hallway. They were partying someplace in Ashbury Heights. Eric snorted some coke. Then they met some sketchy dude who gave Eric a couple of blue uppers. Jaycee didn't know the shit. Hadn't seen it before."

"Blue uppers. Never heard of it. What'd the guy look like?"

"Didn't ask," Garth replied. "You know those places."

"Not my scene."

"Gotcha. People in and out. You dunno half the dudes there. Party drugs passed around like candy."

"So Eric popped something that messed with the coke."

"Looks like it."

"And he's still high?"

"Xavier talked to the docs. Said he's still soaring."

Twelve hours on a high is not cool. I knew that cocaine affected the dopamine receptors in your brain. The drug rushes up to you like your high-octane best friend. It's sparkly and promises to take you to the peak and turn you into a superhero. But it's a lie, and when you land back on the planet Earth, you find yourself in the same old same old, and you crave your return trip to that place of boundless energy and invincibility. But as the song says, "Ain't no sunshine when she's gone. Only darkness when she's away." As with love, so with addiction. Cocaine alters your brain chemistry even when it wears off in an hour, but being high for half a day could burn out your lights. I shared my concern with Garth, and he agreed. Eric could be on a one-way ticket.

"I'll let you know if I hear anything," Garth said.

"All right, brother. I'll return to the city when I know Kat's okay."

"Later, dude," he responded.

An hour later, they wheeled Kat's bed back into her room. She now had a cannula in her nose and was covered by a white blanket. When the nurses left, I walked to her bedside, and she opened her eyes.

"You trying to scare the hell out of me?" I asked.

She gave me a weak smile, but the gleam in her eyes told me she was okay. The Kat I knew was in there behind the trauma and pain meds and anesthesia.

"I'm glad you're here," she whispered.

I smiled and brushed her forehead with my lips. Then her eyes drifted shut again, and I pulled up the chair and sat beside her bed, holding her hand and gently rubbing her fingers.

David and Sara returned mid-afternoon, and I had to leave the room because they allowed only two visitors at a time. I saw Kat's parents in the waiting room. Her father, John Dupree, was a 30-year vet with the Sacramento PD. He was a tough guy in his prime. Now he looks deflated, like a football collapsed on one side. He shaves once a week, so most days, his face resembles an old wire brush with a pale handle. I had his grudging approval after my adventure with Kat in New Mexico. Still, he had an old cop's suspicion of professional musicians who, in his experience, were known for drugs, philandering, and destroying hotel rooms. Her mother, Jane, never stopped thanking me for saving Kat's life, and I kept reminding her that Kat had saved mine, too. She wasn't wary of me but didn't think Kat and I were permanent and wanted stability in Kat's life. I sensed that she thought of me like a TV star on a hit show that would be canceled after a few seasons, a star who would fade from the public eye and resurface only as a celebrity contestant on game shows.

Despite unspoken misgivings, we had a pleasant enough conversation until David and Sara returned, and then her parents visited her room. Sara sat on the chair beside mine and asked how it felt to be shot in an armored vest. I told her it was the hardest I'd ever been hit, but I preferred it to being shot without the vest. We talked about her mom's recovery and San Francisco, where Sara thought she wanted to live when she grew up. Then she asked me about our recent tour, and I told her the good parts. Months ago, I'd given her our *Storm Warning* CD, and she said she was beginning to like blues and jazz but still preferred Billie Eilish, Olivia Rodrigo, Dua Lipa, and Taylor Swift. I said she had good taste in music.

When everyone left, I returned to Kat's room. She was exhausted from the visits and needed to sleep, so I left her alone. I found an outlet nearby, bought running shoes and athletic clothing, and walked on an actual river trail for an hour. My knee protested, but I tried to get my heart rate up. Then I drove back to the hospital, found a decent club sandwich and salad in the cafeteria, took some oxy for my aching knee, and returned to her room, where I spent a fitful night sleeping in that padded chair, my knee still sore from the river walk, waking several times as nurses entered the room to check on her.

Kat was still asleep when I went for coffee on Monday morning. When I returned, I stood by her bed. She must have sensed me there. She moved her hands and opened her eyes. A tear escaped and rolled down her cheek.

I wiped the tear with one finger and dried it on my cheek. "What's wrong?" I asked.

"I didn't see him," she said.

I understood what she meant. When I was thirteen, I was blindsided by an older kid who'd been bullying me. The blows you don't see coming hurt the most. They rattle you afterward. You question your awareness, your training, and your trust in yourself. You wonder if you can handle whatever's thrown at you if the confidence you feel is delusional.

"I've been trying to remember what happened. I never saw him."

"Will it help to talk about it?"

"With you, yes." So we did. For the better part of an hour while the rest of Sacramento woke up. She walked through what she remembered up to the point where the first slug slammed into her vest. She never saw where the bullet came from and didn't remember anything after that. Whatever uncertainties I had about our relationship vanished in those moments alone with her in her hospital room. As I held her hand and we shared those feelings of terror and doubt you have after traumatic events, I felt closer to her than anyone I've known.

Then her day became a blur of nurses and doctors, CAT scans, blood tests, bandage changes, return visits by David and Sara, her parents, and a parade of police officers, including Keith Lau, her commanding officer, and the Chief of Police. I excused myself mid-afternoon, telling her I had to return to San Francisco to check on Eric but would return on Wednesday.

As I hopped back on I-80 and headed west, I drove through a yellow haze that seemed to have aged the landscape. Paul Fisher called me as I was passing a convoy of semis. A side wind was buffeting them, and I struggled to stay in my lane as gusts hit from alternating sides of my car. Paul asked how Kat was doing and then said he would have called earlier, but they'd had a crisis that morning in the city. I wondered what happened.

"We had a mass killing on Market Street," he said, "Five dead. Nineteen injured."

"Christ. Another shooting?"

"No. Vehicular homicide. A woman in a Honda Civic jumped the curb on Market and plowed into pedestrians."

I knew Market Street well and tried to imagine the scene. "She have a medical issue?"

'No. Witnesses say she crossed two lanes of traffic and sped up as she approached the sidewalk. After mowing down one group of pedestrians, she veered toward others who were trying to get out of her way. She intended to do what she did."

"What do you know about the driver?"

"Not enough yet. She was forty-nine. Hispanic. Mother of three. A dental assistant in the South City."

"Doesn't sound like a terrorist to me."

"For chrissake. She wasn't Mother Teresa either. She steered her car into those people."

"I'm not defending her, Paul."

"Good! She's dead anyway. After ramming a police car, she put it in reverse and tried to run over more people. Two officers opened fire. She was dead at the scene."

"Sounds horrific."

"It was. There were mangled bodies everywhere."

I gave him a moment and said, "I'm just trying to understand." The why of any crime is usually the hard part. We can understand who, what, when, and where, but we can't make sense of something like this until we can explain why.

"Me, too," he replied. "No other vehicles were involved, so we don't think it was road rage. No signs of anything political. No manifesto on her computer. No suicide note. Her employer said she was reliable, steady, and always on time. Good worker. So this morning, she doesn't show up for work. Doesn't notify anyone she isn't coming. She drives to Market for reasons unknown and decides to run over two dozen innocent people."

"She have any priors?"

"Nope. Nothing in California. Nothing on AFIS. She looks clean, but we haven't done a full work-up on her yet."

"Maybe the autopsy will turn up something."

"Yeah, maybe. I'm facing a room full of press people in a couple of hours. They'll be asking questions I can't answer. Helluva way to start the week."

"Yep. One mass murder on top of another. What the hell's happening?"

"Damned if I know. Too many people? Too many guns? Full moon? Too much fluoride in the drinking water? Beats the hell out of me."

He told me that mass killings nationwide have been increasing. They took a huge jump in 2020. The usual explanation was COVID. People were cooped up and stressed out. Cabin fever and isolation turned some people manic. Around the country, mass killings topped six hundred that year but didn't decline as law enforcement expected. That pace has continued for years, and we're on track to have more than six hundred again this year. Paul said he was starting to feel like a janitor in a slaughterhouse. The best he could do was pick up the bodies and wash away the blood.

"I need a time out," he said. "I don't know how long I can keep doing this." His voice sounded like a song played too slowly. I could understand his weariness, but I didn't have to live in the sewer like Paul. Kat's shooting had the opposite effect on me. Her shooting was personal, and it made me angry as hell. I wanted to punch someone, but there was no one to punch.

"You'd think after twenty-six years as a cop, I'd be immune, but I'm not," Paul said. "A thing like today knocks the shit out of you."

"I don't know what to tell you. Call me when you want to grab a scotch, kick back, and listen to good music."

"Sure."

"Kat's going to be okay."

"There is that."

"One victory at a time, brother."

I was just under an hour from home when Paul rang off, but the road ahead looked longer. Smoke from the fires to the north swept high over the interstate, obscuring the sun and staining the horizon vermilion.

Rhoda

The Zuckerberg San Francisco Hospital is the only Level 1 Trauma Center in San Francisco, and they specialize in treating people who overdose on opiates, coke, meth, ecstasy, LSD, GHB, ketamine, Xanax, steroids, and whatever else people ingest to slay their demons. It is a losing battle. Last year, San Francisco's death rate from overdoses was more than double the national average. Ten years ago, California voters passed Prop 47, which reduced drug possession from a felony to a misdemeanor, and public drug use became common. Walk down the city's streets these days, and you'll see people stoned, strung out, slumped on the sidewalks with needles in their veins, or dead, their bodies lying by liquor stores, laundromats, and luxury department stores. Ask a roomful of San Franciscans in some neighborhoods if they've seen a dead body on the streets, and most will raise their hands.

So Zuckerberg is a busy place.

The interior of the hospital is not what you'd expect from a place that treats junkies. It's modern, clean, colorful, and filled with art. The walls of the hallway I walked through to reach Eric's room were papered with floor-to-ceiling photographs of tree branches and leaves. I could have been walking through a botanical garden. After checking in at the nurse's station, I was allowed to visit Eric. Jaycee Washington sat in one of the two chairs in the room. He gave me a hopeful smile, but his features sagged, and his ordinarily rich mocha skin looked as dull as the underside of a dead leaf in the fall. We hugged each other, and I sat in the other chair.

Eric lay still on the bed, his eyes fixed on something far away. His lips were parted and cracked. He lay as still as death, but the monitor showed a slow, steady pulse. Jaycee said they turned him every six hours to prevent bed sores and were feeding him through his IV. The doctors knew he ingested something with the cocaine, but they didn't know what. The toxicology report was inconclusive. It showed the presence of cocaine along with two other compounds they couldn't identify. Eric's dopamine levels remained abnormally high, and they couldn't explain why. He was on a forever high—a permanent state of rapture.

I recalled the beatific smile on his face at the club. Now it looked frozen, like a Halloween mask of a demented clown. Eric looked smaller, though he'd been here only three days. He hadn't died, but I couldn't imagine the body lying on the bed reanimating and playing the guitar with soul and sizzle. But my likely loss of a friend and bandmate paled beside Jaycee's loss of his life partner. I gave the gray man beside me a weak smile and felt my throat constrict when he said, "He'll get through this."

Sure he will, I wanted to say, but that felt hollow.

I gave him a moment to savor that hope and then said, "I want to ask you something about that night."

He looked blankly at me. "Saturday?"

I nodded. "Garth said he swallowed two blue uppers, whatever they are."

"Oh. I don't know. That night is a blur."

"You were at the party with him, though. Right?"

Jaycee closed his eyes as though having to remember. "I wasn't there."

"You weren't at the party?"

"No, I was there. But it was crowded, man. I was talking to other people. I couldn't be with Eric the whole time."

"Sure. But you told Garth—"

"You know Eric. He's a performer. He loves an audience. He was on the other side of the room, talking to people I didn't know."

I nodded. "I've played with him for years. He does love an audience." I thought I heard Eric take a deeper breath, and I glanced at him but saw no change. I looked back at Jaycee. "Eric snorted coke that night. He also swallowed some pills, right? You told Garth they were blue."

"I might be mistaken."

"Which part am I getting wrong? He didn't take them. They weren't blue. What?"

He scratched behind his head and held a breath. Then he exhaled and said, "I would have stopped him if I'd known. I didn't, I wasn't . . . there. I came up and saw them in his hand.

"Blue pills?"

He nodded.

"What color blue?"

"They were . . . small. Round. A deep blue, like a royal blue."

"And he took two of them?"

He nodded.

"Where did he get them?"

Jaycee shrugged. "From some guy. A weird guy."

"Weird how?"

"He, uh, was wearing a long gray robe. Dark gray. With a hood. Like Gandalf in *Lord of the Rings*. Like he was in costume or something."

"Race?"

"I didn't get a good look at him."

"Okay, but was he black or white? Asian? Did you see his face?"

"White."

"Hair?"

"Long. Dark. Not black."

"Dark brown. What else?" He looked away and didn't answer. "Jaycee, the doctors don't know what's in those blue pills, but the Gandalf guy probably does. We need to find him. Was he tall, short, fat, thin?"

"Average. On the thin side. He told Eric to take one pill, but Eric swallowed both."

"So you heard his voice. High in pitch? Low? Accent?"

"White sounding. Not Hispanic. Not low or high. He didn't have an accent I could hear, but he said something off. Eric asked for three more of the pills, offered to buy them, and the guy said. . ."

"What did he say?"

"He said he didn't have three more. Except he didn't say *three*. He said *tree*. He said, 'I don't have *tree* more'."

A nurse walked into the room then. She smeared something on Eric's lips and fussed with his IV.

"He's going to be okay," Jaycee assured me. He smiled like a cheerleader but looked like a pallbearer.

This time I said, "Sure. He'll be fine." He needed reassurance more than I needed honesty.

———————

I live in a condo on Pacific Heights. My down-the-hall neighbor is a psychiatrist named Rhoda Merrick, a widow whose husband died of lung cancer eight years ago. She was standoffish when I moved in, but we eventually became friends who teased each other with genuine affection. Rhoda is a tall, striking woman with an attractive but serious face. She has chin-length silver hair with black undertones and dresses in a casual but professional way that is carefully chic—long, gray skirts with knee-high black boots and cashmere sweaters on cool days, and silk blouses with complementary scarves when it's warm. She is proper and poised but has the sure eye of a clinician and a gift for measured nuance in her speech. I would be in love with her if we were age-appropriate, but she's 63, and I'm 34.

Two years ago, I came home mid-day from the studio where the Storm Lake Blues Band had been recording, and I saw a 40-something man lingering by the door to her condo. He had a set of keys in one hand and looked like he'd been trying them in her lock. He wasn't her son, Kendal, and I didn't know any other men who should have a key to her place. So I walked down the hall and asked if I could help him with something. I'm six-two, and he was slightly taller than me, heavier by twenty pounds, and muscular. He looked like he'd done some weightlifting and carried himself like a brawler. He measured me with his eyes and decided it wasn't worth the trouble, so he returned the keys to his pocket and said no. I noted his features and watched as he walked to the elevator and left.

That evening, I knocked on Rhoda's door, and she invited me in for a glass of wine. I told her about the incident and described the guy. She knew immediately who he was and shook her head in disgust. He was a former patient named Roland Meany, she told me, who'd developed an unhealthy fixation on her. Transference, she called it. Although their therapeutic relationship had ended, he kept showing up at her office. He discovered her cell phone number and sent texts saying he wanted to see her again. The texts and then late-night calls became more obsessive and frightening, so she'd contacted the police. They spoke to Meany, and the texts and calls stopped. Then she noticed him following her as she shopped for groceries or walked near the UCSF Psychiatry Clinic, where she worked. But having him appear at her condo and trying to break in was a new and terrifying development. She wanted to phone the police that evening, but I convinced her to let me handle it.

Meany owned a mid-size refrigeration company in the Bayview Industrial Park. I waited for him to leave work one weekday evening. John Sebastiani, a former Navy Seal who runs a small security company, joined me. John and I cornered him as he was about to get into his van, and I warned him to forget Rhoda Merrick, never text or call her again, or go anywhere near her. I told him what would happen if he did. He might have pushed back against me alone, but John can look like a mafia enforcer, and I could see Meany thinking twice about tangling with us. Then Garth roared up on his Harley with five Hell's Angels buddies who frequent Wyman Brothers Motors in Oakland. They were bearded and bulked and heavily tattooed and wore leathers and looked like the devil's wrath in Nazi helmets and chains. The roar of their Harleys echoed through the canyons between warehouses.

Garth walked over, stuck a finger in Meany's face, and said, "This the guy?"

I nodded.

"He fuckin' hear you?" Garth said.

"I think so," I replied.

"If he didn't," Garth growled, "next time we fuckin' tattoo it on his eyelids."

We had a round of beers and a good laugh afterward, and Rhoda never saw or heard from Meany again. She asked me later what I'd done to stop him from stalking her, and I told her I'd given him theater therapy. I said I'd staged a little drama to help him understand the consequences of his actions. She disapproved of my therapeutic approach but acknowledged its effectiveness.

I hadn't seen Rhoda since the mass shooting in Sacramento, but I knew she had a light schedule on Tuesdays. So, after visiting Eric, I returned to my condo, cleaned up, and changed clothes. Then I called the hospital in Sacramento and spoke to Kat. She was sore but doing better and was tired of all the visitors. I told her I'd return to Sacramento tomorrow. I was scheduled to meet with friends that evening at BiblioTech, the city's finest bookstore, but I wanted to talk to Rhoda first. I called her, and she was in, so I knocked on her door.

She answered, wearing a loose-fitting jumpsuit of soft material that flowed around her trim figure like smoke twirling around an elegant figurine.

"Wow," I said. "If I were your patient and you wore that to our session, I wouldn't be able to concentrate."

"You're my neighbor, not a client."

"I still can't concentrate."

"Oh, shut up. Have you had lunch?"

I said I hadn't, and she offered a spring salad with walnuts, goat cheese, watermelon, and a glass of Pouilly-Fuissé. While she prepared lunch, I gazed around her main room. She had a portrait of her late husband, John, on one wall. He had been a distinguished-looking man, and I knew she missed him terribly. She grew flowers, and her condo was festooned with a colorful variety of flowering plants, some of which I recognized but most not. Her main room was fragrant and earthy and full of life. Interspersed with the plants were seven aquariums, including one nearly wall-sized saltwater aquarium with exotic fish and living saltwater greens. She told me she would prefer to own cats but was allergic to them. I once asked why she enjoyed aquariums so much. She said the fish reminded her of some of her clients, those who were well-kept society matrons or trophy wives. "They are beautiful creatures," she said, "showcased in glass cages."

We sat at her kitchen counter for lunch. Her smile rose into her eyes.

I said, "If I were older or you were younger, we'd make a great couple."

"I'd get tired of rocking you to sleep."

I laughed at that thought. "You must think I have an Oedipus complex."

"No, you pretend to be a bad boy with me and enjoy a safe tease." She smiled at me and took a sip of wine. "But I know you have a white knight complex. You are obsessed with saving people you think are in trouble, and you take risks a more cautious person wouldn't take."

"Do I need treatment for that?"

She shrugged. "I'm your neighbor, not your therapist. But as a neighbor, I'd advise you to be careful."

I took several bites of her salad, which was cold and sweet and made my mouth water. "I'm worried about Kat."

"I'm worried about her, too. How is she doing?"

I told her Kat was doing better but would need time to recover, physically and psychologically. It rattled her that she hadn't seen the threat.

"Ask her to talk to me if she feels she has PTSD. Or if you see any signs of it."

"I will. I don't think that will be an issue. She handled New Mexico well, where she was kidnapped, held hostage, threatened with torture, and had to kill people. She's resilient."

Rhoda nodded. "But people manage stressors differently, and the effects of trauma can accumulate."

"Got it. I want to ask you about something else. You've examined mass murderers. Right?"

"Four. For psych evals before trial. Three in California. The latest in Oklahoma."

"You know Kat was wounded—"

"—in that shooting in a Sacramento flea market. I know. And that car yesterday on Market Street. I'm aware of both but don't know the details. I don't follow the news. It's too depressing. I have enough hysteria in my work."

"What can you tell me about mass murderers?"

She thought about that for a moment and then said, "The myth is that mass murderers snap for some reason. That's rarely true."

"People do snap, though."

"Yes, some people have poor impulse control. They get angry and can fly into a rage, but it usually lasts a short time, and they are remorseful afterward. It's called IED—intermittent explosive disorder. But mass murderers are different. There's usually a pathway to violence. They do research, they plan, they prepare, and then they act. They might scout different locations. They stockpile weapons, and if they don't know how to shoot, they take lessons. Or they search the internet for bomb-making techniques. Mass murder is not spontaneous or impulsive. It's a deliberate and willful act."

She gave me some well-known examples, like the two murderers at Columbine High School in Colorado. "They usually have a pathological preoccupation with something—a person or a cause. An ideology, a political figure or party, a girlfriend who rejected them—something like that. Afterward, we discover their fixations in journals or social media."

"If they haven't been violent before," she continued, "they often engage in novel aggression. They try it out on a cat or dog or some inanimate object. They'll drive to the country and shoot up road signs when no one's around, or they'll go somewhere remote at night and fire shots at houses or kill livestock. The murderer I examined in Oklahoma vandalized churches. He got a feel for it before walking into a prayer meeting with an assault rifle and killing everyone there."

"Are they mentally ill?" I asked.

"That's a common question and a tricky one to answer. You're mentally ill, Sonny. You have a white knight complex, which is not normal, and you have an unnatural obsession with older women."

"Only one."

She smiled. "The right question is, are they pathologically ill, and the answer is probably not. Columbia University studied 1,800 mass murderers and found that only eight percent had a serious mental illness like schizophrenia or severe bipolar disorder. Fewer than one in four had less severe mental illnesses like depression or anxiety, and that percentage matches what we see in the general population."

"So people with mental illnesses are unlikely to commit mass murder."

"That's right. No more so than the rest of the population."

"Then why do people do it?"

She shook her head. "There are no easy answers. Early childhood trauma is a common thread. Parental divorce, sexual assault, violence at home, suicides of someone close, bullying at school. They grow up feeling isolated, rejected, hopeless. They loathe themselves and often can't build meaningful relationships. Many of them feel they've been mistreated or abused. Oppressed by their elitist classmates or unfairly denied a promotion. A slight becomes a grudge, and the grudge becomes a pathological need to get revenge by destroying the oppressor, who could be a spouse, boss, coworker, neighbor, or member of a hated group."

"Like gays, blacks, women, Jews, Muslims."

"Right. Then there are the pseudocommando murderers. They buy camouflaged clothing and military or police hardware. They see themselves as Rambos or Seal Team operatives eliminating the bad guys."

"I heard an NRA spokesman on television last night saying that most mass murderers are insane."

"Nonsense. They're probably as ordinary as your next-door neighbor."

"That would be you." I gave her a frightened look. "How did you slice this watermelon? Where's your knife?"

"Better watch your back, buddy." She smiled broadly and said, "One more important sign is leakage. That's direct or indirect communication with someone about what the murderer is about to do. They often express their rage in some form to someone before they act. Teenage murderers sometimes post a rant on social media. Others share their plans with a friend. Most adult murderers are more circumspect, but it's common in mass shootings to discover that the murderers have leaked their intentions ahead of time."

I thought about what she told me as I took a final sip of wine. Then, I cleaned the dishes and put them in her dishwasher while she rinsed the glasses. I thanked her for lunch and the information, and we walked to her door.

"Have you ever heard of blue uppers?" I asked.

"No. What are they?"

"I don't know." I told her about Eric tripping out on Saturday night and what I'd learned since.

"That's a new one," she said. "I'll ask my colleagues who deal with addiction. He took the pills with cocaine in his system?"

I nodded.

"It sounds like a bad drug combination, but I don't know of any polysubstances that would elevate dopamine levels for this long."

"Okay, thanks," I said as we hugged each other.

"Any time."

"You sure I can't interest you in some casual sex?"

Rhoda was a classy woman, but when she laughed, she snorted, and she gave me a mighty snort. "You're dating a police officer," she exclaimed, "and I don't want to be arrested for child abuse. Now, get out of here before I spank you."

"That could be fun," I said, laughing.

I heard another snort as she closed the door.

Philosophers

I drove into a war zone when I left my garage Tuesday evening. Gray, caustic wind buffeted my car as people hurried by before me, bent against the wind, clutching their coats. Some wore COVID masks; others covered their noses with handkerchiefs or scarves spotted with ash. The wind raced between buildings and flung newspapers down streets where the visibility was near zero blocks ahead. The smell of smoke was so pungent I wondered if a nearby building was on fire, so I turned on my radio and went to a news station.

"We have a report of a brush fire west of Escobedo," the announcer said. Escobedo is a farming community in Mendocino County, north of the city. "The fire quickly grew to over two thousand acres and has already destroyed four homes. Firefighters rushed to the scene, but the fire is being driven by Diablo winds gusting to fifty miles an hour, sources say. They aren't sure firefighters can contain the blaze before it reaches Escobedo. An evacuation order has been issued, but some residents have vowed to stay and fight the fire if it threatens their homes."

I felt heartsick the way you do when people are fighting for their lives and homes, and you can't do anything to help them. The Diablo winds form when a high-pressure system over the Sierra Nevadas pushes hot, dry air across the Central Valley and the lower mountains near the coast. When this strong downslope airflow meets low pressure over the ocean, it can create winds exceeding 50-60 mph, turning forest and brush fires into fast-moving infernos. Northern California's Diablo winds are similar to the Santa Ana winds that afflict Southern California.

My skin felt like old parchment, and my mood was as gray as the air. As I drove past BiblioTech and saw people on the sidewalk struggling with the wind, I thought of the woman who plowed her car into pedestrians on Market Street and wondered whether the zeitgeist of our era was best described by uncertainty or fear. You can't distrust people's intentions while sheltering against nature's wrath without feeling that we are at some primal tipping point and our clock is winding down. But the foreboding I felt was also my anger at the guy who shot Kat and killed those people in the flea market. It simmered at the base of my brain, wanting release but having nowhere to go.

I arrived at BiblioTech at seven and parked in the lot behind the building. Before going inside, I called UC Davis in Sacramento and learned Kat was doing well and resting comfortably. Then I called Keith Lau and got an update on what they'd learned about Robert Duggins, the man who shot Kat. When I left my car, I was encircled by my own private cyclone of dust and soot. I pinched my nostrils against the bitter air and walked to the door beside the loading bay where they received shipments. Ari Kirakosian met me inside. He was the owner of BiblioTech and also an importer/exporter. That's his public face. Privately, he was a power broker with a network of legal and not-so-legal contacts in the Bay Area and beyond. He traded information and brokered deals that go largely unnoticed in the newspapers except when reporters questioned why plans for a development changed or why a prominent person suddenly retired or left the area without explanation. Ari was wealthy, having made his fortune at Microsoft and later in market and currency speculation. He quietly funneled that money to places where it leveraged deals or supported his causes.

I met Ari and his partner, artist Catherine Gauthier, years ago at the Monterey Jazz Festival, where the Storm Lake Blues Band was performing, and we've been close friends since. Ari is of Armenian descent, and his cousin Sana Houssain is BiblioTech's night manager. Sana is a grizzled veteran and leader in the Armenian underground in San Francisco. He and five of his Armenian friends helped Kat and me in New Mexico. Without them, we might not have succeeded. That experience made me appreciate their loyalty to Ari and their capabilities as shadow soldiers. Among their skills were forgery, bomb-making, and kidnapping, which, to my knowledge, they employed only to serve noble causes. But I may be wrong about that. The only member of Ari's team I trusted more than the Armenians was Earl Zepeda, who was born Earlene but identified as male and, with Ari's help, underwent sexual reassignment surgery and became a tough young man through iron will and training. In a few years, Earl transitioned from lithe to lethal, protecting Ari's interests with fanatical determination.

I saw Sana and Earl deeper in the warehouse as I sat beside Ari's desk. He flipped through papers on a brown clipboard and said, "Sign it here." I was looking at a bill of lading from SunChip, a semiconductor manufacturer in Taipei. I was listed as the importer, and by signing, I accepted the delivery of 25,000 SCS9502 computer chips for $19 million. The document below the bill of lading was a contract to sell those chips to a technology distributor in Pittsburgh for the same price. This pass-through transaction, which Ari couldn't do in his name, was a dodge. Although I officially didn't know this, hidden in the packing of the SCS9502s were four hundred state-of-the-art artificial intelligence semiconductor chips not yet licensed for export from Taiwan. They would then be routed, secretly, to an A.I. research firm in Silicon Valley that competed with China for supremacy in A.I.-enhanced packet switching. SunChip CEO's grandparents had been murdered by the Chinese government, forcing his parents to flee to Taiwan, so he was always willing to stick it to the Chinese, and I was happy to do my part.

Every Tuesday evening, Ari and I meet with two other close friends in a musty room on the top floor at the back of the building, a private room with dusty bookshelves and well-worn leather chairs. The room looks like a salon from the Victorian era and could be that old. It smells like clothing closeted for decades and has the Western ambiance of worn boots and cheap whiskey. The ghosts in this room hover just beyond your vision, vapors that quickly dissipate when you turn your head, but you know they're there, watching and listening. When Ari and I arrived, John Sebastiani and Julien Kito sat in their chairs having a lively debate over two bottles of wine open on the room's centerpiece—a mahogany coffee table as crusted and scarred as the moon.

We named our group The Philosopher's Club after Julien, a retired philosophy professor at UC Berkeley. Julien is a Japanese-American. His parents were among the first to be interned during World War II. His father ran a printing press, and he was suspected because the government feared he would print pro-Japanese propaganda during the war. They had no evidence of guilt beyond his ancestry, but that was sufficient to justify his incarceration. Julien was born in Torrance after the war, spent four years in Japan as a college student studying Eastern religions, and has written three well-regarded books on Eastern philosophy. He is recovering from throat cancer and speaks in a gravelly voice that betrays a profound intellect.

John, who helped me intimidate Roland Meany, is a one-man American melting pot. Half-Italian, half-Scottish, he dropped out of high school, worked on a freighter on Lake Michigan, fought with the Marines in Afghanistan, became a Navy Seal doing black work in the Middle East, got religion, spent ten years as a Jesuit priest in Chicago, became disaffected with the church, and now runs a small security firm in San Francisco. He is a licensed PI, consults with the San Francisco police, and has ties to the FBI and CIA. He is a multi-faceted tough guy with a soft heart whose steely eyes can bore into you while he pats you on the back and encourages you to pick yourself up and keep moving. You don't know whether to be motivated by his kindness or fear that he'll kick your butt if you don't move.

Julien and John disagreed about the quality of Oregon's Willamette Valley pinot noirs, one from Adelsheim and the other from Eyrie. Ari and I poured a little of each and let the wines slide over our tongues before swallowing. I thought they both tasted fine, but then I'm a Scotch drinker and am not as discriminating about wine as my companions. Our philosopher-king buried his nose in the Eyrie vintage for a minute, savoring the bouquet, and pronounced it divine. Ari couldn't disagree, although, like John, he preferred the Adelsheim. I settled the matter by siding with Julien on the Eyrie, so the group agreed to a draw. When we concluded our wine tasting, Ari settled into his high-back, comfy chair and crossed his legs. He wore a white shirt under a blue tweed sportscoat buttoned at the waist. He set one elbow on his knee, rested his chin in his hand—his classic contemplative pose—and asked me how Kat was doing.

"She's improving. They operated on Sunday morning to repair her liver and a broken rib. I spoke to her this morning, and she said she's sore as hell but okay. She's resting now. I'm driving back to Sacramento tomorrow."

The door opened, and a twenty-something man came in with another open bottle of Willamette wine and a tray of finger sandwiches and raw vegetables. He set them on the coffee table.

"Thank you, Justin," Ari said as the guy left. Then he turned to me. "How are you doing?"

"Okay. Good." I said, not convincingly. "Bad. Angry. She could have died. She was crashing when they wheeled her to surgery. I'm pissed that she was shot, and I'm pissed that the guy who shot her is dead."

"You wanted to kill him yourself?" John asked.

I thought about that as I put some cucumber slices and carrots on a napkin. "If I'd been there, I would have stopped him, one way or another."

"You weren't there, and you can't save everyone all the time," Ari said.

"Kat's not everyone," I replied. The cucumbers were cold and tart.

Julien smiled at me and said, "In Buddhism, they say that anger is like drinking poison and expecting the other person to die."

I laughed. "Yeah, and anyway, the guy is dead. Karma already dealt with him."

"What do the police know about the shooter?" John said.

"He was a banker."

"Not a typical occupation for a mass murderer," John said.

"No, but I'm not sure what is."

We took a moment to get food from the tray, and as we ate, I told them what I'd learned about mass murderers from Rhoda Merrick.

"Duggins doesn't fit the mold," I said. "He was president of a Bank of America branch. He had golf clubs in his trunk but got sidetracked for some reason and wound up following a guy into a flea market and shooting him before going on a rampage."

"Did he know the guy he shot?" John said.

"The police haven't found a connection. The guy he killed was Alberto Flores. A mechanic. Worked in an auto shop in Elk Grove. As far as the police know, Duggins didn't take his car there."

"Did Flores bank at Duggins's branch?" Ari asked.

"No. Keith Lau said he banked at Wells Fargo. His wife ran a stall at the flea market, which is probably why he drove there."

"Where did Duggins get the weapon?" Ari asked.

"Bought it. He carried it in his car. His wife told police he was afraid of being kidnapped. It was a Kimber Rapide 1911."

"That's serious armament," John said. "The Kimber is the Rolls Royce of forty-fives. A well-made, quality piece, and you pay for it. Around fourteen hundred new. It's more accurate than most custom-made handguns."

Julien closed his eyes and tented his fingers. "Why would he need such a weapon? Was he a competitive shooter? Or a collector?"

I shrugged. "They're saying he took shooting lessons at a gun club, but they didn't find other weapons at his home. After SWAT shot him, they discovered a thirty-eight near his body. He had fired it, too, but they think it belonged to a man Duggins killed at the scene."

John refilled his glass with the Eyrie pinot and said, "So he prepared for the incident by buying a gun and learning how to use it. Any other evidence of planning?"

"Apparently not. They haven't found any evidence of premeditation. Like everyone else in Sacramento, he'd probably been to the Folsom Flea Market. He didn't need to scout it."

I took a bite of a tuna salad sandwich. The moment I bit into it, I felt a tangy burst of flavor. It was rich and creamy and had a saucy aftertaste. Delicious. All the sandwiches were exquisite. I asked Ari where he got them.

"San Francisco Meat Company," he said. I was about to make another comment on the food when Julien suddenly spoke.

"The location is not important." We turned and looked at him.

"Why not, Julien?" said Ari.

"He targeted the first victim. Why? The police should focus their efforts on that question. The location is not material to killing Flores. The rest of the shootings, while tragic, are a distraction."

After thinking about Julien's comment, I said, "Maybe it wasn't planned. Maybe the first shooting was road rage. Flores cut him off in traffic. Something like that."

"That might explain the first victim," Ari said, "but not why he kept shooting. People with road rage target the person who pissed them off, not total strangers in mass murder."

I agreed with Ari. Road rage killings are impulsive and focused on the object of their anger. "Something else. Keith said witnesses described him as enraged. Duggins had red hair and a red face. They said he looked like his head was on fire."

John grunted. "Sounds like the berserkers."

"The what?" I said for the rest of us.

"Bear warriors," John said. "Viking shock troops. Berserkers. Norse sagas say they went into battle naked except for bear or wolf skins and fought ferociously, hacking their enemies to pieces, eating them, and drinking their blood. They were shape-shifters who dressed and fought like wild animals. That's where the word berserk comes from. The Norwegian king outlawed them, I think, around the year 1200. When you go berserk, you fly into a blind rage. That sounds like Duggins."

"He was a banker, not a warrior," Julien observed.

"Anyone can fly into a rage," I said.

"But very few commit mass murder," Julien said. "Many orders of magnitude separate anger from mass murder."

I looked at Ari. "What do you think?"

He leaned back in his chair, wiped his mouth with a napkin, and recrossed his legs. "From what I've read, Duggins' actions were out of character. He might have had a seizure or been on drugs. Maybe it was a brain tumor. Something caused him to go berserk."

"We won't know till they finish the autopsy."

John said. "The Berserkers supposedly drank alcohol and ate psychedelic mushrooms before battle. The Nazis gave their soldiers crystal meth so they could fight longer without being exhausted. They didn't feel pain, and they wore down their enemies. But you don't need drugs to feel invulnerable. When I was in Afghanistan, we had a poster on the barracks wall. It showed a scowling, grungy Marine, grenades hanging from his vest, weapons in both hands. It read, 'Yea though I walk through the Valley of the Shadow of Death, I will fear no evil, for I am the meanest son of a bitch in the Valley.'"

I laughed. "I'm trying to picture that poster in a banker's office."

"Yeah, maybe not," John said, "but I'm with Ari. Duggins acted out of character."

"From what I've read, so did the woman who drove her car into those people," Julien said. "The *Chronicle* profiled her in today's paper."

"Fernanda Alamilla," I said. "Paul Fisher said she was 49. A dental assistant in South San Francisco. Mother of three. Grandchild on the way. No priors. No history of violence. No known drug abuse. He said when the cops shot her, she looked crazed, had spittle flying out of her mouth."

Ari sipped his wine, thumping one finger on the side of the glass. "So we have two seemingly ordinary people who went berserk and committed mass murder."

"That's right," I said. "Neither had a record of violence. Or a record of any kind. It's not clear that they targeted their victims. Or held a grudge against anybody. Neither one was alienated, as far as we know, or desperate. They hadn't been fired, hadn't been bullied. They weren't recently divorced and hadn't had a death in the family."

"Suicidal?" John said. "Death by cop?"

"Not as far as I know," I said. "The signs you look for in a typical mass murderer aren't there."

"Yet they murdered many people," Julien said. "We can't know what's in someone's mind. Their motives may always be inexplicable, and we must accept that."

"Quite right, Julien," Ari said. "But acceptance doesn't mean we don't try to understand. The victims' families want to know why their loved ones are gone."

Julien peered into his glass of wine, brooding. He said, "A young man dies suddenly of a heart attack. His family wants to know why he died so young. There may be no reason. It is what it is, and nothing they can do will change it."

"Yes," Ari said, "but to the families of Duggins' victims, that young man's death is a paper cut. Their loss is an amputation."

We sat silently for a long moment, drinking wine while wondering why ordinary people do extraordinarily awful things.

"There's a difference," I said, "between someone like Robert Duggins and Donald Reese, the guy who raped my sister and threw me over a banister when I was 12 years old. Reese is an evil son of a bitch, a bad seed. You expect deviant behavior from a psychopath like him. You don't expect it from a normal person with a good job, a decent family, and a house in the suburbs. Asking why he did it is a reasonable question."

"Reasonable, yes," Julien said, "if we live in a rational world where people do what you expect. Buddhists warn against the tyranny of expectations. People are sometimes inexplicable. To expect otherwise is never to find peace. You have a wanting mind, Sonny, and will find no peace seeking answers when there are none."

"I don't want peace," I told him. "I want justice."

Duggins

I awoke early on Wednesday with a throbbing knee and a bucket of sludge in my head. I dreamed I was chasing a furtive figure through the city's streets. I saw him turn left at an intersection, but he vanished when I reached that corner and looked left. Then I'd see him on a different street, and he'd turn at another corner. The chase lasted all night through streets rimmed with ash. I never lost sight of him, but he remained elusive. He was always half a block ahead, disappearing around another corner. That dream was still hovering when I remembered the time and dragged my feet onto the floor. I don't know why I was chasing him; I just knew he had an answer I sought, a feeling that confounded me. I shook off the cobwebs, shaved, showered, and pulled on jeans and a Monterey Jazz sweatshirt. Breakfast was coffee sweetened with oxy and a power bar as I dashed to my car. The wind had stopped blowing overnight, but the streets wore a pussy-willow veneer of gray particulate.

Kat had been discharged from the hospital Wednesday morning. Keith Lau drove her home in a police van and texted me that he'd stay with her until I arrived. After her divorce, Kat moved to a small split-level brick house in Sacramento's Curtis Park neighborhood, a potpourri of home styles and pinched lawns along narrow streets. Sacramento has been called the City of Trees, and in Kat's neighborhood, lofty sycamores and oaks towered over the houses, their branches forming an intricate web in the autumn sky. The leaves created an umbrella of green, yellow, and brown that painted homes in dappled sunlight and formed a Rorschach pattern on the streets. Fallen leaves blanketed the unraked lawns and spilled onto the sidewalks. It was a neighborhood where people walked their dogs in the evening, kids skateboarded up and over and back down curbs in scratchy staccato, and the smell of hot apple pie reminded you it was dinnertime.

I'd stayed at her house now and then since we met and more frequently since the band's tour ended. I arrived mid-morning and parked along the curb in front. She had a long driveway with a white garage behind her house. A police van occupied the driveway. Dry leaves crinkled underfoot as I walked to her front door. When I opened the door, I heard voices inside. She and Keith sat at her dining room table. A laptop was open between them, Kat's fingers resting on the keyboard. Her face was as worn and faded as an old paperback at a garage sale. Her stringy blonde hair was matted haphazardly and meandered over her head, but her lips rose in a sweet smile when she saw me. I leaned down and kissed her.

"I like this look on you," I said.

"Thanks. I call it hospital grunge."

"Good choice for Halloween. You'll scare the hell out of the trick-or-treaters."

She flashed a weak smile. "I feel as bad as I look. I wish you weren't seeing me like this."

"I saw you slathered in mud in New Mexico. This is an improvement."

That brought a constrained laugh. I saw bandages beneath the top button of her loose blue plaid shirt. I knew she was in pain, so I vowed no more jokes until she felt better. Her eyes were alert, but her mouth was pruned. I asked about the pain. She said it was tolerable, but she grimaced when she moved. Rib injuries make breathing difficult. Any movement feels like a lance piercing your side. A pair of crutches leaned against the wall beside the table, and a vial of Percocet and a glass of water sat beside her laptop. I asked if she shouldn't be in bed, and she shook her head.

"One more minute in bed, I'll become part of the mattress."

"Gotcha."

"I need to work. How long can you stay?"

"Long as you need me."

"Good. Then you're moving in?"

I smiled and kissed her again. Keith watched us, amused. He wore a shoulder holster with a black automatic over his white shirt. A gray plaid sportscoat hung from the back of his chair. I shook his hand and asked what they were doing.

"We're constructing a timeline of Duggins' actions on Saturday morning," he said.

"Anything new?"

He nodded. "A wit named Ralph Klusman called yesterday and said Duggins almost ran him off the road that morning. Klusman was on his way home from Lowe's, and Duggins veered into his lane and nearly sideswiped him. He said Duggins snarled at him and flipped him off."

"He's sure it was Duggins?" Kat asked.

"Klusman memorized his plate and then turned off the road when he could. He said Duggins looked like a maniac. Scared the shit out of him. He saw Duggins' picture in the paper and realized that was the guy."

"What time was this?"

Keith glanced at his notebook. "Just after nine."

Kat typed that in. "He left his house at eight o'clock, according to his wife," she said.

Keith kept reading while Kat typed. "Right. He stopped at the Old Town Roasting Company off Lincoln Highway and charged coffee and a sweet roll to his Visa at 8:22." Keith glanced at me. "He had one of their cups in the beverage holder. It still had a few drops of coffee in it." He looked back at Kat. "He freaked out Klusman by that Office Depot on Folsom. Around 9:05. He shot Flores at 9:12, so we assume he encountered Flores during that seven-minute interval."

"What time did SWAT put him down?" I asked.

Keith read from his notebook: "9:36. He and three other guys had a tee time at Castle Oaks in Ione at 11:06. His wife told us Saturday was their twenty-fifth anniversary. They had plans for a special dinner with friends."

"So he hadn't intended to murder anyone that morning," Kat said. "They had something special planned that night. He expected to be home, so it wasn't suicide or a vendetta."

"Was he acting strangely at the coffee place?" I asked Keith.

He shook his head. "Nothing out of the ordinary. They knew him there. A regular. They said he seemed normal."

"How long was he there?"

Keith shrugged. "They didn't know. They said he usually sits for about twenty minutes on Saturdays having coffee and something to eat, but they didn't notice him leave last Saturday."

"So we can assume twenty minutes for breakfast."

Kat said, "Whatever set him off happened after he left Old Town Roasters and before he gave Ralph Klusman the finger. That would make it 8:40, give or take, and 9:05."

"That's not much time to go from Dr. Jekyll to Mr. Hyde," I said. "Did he stop anywhere else?"

"Unknown," Keith replied. After a pause, he flipped his notebook shut and said he had to go.

"What makes a mild-mannered banker fly into a rage and shoot up a flea market?" I asked.

Keith threw up his hands. "I don't know. He had no history of drug use or violence. There were no illegal drugs at his house or in his car—nothing that says he planned it. It's a mystery."

I heard a car pull into Kat's driveway shortly after Keith left. Two young women came to the door. One was a pretty dark-haired nurse with a long, narrow face. She wore blue scrubs and a brown hijab. She had a medical bag and introduced herself as Amira. The other was Noreen, whose curly brown hair fanned out from her head like a cape on a windy day. They were there to check on Kat and do rehab. Kat's bedroom was down the hall from the living room. I helped her there and then returned to my car for my travel bag and the saxophone I'd brought from home—a gold Selmer Supreme, one of the first altos I bought. I named it after Charlie "Yardbird" Parker, who pioneered the bebop jazz style in the 1940s. The "Bird" loved chicken, which is how he got his nickname. They say he practiced fifteen hours a day as a kid. It rattled his neighbors, and they asked his mother to move so they could have some peace. Bird had the rare gift of perfect pitch. Every alto sax player since him has tried to match it. None have succeeded.

But you have to try, so after Kat assured me I wouldn't bother them, I took out Bird and ran through the scales as I flexed my fingers, and they became more nimble. I was practicing a solo from our latest album when the screen door opened, and Kat's daughter came in. Sara is an eighth-grader who has it all figured out, like many kids her age. She knows where she wants to go to high school (St. Ignacius in San Francisco) and college (UC Berkeley) and what she wants to be when she grows up (a biochemist like Nobel-prize-winner Jennifer Doudna). She's tall for her age and a bit gangly, but she has her mother's good looks.

She listened to me play for a bit and wished she could play like that. She's been learning the trumpet and is a fair early intermediate player. I told her all it takes is years of practice and a love of the instrument. She asked me to teach her something, so I told her to get out her trumpet. I played a jazzy version of St. James Infirmary, a traditional New Orleans funeral march. It's an eight-bar blues number in A minor, and she picked it up within a few minutes. I told her I was impressed. Then she played the melody while I added accompaniment on the sax, creating harmony around the melodic line. As she grew more confident, she smiled at me with her eyes and began embellishing some notes. We were interrupted by applause as Kat and her nurses emerged from the bedroom.

They had changed Kat's bandages and rehabbed her leg. Noreen told us she would need the crutches for two more weeks and a cane afterward, but she'd be walking normally in a few months. Sara disappeared into her bedroom upstairs as the two nurses prepared to leave. Before she closed the door, Amira turned and gave me a coy smile, which Kat noticed.

I shrugged and said, "She must have enjoyed our duet."

"I'm sure that's it," Kat said.

"Maybe I need a t-shirt that says my girlfriend carries a gun."

"I'll have one made for you," she said, smirking as she returned to the dining room table and opened her laptop.

"What are you up to?" I asked her.

"A deeper dive on Robert Duggins. I need to understand why this guy lost it. He grew up in Reno, so I'll start there."

"Think you could lean over your kitchen sink and rest your shoulders on your arms?"

"If this is some weird sex thing, remember Sara's in the house."

"What I have in mind is kinky, and I'm game if you are," I said, laughing. "How about I wash your hair instead? We can pretend we're fooling around."

She gave me a weary smile. "That would help me feel better."

It wasn't my first kitchen sink hair wash job, but I'm no expert. I wrapped a towel around her neck to keep her dry, but that didn't prevent me from getting soaked. Afterward, she told me the simulated sex wasn't that great, and I apologized, saying it was a new technique. We agreed to keep working on it. She said it was painful to raise her arms over her head, so I combed her hair while she sat at her table, re-reading her notes on Duggins. When I finished combing, she started working again. I went to her garage and found a rake and plastic leaf bags. The air was cool and smelled musty and sweet, like rotting apples and pumpkin spice with overtones of burnt toast. I was raking the leaves in her poster-size front yard when I got a call from Paul Fisher.

"What's up, Paul?"

"I have an update, but first, how's Kat doing?"

"Better."

"Good to hear. She's as tough as a hanging judge. She'll be fine in a few months."

"Yep."

"There have been some developments related to your guitar player. We had a drug death last night in the Castro. A gay guy, 26, started zoning out at a drug party. When he collapsed, they called us. He was dead at the scene, and, funny thing, he had a strange smile on his face, like what you described when your guy collapsed. I just texted you a photo of the victim."

"Give me a minute," I said, putting him on hold while I checked my texts. The photo showed a white guy with a prominent nose ring and tattoos on his neck. His mouth was drawn up in an exaggerated smile, dull, tobacco-stained teeth underneath. He had the faraway look of a happy corpse who'd seen heaven as he passed. "That's what I saw on Eric," I told Paul. "It looks like glee laid on with a trowel."

"Yeah. Whatever poison this guy took, he had an enjoyable trip to the grave. I checked with Narcotics and learned there's been a rash of similar overdoses in the past three days."

"Other deaths?"

"None so far. They think the difference is the dosage. The Castro guy took more of it than Eric, but no one at the party knows how many pills he swallowed or where he got them. Like Eric, he'd also snorted coke. I asked for expedited toxicology, and the report just came back. Along with cocaine, he had a higher level of the same substance they saw in Eric's tox report."

"They don't know what it is?"

"No. The lab's never seen it before. They think a new designer drug may have hit the streets. Narcotics is hearing from a few sources about a feel-good product called Rapture. They don't know where it's coming from or who's distributing it. Narcotics contacted DEA to see if they knew anything, but they haven't heard back. This could be an East Coast thing that just made its way here, or it could be from China or South America. Nobody knows."

"Okay, thanks, Paul."

"Sure. I'm sorry about Eric. This Rapture drug is probably what he took, and the prognosis is grim. The low-dose victims are conscious and responsive in a day or two, but the doctors think their dopamine receptors may be permanently damaged. The hospitals don't know how to treat it because they don't know what it is. Okay? Gotta run. Let me know how Kat's doing."

When I finished raking and bagging leaves, my left knee throbbed. I sat in my car and rubbed it. Then, I took two oxys from a vial in my glove compartment and swallowed them with water. Two might be enough if I caught the pain quickly. I slipped two more oxys into my pocket in case I hadn't. When I returned to the house, Kat was on her phone, and I heard her say, "I understand. I'm sorry about your brother." I asked what that was about.

"That was Robert Duggins' older brother. After calling a dozen high schools in Reno, I discovered that Robert graduated from Reno High School in 1989. I didn't find anything remarkable in his yearbook. Then I called the Reno police and asked them to check arrest records from '85 to '89. There was nothing on Robert Duggins, but a Kurt Duggins was arrested in '87."

"For what?"

"Manslaughter. He was 17 at the time but was tried as an adult. He beat his uncle to death in his family's home. Robert was 14 at the time and witnessed the beating."

"So Duggins had some family trauma."

She nodded. "He witnessed a violent death. The brother was convicted of involuntary manslaughter, sentenced to 3 years, and served 22 months in Loveland."

"What's that?"

"Loveland Correctional Institute. Nevada's state prison for juvenile offenders. The uncle was a heroin addict. The boys heard him pleading with their father for money. The father said no more. The next day, the boys returned from school and found the uncle in their house, pocketing their mother's jewelry. Kurt confronted him, and they fought. Kurt was a junior in high school and on the wrestling team. He struck his uncle, and the uncle went down. He fractured his skull when he hit the floor. Kurt said he couldn't stay in Reno after he was released. He drifted south, worked odd jobs, and then made his way to Long Beach and learned to drive trucks."

"How did you find him?"

"I checked for driver's licenses in states he might have gone to and found him in California. He's lived here twenty-one years."

"Good work, detective."

"Routine, but thanks. He's now working as a long-haul trucker for an outfit called Trans-Oceanic. I called their office and was told he was en route to Birmingham, Alabama. I called his cell and left a message. He called me back a few minutes ago and was surprised to hear what Robert did."

"How could he not know? No one in his family mentioned it?"

"He said he lost touch. Their parents are gone. The father died of lung cancer in 2009. The mother has Alzheimer's. She's in a care facility in Reno. Kurt lost track of his brother when he headed south and said he doesn't listen to the news or read papers on the road. I asked if he thought Robert was capable of mass murder. He said Bobby was an angry kid after what happened. Kurt didn't think his brother was a killer, but he admitted he didn't know him well. He said after he was incarcerated, Bobby visited him once and was angry at everyone and everything. He told me if there's a funeral, he's not going. It's not part of his life anymore, and his family in Long Beach doesn't know he had a brother."

Kat hadn't eaten anything since leaving the hospital, so I made soup and salad for the three of us and thought about Duggins while I ate. When Sara finished lunch, she asked me to teach her another song. I asked what she'd like to play, and she said a song that's more than easy but not too hard. I chuckled and said I know about a thousand of those.

While she returned upstairs to get her trumpet, I told Kat, "I get that Duggins was an angry kid. He probably looked up to his older brother. It would have been tough to see his brother kill their uncle and then lose his only sibling to the prison system. But it's a giant step from there to mass murder. Something else happened to him."

Rapture

When my former girlfriend, Marilyn Anne Crittenden, caught COVID in 2020, I spent a week sleeping on the couch while she recovered in our bedroom. Nobody in the world knew what to do back then. Advice from the CDC changed every other week, and the president advised people to drink bleach and shine ultraviolet light up their ass. Mac wasn't sick enough for a hospital, but my taking care of her was like a grease monkey arranging flowers.

At Kat's house, I slept fitfully on a living room couch too short for a guy six foot two, and I swear the sofa was made of steel girders and concrete covered with a thin layer of military canvas. So I was awake at 2:17 when I heard her moving in her bedroom down the hall. She was hobbling on crutches toward the bedroom door when I intercepted her. She said she couldn't sleep because the pain in her chest felt like a drill press, and she needed a Percocet to lighten the load. I guided her back to the bed and brought her a pill and a glass of water. Then I sat on the other side of her bed until she drifted off about an hour later. I don't know if that counts as caregiving, but I did my best.

In the morning, she looked like an extra from *The Walking Dead* and asked for another Percocet. She needed more sleep, so she returned to bed, telling me not to disturb her until noon. I pulled the drapes and closed her door. After Sara left for school, I couldn't practice music, so I looked up Krav Maga studios in Sacramento and found one that opened at nine. Krav Maga is like any skilled sport. If you don't practice regularly, you lose your edge. I packed my gym gear and walked to my car. The air had a jaundiced cast, and my car was coated with fine white ash. As I drove, I turned on the radio and learned that the Escobedo fire had grown to over 18,000 acres and had torched dozens of homes west of the town. I looked north and saw billowing cumulus clouds of smoke rolling east—tumbling balls of gray and white spanning the horizon.

I found American Krav Maga in a strip mall between a used furniture store and a Vietnamese restaurant. The wall opposite the entrance had a giant mural of a stalking tiger painted in yellow, brown, and gold pastels; two other walls had floor-to-ceiling mirrors. It was a cool, modern scene—and busy. Two classes had started as I walked in—a dozen kids in one corner doing warm-up stretches, teens in another lined up in front of heavy bags. The owner, Bob Jordan, was a tall black guy with a shaved head and a pencil-thin beard. The muscles on his arms moved like snakes beneath his skin. He was a black belt like me and taught classes on Friday mornings to the kids, so I worked out with another instructor who'd earned his black belt fourteen years after mine. I can't say I learned anything, but we had an enjoyable hour throwing each other around.

Afterward, I asked Jordan if he knew of a fitness club with a decent indoor track. He directed me to a gym across town called The Well. I put an elastic wrap on my knee but overdid it by walking four miles on the track. Afterward, my knee was throbbing, so I took an oxy and sat in my car, waiting for the pain to subside. I needed to talk to Paul Fisher, but I called Xavier first.

"Hey, bro," he said when he picked up. "What's poppin'?"

I told him how Kat was doing and asked about Eric.

"Been no change, but at least he's vertical. I s'pose that's a change. He can walk with help, but his head is, I dunno, on Jupiter somewhere. Hasn't said nothin'. Doesn't respond when they talk to him. They scanned his brain and said his lights were on but dim, you know? Part of his brain not connected with the rest. I dunno, man, I think the brother's gone."

"My cop friend said there's a new drug on the street called Rapture."

"Never heard of it."

"Designer drug. A guy in the Castro OD'd on it. Some others are on strange trips and in hospitals. They don't know what it is."

"Shit."

"I'm going to find out who's pushing it."

"Won't help Eric."

"Maybe not. But if the labs can analyze the stuff, maybe they can figure out how to treat it."

"Where'd it come from?"

"Nobody knows," I said.

"Well, fuck." He paused, letting the frustration drain out of his voice. "I'm gonna cancel our gigs for the next month. We need a guitarist."

"Could be temporary. Eric might come out of it."

"There you go. Look on the bright side, Mr. Sunshine. And maybe I wave my hand, salt turns to sugar."

"No, I'm with you, X Man. I'm just saying, we should look for somebody to plug the hole in the dike, but make it somebody who could be interested in a permanent arrangement. Somebody fresh. As good as Eric. You know any GOATS?"

"Greatest of all time? Sure, but they're all dead, man. Stevie Ray, B.B., Jimi. And Bonamassa doin' his deal. But I got some ideas. Heard a player the other night. Young gal. Lightning fingers, bitchin' tone. Had a smooth touch and attitude. She sang, too. Edgy voice. I'll make some calls. See what she's about. Gonna be back Saturday?"

"If I have to."

"I talked to K.C. and Garth. We need to meet."

"Count on it."

"Later, bro."

Xavier, Garth, and I were the original Storm Lake Blues Band members. Eric was Xavier's friend and joined us soon after. Eric knew K.C., and we convinced him to join a few months later. It took us a year to develop our sound. We jammed three or four times a week until it felt like a cohesive unit, and then we started writing music. Changing horses midstream is not easy in a band. You learn each other's techniques and timing. You know when a guy is hot and when he's not. As he improvises, you learn to listen, *really* listen, sense where he's going, and know when a counterpoint would enhance the solo or a drum fill would mark a transition. And when you're playing a set, you don't have to think about what's happening when the whole band is in sync, like playing well together, and it doesn't happen unless you're totally in touch with the other guys and trust them. Losing Eric would be a setback, so whoever took his place had to be someone with exceptional skill and the ability to play well with us.

I sat in my car, brooding over it, rubbing my knee, watching people go in and out of The Well. Then I called Paul Fisher. He was still working the Market Street homicide. I told him what I'd learned about Robert Duggins on the morning of the shooting.

"Fernanda Alamilla stopped for coffee, too," he said, "at a Starbucks in South City. She met a friend there, Ana Cervantes. They have coffee there every morning."

"And?"

"Duggins had coffee, too. Interesting coincidence."

"You think bad coffee caused these two incidents?" I asked.

Paul laughed. "Only if it's that bitter crap in our squad room."

"Find out why she ran over those people?"

"Uh-uh. No, Cervantes said Alamilla seemed normal. Until she left. She ordered a latte and said it was too sweet. She complained and got another one, which she said was fine. She ate a chocolate croissant, which she does every morning."

"Maybe she and Duggins had a sugar overload."

"Yeah," he laughed. "The Twinkie defense."

"The what?"

"Before you were born. In the seventies, a former city Supervisor killed Mayor George Moscone and Supervisor Harvey Milk. The shooter claimed he overdosed on Twinkies. That was his defense."

"Sounds like bullshit to me," I said. "Bad actors always have to blame someone or something else for their behavior."

"Yeah. Cervantes told us that Alamilla became fidgety just before they left Starbucks—like her head was twitchy, she couldn't focus, and she didn't know what to do with her hands. Outside, she was disoriented and thought she was driving home. Cervantes had to remind her that she was on her way to work. Then she was concerned when Alamilla drove out of the parking lot in the wrong direction."

"What do you make of that?"

"I don't know," Paul said.

"Could be Rapture, maybe?"

"We don't have her tox report yet, but that seems unlikely. We're getting more reports of bad trips on Rapture, but the people taking it are not turning homicidal. They disappear in a cloud of bliss."

"Kat's digging up more background on Duggins. I'll let you know what she turns up."

Before I returned to Kat's house, I wanted to talk to Ari. When he answered, I told him what I'd been learning about Rapture. "I want to find out where the drug's coming from," I told him. "Who would be the best source in the city? Not law enforcement. They're in the dark."

"That would be Alejandro Crisologo. Several gangs push drugs in the city, including the Colombian and Mexican cartels. There are Chinese importing fentanyl through the harbors. But those people are specialized wholesalers. No one knows the total drug scene better than Crisologo."

"You know him?"

"Oh, vaguely. We've crossed paths a few times on other matters, but I'm a bookseller. He's not in that business."

I smiled to myself. "How would I go about meeting him?"

"You sure you want to do that? He's elusive as hell, and he surrounds himself with junior gangbangers. These are not people who tolerate outsiders."

"I need to find out what's happening with Eric. Rapture hasn't been on the scene long. Someone's importing it."

"Or making it," he said. "Maybe it's Crisologo's product. Maybe he'll discourage curiosity."

"If he's bashful, we'll talk about the blues. Everybody likes music."

"All right, partner. If you want to jump into that snake pit, I'll set it up for you—and put some protection in place."

I returned to Kat's house just after noon. I stopped at a gourmet deli and brought home a Mediterranean wrap, a chicken salad sandwich, a gyro, and three salads. Kat had dressed in sweatpants and an oversized Sacramento PD sweatshirt and sat by her laptop at the dining room table. She was pale but was moving better. We kissed, and I leaned back and studied her eyes. That fierce light I loved about her was returning, and I thought how much I admired this woman with liquid steel coursing through her veins. She hadn't eaten since last night and said she was hungry for something better than hospital cuisine. She ate the wrap and the garden salad. I ate the gyro and a Caesar salad, and we saved the rest for Sara.

"I've been up for an hour," she said. "I found more on Duggins. He enrolled at Boise State in 1990 and graduated in '94. The yearbook says he was in the Boise State Boxing Club for three years."

"No shit." From the photos I'd seen of him, he didn't look like a boxer. "Did he box earlier? The guys I know who got into boxing usually started when they were seven or eight. It would be unusual to start when you reach college."

"I couldn't find any evidence of him boxing earlier. And, get this, he boxed at Boise State for only three years. He started his first year and quit halfway through his junior year."

"Okay, so he got too busy with school or decided he didn't like boxing." I saw the gleam in her eye and knew she was setting me up.

"That's what I thought. But that's not it. I looked up the *Idaho Statesman* on-line—that's Boise's newspaper—around the date he quit the boxing club."

"And you found his name."

She smiled. "There was a brief article in late March of '93 about a bar fight in down-town Boise. It was an altercation between some college boys and three loggers. Two of the loggers wound up in the hospital."

"Duggins put them there?"

"Yep."

"Logging's hard work. They're usually tough guys."

"Duggins was tougher. He fractured one guy's jaw and broke another one's nose. He was charged with aggravated assault, but the charges were dropped."

"Why?"

"I don't know. I couldn't find later stories about the incident. But I read he was represented by a lawyer named Dorothy Varnis. There's a law firm in Boise called Varnis & Locklin. I was about to call them."

"Put it on speaker."

While she dialed, I went to the kitchen and poured iced teas. When I returned, she was asking to speak with Dorothy Varnis.

"She's no longer with the firm," a woman said.

"Okay," Kat said. "Can you tell me how to reach her?"

"I'm afraid Mrs. Varnis passed. Ten years ago."

"I'm sorry to hear that. I'm a detective in Sacramento and—"

"Maybe you could speak to her son, Lon."

"Is he—"

"He joined the firm before she died and is now a partner."

"If he's available, that would—"

The woman clicked off. Kat glanced at me, her eyes registering annoyance. I wasn't sure whether she'd been disconnected or put on hold. After a few seconds, we heard another click.

"This is Lon Varnis. How can I help you?"

Kat explained who she was and why she called and introduced me as her associate. Lon Varnis had heard about the mass shooting in Sacramento and knew the murderer was Robert Duggins.

"I still can't believe it," he said. "He's the last person I would ever expect to do something like that."

"I hoped to talk to your mother. She represented Duggins after that bar fight in 1993."

"My mom died a decade ago."

"So I was told. I'm sorry."

"She represented all of us at my behest."

"All of us?"

"The three of us in the boxing club. I was there."

"I didn't realize that. You weren't mentioned in the newspaper story."

"Fortunate. It wouldn't have looked good on my law school application. Yeah, I was there, along with Bob and Kent Danilov. The cops threatened to charge all of us, but Bob was the only one who threw any punches. My mom convinced the DA that Kent and I had no culpability. She had a harder time convincing them to let Bob off because of the injuries."

"Is there any reason you can't tell me what happened?"

"No. I don't mind. Attorney-client privilege doesn't apply. Uh. Jeez, I haven't thought about that night in a long time. The three of us went to the bar with a couple of girls. Not dating. They were just friends from school. We were sitting at a table in the back, and I saw these three guys eying the girls. They were wearing canvas coveralls and work boots. They'd been drinking for a while, I guess. They looked pretty loaded. We learned afterward that they were loggers. One of them came over and asked the girls to join them. When the girls said no, he leaned on the table, stared at us guys, and said we wouldn't mind if the girls joined him and his friends, would we? That pissed me off, and I told the guy to go fuck himself."

"That might have been the wrong thing to say," I said.

"Yeah, for sure," Lon responded. "You know, when you're young and dumb. Anyway, his two buddies came over. Kent stood up and apologized and said let's forget about it, or something like that. One of the guys pushed Kent back into the table. When he fell, his arm knocked over some beers. That's how it started."

"How did Duggins get involved?"

"We all three stood up, and one of the guys threw a punch at Bob. Wrong thing to do. Bob was one of the best boxers in our club. He ducked and counterpunched with a brutal uppercut, and the guy went down with a broken jaw. Before Kent or I could react, Bob gut-punched the guy who came over to our table and then delivered a roundhouse right that flattened his nose. The third guy backed off when he saw what Bob was capable of. When the police arrived, we looked like the aggressors, and they arrested us. So I called my mom, and she found witnesses to say the loggers provoked the fight. There was some damage, and we agreed to pay for it without admitting guilt. The loggers worked for a forestry company outside of Boise. They didn't want to get fired, so everyone agreed to let the matter drop."

"It appears that Duggins left the boxing club around the time of that incident," Kat said.

"Yeah. He wasn't exactly asked to leave, but the team manager lectured us on how it looked for guys in the club to be involved in a bar fight. It wasn't the image Boise State wanted to project in the community. I don't think they asked Bob to resign, but they might have. He left the club about a week later."

"Are you aware of any other incidents?"

"No. I didn't see much of Bob after that. I was pre-law, and he was finance. We didn't have classes together, but I never heard anything else. He kept to himself, you know? I maybe saw him on campus two or three times in senior year."

"When you knew him in the club," I said, "what kind of guy was he?"

He thought about that. "He was a good boxer, like I said. Quick hands and feet. I mean, he couldn't have gone pro, but he snapped his jabs and excelled at counterpunching. I didn't like sparring with him. He was too aggressive for me."

"Did he have a temper?"

"You could say that. In the ring, if his opponent pissed him off, you know, low blow, whatever, you could see his face get redder, and he'd rip off a flurry of punches that would knock you on your ass if you couldn't duck or parry quickly enough."

"Outside the ring?"

"I never saw him get angry outside the ring. Except for that one time at that bar. He was pissed then, and he put down two scary-looking dudes inside of three seconds."

We thanked Lon for his help and rang off. Kat typed her notes on the call while I sat quietly, thinking about what we'd heard. Thirty years had passed since Duggins was in a bar fight in Boise. People can change. Most people mellow as they get older and softer and learn that avoiding drunks and people with no boundaries is better than confronting them. But I don't know if an aggressive disposition ever changes. Once you're prone to violence, maybe you always are.

"One thing's for sure," I said to Kat. "Until Folsom, Robert Duggins seemed like a white-collar cutout with a home in the 'burbs, but he was no Boy Scout."

Attracting Trouble

In my clearer moments, I am astonished at the human capacity for self-deception. We build narratives of ourselves from our core self-conception and exclude the monsters from our id. If we permitted our shadow selves to share center stage, we could not hold ourselves in high esteem or engender the goodwill of others. We are programmed to be the heroes of our own stories, so we selectively attend to what creates the most acceptable façade. I thought of that as I sat in my car Friday morning and counted the oxys in the vial hidden in my glove compartment. There were fewer than I remembered or could have imagined myself taking. But none had spilled, as I wanted to believe, and the vial had been full when I began this journey, though I excused myself by imagining the contrary. Opioids are beguiling companions, and oxy is particularly wistful and sly. You discover its name on your lease before you realize it has moved in. I looked at the three pills in my palm, reluctantly dropped them back into the vial, and returned it to its hideout.

To my shame, Kat refused to take her pain pill when we left her house an hour later. She needed fresh air and wanted to walk several blocks to Curtis Park. She was adroit in using crutches and put little weight on her left leg, but she could not hide grimacing when she propelled herself forward. I walked beside her and could gauge the ache in her chest by watching tight lines grip her face when her weight shifted. Her stoicism reminded me of Paul Fisher's mask of sanity after he caught a godawful case in 2020 when container ships sat idle for months in San Francisco Bay after COVID closed the ports.

The captain of a ship under Singapore registry notified the police of deaths aboard, and Paul supervised the homicide detectives who discovered thirty-three dead Chinese nationals, including children, inside a shipping container. Their provisions were depleted before the ship could reach the dock, and they'd been locked into the container, which was piled among scores of others, unnoticed by the captain or crew, who claimed to be unaware of the stowaways until the stench of rotting corpses settled over the deck. Paul called me late and asked me to meet him at the Lost Cat Bar on Post. We sat in a dark corner and drank scotch until they told us we had to settle our tab or help clean the place after they locked up.

Paul described the horrific sight of bodies wedged against the doors, piled on each other in a bloated cat's cradle of limbs, fingers shorn of nails, shrunken faces devoid of humanity in a ghastly tableau. He said the horror of their final hours was written in every frozen shriek and the black mat of blood beneath the bodies. As he spoke quietly, I saw tremors rippling through him, the rattling of bones barely concealed behind a countenance that those who didn't know him would describe as peaceful. But I've known Paul for years and saw a man on the verge of disintegration. That he could hold himself together in the face of such horror was a testament to his strength of character. I saw that in Kat, too, as she forced herself to persevere through the agony of each step. Courage in others is a lesson for us in our faltering moments.

When we returned to her house, I saw I'd missed a call from John Sebastiani. He'd texted, too: "Call me right away." Kat sank into an easy chair in her living room and closed her eyes. I went to the kitchen to make coffee and returned John's call.

"What's happening, *padre*?" I said when he answered.

"You need to get back here. There was a shooting at Bibliotech last night. Late. Out by the loading dock. Ari's okay, and Earl wasn't there, but three of Sana's guys were killed."

"Holy shit."

"Yeah. Two of them were with us in New Mexico—Azad and Davros. I'm not sure you knew the third guy, Andreas Derian."

That news hit me like a sharp slap on the forehead. Azad and Davros were good guys. I couldn't recall Andreas. "What the hell happened?"

"I'll fill you in when you get back. You'll get a call from a homicide detective. He's working with another detective in Robbery. They think it was an attempted heist."

"And they want to talk to me because?"

"The crew was loading a shipment of computer chips when the shooting happened. Your name is on the manifest. You quitting music?"

"Long story. See you soon."

I thought about how these deaths would affect Ari and Sana. Their Armenian friends were like family; when the initial wave of grief passed, their anger would rival steam exploding from a burst boiler. John didn't say what happened to the shooters, but if they survived the incident, I wouldn't sell them life insurance. Before I woke Kat, I called Keith Lau and told him what happened. Then I called the home healthcare company that sent Amira and Noreen and said I needed to arrange for extended home nursing care. I texted Sara at school and let her know. She texted back that she could cut her last class and would be home in an hour. Kat understood why I had to leave. I told her I'd be back on Sunday. Keith Lau pulled into the driveway as I was heading for my car.

"You have a way of attracting trouble," he said.

"It knows who to call," I responded. "The nursing agency is sending someone. I want them here around the clock if she needs them. Sara will be home shortly. I appreciate you staying with her until somebody arrives."

"No problem," he said.

I drove back through a wall of smoke from the fires north. Breathing was like sucking exhaust through a bellows. I couldn't see more than two or three vehicles ahead on the highway. Semis in the right lane crawled down the road in single file while cautious drivers on their left edged carefully past. Even with my knee, I could have run faster than traffic moved, but I calmed myself by box breathing while listening to CDs by T-Bone Walker and Etta James. For several hours, I lost myself in the blues, wondering what the hell had happened behind Ari's bookstore.

When I reached the city, I drove to BiblioTech and turned into the alley behind the building. Two SFPD patrol cars and two black sedans were parked in the lot. A small white moving van sat in front of the loading dock, its back doors open, splintered stacks of crates inside the cargo area. It was circled by yellow crime scene tape and had a dozen silver-dollar-sized holes in its opened back doors. The concrete on the back of the building was gouged where bullets had struck, and splotches of red stained the pavement where men had fallen. Evidence techs worked around the van, and two plainclothes detectives were conferring behind it. I parked my car and opened the door. The day was cool and breezy and carried the pungent smell of smoke. One of the uniforms told me I couldn't park there. I said I owned the merchandise in the van and was wanted for questioning.

I'd met one of the detectives before. James Renicke, a 40-something hot dog with a red buzzcut, had interviewed me after I was nearly killed in my condo by two degenerates. Renicke and the other detective ambled over when they saw me. Renicke was dressed casually in black jeans and a blue sports coat over a white shirt. The man with him wore a natty charcoal-gray suit, a buttoned-down stiff white shirt, and a blue striped tie. He had a matching silk handkerchief folded in his breast pocket. He looked Japanese and had the style and bearing of a model for GQ.

"Well, if it isn't Houdini," Renicke said. The degenerates had zip-tied my hands behind my back, and I'd shown Renicke how I rolled over and slipped my hands in front of me so I could defend myself. I think he was impressed despite his inherent skepticism. Renicke worked for Paul Fisher, the chief of homicide. "You keep turning up at my crime scenes," he said.

"Can't help you, detective," I said, holding up my hands. "I was in Sacramento last night."

"I'm sure you can prove that."

"If I need to. Let me catch your train of thought here. You're thinking I drove here last night and tried to steal my own shit?"

He cast a cold eye on me, but his lips were curled in a smirk. "Hey, it happens, tough guy. You rip off your goods, sell them on the black market, and collect insurance. You weren't thinking of defrauding the insurer, were you?"

"You got me," I said, holding my hands out to be handcuffed. Then I dropped my arms and smiled. "You need to do something else with your free time, detective. Lay off the film noir and watch some game shows. Or play solo Monopoly. See if you can beat yourself."

"All right, all right," he said, laughing. "My partner here is Frank Shimizo. He works Robbery."

Shimizo extended his hand, and I shook it. "Sonny Marshall," I told him.

Shimizo put his hands on his sides, his arms akimbo. His white shirt was crisp, smooth, and flat to his waist. This guy was in good shape.

"I appreciate you coming in," he said. "You own the shipment being loaded into the van, I understand."

I hesitated, wondering how wise it was to have signed that manifest. "Yeah, I do."

"Computer chips from Taiwan?"

I nodded.

"Worth a lot of money."

"Nineteen million. Was any of it taken?"

Shimizo shook his head. "The shooting started before things got that far."

"You know who tried to steal it?"

"No. From the vehicle's description, we think they drove a black GMC. But witnesses didn't get a good look at the shooters. Do you know anybody with a vehicle like that?"

I said I didn't.

"The shipment arrived from Taipei on a ship?"

I nodded.

"Why were you storing the chips here? It would be more logical to keep them in a warehouse at the pier."

Good question, detective. Why would I have done that? "I know the owner of BiblioTech. He allowed me to store them here, and it is a secure space."

He nodded and wrote that down in his notebook.

"Did anyone know you were moving the goods last night?"

I didn't even know it. "I don't think so, except for the guys hired to load it."

"Your cargo was headed to the East Coast?" I nodded. Shimizo looked back at the van and then at me. "Hijacking high-value loads is a lucrative racket. A shipment like this would be appealing. Low weight, high dollar, easy to move on the black market."

"I'm more concerned about the men who were killed."

"Of course. Understandable."

"You knew them?" Renicke asked me.

"I knew two of them. I wasn't familiar with the third guy, Andreas something."

"Derian. Andreas Derian. The dead guys worked for you?"

I was so winging it here. I could be an albatross with a seven-foot wing span. "They were being paid to load the shipment. And guard it."

"Okay, well. There are two security cameras on the back of this building. We'll know more after we see the tapes." I hadn't thought about the cameras, and I knew Ari was paranoid enough about security to ensure they were working. "Meanwhile, we'll need a statement from you."

"Sure," I replied, coughing. "If it's all right, I'll meet you inside."

Renicke looked at Shimizo, who said, "I'm fine with that."

Inside, I found Ari and others in his office. Ari wasn't given to ostentatious displays of power, and if the authorities were ever to raid BiblioTech, they wouldn't find anything compromising. His office looked like the back of any local bookstore—metal shelves crammed with books, papers overflowing on top of tarnished metal filing cabinets, and a modest middle-school teacher's wooden desk with initials scratched on the surface. And although it was early afternoon, and a smoky sky cast some light inside, the room seemed covered in a black shroud.

Ari sat in his chair, his chin resting on one fist, the index finger laying on his cheek. He raised his chin in a silent greeting when he saw me. Sana stood in a corner opposite the window, eyebrows heavy, dark circles like coke-bottle lenses beneath his eyes. The bottom half of his unshaven face looked like black sandpaper. John was stooped over a computer screen on Ari's desk, and Earl Zepeda stood to the right of the door. He peered at me with fiery eyes, then walked over, and we fist-bumped. He whispered, *"Jopuntas. Quiero matarlos."* Motherfuckers. I want to kill them.

¿Dónde estabas?" I asked him. *Where were you?*

"La Casa de mi tia," he said. *My aunt's house.*

"¿Sabemos quiénes eran?" Do we know who they were?

"No. Pero los encontraré." No. But I will find them.

"No, hermano. Los encontraremos." No, brother. We will find them.

"Y luego los mato, compa." And then I kill them. partner.

"Sean quienes sean, la justicia los encontrará." Whoever they are, justice will find them.

"Yo soy la justicia." I am justice, he said quietly.

Earl might have been a pro baseball player if genetics hadn't dealt him the wrong hand and he hadn't grown up on the tough streets of San Jose, where the games had no rules. He was fast and athletic, tougher than Oak and strong, having bulked up when he started taking testosterone. He was born with the wrong body and rectified that when Ari paid for his sex reassignment surgery. Earl was a handsome young man and would have been a beautiful woman, but his looks belied a savage intensity. In body and spirit, Earl was a griffin, the mythical creature with a lion's legs and loins and an eagle's head and talons. Revenge was not a complicated concept for Earl. An assault demanded a forceful response, and not in equal measure. Ari had believed in him and made the life he wanted possible. Earl would respect no boundaries in avenging the shots fired at his surrogate father. As he stood beside me, his neck was corded, his shoulders tensed, his talons sharp and pulsing with restless energy. I imagined him crouching in the ready position, waiting for prey. His pupils were deep pools of black beneath a hooded brow.

I walked to Ari's desk. He looked up at me. "What happened?" I asked him.

His face looked like ten years of gravity had sunk it overnight. "We were loading the shipment," he said. "For the airport. I was sending the chips east on a private cargo jet."

"Davros and Azad were loading the crates," Sana said in a voice clogged with wet cement.

"I knew that pickup was wrong," Ari continued, but John cut him off.

"Here it is," John said, pushing a key on the keyboard. Everyone crowded around the screen, and John pushed a key to play the video. Although it was dark, streetlights and lights from the building showed the alley clearly enough. We saw the top of the white van in the lower part of the screen. Its front faced the loading dock. The back doors were swung open. Two men on the left were carrying crates from the loading dock ramp to the back of the van. Davros and Azad. Sana walked back toward the dock. On the van's right side, one man held what looked like an AR-15. I guessed that was Andreas Derian. Behind Andreas stood another man, taller with dark hair, and I saw enough of his profile to know it was Ari.

From the right of the screen, I saw a shadow moving left, and then the hood of a dark pickup with a crew cab appeared. It edged into view, and I could see the distinctive grill of a GMC. The driver was in shadow but looked toward the van through an open window. The truck slowed to a stop. The pickup's horn blared. Instantly, the back crew door swung open, and two figures popped up in the truck's bed. Then two spits of automatic fire erupted from the bed and another from the open crew door. The Armenian closest to the back of the van fell forward onto the crate he was carrying and lay still. The other—I couldn't tell who—dropped his crate and ducked behind it. He stuck an arm out an instant later and returned fire, but the incoming fusillade was overwhelming.

On the other side of the van, Andreas stumbled backward and then raised his rifle and fired an automatic burst. Then we saw a spit of fire from the pickup's driver. His left arm was extended, and he rapidly fired toward the Armenian behind the crate. The entire exchange took less than four seconds. The driver retracted his arm, and the pickup sped away. I saw something drop to the pavement behind the pickup as it did. Then I looked back at the van and saw two figures sprawled on the pavement and another slumped behind the crate.

I realized I hadn't seen Ari or Sana and asked Ari where he had gone.

"I knew something was wrong about that truck," he said. "I dove in front of the van as the shooting started."

"Where were you?" I asked Sana.

"Carry another crate out. Ducked behind the door and shot them, at them, using door for cover."

As we watched the video again, I focused on Ari and saw him leap behind the van just as the pickup's horn blared. That fraction of a second put him out of the line of fire.

"Can you zoom in on the pickup?" I asked John.

He could do that, and we watched the video several more times as John focused on different parts of the assailant's vehicle. One take showed the driver, and although the video was fuzzy and dark, I realized it could be a woman. Her long black hair fell over the left side of her cheek, and one brooding eye was visible beside a long nose as sharp as a knife's blade. She was left-handed and held the automatic as steady as though she were threading a needle. It might have been a guy with long hair, but I didn't think so. When John focused on the bed of the pickup, we saw that the two men shooting from that position were wearing balaclavas. So was the shooter in the backseat of the pickup. Their features were obscured not only by their masks but by the strobing light of their rifle fire. But as the shooting stopped, the one at the back of the bed abruptly jerked and brought his hand up to his neck. As he did, his rifle tumbled out of his hands. That's what landed on the pavement behind the pickup.

"He was shot in the neck and dropped his weapon," I said.

"It was an AK-47," John said. "The police have it. The three behind the driver were firing AKs. You can tell by the sound. The driver was using an automatic like a Glock or a Sig Sauer. It could have been a PL-15." He turned to Ari. "Who knew you were moving the goods last night?"

Ari sat back and closed his eyes. "A few people here," he said quietly. "Me. Sana. The men loading it. Azad and Andreas were driving the van to the airport."

"Who at the airport knew?"

"The carrier. They had the manifest and filed a flight plan."

"Anyone could have paid them off," John said. "What about the buyer?"

"They knew it was being moved last night," Ari said.

I asked John if he had seen the AK before the police tagged and bagged it. He shook his head.

"Have you given the security tapes to the police?" I asked Ari.

"Not yet. They asked for them."

We were quiet for several moments, thinking about what we'd seen on the video. Then John said, "The thieves were surprised. They hadn't expected so many guys moving the cargo. Or Andreas with an assault rifle. I think their plan blew up on them before they could react."

"I don't think so," I said.

"Why not?" Ari asked me.

"The horn. The driver honked the horn, and then hell was unleashed. A horn at night is startling and makes too much noise for thieves. Except for Ari, everyone in the lot froze. But the men in the trunk raised their weapons and opened fire. I think the horn was a signal to start shooting. John's right. They were surprised by the number of men in the lot, but this wasn't a botched robbery. It was a botched hit."

My Heart Bleeds Blue

"Let's have some fun," Le'Andra Kimani said. She'd brought two guitars, took a Fender Standard Telecaster out of its case, and plugged it in. The four remaining Storm Lake Blues Band members had met Saturday morning in Studio B at my recording studio. Although everyone knew it was an audition, Xavier invited Le'Andra to jam with us. Xavier had seen her play, but Garth, K.C., and I were not familiar with her. She told us she grew up in Seattle and had been in the Bay Area for over a year. She was a slender 22-year-old with a smooth caramel complexion and smoky brown eyes. Long gold earrings with ruby tips hung from her earlobes. She slid the guitar strap over her neck and tuned the instrument with long, nimble fingers. I asked how long she'd been playing, and she said since she was six. Her father was a musician in Seattle, and she learned on his knee.

"Ya'll know 'My Heart Bleeds Blue'?"

"Deborah Coleman," Xavier said.

"Yea, brother. You and Garth join me in this fine twelve-bar blues number. It's in B minor. Chorus is 1-4-1-1. Ever'thing else is standard. Here we go."

She stepped up to the mic and played the opening riff. Then the X-Man and Garth joined. The first twelve bars were instrumental. Then she began to sing. She had a low, husky voice and sang with sass and nuance, sliding between pitches in perfect portamento. She would need more heartbreak in her life before she sang like Bessie Smith, but when you closed your eyes and listened, her voice felt like satin sliding over your skin.

When she finished, she flashed us a cocky smile as if to say, "Damn, I'm good. You know I'm good." Then she looked at K.C. and me and said, "You boys up for a little blues number I learned yesterday? It goes by the name of 'Hang Time'."

We wrote that song. It was a track on our first album, *Storm Warning*. That she learned it yesterday blew me away. She played Eric's part well. She created a more blues-rock vibe than Eric, but a casual listener wouldn't know the difference. Her performance earned some fist bumps, and she flashed that seductive smile. We jammed for another hour, just improvising, trading solos, getting a feel for how we could play together, and then she sang a few more blues numbers.

Before she arrived, we'd talked about Eric. We knew he wasn't coming back, hadn't quite gotten our heads around that, and felt sick about what happened to him, but what do you do after such a loss? He was family, but we couldn't let the loss of one of us break up the band. So we tossed around the names of other guitarists on the West Coast who might be available. But we forgot about the others after we jammed with Le'Andra. We agreed she'd become part of Storm Lake if she was down for it. Someday, she'd front her own band. She was too salty not to be a headliner. She wanted a few days to think it over, and after she left, we sat around asking ourselves what the hell just happened.

Before I left the studio, I checked my phone and had a message from John asking me to join them for lunch at Leo's Oyster Bar. Leo's is an *el primo* lunch spot in the financial district. Catherine and Ari were there when I arrived. I met them in a corner where we sat on a maroon leather bench with a ribbed back beneath a bamboo sconce. Catherine's bright red hair was pulled back in a ponytail, her face lean and dimpled when she smiled. She had the regal bearing of a lioness and spoke with a French accent. She greeted me with a kiss on both cheeks and handed me a glass of Balvenie on the rocks. John joined us a moment later, and we ordered fried oysters and deviled eggs. Catherine took my hands in hers and asked about Kat. I told them a few gunshots weren't enough to ruin her picnic. She'd be back soon.

When lunch arrived, John said, "We have some developments. The police found an abandoned truck in San Bruno. It was stolen from the pier yesterday. Somebody drove it into an auto repair parking lot and left it. There were bullet holes in the left side and sandbags in the bed, a wall of them stacked on the left side."

"Sandbags?" Ari said.

"Cover," I suggested. "For the shooters in the bed."

John nodded. "It wasn't a heist. They came to shoot and were ready for a firefight if anyone shot back."

"They came for me," Ari said.

Catherine's eyebrows shot up. "You said it was a robbery."

"That's the narrative the police are spinning," I said, "but I don't think so."

"Nineteen mil in easily moveable goods," said John. "It's logical, and that's what the police think, but I agree with Sonny." He looked at Ari. "It doesn't make sense that the other guys were the target. None of them were high profile. And the shooters brought a lot of firepower. They intended to light up the kill zone. Who would want you out of the way?"

Ari thought about that as we ate.

"I can think of a half-dozen people," he said finally. "Maybe more."

"Business rivals?" John asked.

"You can't be a bookseller and not have people wanting your share," Ari replied.

Catherine and I smiled at each other, she in unspoken acknowledgment of Ari's shadow role, me as an accomplice in her affection for the man.

"Deals gone south?" John said. "Someone settling a score?"

Ari tilted his head in the affirmative. *Could be*, his gesture said.

"Give me names. I'll check them out," John said. Ari gave a solemn nod. "The police are analyzing the blood splatter in the back of the truck, and they dusted for prints. Nothing there. But they found more shell casings in the bed."

I asked John if he could tell where the ammo was made.

He shrugged. "Maybe. I haven't seen the casings yet, but Forensics is done with the weapon. They're giving me a look this afternoon."

I finished eating and pushed my plate away from me. I took a cool sip of the scotch and thought about the assault. "They were careful. They stole the trunk just before they needed it, not a day or two ahead of time when it might have been reported, and license plate scanners could have identified it." I looked at Ari. "How did they know you would be there that night? They drove down the alley when you were outside. That wasn't luck. That took planning, preparation, intel. Their timing wasn't accidental. It was perfect. They knew you were outside."

John nodded. "They had a spotter. We need to look at the buildings opposite yours. Somebody there was watching. I'll get a couple of guys to canvas the buildings." He took a photograph from the breast pocket of his shirt and passed it around. It was a blurry close-up of the driver. "This is the clearest shot of the driver. The Joint Terrorism Task Force has a database of people of interest, including faces. They're running facial recognition software to see if there's a match. I've sent this to one of my contacts in Interpol."

"These people will try again?" Catherine said.

"We have to assume so," John said. "They killed three men and shot up the place, but they didn't accomplish their goal." Then to Ari: "We need to put more protection around you."

"Sana and Earl will take care of it," Ari said.

"No. Earl and your Armenian friends are not authorized to carry weapons. They'd be in deep shit if they shot somebody while protecting you. I have associate PI's with concealed carry permits. I'll assign them. And clear my calendar."

"Promise me you'll take care of him," Catherine said.

John nodded, and I said, "They'll do their best. So will I." Catherine gave me a wan smile. She looked like she'd dealt the Death card in tarot, followed by the Five of Cups.

When I got back home, I talked to Kat. She hadn't learned anything new about Duggins. I filled her in on the BiblioTech shooting, and she surprised me.

"How would you like a house guest?" she said.

"Who do you have in mind?"

"Smartass. I'm on convalescent leave for two months, and I can't spend all that time in this house, and you can't keep camping out here. You have too much going on in the city."

"What about Sara?"

"She's with her dad for two weeks."

"Your nurses?"

"You want me to bring them?"

"If you don't mind. Amira's a real beauty."

"You know what GFY means?"

"Is that a tricky sexual maneuver you try by yourself?"

"That's the one."

"Okay, no Amira. But you'll need home health care. I don't do bandages. Or physical therapy. I'll arrange for it here."

"Thanks. I talked to our HR rep yesterday. They're making me see a therapist before they'll let me return to duty. Standard procedure when you're shot on the job."

"Rhoda's a psychiatrist. She offered to talk to you. If she can't treat you, she'll know someone who can."

"I remember her. Are you still coming back tomorrow?" she asked.

"Unless I get a better offer."

"I could just find a ride and show up at your door."

"Then I'd have to clean my place, and I hate doing that."

"Nice try. I know you. You're not a slob."

"Doesn't sound like there's any way out of this."

"Nope."

"All right, officer. I'll see you tomorrow. Should I bring a moving van for your luggage?"

"A large one."

"You're sounding a lot better."

"I'm feeling better—from the neck up. Below the neck, I'm a train wreck. See you tomorrow, wise guy."

At 7:00 that evening, my doorbell rang. I opened the door to John Sebastiani, who was carrying a bag of Chinese carryout and a bottle of tawny port.

"You eaten?" he said. I told him I hadn't. "Good, I can't eat all this myself and hate Chinese leftovers. All that added MSG gets absorbed, and you forget how bad it is for you."

We got dishes and utensils from my kitchen and set the food on the dining room table. John brought a little of everything.

"You have a regular gig now with SFPD?" I asked as we ate.

"They're short six hundred officers, so they're bringing on security consultants like me."

"Doing what?"

"Investigations."

"Interesting work for an ex-priest."

"I have a full life," he said, smiling between forkfuls of Mongolian beef.

"If you ever write your memoirs, you'll need a huge staff."

"Except half the shit I do is under the counter or classified. If I told you about it, I'd make you a co-conspirator."

"I'm bringing Kat here tomorrow. She's staying for a while."

"Good. Your life needs a woman's touch. Smooth out the rough edges."

"She's a cop. Her edges are rougher than mine," I said. John found two wine glasses in my cupboard and poured the port. We clinked glasses and sipped.

"Not bad," I said. "Where'd you get this?"

"A guy on Columbus Avenue. He was drinking from it in a paper bag. I gave him a twenty for it and screwed the top back on."

"Did you wipe off the mouth of the bottle?"

"Nah. Should I?"

"Classy guy, John."

"Thanks. So, partner, I learned something interesting this afternoon."

"About the shooting?"

He nodded. "I examined the AK-47 SFPD found at the scene. You know what a factory mark is?" I said I didn't. "AK-47s are made in Russia and places like Iraq, North Korea, China—and former Eastern bloc places, Poland, East Germany. The Russians license the design. It's how they extend their influence. Every AK has a factory mark on the front trunnion. It's a symbol they stamp on the metal."

"I'm sure this is going somewhere."

He nodded. "Somewhere interesting. The AK-47 they impounded has a five-pointed star factory mark. That's the Tula factory."

"Which is where?"

"Russia. In a town about 120 miles south of Moscow."

"Okay, so? Aren't most of them made in Russia?"

"Yes, but this is a new weapon. You can find older AK-47s in the States. The semi-automatic ones are legal in some states, and soldiers shipped some back from Vietnam and the Middle East. Most are in the hands of collectors—and they'd show wear. AKs are not shipped here from Russia these days, and you can't own or import them into California."

"So how did this one get here?"

"I've been asking myself that. It's fully automatic and had a 40-round clip. AK-47s like this are like, you know, don't get caught with it unless you don't have to be anywhere for five years."

"How do you know the rifle is new?"

"I took it apart and examined it with a magnifying glass. There were no scratches, tarnishing, or scuff marks except on the base of the stock where it hit the pavement. This baby still had the factory shine and clean oil in its guts. Somebody took it out of the crate, loaded it, and shot up Ari's building."

"What does this tell you?"

"These guys had access to pristine Russian-made fully automatic rifles, and they didn't buy them in this country."

"They brought them in."

He nodded. "I tried to find out where Tula-made AKs are shipped, but no one has that information."

"Have you told Ari about the rifle?"

"Not yet."

"Their crew might still be local. They could have an offshore source for the weapons," I said.

"Could. But why go to that trouble? You can find unlicensed assault rifles here. I could go to underground dealers in the Bay Area and buy AR-15s with bump stocks if I wanted to lay some serious firepower on somebody. I think these guys are not local. They smuggled their weapons into the country because AKs are what they know, probably what they trained on. They wouldn't know how to find dealers who sell assault rifles out of the back of a van outside a gun show and couldn't risk exposure, so they brought their ordnance with them."

"How'd they get it into the country?"

"For sure, not by post," John said. "You could smuggle arms by air concealed in a shipment of baby formula. Something like that. Dicey but possible. But if I were them, I'd load the crates on a ship. The sea is the easiest way to get anything into the country illegally. A freighter from Venezuela stops ten miles out, offloads the crates onto a pleasure boat, and the boat berths at Mission Creek Harbor. No one would inspect it. No one would know."

"Any idea who they are?"

"Not a clue. But if I'm right—"

"Ari's enemies are foreign and have major money behind them. What we're talking about takes months of planning."

"And a deep commitment to the mission."

John is a chameleon. He'd blend with dock workers in a tattered, oil-stained t-shirt, with tousled hair and grime on his cheeks. Clean him up, put him in an Italian suit and French cuffs, and he'd pass for a banker. But it's not an act. He adapts, knows the lingo, and passes himself off well enough to build trust with the unsuspecting, leading them to reveal more than they should. That's what makes him a good investigator. Before he was a shape-shifter, he wore a priest's collar, then lost his faith when he witnessed serial sex abusers shuffled between parishes to avoid accounting for their crimes. He's accepted now that the world is a Hollywood set where the vile and corrupt hide behind the illusion of normalcy. He has not lost his moral vigor, but now he is a protector where the lines are more well-defined, and he is an arbiter of justice.

He phoned me an hour after he left and told me to turn on the TV. KPIX-TV was live with breaking news. A reporter stood outside a restaurant east of Golden Gate Park. Behind him were a half-dozen SFPD patrol cars with flashing lights and a chaotic crowd of cops and civilians milling outside yellow police tape in front of the restaurant. The reporter said a thirtyish man having a late dinner with friends began stabbing people with a steak knife, killing two of his dinner companions and then attacking people at other tables. An eyewitness the reporter interviewed said the attacker was like a madman, screaming and stabbing people indiscriminately. Police were reporting four dead and multiple others injured in a scene witnesses likened to a slaughterhouse. It took the police six minutes to arrive. When he was ordered to drop the knife, the man attacked them and was shot and killed by responding officers. More details are forthcoming, the reporter said, but the city has been shaken by another mass killing in a week.

After watching the news, I poured another small glass of the port, turned off the lights, and sat in my living room. It was dark but for soft light in my windows from the streetlamps below. In my mind, I replayed the day I was attacked by two men in this room, one with a knife, the other with a hammer. Fear can be disabling when someone is trying to kill you. The realization that your life could end in minutes is paralyzing unless you are well-trained and can react with skill and force. Training gives you the muscle memory to respond without thinking. When your mind engages, the initial attack will be deflected, and your attacker will be defeated or on the defensive. But the people in that restaurant were likely not black belts in martial arts, and the shock that their world had become violent would have been incomprehensible to them until it was too late. I was sorry I hadn't been there. I would have put the son of a bitch down.

Collateral Damage

Some mornings, I wake up feeling like I'm not in this world, like my self is a half-inch left of my body. I lay there trying to bring myself together, as though I couldn't find all the pieces and assemble them into a coherent whole. I became aware on this Sunday morning—once I realized it was Sunday—of a cannonball in my bed, depressing the mattress, forming a deep, hot sink in the bed like a black hole in space, a slowly swirling vortex of gravitational immensity I might fall into if I moved toward it. I tried to inch away from the event horizon, imagining I could fool it if I moved stealthily enough, if I could distract it by thinking of something else while my fingers stretched one fraction of an inch at a time toward the edge of the bed. But I felt too itchy for such graceful movement, and that immensity followed me as I tried to roll away from it. I found myself chained to it as though I were a prisoner of its awful attraction, and as I swung my right leg onto the floor, I realized that that orb of misery was my left knee.

I hobbled to my bathroom sink, stared at the ashen man in the mirror, and reached into my medicine cabinet for my bottle labeled vitamins. I took three small white pills from it and swallowed the oxys with tasteless water. I eased the toilet seat cover down and sat on it for a long spell—I don't know how long—until the pain subsided, a nightmare that nagged and nagged and nagged like a glowering aunt I never liked until, finally, I was free of her skulking presence. Then I floated onto my feet and allowed my memory of what I do every morning to lead me through the routines of taking a shower and getting dressed and making my bed and eating something for breakfast, something light—anything, I didn't care what—and brushing my teeth and combing my hair and finding myself in the mirror free of the pain and floating as I remembered that I was driving to Sacramento this morning to pick up Kat, floating and knowing I'm floating and knowing I'm addicted and not caring because being free was worth the price of admission.

Admission. The word echoed like receding footfalls on a wood floor. I tasted it, rolled it over my tongue, and touched its brittle lines and curves. *It's an awful word. Best not dwell on it, Sonny. Let it go. The day is too long, and you are too weak. Enjoy the float.*

On my drive through the city, in a morning turned twilight with the now-familiar dusky haze of smoke from the fires, my cell phone rang. It was David Fetchenheir, my childhood friend who works as a videographer for KPIX-TV in San Francisco. Fetch warned me that I would receive a call from Marcella Delgado, a reporter for KPIX. She had taken a hiatus from the TV station to write a true crime book about our experiences in New Mexico. The word in publishing circles was that three other true crime authors were racing to be the first to publish the story, and Marcella didn't want to be last to cross the finish line. She wanted to interview Kat and me again. She was convinced, Fetch said, that we could remember details now that we'd forgotten earlier, and she knew Kat and I were still together and wanted to ask about our relationship. Were we getting married? Were we starting a family? The world wants to know. I told Fetch I wouldn't have kind words for Marcella if she called me.

After I returned from New Mexico, the media swarmed me like a brood of cicadas. The story appeared on every news channel and in newspapers and magazines worldwide. For weeks, I couldn't look at a newspaper without seeing my picture, and I turned down interview requests from scores of writers and reporters. I had to turn off my cell phone and buy a burner so only a select few people could call me. It was intrusive enough that I talked to Rhoda Merrick about how I felt. I told her I enjoyed people appreciating our music, but I didn't track down Erin Hightower so I could be featured on the evening news. I did it because it was the right thing to do. She said I was wise to avoid the circus and not let it go to my head. Fame is a drug, she said. Many famous people become addicted to it, and when the attention and adoration stop, they experience withdrawal and become anxious and depressed. That's no way to live. No shit, I said to Rhoda. It sounds more like a living death.

I told Kat about Marcella's interest as I loaded her things into my car. She didn't respond. I arranged her bags in my backseat. It was a tight fit. This morning, she had the war-weary eyes of someone who's seen suffering, like a war correspondent who's spent too much time in the zone and witnessed unimaginable brutalities. I wondered if this was a sign of PTSD, if she was flashing back to that day in the flea market. I've learned that Kat is a stoic. She suffers in secret. But every untended wound festers, and I made a mental note to ask Rhoda about it.

"I'll talk to Marcella," Kat said when we'd settled into the car. "I don't mind." She put her hand over mine. "I told you once that it's better to be ahead of the narrative than behind it. I'd rather she got the story right."

As I drove back to the interstate, I could smell flowers above the odor that had become a part of our lives, the smell of burning wood from the north that felt like a stain of burnt umber. The floral overtone was Kat's perfume, rose or jasmine, with a hint of lavender. She smelled like spring, and it lifted my heart. I didn't have to look at her to know how I felt.

"When you're in law enforcement," she continued, "positive press is good. It builds your rep and opens doors. You wouldn't believe how many departments around the country contacted me after New Mexico and offered jobs. Several asked me to interview for their new chief."

"Why didn't you pursue it?"

She glanced around at the haze, the clogged roads, and the power lines snaking along the highway. Then she touched her bruised sternum and the bandage on her leg and said, "And leave all this?" She smiled at me, and I returned it. Then she opened a manila folder from the soft leather case at her feet.

"This is the autopsy report on Paul Duggins," she said. "His cause of death was multiple gunshot wounds."

"Don't piss off a SWAT team. My standard advice to miscreants."

"No kidding. He had four to his chest and one to the right temporal region of his head. He had massive brain damage, but he might already have been dead. The four chest wounds penetrated his heart, right lung, and liver. He also had two non-fatal gunshot wounds to his left thigh and one to his right knee. SWAT team members fired all eight shots."

"How many shots did they fire altogether?"

"Fifty-two. Some bullets also killed a nine-year-old minor named Isabella Suarez, whose body was found beside Duggins. They think Duggins took her hostage and used her as a human shield."

Collateral damage is a syphilitic whore.

"I'm sure they did a tox report. What did it say?"

"His blood was positive for two prescription drugs, amlodipine and metoprolol," she told me. "Duggins had high blood pressure. Toxicology was negative for all commonly used illegal drugs. No coke, smack, crank, black beanies, monkey, or anything else. The guy was clean."

"Monkey?"

"Morphine. The only odd thing they found was an alkaloid similar to . . .." She looked down at the report on her lap and read from it. "Hyoscyamine. That's a chemical found in Datura stramonium."

"Which is what?"

"Jimsonweed. I had to look it up. It's a toxic plant grown in the Americas that can cause hallucinations. I guess some natives use it to induce visions. But," she added, flipping over a page, "it can cause paranoid delusions. Some users say their hallucinations were terrifying, like monsters oozing through cracks in the windows and crawling into their ears, that sort of thing. They say they'd never take it again."

"He had that in his system?"

"No. Not jimsonweed. He had an alkaloid similar to hyoscyamine, but the report is inconclusive. They don't know what it is."

"Is it the same thing they found in the blood of the Rapture victims?"

"No. That's the first thing I thought of, so I called SFPD and asked. What they found in Rapture is not a plant-based compound. It's a synthetic chemical."

I shrugged. "I guess I don't know the difference."

"Alkaloids are organic compounds," she read. "They occur naturally and contain at least one nitrogen atom. The substance in the Rapture victims is synthetic, has no nitrogen atoms, and is not hyoscyamine or anything chemically similar." She looked at me. "You were hoping for an easy explanation of Duggins' behavior."

"It's a missing piece of the puzzle."

"Yeah.

"So it's not Rapture," I said. "Still, he had something in his blood that causes paranoid delusions."

"Maybe. I spoke to the toxicologist in Sacramento. She told me jimsonweed also contains hyoscine and atropine. All these chemicals have medicinal uses on their own. Their combination in jimsonweed causes paranoid delusions, even death. But Duggins didn't have all three chemicals in his blood, just something similar to hyoscyamine."

"I should have paid more attention in high school chemistry."

"Oh, I don't know. I think musicians are more fun than chemists."

I laughed. "Why do you say that?"

She thought about it. "Musicians make waves, honey. Chemists make solutions."

"That could be a slogan on a T-shirt."

"Too late," she said. "I already ordered you one that says, 'My girlfriend carries a gun.'"

I chuckled as the San Francisco skyline became visible through the haze. When we arrived at Pacific Heights, I unfolded Kat's crutches and helped her to my condo. Then I schlepped her things upstairs and got her settled. She sank into an easy chair, lay back, and closed her eyes while I took her bags into the bedroom. She and I had been here together since we returned from New Mexico, but as I hung some of her clothing in the closet and put the rest away in a chest of drawers, I thought back to when Mac lived here. I hadn't had a woman living here since. I felt close to Kat and wanted her here, but putting her things away felt like a shift in our relationship, a move toward permanence I wasn't comfortable with yet. We hadn't spoken of commitments or signed any papers, but you don't need to feel the motion to know a train is moving.

I returned to the main room and poured myself a glass of sparkling water, adding ice and a slice of lime. While I sipped it, I watched her dozing. Mac had sat in that chair many times. I could still see her dark hair fanning out behind her head as she lay against the back of the chair and her sweet smile when she caught me looking. I missed those precious moments when the bond you feel with someone feels absolute and unshakeable. But Mac could not tolerate my obsession with finding Erin Hightower or accept that I risked my life to help others in harm's way. The woman now sitting in my chair accepted it—and joined in the quest. She had more fidelity to the rules than I did, but she was resolute and committed to righting wrongs, and I could talk to her about my obsession. Sunlight through the kitchen window made her yellow hair glow, and as I gazed at her, I realized that having her acceptance was more important to me than I thought. She understood me, even as she urged me to be sensibly cautious.

Hours later, when she woke up, I told her I'd ordered dinner brought in. I didn't think either of us had the energy to go out, and I didn't want to make something and have to clean up afterward. I told her that I'd had a thought as she lay sleeping, and I wanted to invite two guests for dinner. At six, the doorbell rang. Rhoda Merrick stood outside with flowers from her gardens and a bottle of cabernet sauvignon. Minutes later, I opened the door to Paul Fisher. Paul was weary from an unscheduled day's work on the multiple homicides last night and welcomed spending a quiet evening away from work. I didn't want to disappoint him, but I had something else in mind.

After the social pleasantries, an Uber Eats driver rang the doorbell with a delivery from Go Duck Yourself, a Cantonese barbeque from the Hing Lung Company. If you want people to relax and be in the mood for contemplation, serve them excellent food and wine. When we'd finished dinner, I told them I hoped they didn't mind a little shop talk. Then I brought Kat her leather case with the Duggins toxicology report and asked her to summarize what she'd read to me in the car for Rhoda and Paul.

Afterward, I asked Rhoda if she was familiar with hyoscyamine.

She nodded. "It's a common treatment for gastrointestinal disorders. It's prescribed for cramps, irritable bowel syndrome, and pancreatitis—issues like those. I've read about jimsonweed but am not very familiar with it."

Paul rubbed his eyes and looked askance at me. "You're suggesting Duggins killed those people because he took something for a stomach ache?"

I shook my head. "It wasn't hyoscyamine, Paul. It was a substance like it, a substance that contributes to paranoid delusions when someone eats jimsonweed."

Paul turned away and took a deep breath. When he expelled it, he said, "You know what? It's been a tough day. I'm dead on my feet. Thanks for dinner, but I need to get going."

"Paul, do me a favor, and then I'll leave you alone."

He looked at me like I was one step away from plunging over a cliff, and he was ready to push. "Is that a promise?"

I laughed and said, "No."

"I didn't think so. Okay, what? You're on the meter."

"You have the tox report on the woman in Market Street?"

"Fernanda Alamilla," he said. "Yeah. It's on my desk. In a murder book. Along with thirty-five others, not counting the homicides today."

"Can you call someone to read it? I'd like to know what they found in her blood."

After some exasperation, he pushed himself up from the table and took his cell phone from his jacket. He walked away and dialed a number. While he called, Kat asked me what I was thinking.

"Just a hunch." I said, "Duggins and Alamilla don't fit the profile of mass murderers. Duggins was a boxer, but you haven't found any evidence of violence since he left college, right?"

Kat shook her head. "Not so far. Not until Folsom."

"What I've read about Alamilla says she was a normal middle-aged grandmother who made sopapillas and had a great salsa recipe. It's out of character for her to drive her car into people on a sidewalk."

Paul returned a minute later, set his phone on the table, and dropped into his chair. His head was tilted, his forehead knitted, and he gazed at me as though he'd had a revelation. "It's the same."

Kat's eyes opened wide. "Hyoscyamine?"

Paul nodded. "Something like it. Our lab techs don't know what it is, but they wrote that it resembles the same chemical found in Duggins' blood."

We were silent for a moment, digesting what Paul said.

"Bob Duggins and Fernanda Alamilla were not murderers," I said. "They were victims."

"You think they were drugged?" Rhoda said.

"I do." Despite his weariness, Paul gave me a slight smile, the joy of a possible step forward in a baffling case. I said, "Do me a favor, Paul. The guy in the restaurant last night, the one who went berserk with a knife."

"Daniel Niccum."

"Do you have the tox report on him?"

"Not for two or three days."

"Can you expedite it?"

He nodded.

"I'll bet you a 40-year-old Port that he also had hyoscyamine in his system."

He scrunched his mouth and shook his head. He wouldn't take the bet. "That would answer a lot of questions," he said.

"If I'm right, you have a bigger problem. You have a killer out there with a drug that makes people homicidal."

"I don't know of any drugs, legal or illegal, that can do that," said Rhoda. "Unless he made it himself."

"Is that possible?" Kat asked her.

Rhoda shrugged. "Possibly. You'd have to synthesize hyoscyamine or extract it from jimsonweed and then modify it so it had the effect you want."

"How difficult is that?" Kat asked.

"Very. Your average high schooler with a chemistry set couldn't do it, but it could be done."

"So we're looking for a suspect who knows how to make drugs," said Paul. "A pharmacist."

"A chemist," Rhoda said, shaking her head. "Pharmacists dispense drugs. A chemist could make it, a biochemist, I think—someone who's studied pharmacological effects on the brain."

"Maybe he also made Rapture," I offered.

"Humph," Paul said. "Very different effect on people. By the way, we had two more Rapture deaths yesterday," Paul said. "Christ almighty."

"Ari is setting up a meeting for me with Alejandro Crisologo," I told Paul.

He scrunched his eyebrows. "Why?"

"He may know where Rapture's coming from."

"Are you fucking crazy?" Paul said.

"Wait," said Kat. "Who is Crisologo?"

Paul told her he was the biggest drug dealer in the Bay Area. She gave me a wary look but didn't pursue it.

"Are you willing to wear a wire?" Paul said.

I laughed. "He'd wrap it around my neck."

"I'd tell you to watch your ass, but you'd just make some wiseass comment."

"No worries. But you have a bigger problem, Paul. If we're right about a homicide drug, and the guy figures out how to give it to many people at once, you could have an epidemic of mass murder on your hands."

Warm Whiskey

Last year, I caught a show in Vegas by one of the reigning queens of pop music. Her show was a frothy confection of dazzling pyrotechnics and pulse-pounding rhythms at 120 decibels, enough to crack your fillings. But I was impressed with her energy and artistry and have no problem with pop music. It has its place. But it feels to me like a fizzling cherry coke poured over ice. Blues is warm whiskey in a dirty shot glass.

People have different theories about how and where the blues began. Some trace its roots to the tribal rhythms and chants of West Africa. The blues germinated in the cargo holds of slave ships. It took root in the Americas as field slaves used the call-and-response form of musical conversation to express sorrow and defiance while fostering community among the oppressed. The blues evolved during the failed promise of emancipation and reconstruction in the last half of the nineteenth century. Negro spirituals found hope in the promise of salvation while itinerant musicians roaming the hardscrabble roads of the deep south created songs to rub salve on the wounds of people making the most of a hard life. Blues got its legs in the early twentieth century in the Mississippi Delta, the cane fields of Louisiana, and the cotton fields of Texas. By the time it flourished on the West Coast, blues was an electrified, multi-instrumental form that incorporated the drive and rhythms of rock. Blues is one branch of an American musical tradition that produced ragtime, jazz, R&B, gospel, and rock and roll.

I lay in bed Sunday night thinking about the blues and—in the way your drowsy mind morphs from one thing to another—about the murderous rages of Robert Duggins, Fernanda Alamilla, and Daniel Niccum. If we were right about them being drugged, they were not acting out of malice when they killed their victims. You can make people slaves by stealing them from their homeland and forcing them into involuntary servitude, or you can drug them and make them commit mass murder. Either way, you are robbing them of their freedom and dignity. No one has the right to do that.

When I was growing up, one of our neighbors was Marlene Bostwick, a true believer, as religious zealots often are. She saw no shades of gray. People either believed in God and the teachings of the church or they didn't. They were saved, or they were damned, decent or indecent, lawful or lawless, givers or takers. I think the truth is more nuanced. Most people do their best most of the time. They do their jobs, raise families, and find enjoyment without harming others. But a subset of people take advantage whenever they can and don't give a damn about the consequences. They can inhabit the gutter or the ivory towers of corporations. You'll find them in both places. Some are psychopaths with no moral grounding and zero empathy for others. I think the people who created Rapture and the killer drug are in the substrata of humanity who prey on others. They have been with us since we left the caves and will be with us when we reach the stars. You can ignore them, tolerate them, or search for them. I am a searcher. So is Kat, my new love, my partner.

She lay beside me. Light from the city shone through the coverings on our bedroom window and cast a faint glow on her yellow hair, which lay in a raggedy pattern over her cheek. Her lips were open, and I could hear her breath when she exhaled, a soft brushing across the pillow, catching slightly when she inhaled, not snoring exactly, just a hitch as the air was drawn in. She lay on her back, rolled just enough onto her right side so that her head lay on her crooked arm. It was still too painful for her to roll completely onto one side. The fingers of her right hand were curled like a bird's claws. I thought what a magnificent creature she was. Beautiful but rugged, resilient, with a good heart and a fierce commitment to justice.

I turned over onto my back and felt my knee pulsing, a lighthouse beacon across a dark ocean. Rocky shore ahead. Sailor beware. I thought about taking some oxy but fell asleep before I could get out of bed. The next day, she was awake before I was. My knee throbbed as I hobbled to the bathroom and took three oxys. When I left the bedroom, she walked with one crutch and paused every few steps to stretch, arch her back, and rub her breastbone. She was moving with more ease and grimacing less. She'd made coffee, which I appreciated, and I found strawberries and vanilla yogurt in the refrigerator for us. When she joined me at the table, I said, "You're feeling better."

"I'll be doing sprints next week."

"Call Marcela Delgado. She'll want the story."

"She already called me," Kat said, dipping her spoon into the yogurt. "She is coming over on Thursday to talk about her book."

I shrugged. "Your deal." I can't prevent Marcella from writing her book, but I didn't want to answer her questions. I'm focused on the now and don't need to relive what happened.

"I want her to know which superhero you most resemble. I'm thinking mutant ninja turtle."

I laughed. "Be sure she spells my name right."

She flashed one of those smiles that had affection at its core. It was a smile that brought an uptick to my rhythm. "Seriously," she said. "I'll keep her from embellishing the story too much."

"Good luck with that. She's a sensationalist."

"She thinks there's a movie in this."

"Good grief."

She gave me a huge grin. "Who do you want to play you?"

I pretended to give that serious consideration. "Dwayne Johnson."

"The Rock? Same body type," she said, laughing.

"Only if I gained a hundred pounds of muscle and shaved my head."

At 9:00, the visiting nurse arrived. Marcie Bell was a pleasant black woman my age with a Cheshire Cat smile and dyed-yellow cornrows. She had the arms and legs of a wrestler and carried her medical bag like a hammer. I didn't have to ask if she took crap from anybody. I already knew the answer. I'd hired her from a temp nursing agency that told me she could provide nursing care and physical therapy. A twofer. She grinned at Kat like she was tickled to see an old friend and said, "Let's get to it."

While she and Kat disappeared into the bedroom, I went to my music room and soaked a reed. By now, I was floating on a cloud of oxy, but that just put the music on a higher plane, one where the sounds had the pure resonance of the wind gliding through slot canyons. I spent two hours grooving on the newest Storm Lake songs we'd written, but I had a good half hour improvising on a melody we invented the night Eric Young collapsed. This melody had promise, and I found ways to embellish it—magic on wings.

When I returned to the main room, Marcie Bell had left. Kat sat at the dining table with John Sebastiani. He smiled when he saw me, an involuntary reflex. His complexion looked sallow, his eyes ragged, and he moved like he was wearing ankle and wrist weights.

"Trouble sleeping, *padre*?" I asked him.

He tilted his head to one side. An admission, but he didn't elaborate. "Brought sandwiches from Molinari's," he said.

Good, I thought. *Food will plant my feet on the ground.*

San Francisco is famous for its eateries, and Molinari Delicatessen is choice takeout. They have a scrumptious turkey and provolone, which John brought for me. Kat had the same but ate the sandwich without the bread. John brought San Pellegrino, and I drank the blood orange. Delish.

When we finished eating, I asked him if there was anything new on Ari. He frowned and shook his head. "Whoever they are, they've gone to ground," he said. "The stolen truck was wiped clean. No prints on the shell casings. They were careful. Either pros or military."

Kat gave him a startled look. "Military? Whose military?"

"I'm not saying they're military. But it was the kind op a trained unit would carry out. Seals or Delta, a team like that. If they hadn't been surprised by the return fire, they would have accomplished their mission."

"You think they're still here?" Kat said.

John said, "Yep. One shooter in the bed of the pickup was hit in the neck, but there haven't been any reports of neck wounds showing up at the hospitals or clinics. Maybe the wound wasn't serious, and they bandaged the guy themselves. Or he died, and they disposed of the body. They're careful. They're waiting."

"Regrouping," I said. "No plan survives first contact with the enemy. They fucked it up. Now they're figuring out Plan B."

"You don't know why they targeted Ari?" said Kat. John shook his head. "Did they have a timeframe? Was there anything special about the day they tried to kill him?"

John replied, "Not that we're aware of."

"They'll try again," I said. "This was a crew on a mission. They won't leave until they've succeeded. They might have a timetable—or not. They could be real patient."

John mused on that for a moment. "I don't think they'll wait too long. Even if they're well-funded and aren't rushed, they'll want to finish this and move on. No pro likes to sit on failure."

I said, "If we knew anything about them, we could check hotels and see if there's a crew staying somewhere. But there are too many hotels, and we wouldn't know what to look for."

John shook his head. "They could have contacts here. Or be in a rental. That's what we did in Ruidoso. We'll have to wait till they try again. Meanwhile, I've got two guys with Ari, and Sana's people are in the shadows."

"Earl?" Kat said.

John's eyes went wide. "Oh, yeah. He won't leave Ari's side unless ordered to." He stood up, took our dishes to the kitchen, and set them beside the sink. When he returned to the table and sat down, he said, "I've got more news. I spent the morning at City Hall, the Mayor's office. They've put together a task force to deal with this hypothetical murder drug. They're calling it Zombie, as in a bite that turns people into thoughtless killing machines. Paul Fisher called me for an urgent meeting this morning. Very confidential. They don't want this on the news. People would panic."

"Who's on this task force?" Kat said.

John held up his hands and counted off his fingers. 'The Mayor, Paul, the FBI Agent-in-Charge for San Francisco—I can't remember his name—a DEA guy, senior guy, and four homicide detectives who work for Fisher. I want you on it, too,' he said to me.

"Me? What? Bullshit. I'm a musician."

"No, you're an apprentice agent with Sebastiani Security Services."

"Give me a break, John. No way."

"No active role, Sonny, just a thought partner. I want your name cleared so you can receive information without me getting my head in a grinder. Then we can talk about what's happening."

"People would be okay with this?"

"They've already said yes."

"Jesus, John."

He removed folded papers from his jacket pocket and unfolded them on the table. He turned them toward me and handed me a pen and a laminated ID. The ID said I was an apprentice private investigator with John's company.

"Your Armenian friend, Taniel Zakarian, made this up for me this morning." Taniel was one of the Armenian crew with us in New Mexico. "There's an employment form and non-disclosure agreement." Then he pulled a dollar bill out of his pocket. "This makes it legit. Do you swear, etc., etc.? Hold up your right hand."

I did, and he handed me the dollar bill. "You have to say yes."

"Yes, I swear. Do I get a badge?"

"No. No badge. Just the ID. And no gun."

"Works for me. I don't like guns. Any responsibilities?"

He smiled at Kat and looked back at me. "None. Except listen to her and do as she says."

"Sounds dangerous."

"It is," Kat said.

"Okay, I'm gone," John said. "I do have one request. Ari's setting up a meeting for you with Alejandro Crisologo."

"Yeah. I already told Paul I'm not wearing a wire."

"Don't want you to. We want to know if he knows anything about Zombie."

"And Rapture," I added. "That's the main reason I want to talk to him."

"Okay, good, makes sense. Ask about both. Don't tell him Zombie is turning people into monsters."

"I'll ask if any new drugs are making people berserk."

"There's extreme urgency around this, Sonny."

"No shit."

He looked at both of us. "Keep it tight. If people knew, there'd be a rush to the gun shops. We'd have a lot of firearms on the street."

Kat nodded. "And frightened people have itchy fingers," she said. "You need to shut this creep down before San Francisco makes hell look like Disneyland."

After John left, I cleaned up while Kat walked back and forth across the main room. I watched her reflection in the window over the sink as I rinsed glasses and put them in the dishwasher. She was limping more in the dusky light of late afternoon. I asked if she'd taken her Percocet, and she shook her head. Kat is not a masochist, but I think she measures her progress by the amount of pain she can endure. Her brow was a straight line above clenched eyes, and her frown quivered but didn't lose its shape as she forced one step at a time without using the crutch.

In bed that night, I asked about the pain.

"Scale of one to ten, it's a five or six, sometimes higher," she said. "But I know it'll disappear, so I push through it. Pain's just a signal. I can tolerate it."

"It's a warning not to push too hard."

"You know me. The pain tells me I'm still alive. The bastard didn't kill me. I did my job, and no one else died. If this pain is the price I pay, fine."

'You look lovely when you're fierce."

She smiled. "You can't soften me up."

"I just did."

"Nope. Sorry. I'm a trained interrogator. I'm setting you up for the tough questions."

"Are you the good cop or the bad cop?"

"What do you think?"

"I think you're playing the good cop now, but underneath that lovely smile is a naughty girl."

"You know what Mae West said. When I'm good, I'm very good. But when I'm bad, I'm better."

"I've met that bad girl. Is she coming around again?"

She laid her hand on my bare chest and rubbed gently. "Maybe. Probably. Certainly," she said. "I wish we could make love now, but—"

"Pleasure with pain is a bad combo. Unless you're a masochist."

"When the time's right," she said, melting me with her eyes. "My lips still work." We kissed, a long one, our lips parting and coming back together, little breaths exchanged, her tongue arching across my lower lip, and me responding.

When we stopped, her face took a more serious turn. She gazed at me momentarily and said, "You were zoned out this morning when Marcie arrived. Just enough out of sync for me to wonder what you are taking."

"Yeah," I said. "My knee hurt this morning. I took something for it."

"Oxycodone?"

I nodded.

"How much are you on?"

"I shook my head as if to say I didn't know. But I do. Instead of answering, I said, "When the pain hijacks my mind, I can't think of anything else. So, as much as I need."

"I can tell sometimes. It's like a part of you is taking the scenic route. I'm amazed you can play your sax well while on that stuff."

"It puts me in a calm space. Removes the background. All I have is the music, and my tongue and fingers start to flow. You know? Like a cool mountain stream over a rock bed. I follow the flow."

"We could hear you playing. Marcie commented on how good you sounded. I told her you're a professional in the Storm Lake Blues Band. She'd heard of the band but didn't know you were in it. We listened while she worked on my leg."

"We're playing at Cactus Jack's Sunday night if you want to come."

"Front row table," she said, smiling. "Cactus Jack's. We went there after I returned home."

"I know. I'll never forget the black dress you wore."

"That was a memorable evening."

"More so when we returned here."

She kissed me again and then lay back and looked at the ceiling. She said, "Straight talk, okay?"

I nodded, anticipating where this was headed.

She looked back at me. Held my eyes. "I'm worried about your meds. You're taking too much of it. Addicted, maybe, I don't know. But I can't follow you onto the oxy dream boat. I know you're obsessed with helping people. I can live with that because I'm the same way. But If you keep taking oxy, it'll be a solitary journey. You need to deal with it."

I sank back onto the pillow. "It's too painful," I told her.

"Wrong answer," she said. It was a gentle rebuke but firm. "I know you're in pain, but escaping to Never Never Land is a one-way trip. You need to see a doctor about your knee."

"I've seen them."

"Go back. Find a place that specializes in knees."

"I have."

"When? Ten years ago?"

Yes, I said to myself. *About that.* I've had three operations. None worked. Oxy is easier.

"I love you, Sonny, but Oxycodone is your crutch, and if you want me in your life, you need to deal with it."

A White Knight

I woke up thinking about Mac, the woman I lived with for three years. She was everything I thought I wanted in a woman. Mac was an associate fashion designer and would someday create her own fashion line. She was intelligent, beautiful, poised, ambitious, sensual, loving—I could heap more superlatives on this pile. Still, it's enough to say that a man could hardly find a more perfect companion. Except she couldn't tolerate my compulsion to help people in harm's way. She made that clear the afternoon she left me after I confessed that I couldn't lay down my sword and shield and be the safe companion she wanted.

Rhoda Merrick calls it my white knight complex. After my older sister Aileen was raped, I studied Aikido and Krav Maga. If anybody invaded our home again, I was determined to defend myself and my family. I was a pissed-off 12-year-old and learned during that home invasion that words were no deterrent when bad men forced their way into your life. Four years later, I'd just earned my black belt in Aikido when I overheard my younger sister Teagen crying in her room after school. She told me she was being bullied by a group of boys two grades above her. The next day, I cut my last high school class and waited across the street from her school. I followed her as she walked home and saw a pack of boys fall in behind her. I hurried up behind them. When they reached her, a husky punk with pale skin, jet-black hair, and a face like a bulldog grabbed her shoulder and spun her around. He barely had time to say, "You're gonna suck my dick," when I slammed him to the sidewalk. The kid was big and muscular for his age. When he hauled himself up, I told him I was her brother, and he advised me to fuck off. The punks with him spread out around me. I gestured to Teagen to walk on ahead. She gave me a fearful look but turned and walked quickly away.

All except the bulldog had the looks of teenagers pretending to be badass, but the one standing to my right—a pimply red-faced kid—had balled his hands and looked like he needed to prove himself to the bulldog. He lurched at me with a round-house right. I spun and kicked his leading foot out from under him, and he flew face-first onto the sidewalk, bellowing when his nose struck the pavement and pawing blood with one hand as he scrambled away. The one to my left looked ready to jump in, but I was instantly back into my Aikido stance and stared him down. Then the bulldog told me he was going to kick my ass and rushed forward with fists raised. I stepped back, spun away from his direction of movement, knocked his leading fist past me, and slammed my elbow into his face. His head snapped back, and he sank to the ground, blood gushing from his nose. I told this motley crew of pissants that if they ever bothered my sister again, I'd find out where they lived and turn their lives to shit. I made sure each of them saw me watching them after school the next few weeks. They never troubled her again.

I'm not a violent person, but don't fuck with me or those I care for, and don't threaten to harm an innocent person in my presence. You'll regret it.

Part of what attracts me to Kat is that she understands my white knight obsession and accepts it. She warns me to be careful but never says stop. Kat has a loopy grin, one side of her mouth rising higher than the other. She was injured years ago when she tried to serve a warrant, and her backup didn't show up. I found her loopy grin off-putting when I met her; now I see it as her badge of courage, an endearing reminder of the tough cop she is. She doesn't have Mac's fashion model looks, but she is beautiful, more so because she is capable and resilient, and I can't imagine now finding anyone more perfect for me than her.

So I lay there in bed thinking about her ultimatum last night. She had already gotten up. I could hear her in the kitchen. My knee throbbed, and I would have gone to the bathroom and swallowed oxys to start my day on that astral plane any other day. But Kat appeared to me last night as Circe warning of the hypnotic allure of the Sirens. I imagined them as tiny white pills surrounding me with their fluttering wings, singing the most beautiful songs I'd ever heard, whispering in voices so sweet and seductive that I bowed my head in supplication and begged to be untied from the mast. I desired the sweet relief oxy promised and was ready to abandon my post and let my ship veer toward the rocks when I recalled Kat's warning.

I don't know if I have the will to endure it, but I decided to go cold turkey on the drug. I've known many smokers and drunks who swore off their vices until the vice vetoed their earnest intentions. But you take one baby step at a time. In the bathroom, I stared at the mirror on my medicine cabinet but didn't open it and swallow the pills my body urged me to take. After getting dressed, I had breakfast with Kat, opened my phone, and googled orthopedic knee specialists in San Francisco. Most couldn't see me for four or five months, but I found one doctor who'd a cancellation and got an appointment in two weeks. My confidence in him grew when I learned he was an ortho for the San Francisco 49ers. My knee couldn't be worse than men whose professional lives involve repeated blunt-force trauma. Kat gave me a big wet kiss when I told her.

Afterward, I sat at the dining room table rubbing my aching knee when my cell phone rang. It was Paul Fisher, confirming that Daniel Niccum, the guy who knifed those people at the restaurant, also had trace amounts of a variant of hyoscyamine in his system. I asked Paul for a copy of the tox report, along with the one on Fernanda Alamilla, and he said he'd have somebody email them to me. I printed them and added them to Duggins' tox report when they arrived. I needed a chemist who could examine the reports and help me understand what I was looking at.

I was practicing my sax when Xavier McQueen called with the news that Le'Andra Kimani had accepted our offer. The X-Man wanted to get the band together with her this afternoon to practice. I told him I'd see everyone after lunch at the studio. Meanwhile, I ran up and down the major and minor scales in every key and practiced well-worn riffs. I've played them hundreds of times, but your play gets rusty if you don't constantly practice. I call it 'reminding my fingers where to go next.'

Kat made a salad for lunch. While eating, Rhoda Merrick called to say she had a free hour after lunch if Kat wanted to talk to her about what happened at the Folsom Flea Market. I offered to drive Kat to Rhoda's office, but Rhoda said she'd come to our place instead because she knew Kat was on crutches. Then I took a call from Ari.

"I've set up the meeting with Crisologo," he told me. "Tomorrow afternoon. Three o'clock."

"Where?"

"He gave me an address in Fruitvale. I had Sana spot the building on Google Maps. It's an old residential hotel in a mixed commercial and residential area. Wide cross streets with good egress. We can cover it."

Fruitvale in East Oakland is a high-crime area.   Murders, carjackings, robberies, random street shootouts, and smash-and-grabs are common in an area disputed by rival Hispanic gangs. The crime rate ebbs and flows like sludge in a polluted tidal pool. When complaints from residents and merchants reach a crescendo, the police step up their presence, and the gangs slither away, seeking paths of less resistance. As the crime rate drops, the police repurpose their forces, and the gangs are emboldened to renew their territorial ambitions. Then the turf wars raise the body count again—among civilians and gangbangers. The latest tactic of intimidation was to plant a rival's naked corpse in an alley, its hands and teeth missing, the face dissolved by acid. The police were able to identify some victims by their tattoos. Now the tattoos are dissolved, too. I wasn't surprised that Crisologo would have a base in Fruitvale. Ari told me it's one of the many safehouses he uses in the Bay Area.

"Does he know why I want to talk to him?"

"I told him you had a bandmate taken out by Rapture and want to find out where he got it."

"He was okay with that?"

"He knows who you are after all the press you got last year. And he knows you have police connections. I gave him my word that you're not connected with DEA or police narcotics and have no interest in his business, but he'll still be wary. I don't have to tell you to be careful."

"Did he know about Rapture?"

"Never heard of it," Ari said.

"Bullshit."

"Right, but he won't admit knowledge of it. Maybe to you in person."

"Does he trust you?"

"He doesn't trust anybody. He wouldn't have lasted this long by trusting people."

"His gang?"

"A revolving door of gangsters and pushers, most from San Francisco, Oakland, some from L.A. His underboss is a slick dude named Henry. He wears black-frame glasses and a blue pork pie hat. You'll meet him."

"How long has Henry been with him?"

"I don't know. Years. I'm not sure how long. But remember that every king has to worry about ambitious dukes who want to wear the crown. I've observed that Alejandro rotates his palace guard frequently before they can get ideas and sends the previous guards into the field, where they are caught or killed. Henry is probably the only person he trusts."

"He's smart."

"In the gangster world, brilliant. Don't underestimate him."

"I won't. But I'm curious about why he agreed to meet with me."

"I don't want to deflate your ego, but he won't care about you. I think he'll see you as a way to get to Earl. He knows you and Earl are close."

"What does he want with Earl?"

"I'm sure he wants to recruit him."

"No way that would happen."

"Alejandro doesn't know that. His father's from Mexico City. His mother was a black bartender in San Jose. I heard that's where they met. His crew are mostly blacks off the mean streets looking for easy scores. Word is Alejandro wants to recruit more Hispanic soldiers, and Earl has a solid rep in the Hispanic underground."

"He'd never leave you."

I couldn't see Ari, but I knew he was smiling when he said, "Earl is family of the best kind."

"Family by choice."

"Some loyalties can be bought," Ari mused. "And some you take to the grave."

At the lowest point in Earl's life, Ari believed in him and helped him get the life he wanted. I knew Earl well enough to know that nothing on Earth could break their bond. It wouldn't matter what Crisologo offered Earl.

"Good to know," I said. "Could give me some leverage."

"Stay frosty. He'll be guarded by a small army of gangbangers looking to make a mark. His outfit makes psychopaths look like a Boy Scout Troop," he said. "But you'll be guarded, too. I'm sending Earl and some of Sana's crew. You won't see them, but they'll be there. Put Earl on your speed dial."

"I already have."

"Punch his number, and the cavalry will arrive in five seconds or less."

"Got it." I paused for a beat and thought about Ari's recent scare. "You doing okay?"

"Fine," he said. "Catherine and I have cabin fever, but we're well protected."

"John and I think the people that came for you will try again soon."

"He told me."

"Anything I can do?"

He chuckled. "Recommend some good jazz LPs. Artists I wouldn't know."

I smiled. Ari loves jazz and blues. "Better yet, I'll send some LPs your way."

"Much appreciated. Keep your guard up, Sonny," he reminded me as he rang off. "There are unpleasant people out there."

"You, too, *jefe*."

Among our tight circle, we refer to Ari as *jefe* (boss), John—formerly a priest—as *padre* (father), Earl as *hombre* (man), and me as *compa* (partner). We use those names when we don't want people outside our circle to know who we mean. Ari hadn't mentioned *padre* as one of my protectors, but it's a role he's played in the past. I have trusted these guys with my life many times and knew I always could.

I left my condo before Rhoda arrived to talk to Kat. I own a recording studio off Columbus Avenue near Washington Square. That's where the Storm Lake Blues Band recorded our first album, *Storm Warning*, and where we're recording *Storm Damage*. When I arrived, I popped into the office and said hello to Samantha DeGregoris, the studio manager. Sammy is a 56-year-old native Californian of Greek origin with sunbaked bronze skin and a wavy mop of black-and-silver hair. She has thick red lips, luminous green eyes, and the mind of an IBM mainframe computer. She's rail thin and wears gypsy dresses, and people mistake her for the office den mother until they don't follow her directions. Then they meet Lyssa, the Greek goddess of fury, and learn that she remembers everything, misses nothing, and can hear an instrument out of tune three blocks away. She hugged me affectionately before pushing some wayward hairs off my forehead and telling me to scoot because she was busy. Technically, I'm her boss, but no one around here believes that. Sammy is an ancient force.

Everyone else was set up when I walked into Studio A. After a round of greetings, I shook Le'Andra's hand and welcomed her to the band. She had learned three more songs on our first album, so we warmed up playing those tunes. We paused here and there to clarify what was happening in some measures and how Eric typically played them. Le'Andra was quick on the uptake, but we could hear differences in how she and Eric played—a bend a quarter-tone higher or a slide slightly faster or slower than Eric would have done it. That was okay with me. The music sounded good—subtly different—but I saw K.C.'s eyes growing darker as we paused, repeated, paused again, and repeated until we got through a song. Then we'd play it again. And again. Songs the original band had played hundreds of times. When we finished, K.C. stood up from his keyboard and wandered into the break room without speaking.

Xavier and I locked eyes, and I shrugged. I told Le'Andra she was a joy to play with, and we hugged briefly before she left for the day. When K.C. returned to the studio, he said, "Ain't workin', brothers. Ain't workin' for me."

"Eric's not comin' back," Xavier said.

"I know it," said K.C. "I know that. We have a sound, brothers. The Storm Lake sound. She's good. Not sayin' she ain't. But she ain't Eric. We need a guitar sounds more like Eric did. I know players can do that."

Xavier shook his head. "Have to give her a chance, K.C. She's good. She's real good. She'll get there."

K.C. stuck his lower lip out, mulling it over. "I don' like it." He removed his glasses and cleaned them with the tail of his shirt. When he put them back on, he said, "She's gonna want to do her own songs, front the band as singer, turn us into somethin' we ain't."

"She's got a voice," I said. "We work with singers like Gemma. You and Xavier sing. A lot of people love blues vocals, brother. Adding some of her songs to our repertoire won't change who we are."

K.C. gave me a sharp look. I don't know if he thought I'd be an ally in his discontent. He said, "You want to be Le'Andra Kimani and the Storm Lake Used-to-Be Blues Band Now Bein' a Studio Backup Band?"

Garth said dryly, "That name won't fit on a marquee."

K.C. tried to suppress a smile, but it lit his lips anyway. Then his mouth drooped, and he shook his head. "I don' like it. I ain't gonna like it. We gotta sound—the Storm Lake Blues Band sound. The people follow us ain't gonna like a new sound. Won' know who we are."

"Can't march in place, K.C.," Xavier said. "Eric is gone. Gotta move on."

Bands break up or die for many reasons: drugs, arguments over credits, personality clashes, and shifting musical tastes. It can also happen if they never change. Music is a process of perfection and experimentation. You get something right—a riff, song, style, mood, genre. Then you try something new. You innovate, or you get stale. The master of musical shape-shifting was Miles Davis. He was an ever-evolving musical chameleon—bebop, blues, cool jazz, modal, progression, jazz fusion. Best ever. I reminded the guys that the average band stays together only two to three years. We'd been together for five.

"Give her a shot, bro," Garth said.

K.C. shook his head. I added, "When Pete Green left McVie and Fleetwood, look what happened." We all knew the story. Fleetwood Mac was a standard British blues band until Green departed, like Eric, for drug reasons. Bob Welch and Christine joined, and they developed an arena rock sound—in the music world called AOR. Then Welch left to go solo, and Lindsey Buckingham and Stevie Nicks joined. The band reinvented themselves, lost their blues roots, and became commercially successful by producing frothy studio pop. Whether or not fans liked the new sound, you can't argue with success.

The biggest question we had to answer was whether we should re-record the six tracks on *Storm Damage* we'd already laid down with Eric. We planned twelve for the album. We decided to redo five to keep the new sound consistent but leave one as an Easter egg for listeners to figure out which track featured Eric. K.C. reluctantly agreed but left with his soul trapped in a tornado. We weren't sure he would come around, but the rest of us—me, Garth, and Xavier—were committed to Le'Andra. She would keep us fresh and, we hoped, together.

When I returned to my condo, Kat was sitting on the sofa watching television with the sound turned off. She was sipping from a glass of white wine and barely acknowledged me when I came through the door. I asked if she was all right, and she pointed at the screen. I couldn't imagine it was good news, so I poured myself an inch of Scotch neat before sitting down. Then I joined her. The screen showed a wall of flames on both sides of a highway. Flames arcing overhead made it look like a tunnel wrapped in fire.

"Escobedo," she said quietly, her voice catching in her throat. I turned up the sound and learned from the news station that the Diablo winds had whipped up again and driven the wildfire through Escobedo. The camera showed the silhouettes of firefighters in front of the skeletal frames of burning buildings, trees exploding into flame as the camera panned right, and dancing walls of fire in furious advance through the devastation of what had once been a town of 26,000.

Crisologo

When I arrived at the Crescent Hotel Wednesday afternoon for my three o'clock meeting, I didn't expect Alejandro Crisologo to be there. Drug lords don't keep appointments where they can be tracked. They aren't listed in the phone book, not under their real names. You can't google them to find their address or call anyone to ask for directions. People like Crisologo exist in a netherworld of darkness and shadow, like a fuzzy shape in the corner of an unfamiliar room past midnight that might be a boogeyman or a bulky coat hanging on a hook. If Crisologo didn't operate on stealth and deception, he wouldn't last a month.

I had driven through a brown haze across the Bay Bridge. Smoke north of the Bay billowed skyward, disappearing into the stratosphere like a memory. Traffic slowed as drivers gawked at the sight. After arriving in Oakland, I turned southeast toward Fruitvale. The Crescent Residence Hotel stood on the corner of a major intersection, an entire block deep and half a block wide on the main drag. It was a four-story brown brick behemoth, tired on its face and ragged on its edges, evoking a 1940s film noir *mise en scène*. You expected Jimmy Cagney to strut through the front entrance wearing a pinstriped suit and a fedora and find Rita Hayworth in the lounge singing a sultry song to her lover before shooting him in the heart. But there was nothing nostalgic about the Crescent. It was just a relic on a tatterdemalion street with grime caked into its cracks and stained sidewalks where decades of pollution had come to die.

Arriving early, I drove past the building, down the long side street to a fenced lot behind it. The fence, six or seven feet high and topped with menacing metal spikes, barred entry. Behind it, rows of dumpsters were visible, their surfaces a canvas of generations of graffiti, along with a handful of older cars. If Sana's men were lurking there, they were well-hidden. Nor were any nondescript vans parked along the street, where my Armenian protectors might be waiting. But I knew they were there, having arrived long before me. My cavalry, like Alejandro Crisologo, operated on stealth and deception.

The area around the Crescent had long been Hispanicized. Across the street was a mishmash of taquerias, dry cleaners, corner markets, pawn shops, liquor stores, coin laundries, and *farmacias* featuring signs in Spanish, security bars over the windows, bubble graffiti on the walls, and gang tags on the sidewalks. The bottom floor of the Crescent had two businesses on either side of its gated entryway: a tax accountant ("*Soluciones fiscales las 24 horas*") and a beauty salon ("*Apasionada por la belleza*"). I didn't need 24-hour tax service or my hair styled, so at 2:55, when I parked my car down the street from the Crescent, I walked directly to the hotel's front entrance. I took a final glance around but did not see Earl.

The gated entryway was locked, so I pushed a buzzer beside the door. A few moments after the buzzing stopped, a young black woman opened the door beyond the gate and stepped through it. She wore a blue hoodie and a baseball cap with the bill angled straight up. "Wha'chu want?" she said.

"I have a meeting with Alejandro Crisologo," I told her.

"Who?"

Before I could answer, a tall black man came up behind her. He wore a white shirt open to his belly button, revealing three Cuban curb-linked gold chains over sparse, tightly curled chest hair. He had thick lips framed by a short black mustache and goatee. He canted his head back into the room, and she turned and walked away. The grip of a black automatic stuck out of the waistband at the back of her jeans.

"Do fa you?" the brother asked. His eyes narrowed, and his lips parted in a grin that looked more menacing than friendly. I repeated what I'd told the woman.

"Don' know tha man," he said. "You'n tha wrong place." He smiled, then, and a single gold incisor gleamed on the left side of his mouth. If I were asked to nickname the guy, I would have called him Goldilinks after the matching tooth and linked chains. I decided not to mention it.

"Maybe I could talk to Henry," I said.

"Don' know him neither."

"Tell Henry that Sonny Marshall is waiting outside."

He shrugged and walked back inside, closing the door behind him.

I turned and moved beside the door to the beauty salon. The salon's large picture window displayed photos of modern Latino hairstyles, and I wondered how I'd look with an Edgar—shaved halfway up the back and sides with a fringe cut across the forehead. Before I could decide, I heard the inner door open again, and a voice called out, "Yo!"

I walked back to the gate. Henry was shorter than I imagined, no more than five-six. He was clean-shaven except for a bristly mustache, wore heavy black-frame glasses, and had a pork pie hat perched on his egg-shaped head. He looked like a member of a college debating club.

I glanced at my watch. It was 3:09. "I was told I could meet with Alejandro at three o'clock," I said.

"Who told you that?"

"The tooth fairy," I replied. He stared at me but didn't respond. I added, "I am not a member of law enforcement, have never been a member of law enforcement, and am not affiliated with law enforcement now. No weapons and no wires. You know the rest."

"Open your coat," he ordered.

I wore a short brown leather jacket over a blue shirt and jeans. I unzipped the jacket, pulled it open, and spun around, showing him that I had no weapons under my jacket. He unlocked the gate and pulled it aside. I stepped in beside him, and he directed me to spread my arms for a search. He patted down my torso and arms, then patted my legs, ankles, butt, and crotch. Satisfied I wasn't carrying, he opened the inner door and waved me inside. The lobby smelled like old shoes and used condoms. It sagged under the weight of time and neglect, its walls yellowed like an old man with jaundice. What had once been an ornate marble floor wore a sheen of yellow residue. Maybe they polished it with earwax.

The woman in the hoodie stood behind the reception desk, glancing warily at me while she fussed with something on the counter. Goldilinks stood at the entrance to a hallway across the lobby. He cradled a black MAC-10 machine pistol with a suppressor in his arms and smiled at me like we were buddies.

"Why you wanna see tha man?" Henry asked me. He was examining the buttons on my shirt, jeans, and jacket, inspecting more thoroughly for compact eavesdropping devices.

"I'm applying for a job," I said.

Henry gave a mock chuckle and called out, "Got Cedric the Entertainer here. Dude think he a comedian." No one else laughed.

"Am I going to see the man or not?" I said with some edge in my voice.

"Slow your roll, man. Ever'thing be cool," Henry replied. "I be back." He disappeared down the hallway. While he was gone, Goldilinks kept showing me his gold incisor. He was proud of it. Henry returned a few minutes later with an escort, a slender dude wearing a black watch cap, black t-shirt, and black briefs. I could see his briefs because his jeans hung four inches below his waist. He had a Glock tucked under his belt and held his hands out to his sides like he was ready to practice quick draw. His dark eyes flitted around nervously, and I wondered what he was on.

"Come wit' me," Henry said.

I followed him down a long hallway, past closed doors with shadows where the numbers had been removed. The escort fell in behind me. When I glanced back at him, he sucked in his lips and pulled his right hand in toward the Glock. I wasn't worried. No one would make a move while their boss was waiting for me. Gangsters like this guy are not independent thinkers. If they were, they wouldn't be in a gang.

We turned down another hallway, going deeper into the building. From the distance we walked, I guessed we were closer to the parking lot behind the building than the front entrance. That made sense. Crisologo would enter the building through the protected parking lot, not from the lobby entrance on an open street. We stopped at a door with a long vertical crack near the knob. It had been kicked in at least once. Henry opened the door and gestured for me to go in. It was a large room with a desk at one end, chairs, bookcases and filing cabinets along the walls, and a ratty leather sofa opposite the desk. Henry told me to wait here, and he left. As he closed the door, I saw the escort standing opposite the door, his fingers hooked on his jeans. He gave me a blank look as the door shut.

Two large men were in the room with me. Neither wore a shirt, and they were well-built, bodybuilders from a gym or a prison yard—large, tight pecs, shoulders, and biceps. Toned abs. Bodies you get only with steroids and years of dedicated lifting. One wore a black baseball cap backward. He sat on the sofa, pretending he wasn't paying me any mind. He held a silver automatic in his lap. The other sat at the desk. His abs were clean, but he had tats covering his pecs, shoulders, and arms—a vivid, swirling display of dragons, flames, knives, women's faces, and abstract shapes suggesting energy and force. These weren't prison tats; these were professionally done, the kind you get by paying a tattoo artist two month's wages. Framing his tats was a black shoulder holster, a long-barreled handgun holstered underneath his left arm. He had a long, wiry black beard and mustache and stood up when I entered the room.

He walked toward me, giving me a thin smile. "I know 'bout you," he said.

"Yeah? Where do you know me from?"

"Read 'bout you." To the guy on the sofa, he said, "Dude a warrior. Black belt in Krav Maga." Then to me: "Amirite?"

I nodded. "Fourth degree."

"Sump'n else."

"Aikido. Third-degree Dan. I stopped there because I didn't want to teach it full-time."

He smiled at me, his eyes lit. "Yeah, no shit." He held his hands out to his side, an inviting gesture. "Show me."

I looked back at the guy on the sofa. Now he was making eye contact. I said, "No drama." I turned to the desk and saw a gray stapler. I picked it up and held it out to Tat Man. "Say this is a gat."

He reached for his shoulder holster. "Got tha real thing."

I shook my head. "In the dojo, we practice with fakes. That way, nobody gets hurt. Like I said, no drama."

He shrugged and took the stapler from me.

"Shoot me with it," I told him.

When he pointed the stapler at me, I made a lightning move, knocked it to the left with my left hand, and then grabbed it with my right hand when he released it, as he had to do when the stapler twisted out of his grip. I spun quickly to the floor, aimed the stapler at the guy on the sofa, and said, "Bang, bang." Then I whipped onto my back, pointed the stapler at Tat Man, and said, "Bang, bang, bang."

Tat Man's eyes went wide, and his mouth cracked open with a show of teeth. "Fuck me like a porn star," he exclaimed, laughing. He reached down, and I handed him the stapler. Then he grabbed my hand and pulled me up.

"You aight," he said, as in, "you're all right." He set the stapler on the desk and said, "I gotta learn that shit."

We heard footsteps in the hallway, and the door opened. Tat Man moved away from me and assumed a position against a wall as Henry entered, followed by Alejandro Crisologo. He looked to be in his mid-50s, with salt-and-pepper facial hair and short curly hair on his head. He wore thin wire-frame glasses, a natty white shirt with tiny black polka dots, pressed slacks, and a black blazer. He studied me for a moment, his eyes taking stock, like a mortician figuring out how to make a corpse look presentable for viewing or a professor gazing at an unpromising student.

"I'm Criso," he said, not offering to shake my hand as he moved behind the desk and sat down.

"Sonny Marshall," I said. Henry pulled a chair over in front of the desk and gestured for me to sit.

Henry said to Crisologo, "*Esta desarmado. Y está solo. Nadie afuera.*" *He's unarmed. And he's alone. No one outside.*

Henry was wrong about that. They hadn't done their homework. They didn't know that I spoke Spanish.

Henry continued: "*Su gente dijo que quiere saber sobre el nuevo medicamento. Arrebatamiento.*" *His people said they want to know about the new drug. Rapture.*

"*¿Por qué están interesados?*" Crisologo asked Henry. *Why are they interested?*

"*No lo dijeron.*" *They didn't say.*

Crisologo took a pack of cigarettes from his coat pocket and lit one with a gold lighter. Then he said, "You're with Kirakosian?"

"He and I are friends."

"Why do you want to see me?"

"I want to ask about a new drug on the streets. Called Rapture."

"Why would I know anything about that?"

"You're a man of the world," I replied. "You hear things."

He shrugged. "It's not my business." He looked away, as though growing bored with this conversation, but I knew he was totally present.

"I play in a band. Our guitarist is dying because of this drug. Other people have died from it. I want to know where it's coming from. Who's putting it on the streets."

"I can't help you," he said, looking back at me. "If I said anything about this drug, people could assume I have knowledge of it, and I don't." He turned to Henry: "*¿Qué sabes de este hombre? ¿Estás seguro de que no está con las fuerzas del orden?*" *What do you know about this man? Are you sure he's not with law enforcement?*

Henry replied, "*No hemos encontrado ninguna conexión. Si Kirakosian responde por él, creemos que está a salvo.*" *We haven't found any connection. If Kirakosian vouches for him, we think he's safe.*

Crisologo nodded thoughtfully. "How is Ari?" he said to me. He knew I'd heard Henry say Ari's name.

"Okay," I said. "Being safe."

Crisologo nodded. "I heard about that. His army's short a few men."

"Easy. They were my friends." I glanced around the room at his squad. They think they're on the express elevator to fortune, but most will either be washed up in an alley with needle art on their dead arms or receive a graduate degree in human waste in California's penal system, all without realizing how deftly Crisologo has used them to put silk sheets on his bed. But I had no doubts about their capabilities or willingness to do the man's bidding.

"You know anything about the shooting?" I asked Crisologo. He feigned looking offended, but this dance was highly choreographed. He had nothing to do with the attack behind BiblioTech, and he knew I knew that. After a beat, I added, "I just thought that as a man of the world, you might have heard who attempted the hit."

He shook his head. "Not my affair."

I shrugged. "I'm sure Ari would appreciate anything you might hear in the future."

He gave me a negligible nod.

Just then, the door opened, and a young woman sauntered in, moving her head, grooving to a beat no one else could hear. She wore a black leather skirt and jacket with a chrome automatic shoved in the front of her skirt. She had a full head of brown frizzy hair and heavy-lidded eyes. When she saw me, she smiled, revealing a gap between her two front teeth. "Ouuu, ain't he a pretty one," she said. She plopped down on the sofa, covered her crotch with one hand, and rubbed in circles. "Why don' chu come on over here, white boy, and lick my kitty." Her fellow gangbangers laughed at that. Even Crisologo looked mildly amused. Ignoring her disrespect would cost me points with this crowd, so I shifted gears.

I stared at Crisologo, cold and hard, and said, *"Tu chica debe aprender la diferencia entre ser provocativa y ser una gilipollas."* Your girl must learn the difference between being provocative and being an asshole.

Alarm passed over his face as he realized I spoke Spanish. I imagined he was trying to remember what he and Henry had said to each other.

Behind me, I heard the woman get up off the sofa. "Say what, muthafucka?"

I don't think she understood Spanish, but she was astute enough to know I wasn't complimenting her on her manners. Meanness poured out of both eyes as she walked toward me.

Henry raised a hand to stop her and said, "Act right, Chalene. Can't take you nowhere."

"Wha' that muthafucka say?"

Henry said, "Tighten up!"

"I dunno what tha muthafucka say, but he keep talkin' reckless like that, he gon' catch a fade."

"Chalene, go fix yourself a Dr Pepper," Crisologo told her, "with lots of ice. You need to chill. Go on now."

She stood her ground momentarily, communicating with those heavy eyes that I'd crossed the line with her, and she wouldn't forget it.

After she left, Crisologo said to me, "You're not making any friends here."

"I didn't know it was a social club."

Crisologo shook his pack of cigarettes and held it out for me. I declined, and he lit another cigarette for himself. While he did, I glanced at Tat Man. I caught his eye, and the corners of his mouth curled up just a little bit.

Crisologo blew smoke out of his nostrils and said, "Maybe you can do something for me."

"My band doesn't do weddings or bar mitzvahs."

He grinned. A good sign. "I'd like to meet a friend of yours."

"I have many friends."

He nodded, still grinning. "Earl Zepeda."

"Why you wanna meet that bitch?" the bodybuilder blurted from the sofa.

I turned to him. He looked outraged that his boss would want to meet Earl. I told him, "He's the toughest man I know."

"Shit, man, dude ain't even a dude. Know what I'm sayin'? He a fuckin' bitch." The banger didn't look like a conservative, but I guess he had a problem with transsexuals.

"If you want to meet him," I said, "he's right outside. But a word of advice. Don't call him a bitch. You'll only do it once."

Henry said to him, "Shit, Junior. You gonna write a check your ass can't cash."

I turned back to Crisologo, and he said, "Maybe you could introduce him to me."

I shook my head. "Not the right time. If Earl came in now, others would come with him, and there'd be heavy drama. It's too nice a day to make a mess." Then I said to Henry, "*No vine solo. Pero no los verás.*" *I didn't come alone. But you won't see them.*

Henry and Crisologo exchanged a glance. They didn't know if I was bluffing, but they'd have words about it later. They'd be worried about what they missed. Ain't no pride in being outfoxed by another crew.

"Maybe another time," Crisologo said to me.

"*Quizás,*" I replied. "*Pero Earl es como un hijo para Ari. Nunca abandonará a su padre.*" *Maybe. But Earl is like a son to Ari. He will never abandon his father.*

Crisologo pursued his lips. "*Admiro la lealtad.*" *I admire loyalty.*

"So do I," I said. "Another drug just hit the streets. Makes people crazy. Crazy like killing people. Makes them go berserk. That woman who ran over those people on Market. The knifings in the restaurant outside Golden Gate Park. The guy in Sacramento. They all had that drug in their system."

Crisologo glanced at Henry, a question in his eyes. I couldn't see Henry, but I guessed Henry drew a blank. When Crisologo looked back at me and said he didn't know anything about it, I believed him.

"If I were in that business," he said, "I wouldn't put shit like that on the street. Dead users don't keep buying product." Crisologo dropped his cigarette into an ashtray and stood up. "Sorry I can't help you. Give my regards to Ari." He said to Henry, "Walk him to his car, and watch out for Chalene."

"Bitch is extreme," Henry said.

Crisologo walked toward the door. Tat Man opened it for him, but before leaving, Crisologo turned to me and said, "The man you're looking for calls himself Raylan Major."

He nodded at Henry, who took a small plastic bag from his pocket and set it in my hand. The bag contained a half dozen small blue pills. "Found this on the street," Henry said. "Dunno who dropped it. Jax'll take you out."

He was indicating Tat Man. I followed the tattooed giant back through the hallways to the lobby entrance. Before I returned to my car, I told him the name of the Krav Maga gym where I practice.

"Stay cool," he said.

"Always do, brother."

The Spotter

Bulbous clouds of smoke belched from the windows of the burning house, its interior lit by flickering reds and yellows climbing the walls. Through the open front door, I heard someone wailing, a prolonged cry like the caterwauling of an angry cat. I was hesitant to rush in—smoke escaping from the doorway billowed into the night sky, and I was afraid I couldn't breathe if I went inside—but that crying drew me like an obsession. I ducked beneath the smoke but still felt it burning my lungs. Once across the threshold, I saw a room crowded with smoldering furniture; the drapes beside the windows on the far wall waved like iridescent yellow flags as flames consumed them. Then I saw a woman on the floor on the threshold of a doorway leading to a room deeper in the house. She was struggling to lift herself by her arms and cried out again, a raspy wail clogged with smoke. I duckwalked toward her, then felt my shoes dragging on a carpet that had become mushy. Halfway to her, I saw the floor melting beneath my feet, my shoes disappearing beneath molten gray mush. Then the mush hardened like concrete, and I sank to my knees. I began shaking, my bones rattling like a spoon caught in a garbage disposal, and I shook myself—

—awake, my eyes springing open, and I saw Kat sitting on the bed, one hand on my shoulder. "Are you okay?" she said. "You were moaning."

I sank back into the dream, shook myself out of it, and then said, "I'm okay." But I wasn't. My left knee was on fire. It hurt to move it, even to tense the muscles in that leg. I wondered if I'd tweaked it yesterday while showing Tat Man how to take a handgun away from an assailant. But my knee doesn't need an excuse to turn from cranky to belligerent. Despite my cold-turkey intentions, I told Kat about the dream and said I needed oxy this morning. She said she understood. She left the bed and walked into the bathroom, limping much less than two days ago, using only a cane to steady her left leg. She returned with four oxys, said she knew I kept them in a vitamin bottle, and gave me two with a glass of water. I asked how she knew where they were.

"I'm a detective," she said. "I'm giving the other two to Rhoda so she can have them tested. She said your supply of illegal Oxycodone probably comes from China." I gave her a doubtful look, but I didn't know where they were made. "She said Chinese-made opioids are notoriously impure." I didn't respond. She could be right. When you're addicted to a drug, you're not circumspect about what you're swallowing.

I struggled through the early morning, the pain gradually becoming less insistent as the oxy coursed through my system. Kat stayed there for me. She held my hand as we sat at the dining room table, having a breakfast of vanilla yogurt, strawberries, and steaming dark roast coffee. She had showered earlier and looked softly radiant in the diffuse light through the kitchen windows. She smelled like wisteria and lavender, and I leaned into her scent as we rubbed cheeks and then kissed for a long moment.

"You're moving better," I told her.

"My leg still hurts," she said. "But it's more a dull ache than a sting. The PT is helping."

"She coming this morning?"

"Marcie? Yeah. She'll be here at nine."

I told Kat I had band practice today. She knew K.C. was uncomfortable with Le'Andra and asked if that would work out. I shrugged. K.C.'s a professional musician. I thought he'd come around if Le'Andra's playing met his standard, although it meant reinventing the band's sound and style. But you never know what shines a light on another man's soul. K.C. might be anchored in what the Storm Lake Blues Band was, and that's a gone world because Eric isn't coming back. Adapt or die, I say, and maybe K.C. would prefer to move on.

"Okay with you if Sara visits this weekend?" Kat said.

"Love to have her," I said.

Taking up with Kat meant accepting the whole package, and I was okay with that. I liked Sara. She's a good kid, and having Kat here was more than okay. I found myself morphing from enjoying Kat's visit to wishing she wouldn't leave. Every relationship is a compromise and requires ongoing negotiation, but she hadn't asked me to make a deal-breaking choice yet. Giving up oxy was a challenge I had to face with or without her. But neither of us had spoken about a commitment to anything other than what we were now doing. I had a life here, and she lived in Sacramento and had a daughter she shared with her ex. I couldn't see our circumstances changing. I liked my life here. I also enjoyed sharing it with her. I didn't know what the hell I wanted. I just knew that, for now, I wasn't prepared to talk about anything more, but having Sara visit wasn't making a lifetime commitment.

"Maybe we could take her to St. Ignacius," I said. Sara was interested in that high school. "There's no better college prep school in the state."

"I don't know. She might decide she likes it, and I couldn't afford it."

I shrugged. "You don't have to make any decisions now. Let's see if she likes it first." She looked away, thinking, like me, I imagined, about challenges ahead and changes. She took her coffee cup to the sink and rinsed it. Then she poured another cup and carried it to the table. She traced one finger over the back of my hand. "Are you certain about this, Sonny? There's a lot we haven't talked about."

"Let's have a nice weekend with Sara. See what she thinks."

"What do you think?"

"I think the ground's shaking beneath my feet. But we're sitting on the San Andreas Fault. It's either an earthquake or it's you."

"Are you always this full of shit?"

I laughed. "Caught me."

Marcie Bell arrived just before nine. When she smiled, her cheeks lifted her nostrils and put a song in her eyes. You can't help smiling back. The woman is infectious. When she saw Kat walking with a cane instead of crutches, she said, "How you doin', young mama?"

"Better," Kat said

"Lord, we're gonna have you back on two feet in no time a'tall. People gonna say it's a miracle. They gonna put me up for sainthood; they will. Let's go see 'bout those wounds." Then she said to me, "You playin' with your band today?" I nodded. "Play a little somethin' for me."

"How about 'When the Saints Go Marching In'?"

She crinkled her eyes and shook with laughter as she headed for the bedroom. I gave Kat a long, warm kiss before she followed Marcie.

I arrived at the recording studio a little before 9:30 and took the elevator to the top floor. Sammy DeGregoris, the studio manager, stood outside the closed door to Studio A. With her head bowed, she listened to the muted sounds of instruments in the studio.

"Anything wrong, Sammy?" I said.

She glanced at me and then pointed at Studio A's door. "You tell Garth to tighten that snare drum, or I'm going to go in there and do it for him." She shook her head like a lion, swirling her wild mane of black and gray hair, and then marched off. I was chuckling as I opened the door and went in. I told Garth what Sammy had said, and he hit his snare a few times and then set down his drumsticks.

"It's tight, dammit. It's tuned where it should be." He hit the snare several times, canting his head to listen to the sound. Then he hit it again—a long roll of the drumsticks—and shook his head. "Shit. She said that? The batter head or the resonant head?"

"She didn't say. I'd check 'em both."

"Damn woman," he muttered.

Le'Andra sat on a bar stool in the corner of the studio, her Telecaster in her lap, her fingers flying over the fretboard. I said hi, and she glanced at me and flashed a smile, her fingers never breaking the rhythm of whatever riffs or scales were running through her mind. I got my sax out and warmed up, and for a few minutes, the studio was a cornucopia of competing instruments as each musician went inside and played whatever turned their juices hot. When everybody was tuned and ready, Xavier said, "Let's just jam. K.C., you're leading. Garth, give us one twenty."

Garth set his clicker to 120 beats per minute, thumped his kick drum, followed by a flam on the snare, and settled into a snappy rhythm as the clicker shut off. K.C. started soloing, and the rest of us backed him. When he'd had his run, others took turns soloing, and we jammed like that for an hour, with different tempos and different keys, just jamming. Then we practiced the six Storm Lake songs Le'Andra had learned until we felt comfortable with them. We still had some time, so we jammed again. We discovered that Le'Andra could improvise in the style of B.B. King, Stevie Ray Vaughn, Buddy Guy, John Mayer, Albert King, and T. Bone Walker. During an improv in B flat, she began singing:

Come on, honey. Let's keep it warm
Wanna see you rockin' in the storm
Gitchee gitchee, baby, 'fore the night is gone
You betta have alla them lights comin' on.
You know it's time, cause I'm feelin' fine
Need to show me, baby, you got some spine.

I didn't know if she'd written those lyrics or were pulling them out of the air, but we were laughing when the song ended. Garth said, "Where the hell did that come from?"

"Just made it up, brother," Le'Andra replied. "Just making it up."

"You're not gonna do that every song," K.C. said.

She smiled at him, reading the vibe. "Only in the studio trying something new. Can't jam lyrics live unless they're real simple," she assured him. "And I don't do real simple. How you like me now?"

"It's all good," K.C. replied.

"Okay, talk about Sunday," Xavier said. "Let's do the six Storm Lake songs Le'Andra knows and improvise the rest. Le'Andra, can you write the song you just made up?" She said she could. "We'll call it 'Keep It Warm'," Xavier continued. "Should have some bounce to it, so let's play it at one-thirty or one-forty. Leave a middle instrumental section for some sultry sax." He opened his notebook computer and continued: "I'll write down some tempos, chords, and who's leading on each number. Send the set list around tonight. We'll practice the improvs tomorrow. Cool?"

"Yeah, X-Man. But let's mix it up," K.C. said. He meant the blues styles. "Some boogie-woogie, some West Coast."

"A little Chicago?" Le'Andra said. "You guys okay with distortion and overdrive?"

"Long as we don't sound like Metallica," Xavier said.

"I'm down with that," Le'Andra said.

We agreed. It was a good plan. Improvising with pros like this crew was like drinking honey from the hive.

I checked messages as we wrapped and saw one from John asking me to meet him and Paul at Saint Frank's on Folsom. Saint Frank Coffee is known for premiere blends, but as I walked there after parking my car, I remembered that Duggins and Alamilla had both had coffee before going on their rampages. Just a coincidence, I told myself when I arrived. John and Paul had snagged a table by the window and ordered me a Friar Minor, a dark roast blend from Honduras. It was delish, just the boost I needed after five hours with the band. Paul looked like he always does—black suit, white shirt, narrow black tie, black shoes—standard for a guy who's color blind. His prominent nose hung over his coffee cup like an umbrella. John looked incognito in a nondescript jacket over a nondescript shirt. His face had three days of stubble, and he hid his eyes behind aviator sunglasses with bronze lenses. I told them what I'd learned from Alejandro Crisologo.

"Raylan Major?" Paul said, knitting his brow. "Don't recall that name. I'll ask around Narcotics and run him through NCIC." NCIC is the National Crime Information Center, a criminal information database law enforcement agencies use nationwide. If Major had any priors, they might show up on NCIC—might, because any database is only as good as the information you put into it, and only about a third of warrants issued nationwide show up on NCIC. No comprehensive national criminal database exists, but NCIC is better than nothing.

"I also have these," I said, pulling a sandwich bag from my pocket with three Rapture pills in it. I kept the other half of the pills for someone who could analyze them independently. "This is Rapture. Crisologo's majordomo said he found these on the street."

"Right," John scoffed. "His crew's not pushing this stuff?"

"I don't think so. Crisologo said dead junkies don't buy product. He wants live clients who are hooked. Better cash flow."

Paul slipped the bag into his suit pocket. "I'll give these to Narcotics."

"I'd like to talk to a chemist familiar with drug manufacture," I said. "Somebody who could look at the tox reports on the victims. Tell us what they mean."

"Our lab can do that," Paul said.

"Your lab techs are analysts, Paul. They can tell us what it is. I want to know how it's made."

They thought about that for a moment. Then John said, "Dom Bernardi."

Paul nodded. "He'd be good."

"Who's Dom Bernardi?"

"He's a biochemist," Paul said. "He works for a biotech company here in the Bay Area. He's done some consulting work for us. Testified last year in a designer drug case. He does research on drugs and, I think, holds patents on a couple."

"Smart guy," John added. "I have his number. I'll call him. See what I can set up."

We didn't have other news, so Paul left for work, and John and I stood outside for a moment, watching people cross the intersection at Folsom and Spear. "You got an hour?" John asked.

"Somewhere," I said, patting down my pockets. "Must have left it in my other jeans."

"Wiseass." He pulled a slip of paper from his pocket and handed it to me. "Follow me to this address. This is where the spotter was the night they tried to kill Ari."

I nodded, walked to my car, and drove to a place a street over and kitty-corner from BiblioTech. It was a plain brown mixed-use three-story building. I could tell it would overlook the lot behind BiblioTech, where the warehouse dock is. I parked and walked to the building's entrance, where John stood talking to two men. One was Glen Kobayashi, an associate of John in his security company. Glen's a slender guy with a smooth complexion and long black hair he wears in a man bun. I'd met him before. John introduced the other man as Bruce Orr, the building manager. He was an older guy with long black and silver hair and a scraggly gray beard. His nose was creased in the middle and dented like a left-handed brawler had hammered it. He sniffled and wiped his nose with one hand. Then he answered a question John had asked.

"Yeah, so I noticed because the guy had this black metal, uh, thing, like on the toes of his boots, ya know? Covering the toes like. Wouldn't wanna be kicked with them, ya know? Never seen that before."

"They're called toe caps," John said. "What'd the guy look like?"

Orr wiped his nose as he thought about it. "Yeah, uh, older, gray hair, thin. I mean thin hair. Guy was short, maybe little shorter than me. Uh, chubby. And, uh, he had glasses. Wore glasses. Black frames."

"What was he wearing?"

"Besides them combat boots? Uh, blue jacket, white sweater, ya know, white, the kind with the collar round the neck."

"Turtleneck."

"That's it, yeah, turtleneck. Wicked boots. Kick the shit outta ya."

"What was his name?"

"Didn't say. Or it slipped my mind. I dunno. When he didn't rent, I, uh, like it didn't matter."

Orr wiped his nose again as John asked him to take us to the third floor. Orr kept talking nonstop, but I tuned him out as we ascended the stairs. The building was probably forty years old but in decent shape. Most of the spaces were occupied—a small insurance company in one, a travel agency next to it, people coming in and out, the usual on a weekday. When we reached the third floor, Orr led us to an empty office on the side of the building facing BiblioTech's lot. "Guy said they was lookin' for space to rent. That's all. He saw the space. Left pretty quick."

The office was empty and had been for a while. A fine layer of dust covered the floor except where Glen had duct-taped a small disturbed area in the center of the room. The room had been cleaned some time ago, the nail holes in the walls patched and fresh paint applied. I saw footprints around the taped area, all leading to a window on the wall facing

BiblioTech. John waved me toward the taped area, and I could see the faint outline of a shoe print in the dust.

"Show him, Glen," John said. Glen handed me his cell phone with a close-up photo of the shoe print taken from an angle so the impressions in the dust were more visible. I could make out five horizontal bands across the bottom of the shoe, along with faint letters: E S E L.

"It's a distinctive sole," Glen said. "The shoe that made this was a Diesel D-Hammer So D, European. Size 40." He swiped one finger across the screen to another photo of a clunky-looking men's black shoe. "That's called an oval D toe cap," he said, pointing to the black metal cap across the toe. "Italian manufacturer. They're sold all over Europe, and you can get them here."

"Never seen one," I said.

"No, they're rare. And over here," Glen said, walking me to the window, "we found finger smudges on the window sill." The white window sill was smeared with black fingerprint powder, and I could see round indentations where someone's fingers had touched the sill. "Too bad we couldn't get usable prints, but we know someone was here."

John asked Orr if the guy who looked at the office had gone to that window.

Orr wiped his nose. "Nah. Quick look and, like, he wasn't interested."

I looked through the window and had a clear view of BiblioTech's loading dock. The window glass was cloudy from the wildfire smoke that had settled over everything in the city, but what I smelled wasn't smoke from the fires. There was a faint scent of something sweeter, not cologne or perfume. Not aftershave. It was something earthier but with the faintest hint of vanilla. I looked around the empty room and couldn't imagine where that scent originated. The window had a shade rolled above it, a string with a round handle hanging down. I pulled the shade halfway down and buried my nose in it. The scent was more potent, and I realized I smelled cigarette smoke, a cloying blend of tobacco—and something else. Whoever was at the window had smoked, and the smoke rose into the shade and saturated it.

"Do you mind if I open this window?" I asked John. He shook his head. I rolled the shade back up, undid the latch, and pushed the bottom window up. Hanging my head out, I scanned the ground below the window and saw scattered trash on the side of the road, among it some small white objects below the window. John and I went down the stairs while Glen continued questioning Orr, and we found a door to the back of the building. Outside, we walked to the spot beneath the suspect window and found four cigarette butts on the ground. One of them, not as smoked down as far as the others, had an imperial-looking red marking on the paper wrapping. It looked like a royal crest.

"I've seen these before," John said. "European." He rolled the butt over in his fingers, his eyes staring intently. Then he gave a small grunt and opened his cell phone. After a few minutes of searching on the phone, he said, "Son of a bitch." He looked at me. "These are Cardinals." Then he peered closer at the small red crest and said, "Gotcha."

"You going to let me in on it?" I asked.

He smelled the tobacco, inhaling it deeply, then put the butt in a small plastic bag he'd taken from his pocket. "Cardinal cigarettes. They're made in Azerbaijan. Their website says they make three varieties—plain, vanilla, and sweet vanilla. You can't buy them here. It's Azeris who want Ari dead."

"Why?"

John smiled. "We'll ask them politely when we find them."

Arachne

Raylan Major was a ghost.

"I can't find anyone by that name living in San Francisco or the greater Bay Area," Kat said.

"It's an alias," I told her. "It was a long shot."

"Maybe he's listed as Ray Major. I'll try that."

She sat beside her laptop at the dining room table, a lukewarm cup of coffee and a half-eaten strawberry Danish. I sat with my saxophone in the chair on the other side of the table, playing riffs with my fingers without blowing into the mouthpiece. I knew how the notes would sound without having to hear them. The keys made a soft clicking sound when they closed, and to Kat, it must have sounded like muted Morse code, but she didn't complain. The band was practicing later this morning, and I was warming up. Sunlight streaming through the kitchen windows made the room too bright, so I'd put on my sunglasses. I wore jeans and loafers, a black B.B. King t-shirt, and an unbuttoned blue plaid shirt. Kat glanced at me and chuckled.

"You look like a high school kid pretending to play an instrument."

"I've fooled everybody for years," I said. "Anything?"

"The DMV lists six Ray Majors in California," she said, "but only two in Northern California." She jotted down something on a pad of paper. "One in Santa Clara. Forty-six years old. Five foot ten, 185 pounds, brown hair, blue eyes. I have his photo and address. The other—" typing something "—lives in Red Bluff. That's a three-hour drive."

"Possible," I said, "but unlikely. How old is he?"

"White hair. He's, uh, sixty-eight. Let's put him on the back burner for now. I'll check arrest records." She typed while I practiced, my keys softly clicking. Then she said, "One Ray Major arrested for burglary in Riverside. Nineteen years ago. Address in Canyon Lake."

I shook my head. "Southern California. Our Raylan Major is local or within easy driving distance of the Bay Area. Raylan Major is an alias."

"Nothing on NCIC either," she said.

She looked radiant this morning. She'd washed her hair and put some blush on her cheeks and a pink gloss on her lips. I asked why she wore makeup. She looked good without it. She told me it moisturized her skin and enhanced her appearance. When I said she didn't need to improve her looks, she asked about Mac, my previous girlfriend. I said Mac wore a lot of makeup, but she was in the fashion industry. It was expected of her. Mac was beautiful, but I'd come to appreciate women whose faces don't look manufactured—a woman like Kat, who's also a lioness in human form. I wanted to curl up with her and feel those claws, but we had to wait until she felt better.

We hadn't made progress on Raylan Major, so I texted Paul Fisher and asked him if SFPD and the zombie drug task force had learned anything. He responded shortly and said no. When Marcie Bell arrived to do Kat's physical therapy, I retreated to my sound-proofed music room and practiced out loud, absently running through the riffs with only muscle memory as a guide. I kept trying to picture Raylan Major in my mind. Eric's husband, Jaycee Washington, said he was an average, thin white guy with long brown hair and a dark gray robe with a hood. But the man he saw at the party might not have been Raylan Major. The supplier Crisologo identified could have been someone higher in the food chain than the spectral dude at the party where Eric got Rapture.

How do you find a ghost?

You go to a place he haunted.

I called Jaycee and asked about the party he and Eric went to. Jaycee gave me an address and said the woman who lived there was Eric's friend, a Goth princess who called herself Arachne. I had time before our rehearsal, so I drove to the address in Ashbury Heights. It was a three-story dark gray row house with a single-car garage on the lower level of a street that angled sharply downhill. On the floor above the garage was a shop named Olympia Tapestry. Displayed behind a broad picture window were three brightly colored tapestries. Crystals were suspended from the ceiling above them, and a sign in the window said that horoscope readings were available within. An ornate Zodiac was carved into the door.

After I knocked, the door opened just a crack, and a woman said, "We're not open."

"I'd like to speak to Arachne," I said.

The door opened a little wider, and I saw a pretty, slender woman, maybe 25, with long black hair. She had pale skin and black bangs hanging just below artfully crafted eyebrows. She wore black lipstick, black eyeshadow, and mascara, which made her eyes luminescent on pearly skin. She reminded me of Geishas with their painted faces. I couldn't see much of her below her face, but in my peripheral vision, I glimpsed a lot of skin and got the impression that she was nude.

"You're a Gemini," she said, regarding me with curious eyes. "Romance will blossom for you tonight."

"I hope so," I replied, bringing a smile to her black lips. I could smell fragrant candle smoke in the room behind her. As she looked me over, she raised a hand to her chin and traced a line down her throat with one finger.

"What do you want with Arachne?"

"You hosted a party here several weeks ago."

"Arachne has many parties."

"A mutual friend attended this one. Eric Young."

Her eyes dropped for a long moment. I thought she might be examining my shoes. "How is Eric?"

"Not well."

She pinched her nose. "It smells like a fireplace out here. Come inside," she said. She opened the door and turned away from me. She wasn't nude, but everything she wore was black—a tiny satin camisole, panties and a garter, thigh-high stockings, and long boots with thick soles and five-inch heels.

"I can wait if you want to get dressed."

She gave me a come-on smile and said, "I am dressed."

I tried not to dwell on it. "I'm an Aries, by the way."

She looked curiously at me and said, "You will put a lot of energy into your relationships today. You may prefer to work alone, but a new relationship you form today could be enduring."

I wondered if she was referring to herself. If so, it was one of the more inventive pick-up lines I'd ever heard.

"Don't be afraid to try new things," she continued.

Her showroom was filled with tapestries in various designs and motifs, and in every corner of the ceiling, there were large spider webs made of spun glass. I gazed at the tapestries. They looked beautifully woven, with rich dark colors and intricate patterns, although I'm no judge of fine tapestry. "Is this your work?" I asked.

"Some is. Do you like it?"

I nodded. "They're beautiful, but I don't know much about tapestry."

"You don't need to," she purred, tilting her head slightly and observing me from an angle. "Just enjoy what you see."

"That's how we should appreciate art," I said. She stared at me, amused. Flickering candlelight made her eyes sparkle. "I want to ask you about Eric."

"I was so sorry to hear what happened."

"Jaycee Washington said he got the drug at your party. It's called Rapture."

"Arachne's party."

"Right. Was her party here in the showroom?"

"It was upstairs in the apartment. Would you like to see it?"

"Intriguing offer. Jaycee said Eric got Rapture from a guy wearing a long gray robe with a hood."

She put one finger to her lips. Her nails were black, too, overlaid with gold spider web nail art. "You a cop?"

"I'm a musician. Blues and jazz."

"Much better. Are you sure you're an Aries? I see a major turning point in your life coming soon. The next knock on the door could be it. Don't hesitate to answer."

I laughed, and she cracked a smile. She had very white teeth. Beneath the smell of the candles throughout the room, I sensed a subtler scent: vanilla and something woody, maybe rose. I felt the urge to move closer to her and realized her perfume's effect on me. I stood my ground.

"I think the guy might have called himself Raylan Major."

She chuckled at that. "I don't know if he deals. Maybe he was carrying. It was a party. People share."

"He a friend of yours? Raylan Major?"

She shook her head. "Not totally. I mean, like, I barely knew him. We met at a Cosplay convention."

"What's that?"

She pouted, giving a look that said I was totally out of touch. "You know, Cosplay. Costume play. You're obviously not into it." She made me feel like a dork. "You dress up like a character from a movie or a comic book or something and pretend to be that character."

That's where her Arachne persona came from, although I had no clue who Arachne was. I made a mental note to look it up. "I usually dress up as a musician," I told her.

"It's a good look on you." She put her hands on her hips, which drew attention to her lower body. I stayed focused on her face. "Anyway, his name isn't Raylan Major. His character is Wraithlan Mager." She spelled it for me.

"Who's that?"

"Jeez, dude, you really don't know what time it is. Wraithlan Mager is from the *Nekromanti Saga*."

I must have looked like I had no idea what she just said. She pouted. "The book by Aksel Larsen. You know, the Danish writer? Dude, get real. Wraithlan Mager is, like, this super powerful evil wizard."

"I'm behind on my reading. So, do you know this guy's real name?" She canted her head like a dog when it tries to understand what you're saying. Her long hair fell away from her ear. She wore black earrings, too. She was nothing if not consistent. "I get that he dresses up as a wizard," I said. "Does he have another name?"

She said, "I don't care who he is in his other life," as if that should have been obvious.

"I don't suppose you know where to find him."

She raised her hands, palms up. "Clueless."

"Do you have his number?"

She gave me a coy smile. "Men call me," she said. "I don't call them."

When I thanked her for her time, she said, "You sure you're not a Leo? Something new and wonderful can start for you today. Don't be afraid to act on your impulses."

I took one more look at this bewitching, raven-haired beauty, thanked her for her advice, and then escaped. I didn't know Raylan Major's real name or where to find him, but I knew what he pretended to be.

How do you find a ghost? You go to a place he might have visited. I knew of a large costume shop on Haight Street.

Haight Cosplay was a phantasmagoria of masks, wigs, costumes, hats, and makeup. You could be anything you wanted to be in there—except real. But, hey, if fantasy is your thing, you could lose yourself in that place. The woman at the register was a 60-year-old graying blonde wearing makeup that weighed more than she did. I wished I had a ruler to measure her painted eyebrows. They were at least a half-inch thick, but I might have been off by a sixteenth. I asked her if she remembered any Cosplay customers looking for a Wraithlan Mager costume.

"I can't talk about my customers."

I wasn't aware that privileged communication extended to sales clerks. But rather than piss her off by pointing that out, I said, "One guy who thinks he's Wraithlan Mager is pushing drugs that are killing people."

"Not my problem," she said. Two teens walk through the door. The girl had bright blue hair. They went to a rack of costumes and fingered through them. "I got customers."

"I'm happy to return with a warrant and the Chief of Homicide."

She glared at me like I was the most enormous manure pile she'd ever stepped in. Then I watched the deeper lines in her scowling face soften as she decided that stonewalling me wasn't worth the trouble. "One guy came in three, four weeks ago. I don't know his name. He bought a hooded cloak with Jacquard trim. He said it was for Mager."

"What color was it?"

"Red. Velvet. But Wraithlan Mager also wore black cloaks."

"Dark gray?"

She shrugged. Sure, why not?

"White guy?" I asked. She nodded. "What color hair?"

"Dark brown. Long. But in Cosplay, Mager can have blonde hair. Or silver. Depends on which volume of the *Saga* you're into."

"Did he use a credit card?"

"Cash."

"Had you ever seen him before?"

She shook her head. I thanked her and was walking toward the door when she said, "You may hide from danger, but you can't escape. Death permeates the air like a mist."

"What?"

"Something Wraithlan Mager said. It's in one of Aksel Larsen's books. Death arrives as a welcoming stranger."

"I'll keep that in mind," I said.

Band practice was smooth and productive. Five hours of blues improvisation revived my spirit like nothing else could, but I let my mind wander now and then to a man in a red velvet cloak who dispensed a drug that cost people their minds. That's a Biblical level of hatred, a Valdemortian disregard for human life that is hard to fathom.   I remembered what Rhoda Merrick said about psychopaths—they have no empathy and no conscience—and felt a smoldering need to bring this guy down hard.

How do you find a ghost? You go to a place he haunts. But the next Cosplay event in the Bay Area wasn't for seven more months. I looked it up.

When I arrived home at 4:30, John Sebastiani, Ari Kirakosian, and his partner, Catherine Gauthier, were there. I was surprised to see Catherine. She's a dedicated painter who rarely leaves her studio on the top floor of the BiblioTech building during the workday. They sat around our dining room table with Kat. Two open bottles of wine sat on the table.

"What's going on?" I asked.

"I have a team installing better security at BiblioTech," John said. They were adding cameras, motion sensors, security lights, and keyless biometric fingerprint digital door locks on the top floors. When they were finished later this evening, only authorized people could enter the living quarters and office areas above the bookstore.

"You think the murderers will return to BiblioTech?" Kat said.

"It's where I spend much of my time," Ari replied.

"I can't live in a cage," Catherine said. She had been sitting quietly, both hands cradling a wine glass. The *joie de vivre* I usually saw in her had vanished, along with the shine in her eyes. They were now dark pools of sadness and fright.

Ari put one hand over hers, but if he meant to appease her, it failed. "It's just until the threat passes," he said. She gave him a sullen glance, then took a sip of wine. Catherine was a free spirit and would not be contained long. I was surprised she hadn't returned to Paris until this was over.

John said, "The extra security is a good idea anyway."

Kat asked if they had a lead on the assailants.

John shook his head. "No, but the AKs they used were made in Russia, an ally of Azerbaijan, and we know the watcher was an Azeri. He wore shoes common in Azerbaijan but rare here, and he smoked a brand of cigarette made and sold in that country."

"Why would they want to harm you?" she asked Ari.

Ari pursed his lips and thought about that for a moment. "It's complicated, like every Middle Eastern conflict. Armenia and Azerbaijan are at war," he said. "Cold, now, but Azerbaijan invaded Nagorno a year ago. Hundreds of Armenians were killed. Technically, there's a truce, but incidents continue, and there's been some ethnic cleansing. After last year's hot war, hundreds of thousands of Armenians living in Nagorno fled to Armenia. Settling them has been a nightmare."

"Why are they fighting?" Kat said.

"We Armenians have been conquered many times since the 7th Century B.C. But we are fiercely independent and have resisted assimilation. The most recent troubles started in 1923 when Stalin carved out a piece of Armenia and called it the Nagorno-Karabakh Autonomous Oblast. The majority of the people in Nagorno were Armenian, but they were governed by the Azerbaijan Soviet Socialist Republic."

"Armenia was part of the Soviet Union then," John added. "When the Soviet Union broke up, Armenia became independent again."

"For centuries, Armenians and Azeris coexisted peacefully," Ari said, "although they are culturally and ethnically diverse. Armenians are Indo-Europeans and Christians. Azeris are ethnically related to Turks and are Muslims."

"I still don't understand why they targeted you," Kat said.

"I give money to the Armenian cause," Ari explained. "Millions to help those who fled Nagorno resettle in Armenia. Also, money for the Armenian militias who continue to resist Azerbaijani terror. Earlier this year, Armenia suspended its participation in Russia's military alliance of former Soviet states."

"So tension is heating up again," Kat said.

Ari nodded. "We think the Russians funded the assassination attempt to punish Armenia for threatening to leave its military alliance."

"They want to dry up a funding source," John said. "So they sent a hit squad from Azerbaijan to carry out the assassination."

"What will you do when you find them?" Kat asked.

"We'll neutralize the threat," John said.

A cloud passed over Kat's face. I knew she wouldn't accept that ambiguity. "They're murderers," she said. "You need to turn them over to the police."

"We will," said John, "if we have enough evidence to convict them."

"And if you don't?" she replied.

"Maybe they'll confess," John said lightheartedly. No one laughed.

"If they don't?" she said, her voice rising.

"We'll ensure Ari's and Catherine's safety."

Kat brooded over that for a moment. She was drinking water and took a long sip while she studied John.

"I'm a police officer," she told John. "I have a duty to the law."

"I know," he said.

"I don't want Sonny involved," she said.

John glanced at me and then back at Kat. "He won't be."

Kat locked eyes with him. "I need your promise on that."

"You have it," John said.

Kat gave me a stern look, wondering, I think, whether I sanctioned what she imagined would happen if the system could not bring the Azeri assassins to justice.

Turning back to John, she said, "If you do anything illegal, I can't know about it."

"You won't."

"I'd have to arrest you, John."

"Won't put you in that position."

You can't dance on the cliff's edge without knowing what one false step would mean. But if you sit in a chair on the side of the dance floor, the people with one foot in the abyss will shimmy all over you. Kat believes in law and order, and I admire her desire to see justice done using the rules lawmakers have laid down for civilized conduct. The people who tried to kill Ari—and did kill three of his compatriots—disrespected those rules but would turn them to their advantage, if necessary, to escape responsibility for their actions. Laws serve the common good. Through arrests, trials, convictions, and sentences, laws can serve justice cold. But sometimes justice must be served hot.

A Tidal Wave Named Sara

On Saturday morning, a yellow fog drifted over the San Francisco Peninsula, obscuring the buildings around my condo and the street below like the mist of Achlys, who, to the ancient Greeks, personified sorrow. Achlys' mist blinded mortals, dropping a shade over their eyes as a prelude to death. From my kitchen, I could follow the air currents by watching the flow of brown particulates in the yellow fog as they wove past my window, settling over the city like a shroud. Another wildfire had started east of Oakland. It had consumed eighteen hundred acres and forty-six structures overnight and was zero percent contained as of six am. The morning news reported some loss of life, although the number was unknown. There were too many people still unaccounted for. I closed the kitchen windows to keep the worst of the smoke outside. Kat had inhaled some smoke during the Folsom Flea Market incident. Her respiratory system was healing, but I heard her coughing beside me in bed this morning.

While she slept, I made coffee and cut up a cantaloupe for breakfast. I took the fruit and a cup of yogurt to my study and turned on my laptop. After reading the news, I searched for Arachne and learned that in Greek mythology, she was a mortal who was a master weaver. The goddess Minerva, who also wove tapestries, challenged Arachne to a weaving duel, which Arachne won. That so incensed Minerva that she changed Arachne into a spider, which explained the spun-glass webs on Olympia Tapestry's showroom ceiling. Then I searched the county tax assessor's records and learned that the house on Ashbury Heights was owned by Susan Smotherman, aka Arachne, the seductive Black Widow. When reality is tiresome, you can always remake yourself as a Cosplay character.

Next, I searched for Wraithlan Mager and discovered he was a charismatic wizard in Larsen's *Nekromanti Saga*. He was supremely intelligent and elusive, possessed an unusual mastery of magic, and was a spellcaster. Wraithlan was a dark lord who emerged from the sea, initially a savior to the people of an island kingdom who were threatened by an army of trolls. By giving magic potions to the trolls, he turned them all to stone. Then he cast spells on the islanders and enslaved them. He could not be defeated because he was insubstantial, a wraith, and arrows and axes passed through him. In the end, he displeased other gods and was banished to the netherworld but still resides in the shadowy realm of nightmares. I found Wraithlan Mager's tale challenging to follow but left understanding that our self-proclaimed wizard considered himself a smart and determined master of potions like Rapture.

How do you find a ghost? You talk to other people who've seen him. But the police hadn't turned up anyone with a better description than a *thin, average white guy with long brown hair wearing a long, dark, hooded cloak.* The police sketch artist, talking to witnesses who'd been to different parties where Rapture was distributed, produced conflicting sketches that looked like any thin, average white guy in the city if most of his features were obscured by a hood. He might have had a cleft in his chin. His eyes might have been close together—or not. His nose might have been rounded—or blunt. No one agreed, and many witnesses were high when they saw the wizard. They barely recalled what day it was.

Kat knocked on my door and peered in. "We have a visitor," she said.

It was Rhoda Merrick. When I left my study, I pretended to be surprised. "I hoped my two girlfriends would never meet," I said.

Rhoda looked chic in a black turtleneck and gray skirt. She stood at the dining room table with a cup of coffee and sat down. "I've been trying to house-train him," she told Kat. "Clearly, I've failed."

"Rhoda told me about you flirting with her," Kat said, sitting beside Rhoda.

I gave Rhoda a disapproving look. "That was our secret."

"If you flirt with anyone else," Kat said, "I'll have to arrest you."

"On what charge, officer?"

"Reckless Endangerment."

"Who would I be endangering?"

"Yourself," Kat said.

I laughed and sat on the other side of the table, worried when I realized they had me outnumbered. "I would plead insanity. Then you could treat me," I said to Rhoda.

She folded her arms and shook her head. "I'd have you committed. Any man who fooled around on Kat would be mentally ill and beyond help."

"Good point," I said, "but I have proof that I'm sane."

They looked at each other. Kat said, "This should be good."

"People with serious psychological problems often don't know it," Rhoda responded.

I told them about my encounter with Arachne. "Candlelight, pretty woman, strong perfume, sexy underwear, and she invited me to her bedroom."

"And you resisted? You're truly a man of steel," Rhoda said.

"To quote Paul Newman, why go out for a hamburger when you have steak at home."

Kat smiled at me. "I still think the woman is dangerous," she said.

Rhoda looked at her. "I could ask the Chief Medical Officer to declare a public health emergency."

I thought, *my neighbor doesn't know how close we are to that, but the problem isn't a pretty young woman dressing as a spider.*

"I did learn something important from Arachne." I told them about our suspect pretending to be Wraithlan Mager.

"What you're describing," Rhoda said, "sounds like narcissistic personality disorder. Most people in Cosplay are normal people who enjoy dressing up and engaging in playful fantasy. But your suspect identifies with a powerful sorcerer and dispenses a drug instead of casting a spell. He's a manipulator. He'll have an inflated sense of himself. He'll believe he's special and thinks others envy him."

"A psychopath," I said.

"Probably, although not all narcissists are psychopaths. Psychopathy is also associated with borderline, sadistic, and antisocial personalities. But your suspect knows what Rapture is doing to people. He keeps distributing it, so he doesn't care that it harms his victims. He might even enjoy that, which shows a lack of empathy. He's probably very intelligent. He'll have fantasies of success, power, and command over others. He may think he's omnipotent and imagines that he'll never be caught. If he decides to quit, it will be on his terms, not yours."

I nodded. "I want him to keep thinking that way. That's how you defeat opponents using Krav Maga. They think they're smart and tough, which makes them vulnerable to attacks they don't see coming."

"How can we spot this guy?" Kat asked.

"Not easily," Rhoda said. "He'll be well adapted to how normal people behave. If you went to a Cosplay gathering, you might see him in his regalia, but I'm guessing he's too smart for that."

Rhoda took her last sip of coffee. Kat asked if she wanted more, and Rhoda shook her head. Then she gave me a serious look, and I caught the shift of gears. "How's your knee?" she asked me.

"I need a new one," I said.

"Kat said you have an appointment."

"Soon."

She took a small blue pill container from a pocket in her skirt and set it on the table. "I brought this for you."

It was a bottle of Oxycodone. Forty-five pills.

"I'm now officially your physician," she said. "Come to my office to complete the paperwork, so everything is legal. Kat asked me to test the painkillers you've been taking."

"She told me."

"I don't want to know where you've been getting Oxycodone, but if it's a physician, he should lose his license and be thrown in jail."

"Why?"

"The pills you've been taking contain 0.4 milligrams of fentanyl. Chinese underground drug makers add fentanyl to make their counterfeit Oxycodone more addictive. A lethal dose of fentanyl is 2 milligrams. Taking five of them in a day could kill you. I also brought Narcan for Kat—in case you overdose when I'm not around to save you."

She told me to take no more than three of the pure oxy pills a day, two when the severe pain was coming on and one four hours later to manage the pain. Then she asked for my stash of counterfeit oxy. I gave her the motherlode, reluctantly—around 200 pills—and she said she would dispose of them safely at her clinic. It felt like a watershed moment, like saying goodbye to a friend who's stuck by my side through the worst of times. I couldn't refuse, but it felt like Rhoda and Kat were ferrying me across the Rubicon. Whatever landscape I found myself in was one I hadn't inhabited for twelve years. You know how you feel when someone cares enough about you to protect you from yourself? We all need friends like Rhoda and Kat. Well, Kat's much more than a friend, but you know what I mean. People who care enough to tell you when you're full of shit and pick you up when you stumble.

I hadn't been to St. Ignacius College Prep since they remodeled it in 2023. When we walked through the main entrance, I thought that if you had to go to high school, this is the place to go. The remodeled campus is modern, large, and high-tech, fulfilling students' dreams while straining their parents' savings accounts. I didn't have to ask Sara what she thought of it. The awestruck look on her face was a portrait of wonder. She arrived mid-morning at my condo with her father, David. I showed Sara around the place while David and Kat talked privately. Sara was amazed at my sound-proofed music room where I practice the sax without annoying my neighbors. She stood outside with the door closed while I played a few riffs and said she wasn't sure when I was blowing notes and when I wasn't. That's the point, I told her.

After David left, Kat had a thoughtful look on her face but gave me a slight shake of her head when I raised my eyes at her. So we got Sara settled in the guest bedroom and prepared to leave for St. Ignacius. When John Sebastiani was a Jesuit priest, he'd been friends with Father Jeremy Kennedy, who is now the President of St. Ignacius. John arranged for us to tour the campus and talk to their Director of Admissions. We arrived just before eleven and parked on 37th Avenue in front of the main entrance to the school. Although it was Saturday, hundreds of parents and students were on the campus. When we introduced ourselves to Fr. Kennedy, he told us that four of their athletic teams were playing today—football, men's and women's water polo, and women's volleyball—which explained why the campus was so busy on a weekend.

Sara was a miniature version of Kat with longer blonde hair. Her front teeth were a little prominent for her face. It looked like she hadn't quite grown into herself, and some parts were still out of proportion. But I could see in her eyes the yearning to become the person she eventually would be, that awkward transition from kid to young adult when she's eager to give up childish things but hasn't mastered thinking and acting independently and isn't confident in her decisions, resisting her mother's guidance but afraid to act without it. She looked intimidated as we walked through the main entrance. Then Fr. Kennedy and their Director of Admissions, Mrs. Somebody (her name went past me too quickly), introduced Sara to two students, a junior and a freshman, whom they drafted to give Sara a tour and talk about the school. I watched Sara's face transform from trepidation to excitement as they led her away. I tried to recall the emotional currents that ran through me at her age—all the fascinating discoveries, disappointments, hopes, fears, dreams, and hormonal urges that course through a young teenager's soul, and I envied Sara for the brave new world she was starting to explore.

While Sara was gone, Fr. Kennedy and his administrator showed us around the school and discussed the admissions process. The deadline for applying to St. Ignacius was weeks away. Kat would have to act quickly if Sara wanted to apply for next fall. They admit only one in four applicants, so Sara's admission wasn't guaranteed. But Fr. Kennedy spoke highly of John Sebastiani, and I thought that connection would give Sara an advantage. Kat and I had lunch at a bistro nearby, and she worried that Sara might get her hopes up too much. I'm not a parent, but I could imagine how you pray your child doesn't suffer a crushing disappointment over something she sets her heart on. Kat ate with anxious eyes and didn't finish her lunch. I hadn't seen her worry like that and was torn between saying nothing or reassuring her that everything would work out. I didn't know that it would, so I chose the wiser course and said nothing.

When our band is playing, I'm sometimes fearful that I won't remember a solo I have to play in a few minutes, and I get a hollow feeling in my gut that I'm going to blow it and look as incompetent as I feel. When the moment arrives, the fear somehow vanishes, and I ease into the groove, unconsciously playing well. Call it performance anxiety or stage fright. I usually recognize it for what it is and try not to worry about my performance, relying on training and practice to work their magic. I wanted to ease Kat's fears, but they're her fears, and she has to cope with them the way she conquers every cop's fears about approaching a suspect or knocking on the door during a domestic disturbance call. Yeah, I know, worrying about your child is different, but fear is still fear, no matter how it chases you into a dark alley or conceals itself under your bed.

When we picked up Sara mid-afternoon, her smile lit up the inside of my car, and she couldn't get the words out of her mouth fast enough. She had to breathe now and then, but otherwise, the wall of excited noise from the backseat was deafening: how dank (excellent) the school was, how many clubs they had, how good the girl's soccer team was, how great the student center was, how she loved the classes they offered, and all the athletics, and two theatres, and how they have small classes, a teacher for every twelve students, and how the two girls she met were totally dope (awesome), and so on through the drive back to my condo. For all Sara knew, we were transported home on a magic carpet. She saw nothing else. Inside the condo, she opened the information folder they'd given her and went through it again.

When Sara sensed that we'd heard enough, she took the St. Ignacius folder into the guest bedroom and shut the door. Kat looked like she'd been run over by a semi. I poured us a glass of wine, and we sat at the dining room table.

"What's happening?" she said.

"Your little girl is growing up."

"She's single-minded. She always has been. When she gets on a track, she doesn't stop."

"Sounds like her mom."

A half-hour later, Sara joined us at the table with a hesitant but hopeful look on her face. Then, glancing at the guest bedroom, she said, "If I go to school there, that could be my room. But I think the desk should be in front of the window."

Kat choked on a swallow of wine and said, "We don't live here!"

"You do," Sara replied. "Sort of."

I couldn't read Kat's face. It was morphing too quickly between shock, surprise, and horror at her daughter's presumptuousness. "I'm visiting," Kat insisted.

"Yeah, but you and Sonny—"

I interrupted Sara by saying, "Let's go see what that would look like." She and I went to the bedroom and moved the furniture around so the small desk sat before the window looking out on the city. It was a great view, and when I looked into Sara's eyes, I could see her mind racing with other designs for the room. Her eyes were alive with creative imaginings.

"How's that?" I asked about the placement of the desk.

"Perfect." She smiled at me, and if I wasn't already in love with this little princess, it happened at that moment.

Her mom appeared in the doorway. "Sara, this is Sonny's place. We don't have the right to tell him what to do with it."

"It was just a suggestion," Sara pouted.

"I like it," I said. "I don't know what's wrong with me that I didn't move the desk over there years ago."

"Don't encourage her," Kat warned.

I smiled at Sara and she gave me a conspiratorial wink. "It's okay to dream, right?"

"Like totally," Sara said, giving Kat an anguished look.

Before a wedge was driven between me and Kat, I said, "Hey, who's hungry?" We had universal agreement on that thought. "What kind of food do you like?"

"Pizza!" Sara shouted.

"Oh, please, something more nutritious," Kat said.

"I know just the place," I told them. "Best pizza in town and lots more nutritious alternatives."

After dinner, Sara disappeared into her room. When Kat and I said goodnight to her, she was lying on the bed reading the St. Ignacius brochure.

"She has stars in her eyes," Kat said when we returned to the dining room.

"You'd better get started on the application."

She nodded apprehensively. Then we sat at the table and read through the application form. "What if she gets accepted?" Kat said.

"We'd have some decisions to make."

I still wasn't sure about committing to Kat for a lifetime, but I felt my uncertainty wavering like a gossamer veil fluttering in a breeze. I envisioned myself walking on loose sand, my feet sinking deeper as the sand shifted with each step. I took her hand, intertwined our fingers, raised her hand to my face, and kissed it. "We made that decision months ago," I concluded, "when we returned from New Mexico and you joined me here."

She gave me a long look, searching for the assurance that makes a big decision safer. "Sara's a good student," she said, taking up a pen and beginning to write on the application.

"John will speak with Father Kennedy," I said. "We have influence. He and I and Ari. Would you like more wine?"

She shook her head. "Coffee."

The next day, David Hastings returned just after lunch to pick up Sara and return to Sacramento. He brought his new wife this time, Linda Fincher, an elementary school teacher. She was a late-twenties brunette with a robust figure and large, rectangular earrings that dangled from her earlobes like surrealistic window frames. I could easily imagine her herding fourth graders. She wore a green striped blazer that didn't quite match her tan slacks, and I noticed she wouldn't hold eye contact with Kat, but it must have been an awkward situation for her. I sensed that she and David would be compatible. She looked pedestrian—and safe.

When we said our goodbyes, Sara clung to her mother for a long moment and then gave me a hug. I kissed her on the top of her head, and she raised her head and whispered, "See you soon," like it was our secret.

That night, the Storm Lake Blues Band played at Cactus Jacks. We had a large, appreciative crowd and played well. The audience would not have known that we were improvising most of the night. Kat sat alone at a table near the stage. Throughout the evening, single men approached her and she politely waved them off. One tipsy guy lingered too long until she flashed her badge at him.

When we returned to the condo at 2 am, she said, "Le'Andra is fabulous."

"Good singer. Great guitarist. She'll be a star someday."

"And beautiful."

I nodded. "Good bones. I don't know how long she'll be with us. I'd give it two years. Max. We'll cut some albums. Feature her on the cover. Then she'll move on. She'd have to. We'd hold her back."

"That's okay with you?"

"It's not up to me. That's music. That's the world I'm in."

We made love that night. The first time since the shooting. It was slow, every move thoughtful, but we found ways to be intimate without pain. Afterward, she lay on her back, gazing out the window. Smokey air floated past like a ghost's wings, thicker wisps disappearing as others thickened and wafted slowly in the breeze.

"When David arrived yesterday, he told me Linda is pregnant," she said. "They're having twins."

"How far along is she?"

"Eight weeks."

"Sara didn't mention it."

"She doesn't know."

"When are they going to tell her?"

"Tomorrow. They wanted to get the ultrasound first."

"How do you think she'll respond?"

"I don't know," Kat said. She was quiet for a moment, and then added, "She loves her father, but I don't think she . . . respects him. If that makes any sense. She knew about his affairs. And always felt he betrayed her as much as me. This development might feel like another betrayal."

"She could be intrigued by her half-siblings."

"Or not. She might see it as her father moving on, starting a new family with a younger woman."

"Have you thought about moving here? If she gets into St. Ignacius."

I could barely see her face in the darkness. Her eyes were deep and unknowable, but a smile grew on her face, her white teeth glowing faintly. "I have a job in Sacramento," she said.

"The SFPD needs almost six hundred more officers. They'd be foolish not to have the Law Enforcement Officer of the Year join them."

"You think they'd hire me? I'm a detective sergeant, not a rookie."

"I'm good friends with the Chief of Homicide. He has some clout. And you and I are about to be swept away by a tidal wave named Sara. She's already deciding how she wants to decorate her bedroom."

"You'd be okay with a teenager living here?"

"Only if her mother's part of the package."

Dom Bernardi

I felt like I was slogging through wet cement, but when I looked down, I saw that my feet had sunk into a soggy layer of sand and water. The air was fetid, and I realized I'd wandered into a swamp. Carpets of green moss hung from the waterlogged branches of distant trees, and the hot air was thick with moisture. It beaded on my bare arms and dripped from my brow. I tried shaking off the sweat, but any movement brought a bitter seeping of salty moisture into my mouth, and I gagged, drinking the salt of my sweat. I kept slogging ahead, though I was lost and didn't know which way to turn. Then I heard a man's voice. He was sniggering, like an insect, taunting me, although I couldn't make out the words. I saw his shape flitting through the trees along the shore, but I couldn't make him out. His face and words evaded me. No matter how I turned, I saw only a flicker, just a quick dash of movement among the shadows. He'd vanish, then I'd turn and glimpse movement in another direction, perplexed at his ability to move so quickly, never being in one place long enough to get a clear view of him. His snickering turned to laughter, and as I sank deeper into the mire, I could hear his taunts reverberating through the quagmire like echoes of echoes—but a wind had come up. It might have been the rustling of leaves, the moaning of branches, and the scraping of predators just out of sight.

I woke up agitated, nursing my left knee. It still felt stuck in quicksand, stiff and resistant as I massaged it. It was Monday morning, I realized, as the day emerged from the fog of sleep. John and I were meeting with his contact today, Dom Bernardi, the biochemist. I limped to the bathroom and took two of Rhoda's pure oxys with warm swallows of water. My throat felt raw from the smoke outside, which now had crept inside and seemed to coat every surface.

Kat sat at the dining room table, a study in contrast. She looked rested and content as she ate a breakfast of oatmeal and raisins with milk. She flashed a smile when she saw me and stood to kiss me. She'd slept well, she said, and now that I was up, she would shower. While she did, I stepped into a pair of black slacks and loafers, put on a plaid shirt, and grabbed a blue sportscoat. After her shower, I told her I had to run, kissed her, and took the elevator to my car.

Ceres Biosciences was one of the dozens of biotechnology companies in the Bay Area. It was located on University Drive in Berkeley, near the University of California, a light brown, five-story building indistinguishable from others near the university campus. GPS guided John and me to it, but we could easily have missed it if we'd been navigating on our own. I parked in the Visitor lot, and we tried several doors before locating the main entrance. I wondered if Ceres Biosciences was deliberately incognito or had chosen a subpar architect when they designed their building.

The foyer was bland and sterile—plain stress-bearing columns, a bright metal reception desk, tinted windows, space-age minimalist chairs, a colorless receptionist of subdued sexuality in a black blouse and prim dark bun. She confirmed on her screen that we were scheduled visitors, pointed at a log for us to sign in, and placed two visitor passes on the counter, neatly aligned. Beyond us giving our names, no one had spoken a word. The young man who came to collect us showed a bit more personality. He was pasty thin in a crisp blue shirt and tan slacks, but he wore a black polka dot bowtie and had eyes that looked permanently amused. He talked nonstop, mostly about nothing, as he ushered us to the elevator and took us to the third floor. Still, we learned that Dom Bernardi was an esteemed scientist with many awards. He was on vacation last year in Tuscany and returned with Tuscan olive oil for everyone in his lab and the most delicious Pecorino Romano. It's scrumptious shaved onto a pear and glazed walnut salad, the young man informed us.

The third floor was a maze of labs—glass-walled, clean tile floors, card-coded door locks, and scores of people wearing white lab coats working quietly at counters lined with computers, beakers, tubes, centrifuges, and other medical research equipment I couldn't identify. The lab technicians and scientists we saw through the windows seemed to be working with purpose and patience, doing work I would find mind-numbing, like playing scales all day on a musical instrument to a metronome marking a slow, steady beat. I would crack under the monotony, but I couldn't see a hint of boredom or discontent on anyone's face.

Dom Bernardi was the opposite of everyone else we saw at Ceres Biosciences. Gregarious and bouncy, he leaned into you when he talked and had a broad smile covered with a mustache brush. His black-hair-turning-white rose from his forehead like a neatly trimmed hedge, and he had thick hands, like Mickey Mouse, and short, chubby fingers. Like a benevolent walrus, he looked gentle and wise, but I reminded myself that first impressions reveal only the façade, not the man. He unlocked the door to his lab and welcomed us inside. I worried we'd track in dirt from the unclean world outside and contaminate an experiment, but he didn't seem concerned. I asked him what kind of research they were doing there.

"Among other projects, we're using CRISPR to modify genes in a corn virus," he said.

To me, that sounded like playing "Chopsticks" on a piano for twelve hours straight, but Dom explained that when they succeeded, the modified virus would no longer replicate in infected plants, which could boost corn production by 25 to 30 percent. Okay, I saw the utility in that. As we walked around the lab, Dom introduced us to Madison Sato, a grad student in biochemistry at UC Berkeley, and Dwayne Karmagen, his assistant lab director. Karmagen had long brown hair, parted in the middle, and wore it in a ponytail. He looked like a street tough, with scars through one eyebrow and across his upper lip, but he had a soft voice and the odd manner of looking away from you when he spoke. He wouldn't survive on the mean streets where intense eye contact invites confrontation, but no eye contact is a sign of weakness. Sato had a perfectly oval face and wore thick-framed black glasses that matched her hair. Dom Bernardi said she was a third-generation Japanese-American and more intelligent than the last five Nobel prize winners in Chemistry.

"Smarter than you?" John asked him.

"Leaps and bounds," Bernardi replied. "Leaps and bounds."

"What is CRISPR?" I asked. I'd heard of it but had only a vague idea of what it was. Dom canted his head toward Sato.

"Clustered regularly interspaced short palindromic repeats," she said. She probably interpreted the blank look on my face as confusion, so she added, "It's a genetic engineering tool that allows us to modify the DNA or RNA of a gene selectively."

"And you're using it to modify the genes of a corn virus?"

She nodded. "We're modifying the RNA of the High Plains Disease virus."

"I think I caught that once," I said.

She laughed. "Then you must be a corn stalk."

"I am." I gestured to myself. "This is a clever disguise." She chuckled, revealing unusually long canine teeth. I said, "Could CRISPR be used to create designer babies."

"People worry about that," Sato said. "No, not yet, maybe not ever. But gene editing has incredible potential. Last year, CRISPR was used to engineer Casgevy, a cure for sickle cell disease."

A timer dinged on the counter behind her, and Sato said she had to return to work. So we walked past another row of equipment and lab technicians busy at their workstations. One guy wearing a white lab coat too long for his body wore earbuds and was tapping an index finger to the beat of whatever music he was listening to.

John said, "Can CRISPR create designer drugs? Like LSD?"

Bernardi nodded and said, "LSD is synthesized from ergotamine. That's an alkaloid in ergot, a fungus that infects grains, but it was first synthesized in 1938, long before we had CRISPR."

Karmagen looked hesitantly at Bernardi as if expecting him to continue. When he didn't, Karmagen turned to us. "Dom is right. CRISPR is a tool for modifying organic molecules like those in ergot. We could use CRISPR to create recreational drugs like LSD if we were working with organic compounds. But if somebody wanted to create designer drugs with inorganic compounds, all they'd need is the right knowledge, some basic lab equipment, and a chemistry set."

"Is that why you wanted to see me?" Bernardi asked.

"Yes," John said. "We need to know how designer drugs are created."

We came to a long row of black scientific instruments resembling the eerie monoliths in *2001: A Space Odyssey*. They were rectangular, as tall as most people, deep black, and arrayed like dominoes along one wall. One was open and partially dismantled, and a technician worked on it. He was a slender guy with short blond hair. He wore shorts, sandals, and a Hawaiian shirt that read, "It's Five O'clock Somewhere." He looked briefly at us, then returned to the instrument he was repairing.

"What are those?" I asked.

"Third-generation DNA Sequencers," Bernardi said. "They automate the process of determining the exact sequence of nucleotides in a DNA molecule. We analyze a DNA or RNA sequence with these machines and then modify the molecules with CRISPR."

"Dom, we have a situation now," John said. "A designer drug called Rapture hit the streets that is putting users into an extreme state of nirvana."

"It's killing them," I added, "if they're also on cocaine."

"You think someone's using CRISPR to make this drug?" Karmagen asked.

John shrugged. "We don't know how it's being made or where it's coming from," he said. "We brought the tox reports from four Rapture victims. We hoped you could tell us more by seeing the chemicals in their systems when they died."

"I also have some of the pills," I said, handing Bernardi a plastic bag containing three Raptures.

"Where'd you get those?" Karmegan said.

"From a drug cartel. They said they found them on the street."

Bernardi shook his head in disgust and then glanced at Karmagen. "Okay, I don't know how much help we'll be, but we'll take a look."

Karmagen glanced at his watch and then approached the technician working on the gene sequencer.

"How much longer, Chase?"

"Another hour," the man said. "Maybe less. I have to test the circuit board. Then calibrate the unit." He looked at me with a curious expression, like a spark of recognition. After hesitating, he said, "I know you from somewhere?"

"I don't think so."

"Yeah, you're familiar. I've seen you someplace. Wait, uh . . ." He touched a finger to his forehead. "You, like, play in a band, right?"

I smiled. "Sax player. Storm Lake Blues Band."

"Yeah, yeah. I've seen you guys. Can't remember where."

"We play a lot of clubs in the area."

"Yeah, no, no, you were in the news, right? I never forget a face. Tere was a picture of you in the *Chronicle* a while ago."

"Last year," I told them that the band had just returned from a tour and was bringing in a new guitarist after losing our previous one. I said we played at Cactus Jacks last night, playing jazz and blues.

Karmagen glanced at the technician with an annoyed look and gestured toward the DNA sequencer the guy was working on. He gave Karmagen an "okay, okay" look and returned to the unit. Karmagen said he liked blues music but hadn't heard of us. I told him he could find our performance schedule on our website. Then I turned to Bernardi. We weren't there to talk about music; these people were busy. I said, "The guy pushing Rapture dresses up like a fantasy character, Wraithlan Mager, a wizard. He's been seen wearing a dark cloak with a hood. He might go by the name Rayland Major."

Bernardi and Karmagen gave us blank looks. The name meant nothing to them.

"There's another drug on the streets," John said, "that's turning people homicidal." He told them about the three incidents at the Folsom Flea Market, Market Street, and the restaurant outside of Golden Gate Park. "We think all three murderers were under the influence of another drug we're calling Zombie. You have their tox reports, too." He indicated the bundle of documents in Bernardi's hand.

"The police and DEA haven't heard of these drugs outside of the Bay Area," I added. "We think they're being made locally."

"By the same people?" Karmagen asked in a skeptical tone.

"Doesn't seem likely," John said.

"The pharmacological effects sound very different," Karmegan said.

Bernardi thumbed his lower lip and turned to Karmagen. "What pharmacodynamic would cause someone to become homicidal?"

Karmagen shook his head. "Something affecting the amygdala, I imagine," he replied. "That might cause rage and loss of impulse control. It might also affect their prefrontal cortex."

"Which could affect their judgment," Dom said. "No inhibitions. Do you have the police reports on the homicide drug?" Bernardi asked John.

"I can email them to you."

Bernardi nodded. "I'd like to know how the people got the drug into their system. That would tell us a lot."

"We still don't know that," John said.

"How were they acting before they started killing people?"

"Normal until right before the event. Then some agitation. Disorientation. Anger."

Bernardi glanced at the tox reports and said, "I assume there's some urgency on this. I'll read these this afternoon."

"I can look at them, too," Karmegan said.

Bernardi nodded. We thanked them and left. The woman at the reception desk glanced at us, showing no sign that she recognized us, and then returned to some anal-retentive task in front of her. She was probably stapling forms and ensuring that the staples were perfectly aligned.

As we were driving back across the Bay Bridge into San Francisco, John took a call on his cell phone. "Oh, shit," he said into the phone. "Are they all right?" He listened momentarily and said, "I'll be right there." He turned to me. "That was Sana. Someone just firebombed BiblioTech. Ari and Catherine are okay. You have time?"

I said I did, and he raced across the bridge. I could see gray smoke rising in the distance, where BiblioTech was located. When we arrived at the scene, the street was cordoned off with yellow tape. Beyond the tape was a maze of fire trucks, police cars, and ambulances. John double-parked on the next block and threw a plastic "SFPD Official Business" sign onto his dash. Then we hurried to the building. John's ID got us through the cordon, and we saw Sana on the sidewalk across the street from the main entrance. Store employees crowded around him, some faces pale, others stricken.

We could not see flames, but smoke rose from windows on the bottom three floors. Firefighters had smashed glass from inside, and it lay in glittering crystal disarray on the sidewalk and street below the building. Hoses snaked along the street, but some firefighters were disconnecting them from hydrants, and the hoses were deflating. The main entrance bustled with activity as cops, EMTs, firefighters, and people in plain clothes entered or left. John asked Sana what happened. He said a bomb exploded in the men's room on the first floor, blasting flames and debris into the stacks outside the bathroom. Two customers outside were killed in the explosion, and eight others were injured. They don't know if any customers were in the men's room when the bomb detonated, but the bookstore was busy, so Sana thought it was likely. A few minutes after the first blast, another bomb exploded on the third floor beside the elevator leading to the upper floors where Ari's living quarters were. Firefighters told Sana that both bombs contained an accelerant, probably gasoline. The building's fire sprinkler system activated within seconds of the explosions and kept the fire from spreading, but the damage inside was extensive. Customers were evacuated without further injury and were now clustered at the other end of the block, where detectives were questioning them.

"Where were Ari and Catherine?" John asked.

"Top floor," Sana said. "Still there. But okay."

John walked away and made a call on his cell while Sana and I watched the activity at the main entrance. Sana's brow looked permanently furrowed, his eyes as dark as the black stubble on his jaw. BiblioTech was his life, and I'm sure he felt an injury as grave as the ruin to the building and the lives lost in what the media will label a terrorist attack, but those of us close to Ari knew better. This was another attempt on his life.

"There are surveillance cameras inside," I said. Sana nodded. "On every floor?" He nodded again. "Then we should see whoever planted those bombs."

"We will see them," Sana said.

"Where is Earl?"

"With Ari."

I nodded and peered at the upper levels of the buildings around us. The Azeri team that planted the bombs wouldn't know if Ari survived. They might be waiting for him to leave one of the exits. I wondered if they had snipers stationed on the upper floors of adjacent buildings. Maybe the fires weren't intended to kill him, just to flush him out. John must have had the same concern. Ten minutes later, an SFPD tactical vehicle was let through the cordon and parked as close to the main entrance as possible. John crossed the street and organized a cluster of police officers by the door. Then I saw Ari, Catherine, and Earl being led to the armored vehicle and whisked inside. They were bent over and surrounded by police. John ran back across the street and spoke to Sana. Then he hustled me back to his car on the next block and said, "We're going to your place. Okay if Ari and Catherine stay the night there? Just till we can arrange a safe house?"

"Of course."

"You sure Kat won't mind? It's going to look like an armed camp."

"She'll love it."

And she did. I phoned Kat from John's car. By the time we arrived, Sana and five of his Armenian crew were there, all heavily armed. Kat had notified Rhoda Merrick, the only neighbor who lived with us on the top floor, and had briefed Sana's crew on the layout of the building. When John and I arrived, she was directing the Armenian surveillance team and organizing security with Sana. Ari, Catherine, and Earl arrived momentarily, and Kat directed Ari and Catherine to the guest bedroom after two Armenians tacked a plywood sheet over the window.

Catherine was pale and listless. She collapsed in a chair in the bedroom and lay her head against the wall, her eyes closed. Rhoda knocked on our door mid-afternoon. She said she canceled her afternoon appointments when she heard what happened and asked if she could help. We introduced her to Catherine, and Rhoda sat with her in the bedroom, talking softly.

While Sana organized cots, food, and water for our armed guards, Ari, John, Earl, and I sat at the dining room table. Kat joined us. "You have to assume one or more of the Azeri team followed you here," she said. "We need to make a show of the security around the building."

Sana heard her and said he'd send more security. He turned away and lifted his cell phone.

John nodded. "I don't think they'll try again tonight. Tomorrow, we'll find a safe house outside the city, someplace that can be well guarded." He looked at me. "We'll use your underground garage. Three dark sedans with tinted windows will leave and go in different directions. Ari won't be in any of them. He and Catherine will be in another bullet-proof car later."

Ari shook his head. "It's a good plan, John, but what they did today can't happen again."

John nodded. "First, we must get you and Catherine to a safe place."

"Yes, for a few days," Ari said. "Then we must stop this."

"Agreed," John said, "but we don't know where they are."

"Then we must bait them into the open," Ari said.

"With what?" said John.

"With me," Ari said. John shook his head, but Ari insisted. "We need to make it easy for them to find me. They will come. They can't resist. Then we'll stop this."

Earl sat smoldering in the chair beside me. Just above a whisper, he said, "*Haré sopa con sus cabezas.*" *I will make soup with their heads.*

"What did he say?" Kat asked me.

I smiled. "Earl said he's hungry."

"Tell him we have food on the way," she said. Earl speaks English but prefers Spanish. He understood her but sat in stony silence.

I leaned toward him and said, "*Pondremos a estos bastardos en un agujero profundo y los cubriremos por la eternidad.*" *We'll put these bastards in a deep hole and cover them for eternity.*

Earl stared at me, his deep, dark eyes glistening. "*No te preocupes, hombre,*" I whispered. "*Tu padre estará a salvo y vivirá una larga vida.*" *Don't worry, man. Your father will be safe and live a long life.*

"*Y la madre que me adoptó.*" *And the mother who adopted me.*

"*Sí, Santa Catalina, también.*" *Yes, Saint Catherine, also.*

Throughout the evening, Kat was in full cop mode, organizing the armed camp with no-nonsense efficiency, directing the food and clean up, getting cots and bedding set up in the main room, and creating a schedule for sentries. She still walked with a slight limp but seemed to gather strength as she took charge.

Sana's team brought in hand radios, motion sensors, night-vision binoculars, and two combative German Shepherds and their handlers for the first floor and the parking garage. Rhoda thought it was overkill, but after hearing about the deaths at BiblioTech, she agreed that extraordinary protection was warranted for Ari but also for other residents in the building, all of whom had been notified of an unusual amount of security because of an unspecified foreign guest with diplomatic connections. Rhoda said she felt safe enough in her apartment, but Kat posted a guard outside her door and several outside ours.

As the evening wore down, Catherine joined us in the main room and had a glass of wine. She asked me to play for them, so I got out my sax and took requests. For an hour or more, I played the blues: *Trouble in Mind, Same Old Blues, The Sky Is Crying*, and *St. Louis Blues*—long-time favorites. Thinking of those who lost their lives today, I finished with Clapton's *Tears in Heaven*. Then worry gave way to exhaustion, and I wiped off my sax, put it away, and sank into my bed. Kat stayed up and would be awake most of the night, making coffee and ensuring that the sentries stayed alert. I learned in the morning that Sana's crew had christened her "Nakharar," the Armenian word for "Chief."

Evidence

Ari sat with one leg crossed over the other, an unlit cigarette dangling between two fingers on his right hand. I thought he would be anxious after yesterday. A normal man would be. But Ari was a rock, magnificent and tall, unfazed by the turbulent sea crashing against his flanks. He gazed at my dining room table, his lips pressed together. Then I saw the corners of his mouth curled up, not in a smile but in the calm contemplation of one who has elected to stand with his neck in a noose and invite his enemies to hang him if they can. John sat to Ari's left, his eyes searching the table for answers. John took yesterday's assault personally, and I doubt he got much sleep. Sana sat to Ari's right. His face bore enough weight for everyone at the table—his brow creased like a bulldog's face, the stubble on his jaw as black as hate, his dark eyes bottomless. My main room looked and smelled like a bunk house, men asleep on cots around the perimeter, their weapons on the floor beside them, two sentries alert inside the door, their radios squawking now and then with reports from other guards throughout the building. One man in camo gear stood on a stepstool, peering through the window above the kitchen sink. A layer of male stink permeated the room, the product of the tension, sweat, and testosterone of a ragged army in a siege.

I poured myself a cup of coffee and joined my friends.

"How's Kat?" Ari asked.

"Asleep. She was up most of the night."

"That's what Sana said."

"Catherine?"

"Okay," Ari replied. Then he reconsidered and shook his head. "Your neighbor came for her earlier."

"Rhoda."

Ari nodded. "They're at her place, having breakfast. Taniel went with them." Taniel was one of Sana's Armenian crew. He was with us in New Mexico when we rescued the children.

"You can trust Rhoda," I assured Ari.

"I trust Taniel," Sana growled. Ari and I exchanged a small, private smile.

"I got a text from Paul Fisher," John said, looking at Ari and Sana. "The police will be here in an hour to question you."

"All these guns?" I said, looking around the room. California has the most restrictive gun laws in the country, and my main room looked like a firearms convention.

"They're legal," John said, "and all these guys work for my security firm."

"How'd you manage that?" I asked. I knew it wasn't true. John likely didn't even know some of the Armenians camped in my condo.

"Partner, while you got your beauty sleep last night, some of us were busy."

"You think overnight hiring is going to fool the cops?"

"Oh, we might have done some backdating here or there," John said with a weary smile.

Before she'd lay down to rest, Kat told John and Ari they needed to disclose what they knew about the Azeri hit squad. Failing to do so would amount to obstruction of justice, and it was better to have the whole of SFPD looking for the Azeris than just the team John and Sana could muster. Ari had many contacts in the Bay Area and allies beyond the Armenian community, including some Azeri Americans who valued peace above loyalty to their former homeland. None of those contacts knew of the hit squad from Azerbaijan or where they might be hiding.

Before the police arrived, Sana opened his laptop and accessed BiblioTech's cloud storage to review the security tapes inside the store. We looked over his shoulder as he parsed through the video images of the third floor. The camera nearest the elevator showed dozens of customers passing back and forth, none remarkable or suspicious, until a dark-haired woman approached the elevator carrying a large purse. She set the purse beside a bookcase next to the elevator and then appeared to be browsing the books in that bookcase. She glanced at her wrist several times while she leafed through a book. Then she set the book back on a shelf, bent down and opened her purse, reached inside, glanced around, took her hand back out, closed the purse, and stood up. She rechecked her wrist, probably looking at a watch, and then walked away.

"When did the first bomb explode?" I asked.

John said, "The bomb in the men's room went off at 1:46."

Sana had paused the video when the woman walked away. The time stamp read 1:42. I said, "She set a timer and left enough time for her to get downstairs and out of the building before the first bomb exploded."

Sana restarted the video. Every ten or fifteen seconds, we saw people pass by the elevator. None seemed to notice the purse. When 1:45 appeared on the time stamp, we saw an elderly man pause at the bookcase. He reached for a book and opened it. At 1:46, he abruptly turned toward the staircase just out of the camera's view. Then he looked back at the book and continued reading. At 1:47, we heard the fire alarm, and the startled old man shoved the book back into the bookcase and quickly left. Between 1:47 and 1:49, several more customers rushed by the bookcase and headed toward the staircase. Twenty or thirty seconds after 1:49, a young bearded man walked calmly past the elevator. Sana said he was an employee. Then, at 1:50, two girls came into view, teens wearing jeans and dark hoodies. One carried a backpack. When they reached the bookcase, one girl ran her hand along a shelf and picked out a book, which she dropped into the backpack. Smoke was now visible at the bottom of the screen, likely rising from the staircase just out of view. One of the girls noticed and tugged at her companion's sleeve, and both girls rushed toward the stairs. They were nearly out of sight when the time stamp turned to 1:51, and the purse exploded in a burst of white light and debris, followed by dense black smoke and a wall of flames. Seconds later, the fire suppression system began raining water onto the flames.

"What happened to those girls?" I said.

Sana said he didn't know. We couldn't deduce much about the dark-haired woman. From her height beside the bookcase, we estimated that she was around 5'8", medium-weight, not slender, but not heavy. She had chin-length dark hair, but her face was concealed behind a COVID mask, which was not unusual in a city now frequently choked with wildfire smoke.

"She drove the pickup truck behind BiblioTech when they tried to kill you," I said to Ari.

John nodded. "Most likely."

Then Sana uploaded the video from a security camera on the first floor. We could see the men's room door. He forwarded the footage to 1:30, and we watched for sixteen minutes as men entered and left the restroom, including one dark-haired man carrying a briefcase and another man in a wheelchair. At 1:44, the man with the briefcase left the men's room. It looked like the briefcase was lighter, but that may have been my imagination.

"He could have planted the bomb," John said.

At 1:46, a massive explosion blew out the restroom doors and flooded the area outside with debris and a burst of roiling smoke and flames. We saw three or four people knocked sideways by the blast and one woman standing just outside the door engulfed in fire. Within seconds, people rushed to her and swatted the flames, but Sana told us she later died.

As we watched the aftermath of the explosion and the fire suppression system showering cones of water to douse the flames, I realized I hadn't seen something I expected to see. "The guy in the wheelchair," I said. "He didn't leave the bathroom."

Sana shrugged. "He was killed. Wheelchair in men's room. Found broken wheels, handle."

"I don't think so, Sana. Rerun the video." The man in the wheelchair was large, with short dark hair. We saw him from behind as he wheeled himself into the men's room at 1:35. At 1:44, we saw a large man leave the room. A body like a small car. He must have weighed 280. Short dark hair, curly, a round patch hanging over his forehead, a colossal head, squat and square, clean-shaven, small eyes and ears flat against his skull. He walked out of the men's room and directly out the store's front entrance. Two minutes later, the men's room exploded.

"You found parts of the wheelchair because it was the blast's epicenter," I told Sana. "Ten to one, the arson investigators will find parts of the chair embedded in the ceiling. It had a joystick controller. It was an electric wheelchair, but he used his hands to wheel himself into the room. The joystick didn't work. They'd replaced the motor and battery with a bomb."

"Get a still shot of his face," John told Sana. The woman will be hard to ID, but not him. We need to get his picture to the police and Ari's contacts."

"Take it to the Azerbaijan Cultural Center in the city," Ari said to John. "Someone there may have seen him.

"Would they tell us if they had?" I asked Ari.

"These people are now terrorists. They killed civilians and will be hunted by the police. I'll call a man I know there. They'll talk to you."

Paul Fisher and two other detectives arrived shortly after Kat woke up and showered. She was getting a cup of coffee when Paul knocked on the door with the two detectives investigating the shootings at BiblioTech last week, James Renicke and Frank Shimizu. Renicke looked like he'd slept in his clothes, a rumpled tweed sportscoat and brown slacks creased in the wrong places. Shimizu was dapper in a blue pinstriped suit and yellow polka dot tie. As was his custom for a color-blind detective, Fisher dressed in all black.

Renicke gave me a once over and said, "You again?"

"This isn't a crime scene, Sergeant Renicke," I responded.

He glanced around at the motley crew on the cots, their weapons on full display. "Not yet, but I'm patient. You own all these weapons?"

John stepped forward and handed Renicke his business card. "You can talk to me about that, Jim. These security guards work for me, and we've been hired to protect a client."

Renicke returned John's card. "Don't need this," he said. "I know who you are."

Paul glanced at me with a look somewhere between annoyance and amusement. "You mind if we sit down?" he said. I waved him toward the dining room table, and the three cops sat with Ari, Sana, and John. Kat pulled up a chair and invited herself to the discussion. Paul glanced at her and nodded.

While they talked, I took a call from David Fetchenheir, my videographer friend at KPIX-TV. He'd been at the scene yesterday, filming the story for the evening news, and he said the network was anxious to talk to Ari. Did I know where he is? I didn't want to lie to Fetch, but I couldn't tell him Ari was in my condo. We'd give away Ari's location and be besieged by the media, some of whom might be Azeri assassins masquerading as reporters. I told Fetch I had no idea but would call him as soon as I knew something.

While I eavesdropped on the conversation at the table, I poured another cup of coffee, an aromatic blend from Kona, and added a pinch of nutmeg. The hot aroma was as soothing as a deep massage. Ari was saying that Sana needed to return to BiblioTech to assess the damage and recover what could be saved. Paul said they had all they needed from Sana, so he left with several of his crew.

John and Kat summarized what we knew about the possible Azeri connection and the motive behind it. Renicke asked me about the cigarette butts I found in the alley outside the window we thought the Azeri spotter was located. He warned me about tampering with evidence, and John said he had the butts in an evidence bag and would hand them over to the police. I added that if the police had done their jobs, they would have investigated that building and found the butts themselves. Paul advised me and Renicke to take it down a few notches. Then Paul told us that since the bombing was a federal crime, the FBI and ATF were now in charge of the investigation, and we'd be hearing from them.

John took a call as the police were finishing. Shimizu was polite and thanked us for our time, but when Renicke walked out, he said, "I hope I never have to come here again."

"My fondest wish, too, detective," I said. "Have a nice day."

As Paul walked out the door, he gave me an eye roll. "You should transfer Renicke to Public Relations," I said. "He's a natural."

Paul waved for me to step outside with him. When the door was shut, he said, "Jim's skeptical because your friend Kirakosian plays on the edges of the law. There's never quite a prosecutable case, but there's deep suspicion downtown. You need to tread carefully. And Sebastiani—I like the guy, and he's helping on the Zombie case—but if anybody looked carefully, I think they'd find that none of those Armenian gangsters work for John's security firm."

"They're not gangsters."

"We can quibble on the word to use, but I'm not going to push it—for now," he said, giving me an exasperated look. "We have bigger problems to solve. But be careful, Sonny. Your friends will drag you and Kat Hastings into the mud, and you won't get out of it clean."

"Thanks for the advice," I said, patting him on the shoulder.

"Yeah." He gave me a weary, close-lipped smile. "I know you're not gonna drop this and go play music. So call me when you know something. Then we'll arrest some bad guys, put 'em away legally, and go have a drink."

"I'll call you."

That sad smile grew on his face again, and he turned away.

When I returned inside, John said, "Dom Bernardi wants to see us."

"He has something?"

John nodded. "He wants to explain it in person."

"I'm going with you," Kat said. She limped to the bedroom and returned with her cane and a light blue jacket. Ari said they hadn't found a suitable safe house yet, but he hoped by later this afternoon. I told him they could stay with us as long as needed. I threw on a black leather sportscoat, and we headed to my car.

We met Bernardi in a small conference room on the first floor of Ceres Biosciences in Berkeley. Whiteboards covered three of the four walls, filled with mathematical equations and numbers written with blue markers. We sat at a small white conference table in red plastic chairs. Yellow pads and pencils were neatly aligned in the center of the table. I felt like I was in primary color heaven. Bernardi entered with a mug of coffee and a stack of papers. He wore a blue shirt under his white lab coat.

"Dr. Bernardi," Kat said, extending a hand. "I'm Detective Katrina Hastings from Sacramento."

He wasn't expecting her and did a double take. He may have been surprised to see a woman or was taken by her beauty. He recovered with a broad smile and a handshake. "Call me Dom, please."

Kat gave him a disarming smile and sank into a chair. We pulled out chairs and joined her.

"I appreciate your call," John said. "Didn't expect it so soon. Did you have a chance to read those toxicology reports?"

"Yes-s-s-s," he said, looking puzzled. He dropped the stack of papers on the table and scratched his head. "Understand. I've read a million of these. You get the picture very quickly. High levels of cocaine—easy. High concentrations of diphenhydramine—sleeping pill overdose. High troponin enzymes—heart attack. I can tell you (snapping his fingers) right away what happened to most people. But these (patting the stack of reports with a heavy fist) were a mystery."

"How so?" I said.

"The people who died of the Rapture drug had an unusually high level of methylenedioxymethamphetamine in their system. Commonly known as MDMA or ecstasy. But the molecules had been modified."

"By CRISPR?" John said.

"Possibly. I've never seen that molecular configuration, but it could heighten hippocampal disruption and severely alter serotonin receptor function."

"Okay," I said. "What's that in English?"

Dom's eyebrows dropped heavily over his eyes as though he were deep in thought. He had thick red lips, and the bottom lip stuck out, giving him a doubtful expression. "It would elevate feelings of well-being. Serotonin creates feelings of happiness and fulfillment. It regulates mood and appetite, among other things. The other happy chemical is dopamine, which cocaine triggers. Combining the two would be like taking a time-release capsule of never-ending euphoria. They'd cause significant psychological changes. Lengthy exposure to cocaine destroys brain cells, but even brief exposure can alter brain function."

"Some users of Rapture recovered," John said.

Dom nodded. "I expect they'd be the ones who weren't on cocaine. The mix of coke and Rapture would be deadly, but the victims wouldn't realize how much trouble they're in. They'd be oblivious until they were no longer aware of anything."

"Would a strong dose of Rapture have the same effect?"

"Probably," Dom said. "depending on the dosage."

"What about Zombie?" Kat asked.

"Completely different chemical signature—and a completely different effect," Dom said. He picked up one of the tox reports and leafed through it as though reminding himself what it said. "The victims of that drug had high levels of scopolamine in their blood. And a modified form of hyoscyamine."

"Jimsonweed," I said.

"Yes, from jimsonweed, but altered. The modified form of hyoscyamine may have increased its potency. These chemicals affect a part of the brain called the amygdala, which regulates emotions."

"Like aggression," Kat said.

Dom nodded. "Rage, aggression, anxiety. Alcohol is thought to excite the amygdala. Oxytocin inhibits it. Your drug, Zombie, in a high enough dose, could hijack the victim's amygdala and cause uncontrollable rage. At the same time, it suppresses the prefrontal cortex, which regulates judgment. The combination would cause uninhibited aggression."

"I witnessed it firsthand," Kat said. Dom tilted his head and looked curiously at her. "I was a first responder at the mass shooting in Sacramento a few weeks ago."

"Oh?"

"The perp shot me in the leg, and I took a hit in my ballistic vest."

Dom scrunched his mouth and shook his head. "I couldn't do your job."

Kat smiled at him. "It's not for everyone."

"How much of the zombie drug would be a high enough dose?" John asked.

Dom raised one hand to his face and laid his index finger under his nose, a classic thinking position. After a beat, he said, "Without clinical trials, I couldn't be sure. This is a new drug. No one knows, but I'd guess not much. Maybe a quarter of a milligram. Maybe less, especially with what else I found. The toxicology reports on each set of victims showed high quantities of fucoidan and HSA."

"Which is what?" I said.

"HSA is an endocytotic mechanism. That's a process that facilitates drug transmission across the blood-brain barrier." He read the blank looks on our faces. "I know, I know. Let me explain. The blood-brain barrier is a semi-permeable membrane that prevents harmful substances and pathogens from crossing into the brain. It keeps the nasty stuff out, in other words. For drugs to rapidly affect the amygdala, you need some way to get the drugs through the blood-brain barrier. HSA, or human serum albumin, is a compound of nanoparticles that can cross the barrier. Think of small particles that can pass through a large kitchen strainer."

"Fucoidan," he continued, "is a sugar molecule found mostly in brown seaweed. It turns out to have many medicinal benefits. People take fucoidan supplements for hair growth, sleep, energy, weight loss, and liver cleansing. It's an antioxidant and an anti-inflammatory, and it can also cross the blood-brain barrier. We shouldn't have found these two chemicals in the blood of these victims. That's highly unusual. I've never seen it in hundreds of toxicology reports. The only reason for them would be to facilitate the absorption of the designer drugs into the brain."

"To make them act faster?" Kat said.

"That's right. Without the HSA-Fucoidan compound, both drugs might have taken hours to affect their victims. The drugs, taken orally, would have to be metabolized in the digestive system before entering the bloodstream and reaching the brain. Digestion is the slowest means of drug delivery in the human body. But with the compound, the victims would have had just minutes before starting to experience the effects of the drugs."

"And those compounds were present in the blood of both Rapture and Zombie victims?" Kat said.

Dom nodded. "It's a signature, just like bomb makers have characteristic ways of making bombs. Once they figure out how, they make all their bombs similarly. The use of fucoidan and HSA in both drugs is a signature of the drug maker."

"You think the same person made Rapture and Zombie?" I said.

"More than likely," Dom said. "That's why I wanted to see you so quickly. I think you're looking for one perpetrator."

"A person who knows how to use CRISPR," John said.

Dom nodded. "Someone with an education in biotechnology, but thousands are in our area." Northern California was a hub for biotech research.

"Okay," John said, "but it would be someone with access to CRISPR. That should narrow it down."

Dom shook his head sadly. "A guy in San Francisco makes and sells home CRISPR kits out of his garage. You could buy one, do a little home study, and try to design two-headed dogs or phosphorescent roses."

"Or drugs like Rapture and Zombie," Kat said.

Dom scrunched his mouth and nodded. "From the police reports, I'd say he's getting the drugs into his victims orally. He's spiking their drinks or food."

"Coffee?" I said.

"Like coffee," Dom continued. "The drug combo would get into their brains quickly. I think the euphoria drug was probably a test, his way of doing human trials on the HSA-Fucoidan mechanism for rapid brain absorption. I think his ultimate goal is to turn people into mass murderers."

Wildfires

How do you find a ghost? You hold a séance and speak to it through a medium, if you know a real medium, which I don't. Or you place your fingers on a planchette, a heart-shaped piece of wood that sits on an Ouija board, and encourage the ghost to speak to you by moving the planchette to the letters of the alphabet displayed on the board, spelling out its message. If the ghost doesn't communicate, you can try to provoke it. You can invade its space, flick the lights on and off, make shrill noises, unsettle it, and incite it to respond. As we left Ceres Biosciences, I didn't realize we had done that. But ghosts have the advantage of being unseen, their presence imagined but not palpable. We didn't know we had provoked the ghost until he became manifest, spewing death like an angry and vengeful god.

The heavens glowed red as we drove back toward San Francisco from Berkeley. To the north and east, the wildfires grew fatter, their thirst unquenched by the rivers of water firefighters poured from aerial tankers or the clouds of fire retardant that painted the torched landscape scarlet. Separate wildfires raced toward each other like lustful teenagers eager to mate, and reporters announced on the radio that fire crews had to choose which battles to fight and which to concede. Northward, the sky's blue was tarnished by dense, boiling columns of inky smoke, twisting and churning as it darkened the day and raised a black curtain between the Bay Area and the rest of northern California. It felt isolating and vindictive, and I wondered, as I stared at that encroaching shroud, how much more hell we could endure.

As we drove west across the Bay Bridge, we saw a column of firefighters on the opposite lanes speeding east—twenty or so light green Forest Service trucks and buses carrying crews, followed by a long column of dark green Humvees belonging to the California National Guard, escorted by a half dozen CHP pursuit sedans, their blue and red lights flashing. Overhead, the sky was alive with Sikorsky helitankers, dipping their snorkels into San Francisco Bay and then swooping east with a bellyful of water, and Boeing global supertankers lumbering from the Redding Air Attack Base or SF International to fields of fire so vast they were visible from space.

"It feels like we're at war," Kat said.

"We are," said John, his eyes flickering red and blue as he watched the emergency procession speed past.

"At least the firefighters know their enemy," Kat said, watching the caravan receding. I could see the consternation in her eyes. She was a fighter, but like a blindfolded kid trying to crack open a piñata filled with treats, she wielded a powerful stick but didn't know which direction to swing it.

I thought about Kat's observation as I drove. The firefighters know their enemy. Wildfires reminded me of the best dancers in the clubs we play. Most people dancing in clubs are average, gyrating their hips and waving their arms, sometimes in sync with the beat. But now and then, we see a couple who've taken dancing lessons. They know the moves and have the technique. They show off because they're proud and enjoy displaying their skill. Wildfires are like that. They're terrible and savage, but they want to strut their stuff. The larger they grow, the more smoke they create and the prouder they become. Fighting them may be challenging, but you know where they are. The enemy we hunted was invisible and elusive, I told Kat and John. "He's proud but shy."

"Can't blame him for not wanting to get caught," John quipped.

But Kat shook her head. "I've been thinking about what Dom said about human trials. Maybe he's not as shy as you think. Maybe he's been hiding in plain sight."

"How so?" John asked.

"He mixed that blood-brain compound with Rapture and Zombie, right? Why do that unless you can't wait an hour to see the drugs' effects? If you're conducting a human trial, you want the drug to act quickly, but not too quickly. You want time to get out of the line of fire, but you still want to observe the drugs' effects."

"You think he was there at the Folsom Flea Market?" I asked.

She looked at me, the light of discovery in her eyes. "Yeah. I think he followed Robert Duggins into the market and left when the shooting started. He would've wanted to escape before the first responders blocked the exit, but he also wanted to watch his creation work."

"Then he followed Fernanda Alamilla onto Market Street," I said.

She nodded. "Likely. I'll bet he was in that restaurant when Daniel Niccum stabbed those people. He would have been in the crowd that fled the restaurant when the rampage started. With all of them, I'll bet he timed how long it took for Zombie to turn people into murderers."

John said, "We should think of this guy as a scientist, not a killer. He's methodical and organized, not erratic or impulsive."

I nodded. "Maybe he's experimenting with dosages."

"If someone got too much of either drug, what would happen?" Kat said.

We were nearly in the city, and traffic was slowing. The air was a brown haze, giving the skyline a sfumato effect like the Mona Lisa. The haze softened the transition between buildings and obscured the distinction between light and shadow, making the day mysterious and uncertain.

"I don't know," I said. "Maybe it would fry their brains before they could act. Eric got a high dose, and it torched him quickly. Other victims of Rapture took a lighter dose and recovered."

"Is he acting alone?" Kat said, more to herself than us.

As she puzzled over that, I said, "He wears a hooded cloak to the parties where he's pushing Rapture."

John nodded. "Yeah, but in parties, people are close together. They talk, they laugh, they introduce themselves. The purpose is to connect with others, so if you want to avoid detection, you wear a disguise. And you don't linger."

"I agree, John, but he's not wearing a cloak when spiking people's coffee with Zombie. A hooded guy would have been noticed, and no witnesses reported it. He probably looks average. Nothing odd or distinctive. Just a guy. He fades into the crowd. You go into a coffee place. How many people do you notice?"

"None," John said, "unless they're striking in some way. A hot woman. A guy with facial tattoos. Somebody with green hair. Like that. Otherwise, I couldn't describe them two minutes after I leave."

"He wouldn't trust people," Kat said. "The stakes are too high. He'd worry about informants. I think he works alone—no lab assistants. No co-conspirators. No one to sell him out to the police."

"There are more than eight million people in the Bay Area," John said. "That's one needle in a huge haystack."

"We'll find him," I said. "He's not going to stop. He hasn't reached the grand finale. The brilliant, sustained display of fireworks at the end of the show. The band's final song, that long, raucous number that leaves fans exhilarated and breathless. He's experimenting now, taking baby steps, but I think he wants to dazzle us. We'll catch him because he can't stop until he does."

When I dropped Kat off at the condo, John left for his office in Hunter's Point. I grabbed my gym bag and drove to the Bay Area Krav Maga Institute for a workout. The Institute is in a nondescript brown building. Inside is a large gym equipped with punching bags, blocking pads, and various gear to make self-defense training safe. The walls are lined with mirrors, and the floor has thick pads. When I arrived, Danny Seitz, the manager, was leading a women's class at the far end of the gym. Two dozen other people were practicing on the mats. I recognized several people, including a surprise—Crisologo's warrior, the tattooed giant named Jax. He was the gang member who wanted me to demonstrate a Krav Maga move. When he saw me, he motored over, his prominent, bearded chin protruding like a snowplow blade.

"Member you," he said, thrusting out his paw. I shook it.

"You're Jax, right?"

"Jackson. Yeah, man. Jax."

"What're you doing here?"

"Getting' it on, brother. Wanna learn this shit. Know what I'm sayin'?"

"I hear you, bro. Great place to do it," I said. "But Krav Maga is about self-defense, right?"

"Yeah, dig it," he replied. I wasn't sure he did. This guy was a battle tank with skin art, part of a drug gang known to make opponents disappear and impose their will with violence. I told him the purpose of Krav Maga is to defend yourself by de-escalating conflict if you can. If you have to fight, you want to win quickly and disengage. Krav Maga is the most lethal martial art, but the goal is to use the least force necessary to neutralize the threat.

Jax said he was cool with that, but my gut said teaching this guy Krav Maga would be like arming a missile with nukes. Krav Maga is a discipline and an attitude. It takes years of practice to master it. Jax was an imposing physical specimen with an intimidating façade, but I didn't know what was in the guy's heart and mind. Maybe he wasn't looking for a more efficient way to inflict pain. Judging people by appearance is like thinking you bought the winning lottery ticket. You could be correct, but most likely, you're wrong. When he asked if I'd work with him, I said I'd arrange classes with a Krav Maga master but would partner with him whenever he and I were in the gym together. He smiled, looking like a serial killer in a horror movie, and shook my hand with a vise grip that would have broken my fingers if I hadn't squeezed back just as hard. I didn't know what to make of this dude, but he came here looking to learn, and I'd work with the brother until he gave me a reason not to.

I was introducing him to Danny when John Sebastiani flew into the gym and yelled, "Got a situation!"

I threw my gym bag in the back seat of his Range Rover and jumped into the passenger seat. "What's up?"

"Shooting in progress," he said as he whipped his car around and headed west, speeding through intersections with his horn blaring, whipsawing around other vehicles in a high-speed pursuit that would have scared the hell out of me if anyone other than John had been driving. "House on Ocean Avenue. Three bodies on the sidewalks. Shooting the shit out of first responders. Fisher called me in. Thinks it might be Zombie."

"Where's SWAT?" I screamed. His windows were down, and the wind blasted through the car at gale force.

"On the scene," he yelled.

"Why the hell are we going there?" I like John and would have his back no matter what, but this was insane.

"Fisher called in the Zombie Task Force. That's us."

"Christ, John. I'm a musician. The most I can do is throw my sax at the shooter."

"Hang this around your neck," he said, tossing a lanyard at me with a laminated sign that read "SFPD Consultant."

"SWAT will handle the shooter," he said as he wheeled around a corner so fast it threw me into the passenger side door. "We'll scan the area for Raylan Major. If Kat's right, he'll hang around to admire his work."

Ahead, we could see a circus of flashing lights and black-and-whites pouring into the area north of San Francisco State. Blocks ahead, we were stopped by a police cordon, police cars blocking the intersection, and yellow crime scene tape stretched across the road manned by a bevy of uniformed officers. Civilians crowding the street were joined by more fleeing the area ahead, where we could hear the rapid, staccato pop of gunfire. John and I left his car and ran to the blockade. The police sergeant directing traffic at the cordon let us through when he saw our lanyards. Ahead were a half dozen black-and-whites strewn haphazardly on the street in front of a large white house with a green two-story, shoebox-shaped addition perched above the garage. The backyard was fenced, and the front of the house was nearly concealed behind tall junipers. The air above the street was clouded with gun smoke and smelled sweet, acrid, and sulfuric.

A SWAT armored van sat across the street from the house, the side facing the house pockmarked with divots. SWAT members kneeled behind it, their assault rifles spitting a continuous stream of fire. We could see a dark lump, a body, on the sidewalk in front of the house and two dark lumps in the street beside police cars pocked with bullet holes and silver divots. Two cops down, not moving. There were other bodies on a lawn across from the house and the sidewalk opposite. I counted six people down. The firing from the house stopped when we approached, and the police ceased fire. In the lull, smoke rose from the street. I thought the shooters might be dead. Then, a rapid burst of fire came from a window on the third floor, and SWAT and uniformed officers responded with a fusillade that tore through the window and disintegrated the green siding beside it. After a moment, firing from the house resumed at a different window, followed by a retaliatory response from the police. I thought the house would be riddled with holes, but police fire seemed only to mar the siding. We learned later that the house was heavily fortified, and few of the police bullets penetrated the interior.

John and I peered around and saw a few curious onlookers, most huddled behind cars or trees, a few peering from behind house corners, but we saw no one who resembled the drug maker we imagined. No younger men with long dark hair, no hoodies or hooded cloaks, no one remaining calm while others looked on in horror, and no one sneaking away while the drama unfolded. I saw confusion, fear, and concern but no scientific detachment on those faces. When I looked back at the house, I saw a long spit of fire from a casement window just above ground level, and in a split second, something struck the side of the nearest black-and-white. It exploded in a thunderous mushroom of smoke and fire. Burning fragments flew across the street and rained on the other police cars and the cops behind them. The black-and-white's carcass was a blackened skeleton now engulfed in fire.

"RPG," John yelled. Rocket Propelled Grenades were Soviet-block weapons used by the enemy in Vietnam, Somalia, and the Middle East. I was shocked to see one used in San Francisco. The blast drove everyone away from the house. Then more automatic weapons fire erupted from a third-story window. Cops scrambled away as bullets tore up pavement, car bodies, and tires. They were confronting at least two barricaded shooters, and I heard the SWAT captain order his teams to pull back from the house as he assessed the evolving threat. John and I had taken cover behind the nearest black-and-white, a half block from the house. I heard a series of thumps as bullets hit the ground behind us and the metallic slap of bullets hitting the sides of the police car. Paul Fisher ran up behind us, ducked below the windows, and landed on his butt.

"Tell the choppers to clear the area," he screamed into his radio. "We dunno what else they have in there." I hadn't noticed state police helicopters above us, but I glanced up and saw two circling the house. After a few seconds, they veered away. Paul looked wild-eyed and disheveled, his ordinarily neat hair matted and spiky. "Ain't this a shitshow?" he yelled to me. Before I could respond, his radio squawked. Paul listened and then said, "No, hold the Bearcat. They have RPGs. They'll blow the hell out of it."

The Bearcat is an armored vehicle SWAT uses in active shooting situations. They intended to drive it in to rescue the people lying on the street—or check to see if they were dead—but SWAT couldn't risk it now. They'd have to neutralize the threat in the house before they attempted a rescue.

Paul took another call and responded, "It's yours, Geraldine." Then he looked at John and me and said, "Turning over tactical command." As the firing from the house continued, bullets zipped over the car we were using for cover. Several clipped the top of the car, shattered windows, and zinged past us. Shards of glass showered us, and we shook them off. "Christ Almighty," Paul said. He looked back at us as police poured fire onto the house, and the shooters returned it. It was hard to hear Paul above the cacophony of gunfire. "House belongs to a couple," he yelled. "Neighbors say they're survivalists. Dunno what set this off, but they have an arsenal in there. Hardcore, say people who've been inside. AR-15s, RPGs, AK's, full-auto shotguns, body armor, thousands of rounds of ammo, God knows what else. They might have C-4, pipe bombs, grenades. We dunno what."

"Why'd you call us?" I asked.

"Thought it might be our guy," Paul yelled. "Neighbor saw people going in carrying weapons cases. Before the shit hit the fan, they heard screaming. Then shots. One guy ran out and drove away, and another ran out, screaming like a maniac. He jumps in a truck and drives off, firing random shots at houses. Then two more people run out, enraged and screaming like hell, and climb in a lifted truck and peal out. Neighbor says a final guy ran out the front door, shooting back into the house, then he's shot and killed. That's the body over there in front of the house. Fucking shitshow."

"John said you thought it was Zombie," I yelled above the gunfire.

Paul gave me an exasperated look. "Dunno. Too much shooting, too many people down. Thought it might be our guy. Like everyone in that house went berserk. All at once. Too much violence. Never seen it this bad. Could be the Zombie guy."

John nodded and said, "We didn't see anybody who looked promising."

"Sorry to bring you down. Thought he might have done this," Paul yelled as more SWAT arrived and began inching their way along neighboring houses, trying to get into an assault position. "Too bad we don't have tanks," Paul said. "We may have to blow up this goddamn house." He took another call on his radio. "Right, right," he said after listening to the call. Then to us: "We're clearing the area. Five-block perimeter." He held the radio to his ear.

With the ongoing gunfire, it was hard to hear anything. The shots hitting close to us caused your heart to seize as you anticipated bullets striking even closer. I've never been in combat, but I imagined this must be what it feels like to be under a sustained attack. You don't know how to turn because any direction might be wrong. You're hyper-alert, high on adrenalin, tense, body poised to duck, run, cringe, lunge, or strike, whatever instinct you act on to save your ass. I realized I'd been holding my breath for long minutes and forced myself to exhale, but the breath caught in my throat as more bullets whizzed by.

Then I heard Paul yell, "For chrissakes!" He turned to me and John. "Another mass shooting. Warehouse area. Custer Avenue. By Pier 90. Diverting resources there." He listened to the radio as he spoke to us. "It's the lifted truck. Crashed through a . . . what? Say again, over. Okay, okay. Two shooters. Copy. Male and female. And what?" As he listened, he told John, "You need to go there. Our guy could be there." As we got to our feet, bent over, Paul ordered the patrol officer beside him to give him his radio. He handed it to John. "Take this. I'll radio updates. They're in the warehouses on Custer. Be careful, awright? Look for our guy. Go, go, go!"

Carnage on Custer

As John raced toward Pier 90 on the eastern edge of the city near the Islais Creek Channel, I felt my knee pulsing. Running back to John's Range Rover left my knee burning and tight, like an angry boil needing to be lanced. I dry-swallowed the only oxy I had in my pocket and tried to ignore the pain. As John weaved in and out of traffic, Paul radioed that the shooting continued in a warehouse on Custer, and black-and-whites were converging on the area. The 9-1-1 caller said a truck had crashed through a wall into an office area. When people came to help, a man and a woman jumped from the truck and opened fire. At least three people were dead. The caller was injured and hiding under a desk. I felt my heart racing, driven by the intensity in Paul's voice, John hurling us through the smoky streets, cars swerving out of our way as John blared his horn, sirens screaming in the background, the whole frantic rush of blood and adrenalin setting my mind on fire.

Custer is a short street named after General George Armstrong Custer of Little Bighorn infamy. It sits in the industrial heart of east San Francisco, an area of cement plants, storage facilities, shuttered factories, and warehouses. It's an area the city left behind, strewn with grime and graffiti, home to the homeless, whose encampments stretch down gray streets along galvanized aluminum fences, streets punctuated here and there with abandoned cars, some resting on cement blocks, their tires missing, as well as lifeless trees that should have added natural beauty to the area but appeared as forlorn as the decay around them. Still, hard-working people worked here who managed the flow of industrial products from the ports to the factories and stores up and down the coast and throughout the heartland. They were now actors in the drama of violence that sometimes afflicts the unwilling and unprepared.

When John and I arrived at Custer Avenue, we saw the lifted GMC pickup, its chassis high above its wheels. It had crashed through the large front windows of an auto parts warehouse that ran half the length of a city block and left a gaping hole in the side of the building. The butt-end of the truck looked like an ostrich with its head buried in the building, and the body of a large man lay beside it, blood pooling from his waist to his feet. We slid to a stop 10 yards from the body and clambered out of John's car. We could hear the muted but continuous popping of gunfire from somewhere deep in the building. There were red splotches of blood leading into the building where window glass and part of the door to the office had been pulverized. Three black-and-whites swarmed in behind us. Cops scrambled out of the vehicles wearing black body armor and yelled at us to clear the area until John showed them his SFPD credentials. We ducked when bullets pinged into the side of one of the black-and-whites, shattered glass pelting us like rain. A uniformed cop with corporal's stripes on his sleeve ordered us to stay where we were, but John and I followed when they swarmed into the building.

The office inside was a crumpled mess of scattered desks and desktop computers, the floor flooded with paper, debris, and blood. One body was pinned beneath a flattened desk, its limbs in disarray. Another lay in a bloody heap in the bathroom beyond the office. All that remained of its hollow wood door were wood fragments dangling from hinges surrounded by BB-sized holes where a shotgun blast had peppered the wall and blown the body through the gaping hole in the door. John eased toward another open door into the warehouse, where several cops had disappeared. We could hear shots beyond, but in between shots, I heard someone whimpering. One desk in a far corner remained upright but had been knocked sideways into a credenza behind it. A large silver coffee urn sat on the credenza, and brown fluid sprayed from holes punched in its side by shotgun pellets.

I ran to the desk and found an older, overweight woman trembling in the kneehole beneath the desktop. She held a cell phone and wore a dark blue pantsuit glazed with blood and dust. Blood ran down her face from an open wound on her head, and she was grasping her right arm, which had a foot-long scrap of wood sticking in it, I couldn't tell how deep. The ragged stick was half an inch in diameter, and her hand shook as she tried to staunch the blood flowing around it. Her face grew paler, and her head sank back when I knelt beside her. She hadn't lost that much blood and wasn't in mortal danger, but she was traumatized.

"Get it out," she begged. "Get it out."

"Wait for the paramedics." I saw a stained tea towel next to the coffee urn and grabbed it. I laid it over the scrap so she didn't have to look at it. "You're going to be okay," I said.

Her eyes rolled back, her mouth fluttering, and she groaned, "No, no, no, no, no, no."

"You're hurt, but you'll survive," I said calmly.

Her phone was still connected to the 9-1-1 operator. I lifted it and spoke into the phone, "This is Sonny Marshall. In the auto warehouse on Custer. Woman you've been talking to needs medical help. Might be in shock. Shooters still active but this location clear. Other people down. Need paramedics urgently." I set the phone back in her right hand.

"I'm going to move you," I told the woman. She didn't respond as I edged her out of the confined space in the kneehole and laid her head on a sweater I found beside her overturned chair. Then I raised her legs and placed a thick book beneath her calves. I could hear shots continuing in the distance. I took off my jacket and laid it over her torso. "You'll be okay," I told her. "Paramedics are right behind me."

I scrambled toward the door leading to the warehouse. John had crouched behind a large wood crate, his gun in his right hand while he talked on his cell phone with his left. Two cops had advanced to tall stacks of crates ahead of John, but another lay on the floor in a path between the stacks. I couldn't see if he'd been shot, but he wasn't moving. Several other cops were out of sight to my left. In the chaos, I couldn't tell what was happening beyond the stacks of crates in front of me, but gunfire continued, the booms of repeated shots echoing in the enclosed space, and the zings of bullets passing overhead, striking the metal roof and walls behind me. During a pause in the firing, I ran up to John and ducked beside him.

"The male has an auto shotgun and an assault rifle," he screamed as gunfire erupted again, a steady stream of shots from an automatic. "Got a quick look at him. Has a backpack and bandoliers. Clips for the AR-15. Stay back."

I shook my head and crawled toward the cop lying still on the floor, staying as low as I could. I reached for one of his wrists and felt for a pulse. He was gone. As I crawled up beside him, I saw an entrance wound above his right ear, blood matted around a black hole. His radio was affixed to his armored vest and squawked, so I turned it off. I crawled to his handgun, which lay a few feet ahead of him, stuffed it into my jeans at the small of my back, and continued to the stack of crates to my right. When I reached it, a cop at the far end of the crates saw me.

"Security," I screamed, holding up my lanyard. He nodded and ran toward me, his eyes wide with fear. He was a young white guy, not long out of the academy. He still had some acne on a face otherwise as smooth as a peach. He was shaking but trying to conceal it. "I think she's trying to flank us," he cried. "Jesus Christ!"

"Where is she?"

"I dunno." He jerked his head toward the end of the row of crates. "Back there. She's . . . she's moving. She keeps shooting. She—"

"What's your name?"

"Daniels."

"Let's cut her off." I jumped up and ran toward the end of the stack where he'd been perched. I heard Daniels come up behind me. I peered around the corner and saw long rows of crates, some stacked four high. Slanted rays of light poured through bullet holes in the metal wall of the building. I was ready to jump to the next row of crates when I caught movement and saw the woman doing the same. She edged around a corner, laying down suppressing fire as she ran to the next row. Bullets whizzed past and slammed into the wall behind me. I knew she'd pause before attempting the same maneuver, so I held the gun out with my right hand and sighted down the rows of crates. When she burst from cover and started firing, I fired three rapid shots, my gun jerking upward in recoil. I missed, but she threw herself backward and ducked behind the row she'd emerged from.

"Fuck you!" she screamed, followed by a guttural howl.

This is no frenzied civilian amped on Zombie, I thought. *She knows about fire and maneuver. This fucking woman is trained.*

I waited for her to move again. While I did, I heard the periodic boom of the man's auto shotgun accompanied by a chorus of automatic fire from his assault rifle. He sounded deeper in the warehouse. Returned fire from the cops echoed through the building's chamber, creating a constant chatter of gunfire. The air smelled of sweat and cordite.

I fired a warning shot down the line of crates and then turned to Daniels. "Lay down covering fire for me. Okay?" He nodded. "Fire down along the wall to keep her in place. Don't shoot me in the back."

I leaped out and scurried to the next row of crates, the young cop's shots zipping behind me and pinging into the walls. As I hunkered down behind the crate at the end of the row and peered toward the last place I'd seen the woman, I felt Daniels slam into the crate behind me.

"What are you doing?" I said to him.

"Coming with you," he replied. Just then, the woman fired again, four or five quick shots, and I knew she'd advanced to the next row. She couldn't have been more than three rows in front of us now. I peered around the crate. When I didn't see her, I pointed the gun toward where I thought she'd be. Within seconds, she inched her head out, and I fired once. This time, my aim was better. The bullet split the wood on the crate just above her head, and she jerked back.

"You motherfucker," she screamed. She cut loose with a full volley on automatic, rounds zipping and pinging around us like angry hornets. When she paused to reload, I jumped out and ran to the next row of crates, kneeling at the edge and sighting my handgun at the next row. The young cop scurried up behind me, firing his weapon as he ran. When she leaned out to move again, I fired two quick rounds, both going into the crate before her. I caught a glimpse of her face before she ducked back. Her features were distorted by rage, deep lines converging on black marble eyes, teeth bared in a frozen grimace. With that godawful howling, she was the stuff of nightmares.

Firing continued on the other side of the warehouse. I heard someone cry out and something else being ripped apart. The constant clanging of bullets was unnerving. Some tore through the metal walls, but others ricocheted through the interior like pinballs. I wasn't afraid of threats I could see, but I was anxious about catching a stray from behind.

The shooter in front of us ripped off another long burst on automatic, screaming with every ounce of her breath. "I'm gonna kill you," she yelled.

"What the fuck are you waiting for?" I yelled back.

She might have been sighting down on me, so I didn't peer around the corner and risk catching one in the face. She was probably a better shot than I was. I also didn't know how many rounds I had left in the handgun, so I got in the prone position with the gun aimed toward the corner of the crate and told the cop to get ready. If I had only one shot left, I wanted it to count.

Moments passed, and she didn't appear. Then I heard the guttural roar of an engine starting, followed seconds later by an explosion that shook the building with an earsplitting screech of tearing metal. The roof above the wall next to us buckled. I thought the whole damn warehouse might collapse, but the wrenching of metal and rattling of the walls ended with the building punched outward but still standing. Then I heard a sharp impact on Custer Avenue outside, the screeching of heavy objects being dragged, men shouting, and then a resounding boom.

"What the fuck?" Daniels cried.

I got on my feet and edged toward the end of the row. A massive hole appeared on the side of the building, from the buckled roof to the ground. Blinding sunlight streamed through the gap. I ran to the rows of crates ahead of me, and the woman wasn't there. Through the gaping hole in the side of the warehouse, I saw the orange backside of a large forklift across Custer. The woman had driven it through the side of the warehouse, careened off a police car, and crashed into the opposite warehouse. Uniformed cops were picking themselves up after diving for cover, and in the chaos, I saw the woman climb down from the forklift. She sprayed the street with automatic fire and then leaped through the hole she'd punched in the other warehouse. Daniels appeared beside me, shielding his eyes from the sudden glare. I tucked the handgun into my jeans and told him to follow me. Then I stepped out onto the street, climbing over bent beams and crumpled corrugated iron siding, and sprinted to the forklift with Daniels at my side. In the confusion and panic, I didn't want any uniforms to shoot me, and I thought they wouldn't with a uniformed cop running beside me.

The forklift protruded from the side of a white block-long building with the sign "Bayer Brothers Moving & Storage." A dozen cars and trucks were parked in front of it. The forklift had demolished the side of a gray pickup and rammed it sideways into two other trucks. The street was a jumble of shattered cinderblocks, broken glass, and bent metal. I picked my way through the debris, hoping the woman wasn't lying in ambush behind the forklift, and pressed my back against the wall.

"You have any spare clips?" I asked Daniels. He nodded and removed one from his service belt. I ejected the magazine from my handgun and rammed the full one in. "You ready?" I said.

He nodded, breathing hard, adrenalin-filled light in his eyes. "Yeah. You're security," He said. "You know this place better than me." His false assumption didn't register until later. When you're in the shit, your mind is laser-focused on what's in front of you and what you have to do. I scanned the interior of the building—what I could see of it past the forklift—fluorescent lights on the ceiling, stacked boxes, pallets of things wrapped in plastic, furniture covered with cardboard and tape. There was a scuffling sound behind me as the cops in the street started moving toward us, but there was no sound inside. Then a man screamed, "Jesus Christ, no!" followed by three gunshots.

I braced myself and ran into the building, scooting past the forklift and rushing to the right side of a rectangular stack of furniture. The shots came from deeper in the building. Daniels brushed up against me, breathing hard. "Cover me," I said, running from one furniture stack to another. My mind felt acutely aware, sensing sound and movement and the intensity of now. I saw a man down to my left. He held a hand to his abdomen and was moving his head, but I couldn't stop for him. I raced ahead to my right, hoping to cut off the shooter, but I still couldn't see her. I didn't know where she'd gone, just that she was on the move.

I could hear more cops crowding into the building behind me. I turned and saw Daniels creeping closer, his gun held up in a two-hand stance. "Stay close," I said, and then I heard footsteps ahead, someone moving to my right. I burst forward and chased the sound, skirting around more piles of boxes, rushing into the maze, and I came to a crossroads, aisles crisscrossing where smaller forklifts could move goods from here to there. I didn't know which way to turn, but my instinct was to run to the right, so I did that. Dashing ahead, deeper into the warehouse, I paused after turning the corner at a tall stack of boxes, and then she stepped around the corner a few yards ahead of me, and we made eye contact.

She wheeled toward me with her assault rifle. I jumped back into Daniels, knocking us both backward as she cut loose on automatic, spraying bullets into the boxes I'd jumped behind. Wood chunks and splinters chewed through the air, causing an explosion of particle board fragments, wrapping tape, and shredded plastic. When the firing stopped, I leaped out and ran toward her, hoping she was reloading. I plowed into her as she was slapping another clip into her rifle.

She was a solid woman with meaty arms and legs. I knocked her off-balance, and she tumbled to the floor, her rifle skidding a dozen feet away. She snarled at me and scrambled toward the rifle, but I lunged and kicked one foot out from under her. "Get the rifle," I yelled to Daniels. He was a blur in my peripheral vision as he ran for the rifle. He reached it just as she picked herself up off the gray floor, her fierce eyes jittery with indecision. She was calculating whether to charge me or him. I pointed the handgun at the space between her eyes and felt my trigger finger tensing. I wasn't deciding whether to kill her. My impulse was more primal than that. I wanted to punish this animal for what she'd done. And I wanted revenge for the fear I'd felt when she was shooting at me. The rage burned in my heart for a long moment before it flickered out. But I knew if she attacked me while I held the gun, I would kill her. So I lowered the gun to the floor and slid it toward Daniels.

She watched it slide away from me. Then she came at me like a rabid dog, her face screwed up in rage. When she'd nearly reached me, I pivoted to my left and spun, slamming her in the back as she flew past me. The blow knocked her into a heavy stack of cardboard boxes, and she fell to her knees, screaming.

"What should I do?" Daniels yelled after he picked up my handgun.

"Don't shoot her," I yelled. I saw two other cops running through the aisle toward us. "Don't shoot her," I yelled to them.

She didn't hesitate when she got back to her feet. She lunged at me, fingers clenched like claws, a fierce eagle descending with its talons raised. I grabbed one arm, spun and threw my hip into her torso, and flipped her onto the floor. She hit her head and was stunned, but she wasn't finished. She rolled onto her feet and tried to plow her head into my stomach. I leaped backward and drove my elbow into her back. That dropped her to the floor, and I jumped on her and pinned her arms. She still struggled furiously, spit flying from her mouth, and I yelled to the cops now surrounding us to cuff her.

"She's amped on drugs," I told them. "Out of her mind. Don't let her bite you. She will if she can."

She was still raging as two cops subdued her and snapped on handcuffs. Two more cops helped pick her up and lead her away, her mouth snapping in a frenzied assault on anything within reach. I sank against a stack of boxes and realized I was out of breath. Daniels walked up and squatted beside me. "Here's your weapon," he said, trying to hand me the gun I'd been using.

"It's not mine," I told him. "Belonged to an officer in the other building. I don't think he made it."

He studied the handgun, nodded, and sat down beside me. "What are you? Special Forces? Navy Seal? What?"

I looked at him. "No. I'm a musician."

He stared at me with his mouth open, and in the calm after the storm, I fought to keep from laughing. I explained that I sometimes played in a band (the sometimes part was not genuine) and worked for John Sebastiani's security firm (complete lie), and we were consultants to SFPD. I was crashing from an adrenalin high and didn't want to explain—or get my ass in trouble for engaging in a firefight in the city using a dead cop's handgun. I hadn't misrepresented myself (too much), but the police frown on civilians shooting up the place. I trusted that John and Paul could handle any questions later.

I sat there a while longer after Daniels left, rubbing my aching knee and reflecting on my state of mind. I was angry enough at the woman to have killed her. I was glad I didn't when I had the chance. But the rage I'd felt choked reason and drove me within a finger twitch of taking her life. I don't know how I came out of it, but I knew we had to take her alive.

John walked in and saw me. "How you doing, *partner*?"

"Been better. Been worse, *padre*," I said. "What about the guy?"

"Dead. We cornered him. Police shot him."

"We got the woman."

"I saw her," John said.

"It's got to be Zombie," I said. "She was out of control."

"Yeah."

"Raylan Major wasn't here. I didn't see anybody."

He shrugged. "Nah. He was probably at the other scene. Vanished by now."

"What's happening there?"

"SWAT breached the house. The shooters are barricaded in a reinforced basement. Paul says it's like a fortress."

"They won't find him there. He's too smart for that."

He regarded me like soldiers do when they've been through hell together and survived. Then he sat beside me and stared into the darkness above the ceiling lights as though answers might be hiding there. "He's escalating," John said. "We have to find him quickly."

Yeah, I thought. *But how do you find a ghost?*

Heavy Metal

I sat on my sofa, my head resting on the back, eyes closed. After the firefight on Custer Avenue, I'd endured three hours of interrogation by the detectives investigating the crime scene, then two more hours with the Zombie Task Force. John drove me home. He was as whipped as I was and returned to his place.

Kat had spent the day at SFPD, meeting with Paul Fisher before he was called to Ocean Avenue and meeting with other SFPD brass. She called it a courtesy visit but also planned to visit the California Bureau of Investigation regional office in San Francisco. She wouldn't say she was exploring law enforcement jobs in San Francisco, but we both knew I couldn't move to Sacramento. If Sara were admitted to St. Ignacius, we'd face a major decision about our future sooner than expected. Kat was last year's Law Enforcement Officer of the Year and had just been shot in the line of duty, which made her a wounded warrior. You don't have to be a cop to know what that means to fellow police officers. So she was given the grand tour and met with the Chief of Police. When I came home, she downplayed the visit's importance but said it had gone well.

While I decompressed on the sofa, she took a shower. I could hear her soft sounds through the closed bedroom door as I lay in a stupor. Then the door behind me opened, and she dropped onto the sofa. She smelled as warm and lovely as a spring day. She put a hand on my shoulder and kneaded it gently. "You look like hell. How do you feel?"

"Like I just spent the day in the front row of a heavy metal concert."

She laughed. "Sounds intense."

"Insane volume. Massive overdrive. Power chords banging into each other. The whole frenetic scene pounding your senses like a blacksmith's hammer."

"You don't care for heavy metal?"

"It's like chugging flaming shots of Grandaddy Mimms 140 High Octane whiskey. I prefer soul on ice to a mind on fire."

She patted my head and laughed. "I'll fix you something better," she said. I heard her clinking a glass in the kitchen. My gut felt as tight as an overwound clock. My knee ached, and I rubbed it with one hand. When she returned, she handed me a glass of Macallan's scotch, neat. I took a sip, savored the strong sherry aroma, and let it slide smoothly down my throat like toasty butter.

"I like *Hallowed Be Thy Name*," she said.

I took a sip and nodded. "Iron Maiden. Pulse-pounding, tempo changes, dueling rhythm and lead guitars. Yeah, good song, a heavy metal classic," I admitted.

"*Paranoid*?"

"Black Sabbath. Not my favorite of theirs. I prefer *Heaven and Hell*."

"I thought you don't like heavy metal."

"Doesn't mean I don't know the music," I said, looking at her. I told her what happened at the house on Ocean Avenue and the warehouse on Custer, the madwoman I'd almost killed.

Kat had poured herself a glass of pinot grigio. She held it with both hands and rested her lips on the rim of the glass. Her eyes were far away. When I finished telling the story, she said, "I have trouble seeing her as a victim." I knew she would. Kat draws fine lines when it comes to right and wrong.

"When we rolled up and saw the body outside by the truck, I was numb. You don't expect death."

"You've seen death before," Kat chided, referring to our adventure in New Mexico. "You've caused it."

"In a fight for our lives, yeah," I replied. "But not the kind of death I saw today. You step out of the car and into the blood. Its coppery stench engulfs you. You know the guy was alive minutes ago. Now he's gone. An average guy just living his life, going to work, having a normal day. Now he's decomposing on the asphalt. It's surreal."

"I know," Kat said. "I saw it at the flea market."

I nodded. She was a police detective, and death was no stranger. "Then we heard the shooting inside. We rushed in, and when I saw her, I recognized the rage in her face. That's what I was feeling. I saw myself in her. It felt . . . like the fire in a crematorium. A searing blast of heat. I wanted to obliterate her for all the pain she caused."

"You didn't."

I rolled the scotch around in my mouth and thought about that moment. "No. I didn't. We drove there to find Raylan Major, and the evil son of a bitch was there. I saw him in her eyes."

"She killed those people, Sonny."

"She pulled the trigger, but he killed them. Rayland Major sees himself as a god. Dom Bernardi thinks he created Rapture to experiment with a formula that would cross the blood-brain barrier quickly. Then he created Zombie to turn people into mass murderers."

She sat silently for a moment and then said, "Now the police have a live victim of Zombie. That's something."

"If she comes out of it, maybe she can describe Major. Maybe she got a good look at him."

"We have to catch a break sometime," Kat said.

"In the law of averages, we're due." But it's never that simple, and we were still paying the madman's bills.

We'd just decided to go out to eat. For her to celebrate, for me to chill. Then Paul Fisher called and invited himself and John Sebastiani over for dinner. He said he'd bring Chinese takeout. They arrived an hour later. Paul set a large brown grocery bag on the dining room table, and we walked through the routine of taking out the oyster pail boxes of food and chopsticks, setting out paper plates, getting wine, beer, or scotch, and taking our places around the table. The food was hot and aromatic, smelling of ginger and garlic, scallions, and oyster sauce, and we pulled apart our chopsticks, scooped food onto our plates, and ate silently for a few minutes. Then Kat thanked Paul for meeting with her and setting up introductions throughout the department. He said he was happy to, but the day was heavy on his features, and none of us, even Kat, could escape the weariness that stains your soul when you've witnessed human destruction on a larger stage. It was like sitting through a horror film and having the terror etched into your brain like acid on metal.

After we ate, Paul pulled out his notebook and flipped to a worn page. He studied it momentarily, then said, "The house on Ocean. Dianne Hixon, 57, and Jerry Sonheim, 53. Married. Survivalists. Arms traffickers. She's a former Marine, Afghan and Iraq War vet, and a sharpshooter. Now teaching eighth graders. Was, I should say. Had an ongoing podcast on urban homesteading. He was a plumber, self-taught, former militia member. The Lawful Patriots Brigade out of Texas. Second Amendment fanatic. White supremacist. One conviction in Idaho for selling guns without a federal license."

"Are they in custody?" Kat asked.

Paul shook his head. "They barricaded themselves in the basement. SWAT saw black smoke rising from a chimney and worried about explosives. Couldn't chance a blast that would take out the neighborhood and a lot of police. So they flooded the basement with tear gas. Both dead. Not from the gas. We think Sonheim shot Hixon, then killed himself."

"Were there explosives?" I asked.

Paul nodded. "Nine cases of C4. Blasting caps. Det cord. But all of it packed for shipment. They were selling it."

"Where'd they get it?" John said.

"Unknown. The basement also had . . . ." He flipped to another page. "Sixteen cases of AR-15s, seven cases of AK-47 knockoffs, hand grenades, handguns, hundreds of them—they're still inventorying that stuff—bump stocks, silencers, automatic shotguns, thousands of rounds of ammunition, and Russian-made RPGs like the one that destroyed the SWAT van. God knows how they got hold of those. Assorted other rifles, knives, and three IWI Negev NG-7's—those are Israeli Army machine guns. It was a fortress down there."

"Were they on ATF's radar?" Kat said.

"I'm not sure. We're still downloading info from various agencies. But there are people like them scattered throughout California and everywhere else. Underground gun dealers trading in illegal weapons. Making some components themselves. Sonheim had a full metalworking shop in the basement. They sell arms to militias, collectors, kooks, Mexican mafia, cartels, whoever wants lethal shit they can't get elsewhere. These people don't go to gun shows. You won't even find them dealing guns on the street. They are strictly underground."

"They have some of the best op sec in the world," John said.

"Op sec?" I said.

"Operational security."

"So if I wanted to buy a handgun with a silencer, how would I find people like them?"

"The dark web," John answered. "The underground arms network. Militia channels. Word of mouth among people they trust."

Paul said, "We think they were doing a private arms swap."

"What's that?" Kat said.

"Gun nuts, collectors, or buyers. People known to keep their mouths shut. You invite them to your place—a garage or basement, a mobile home, a truck in the desert—to buy and sell weapons. A private showing. Talk shop. Compare guns and trade or buy. We think Hixon and Sonheim invited a small group to a private swap."

"What the hell happened?" I said.

"Somebody spiked the punch," Paul said.

"The punch?" John said, his eyebrows raised.

"Lame joke, sorry. Somebody put Zombie in the coffee and a pitcher of ice water in the kitchen. We had it tested right away. Everything had Zombie in it."

"He wanted to poison the whole house," I said.

Paul nodded. "If you want to trigger mass murder, what better way than to infect a group of weapons fanatics? A neighbor saw one guy leaving before the place went ballistic. That must have been Rayland Major."

"Description?" Kat said.

"White guy, medium build, long dark hair, sunglasses, dark baseball cap, no logo. Wore jeans and a dark hoodie."

"Thousands of guys like that in this city," John said. "Ten thousand more in the Bay Area."

"Did the neighbor see what he was driving?" Kat asked.

Paul pouted. "He was too smart to park in front of the house. The neighbor was raking leaves and didn't pay attention. Saw the guy walking out. That's all. He said the couple in the house were odd, kept to themselves, never invited neighbors over, but had visitors now and then. The house was a fortress, by the way. Fortified walls, reinforced concrete over the basement, filtered air system, underground water tanks, motion sensors, surveillance cameras with 360 coverage, solar panels on the roof, ham radio setup, and enough emergency food to last years. They were ready for Armageddon."

"Armageddon came to them," I said.

"We saw bodies outside at the scene, one in front of the house," John said.

Paul checked his notes. "That would be Juan Varga. He owned Target Gun Exchange in San Jose. Small firearms shop. He was shot five times. Took one to the head. We suspected this shitstorm might be Zombie related, so I had Forensics do quick toxicologies on the dead. Varga was clean. No Zombie in his system."

"He didn't drink the coffee," I concluded. "He must have run when the insanity began, and somebody cut him down."

"But Hixon and Sonheim tested positive for Zombie?" Kat said.

"Oh, yeah," Paul replied. "Heavy doses. Both."

"What about the two at the warehouse?" John asked.

"Robert Kruzik, 49, dead at the scene," Paul said, consulting his notes. "Tanked up on Zombie. Same with his daughter, Caroline, the one you took down," he added, looking at me. "She's 27, a pedicurist if you can believe that."

John chuckled. "If you go to her for a pedicure, don't sass her. She'll rip your toes off."

Paul was too weary to respond to that. "She's at San Francisco General, sedated. We're hoping to interview her when the drug wears off."

"Will she be charged?" Kat asked.

"Up to the DA," Paul said. "Probably, but diminished capacity, I don't know."

"She seemed ex-military to me," I said.

Paul nodded. "Army Ranger, one of the first women to graduate from their Ranger School." He looked at his notes. "One more guy came out of the house. Glenn Bando. From Daly City. He drove to a tire store, shot two employees there, killed one, then made it to Granville Way, a dead-end street. Black-and-whites blocked him in. A police sniper was ready to take him out, but Bando shot himself with a World War II Remington 45 under the chin. Investigators at the scene on Ocean think Bando was a collector. They found a 1941 M1 Garand at the house. A tag on it bore his name."

"Did he have Zombie in his system?" Kat asked.

Paul nodded. "His blood work showed a smaller dose, but the team at Granville said he was out of his mind. I guess it doesn't take much to send somebody into a rage."

"Something curious about this," I said. "If both Kruzik's were amped on Zombie, why didn't they kill each other?"

"Same question about the couple at the house on Ocean," John said.

"He did shoot her," Kat noted.

"Not till the end of the siege," Paul said. "They fired a lot of angry rounds at us and their neighbors before the murder-suicide."

We had no answer to these questions. Dom Bernardi might have an idea, and I made a mental note to ask him. Everyone but Kat looked exhausted. I asked if they wanted coffee and got tepid nods from Paul and John. While I went to the kitchen for coffee,

I heard Kat say, "The people they invite to these private gun swaps are only people they trust. That means they trusted Raylan Major, whatever his real name is."

"Yes," Paul said, an uptick in his voice. It sounded like he'd thought of that but hadn't considered its significance.

"They knew each other," Kat said. "They'd know how to contact him, so maybe his real name and number are on somebody's phone."

"The lab is checking their phones now," Paul said.

I brought back coffee for everyone but Kat, who was still drinking wine. As I sat down, she said, "Does it seem likely that Raylan Major, a rogue biochemist, is also an arms trafficker?"

"Where are you going with this?" John said.

"I'm trying to figure out how Major knew Hixon and Sonheim. There were, what, seven people in that house?"

"That we know of, yeah," Paul said. "Hixon and Sonheim, the Kruziks, Bando, Varga, and Major."

"Why was Raylan Major invited? It wasn't to pass out Zombie like party favors," she said.

"He obviously has an interest in guns," I said.

"It doesn't feel right. This is a man with too many interests. He has a day job somewhere, presumably. He makes designer drugs. He's into Cosplay and dresses up as a medieval wizard. He frequents the drug party scene. And he also traffics weapons in the underground?"

"Maybe he's not a trafficker, just a collector?" John said.

"I don't think that's the connection," Kat said. "I think he's a survivalist, and that's the connection. We had a missing persons case in Sacramento two years ago. Young woman. Her parents called when she failed to return from a weekend trip with her boyfriend. They'd gone to Nevada for a prepper's meet over a long weekend. He was big into that. He claimed she'd met another guy and run off with him. We didn't buy it, and we found her body three weeks later buried near a plot of land he owned outside of Stockton. A cadaver dog found her. Anyway, I got to know some of the prepper crowd. They think the shit's going to hit the fan, and they're prepping for it all to come crashing down. Weapons are a big part of their preparation, but the people highest in the prepper food chain are the survival experts, the ones designing bunkers like the one you described on Ocean Avenue."

Paul looked thoughtfully at her. "It's possible. Maybe he's prepared for the end of times and wants to speed it along."

"If Hixon and Sonheim knew him as a fellow survivalist, if he advised them or helped them build their complex, and they thought he was trustworthy, they would have invited him. Or maybe he knew of the swap and invited himself. However that happened, they trusted him enough to leave him alone in the kitchen, where he put Zombie in the coffee."

"Not a very friendly thing to do," John quipped.

"He's a psychopath," Kat said. "And he's burning bridges. He wouldn't care who he hurt." She looked at Paul. "I'd suggest you ask ATF to pressure the gun traffickers they know for names. Match them with whatever you find on Hixon's and Sonheim's phones. But you should also look into the survivalist groups in the Bay Area, and there are more than you think. You wouldn't be looking for the individuals stockpiling freeze-dried food in their homes. You want the major players with sophisticated bunkers or compounds—the gurus. Then crosscheck with the Bay Area Cosplay community. Somewhere in the intersection of those groups, you'll find Rayland Major."

"Good thinking, Kat," Paul said. "You should come to work for us. You'd make a fine detective."

She gave him a big, toothy smile. After they left, Kat said, "We had a visitor today." She handed me a business card. It belonged to Artie Forsberg, our building manager.

"What did Artie want?"

"He had a young couple with him. He said they were interested in the vacant unit on the second floor."

I nodded. "2A. The Iszley's moved out last month. It's been listed. Why did they come up here?"

"He said they wanted to compare the layout of your condo with the vacant one."

"Bullshit."

"I didn't let them in. I told them I'd been injured and didn't feel well."

"What did these two people look like?"

"She was in her mid-thirties, with black hair in a bob. Pale. No makeup. Plain looking. She put on a smile when I glanced at her, but it was forced. He was younger, with short black hair, black stubble on his face, and slightly dark complected. He looked too young for her, maybe late twenties. Nice looking guy in a rugged way. An athlete. Strong cheekbones. I just got a glance, but those were my impressions."

I glanced around the main room. We hadn't put it back together from Ari's and Catherine's stay. Cots and bedding were still stacked along one wall.

"What do you think?" Kat said.

"I think two members of the Azeri hit team paid us a visit."

Pulling the Plug

We had no respite from the wildfires. The flames had now reached the Central Valley and were marching through fields of cereal grains and tomatoes, through the orange groves and apple orchards, through cherries, plums, and pecans, and through homes, farms, and lives. Firefighters were draining lakes and ponds, converting irrigation equipment to water sources, and using every resource to stem the relentless red tide sweeping across the most fertile land on the West Coast. Squadrons of flame-retardant tankers so filled the skies that it looked like an invasion, an impression matched by regiments of hot shot crews deployed through the once verdant hills and valleys like an invading army. Winds gusting to 30 mph were catapulting burning embers hundreds of yards ahead and starting new conflagrations. A reporter on the morning news described the dim landscape as a war zone and revealed that more than a hundred thousand acres had already burned.

From our main room window, Kat and I observed a forbidding wall of smoke on the eastern horizon. It resembled a yellow cliff with veins of black and gray. The sun backlit the smothering clouds, giving them an eerie incandescence. Below us, the sleepy city was awakening to another day of bad news turning worse. I'd slept hard for six hours, then woke to the smell of wood smoke, thought briefly our home might be on fire, and then remembered the wildfires north and east of the city. I tried to go back to sleep but kept seeing Caroline Kruzik's manic face—a boiling stew of rage and hatred. She came at me relentlessly, hissing like a serpent, and I lay there with a sense of foreboding before accepting I was more awake than asleep and planted my feet on the floor.

Now, Kat and I stood shoulder to shoulder at the window, steaming cups of coffee warming our hands.

"How's your knee this morning?" she asked.

"It hurts. I put too much stress on it yesterday."

"You should take some oxy."

"I already have. Two of them. They're not helping."

"When do you see the doctor?"

"Next week."

"Hang on," she said.

"Giving it my best shot."

When she left to get breakfast, I stood in the quiet of the morning thinking about the man Alejandro Crisologo mistakenly called Raylan Major. We now knew his fantasy character was Wraithlan Mager. A wraith is a ghostlike image of someone, generally seen around the time of their death. A mage is a sorcerer or magician. I understood why our psychopathic druggist chose that fictional character as his doppelganger. He was a ghostly wizard. Still, it felt like we were tightening the noose. If Kat was right, his name would appear on someone's list—survivalists, Cosplay devotees, gun nuts. Caroline Kruzik might know him. We had very little else to go on, and his crimes were escalating.

We sat together at the table, watching the early morning news program on the local CBS channel. The lead story was the wildfires and efforts to contain them, but the announcers moved quickly to yesterday's shootings. The press had gotten wind of Zombie and were running with breaking news about a new designer drug that made people homicidal. As usual with a hot lead, the media was beating the story into a frenzy, and the panic level in the population was rising. SFPD was under fire for not informing the public about the threat earlier and for not stopping this maniac. Kat shook her head in disgust. Police work was difficult enough without the media inciting the public to demand the impossible. "I'm going to call my old prepper network contacts today," she said, "and see if they know anyone matching Mager's description."

After Kat left for the bedroom to get dressed, I called Artie Forsberg, our condo's property manager, and asked about the couple who wanted to see our unit.

"They was from Spain," Artie told me.

"How do you know that?"

"I asked. They had accents. I said, 'Where you from?' They say they movin' here from Madrid, whatever, someplace like that. That's what they say."

"Why did they want to see my place?"

"Yours or Merrick's. The shrink. I knew she was workin', so I thought you'd be home, maybe, or your girlfriend."

"Kat."

"Right. Her. Say she didna feel okay, so that was that."

"You could have just shown them the empty unit, 2A."

"Yeah, yeah, did that. They wanted to see someplace furnished. You know? See how it look with stuff in it."

"On the top floor?"

"Sure, why not?"

"That seems odd."

"Hey, see enough people," Artie said, "ain't nothin' odd no more." I was hanging up when I heard Artie say, "Oh, one thing."

"Yeah?"

"They was askin' 'bout all the security las' week."

"How'd they know about that?"

"Didna say. I told 'em we had a VIP-type stayin' here. Diplomat. Somethin' like that."

I thanked Artie and then called John Sebastiani. "Hello, *padre*," I said when he picked up. Calling him *padre* is a signal that our conversation might be overheard.

"How can I help you, my son?" he responded.

"I'd like to go to confession," I said.

"I'll be in Old Saint Mary's Confessional in one hour."

"I'll see you there. Thank you, Father."

Old Saint Mary's was our code for Saint Frank Coffee in Russian Hill on Polk. After leaving my condo, I drove in circles for a dozen blocks until I was reasonably sure I wasn't being followed. Then I drove slowly past Saint Frank, spotted John sitting in his car, and he followed me four blocks away, where I parked in the first open space. John swept my car with his bug detector and found none. As we walked to Saint Frank, I told him about the two people at my condo and my talk with Artie.

"Those two knew Ari was there," I said.

"Fuckin' A, partner. They were going to connect the two of you sooner or later. We can use that."

"How?"

"I have an idea. When you drive home, park your car on the street. They're watching you, so let them plant a tracker on your car. Tomorrow, park in your underground garage.

I'll give you a bug detector. Scan your car where they can't see you doing it. You'll know if the car's been bugged. When it is, we'll set a trap."

"How are Ari and Catherine?"

"They're okay. They're in a safe house in Marin County. Earl's there with four of Sana's guys. I want you to call Ari and tell him you want to get together for lunch. Wait until later this afternoon, after I've briefed him. Assume they've tapped your phone, so be careful what you say."

As we reached Saint Frank, I got a call from Xavier McQueen. "I'll be at the studio shortly," I said. We had band practice this morning.

"Nah," he said. "Need you over at Zuckerberg." That was the hospital where Eric Young was taken after his Rapture overdose.

"What's up?"

"They're gonna pull the plug," he said in a voice thick with sadness. John ran back with me to my car. Before I pulled away, he gave me the portable bug detector—a black wand-like device—and told me how to use it. Zuckerberg San Francisco General was a short drive away. They'd moved Eric to a private room, surrounded by Jaycee Washington and his parents. Garth, K.C., and Le'Andra stood in the hallway by his door, along with a half-dozen gay men I didn't know, friends of Eric's. Many had puffy eyes and drawn expressions and stood solemnly, as in a tableau. I imagined them as the youth of Greece gathered around Socrates on his deathbed. Thanatos would hover in the shadows behind them. He, the god of peaceful death, would be joined by Hypnos, the god of sleep; Atropos, the goddess of death who cuts the thread of life; Erebus, the god of darkness; and Charon, the demon ferryman of the dead. I don't know why, at this moment of Eric's death, I thought of Greek gods, but in his person, flawed as he was, he always seemed ethereal to me, a man not entirely of this world, a guitarist of distinction who played so beautifully, as though his fingers possessed a rare gift.

"They've been waitin' for you," Xavier told me. "He quit breathing on his own last night. Time to go pay your respects."

Eric was attached to a ventilator, his sunken frame nearly swallowed by the bed. His beautiful mahogany cheeks had withdrawn since I last saw him, and he looked a hundred years old. He still wore that beatific smile, Rapture's signature, which I now despised. I was grateful that he hadn't suffered these last weeks, that in what remained of his mind, he still reveled in whatever paradise the drug bestowed. But I wished my friend could still feel the hurts, regrets, and longing each of us feels in the normal course of living. Eric was beyond that now and would soon be lost in the darkness. I held his hand for a few moments, said my condolences to his family, and wiped away my tears as I turned from the room.

I commiserated with my bandmates and Eric's friends but couldn't stay longer. I didn't want to be there when they took him off life support. As I left the hospital, I kept hearing The Byrds singing, "Turn! Turn! Turn!, their song is based on the passage from *Ecclesiastes*. There is a time to every purpose under heaven. A time to be born and a time to die. A time to love and a time to hate. A time to hate. Bubbling up from my emotions, beneath all the grief I'd felt at Eric's bedside, was burning hatred for the psychopathic son of a bitch who put him there.

Fort Mason

Three years ago, the Storm Lake Blues Band performed at a charity event in Fort Mason's Festival Pavilion, a sprawling venue on an old army post in the northern Marina District. It was one of those golden evenings when a soft breeze blew across the bay, the smell of salt and seaweed complementing views of Alcatraz and the Golden Gate Bridge. After playing, we sat outside on a balcony overlooking the bay, sipping oaky Scotch and watching the fog roll in. Wisps of white wrapped around us like the gossamer skirts of angels' gowns.

I hadn't returned to Fort Mason since that magical evening. When John and I drove into the old post on Thursday morning, I was reminded how uniformly drab it was. The post closed in the early Sixties, leaving rows of white warehouses and port facilities with red terracotta clay roofs and red windows. The buildings have been repurposed and now house art galleries, museums, coffee bars, food markets, and restaurants. The streets are wide, parking is plentiful, and Fort Mason sits on the bay, so ingress and egress by water is easy. It is isolated from the rest of the city, walled off on two sides and bordered by water on the others. In the summer, Fort Mason is overrun with tourists, but in late October, the crowds had thinned, reducing the opportunity for collateral damage if you are planning an ambush.

We wanted to lure the Azeri assassination team to a remote location that would entice them to strike. We chose D'ellaria's, a chic restaurant on the ground floor of Landmark Building F, the last in a long row of large former Army warehouses. It sits near the Festival Pavilion and has a commanding view of the San Francisco Bay. D'ellaria's main room is bathed in gold and has rosewood ceilings, black-and-white tiled floors, and Art Deco walls.

The luxurious ambiance is matched by a fine selection of West Coast seafood delicacies, featuring cioppino, a seafood stew invented in San Francisco by Italian fishermen using leftovers from their daily catches. D'ellaria's had two distinctive features that made it suit our dark purpose. It had a private dining room in an alcove off the kitchen, and it was owned by one of Ari Kirakosian's dear friends, Louis Lombardi.

Chef Louie allowed us to use the private dining room for a lunch meeting, although that room is usually reserved for exclusive dinners. He agreed to a few modifications and let us substitute Sana's men for his regular wait staff. John and I inspected the room as dawn's yellow glow cast long shadows into the bay. The air was crisp and smoky; it felt like fire had coated your bones. The water across the bay was ruddy and unruly. If our plan worked, the Azeri hit team would conclude it was a good location to eliminate Ari—an isolated, confined space with easy access to main roads or water for their escape.

I called Ari last night and asked him to meet me for lunch at D'ellaria's. We assumed the Azeris had bugged my phone, but we also knew the GPS tracker was under my car, so we reasoned that they would follow me to Fort Mason. I returned to my condo mid-morning and told Kat I was meeting Ari for lunch. I didn't tell her we planned to end the Azeri threat if they swallowed the bait. I didn't see any cars following me as I returned to Fort Mason, but with a GPS tracker on my car, they didn't have to be close.

Ari arrived with Earl Zepeda and two Armenian guards, Davros Hakimian and Hovig Gregorian, at a quarter past noon. We situated Ari at the head of the table opposite the door leading outside. The only other entry into the room was through the kitchen. In front of his knees was a panel of bullet-proof glass Sana had obtained. If gunfire looked imminent, Ari would drop behind the panel. Earl and John sat on either side of him. Hovig and I sat beside them. Davros dressed as a waiter and acted as our server. John had posted lookouts outside and talked to them through earbuds.

While we waited for the Azeris to make their move, we ordered lunch, although no one had an appetite. We nagged John for news from outside until he told us to shut up and said he'd let us know if his lookouts spotted suspicious activity. After eating whatever we could, Sana's man bussed the table, and we sat nervously, waiting for the Azeri hit team to be spotted. I'd eaten only a few broiled shrimp, which weren't friendly to my stomach.

"Maybe they saw through it," John said.

"It's an obvious place to stage an ambush," I said. "But I wouldn't walk in here unless I knew the layout. They could be waiting outside for us to leave."

"Or they've given up," Ari said.

John shook his head. "We can't assume that. They're smart. They'll pick the best opportunity to execute their mission and get away safely. This setup is perfect."

"Maybe too perfect," Ari said.

"Then we'll keep trying," I said. "We're as stubborn as they are." I set my napkin on the table and got up. "I'm going to check the dining room."

"Follow him," Ari told Earl.

As I left the private dining room, I passed through the kitchen and into the main restaurant. I was searching for a Middle-Eastern-looking dude with high cheekbones—the guy Kat described who'd come to our condo with a woman. None of the men in the room fit that description, but I saw a single woman sitting at a small table along the south wall. She had chin-length dark hair parted on the right side of her head. Long strands hung over her left eye. She had a swarthy complexion and wore a sullen expression that looked bone deep rather than born of a bearish disposition. She held a fork in her rough left hand and pushed the food around her plate while scanning the room now and then as though looking for someone.

There were two other single women having lunch. One was absorbed in her cell phone; the other read a paperback while she ate. The dark-haired woman felt wrong. Others in the room wore touristy garb or business casual and were absorbed in their tiny islands of conversation or sitting comfortably alone. This woman wore black tights, black ATAC storm boots, and a loose-fitting dark brown sweater. She looked like a warrior, and she was left-handed like the woman driving the truck the night of the botched assassination attempt. I debated whether to approach her. Many young women in San Francisco wear combat boots, but I had to be sure. I casually walked in her direction and stopped at her table. "Are you enjoying your lunch?"

A look of annoyance crossed her face like a flicker of lightning. She studied me as though trying to place me, then gave a slight nod.

"I'm the assistant manager," I told her. "We like to know that our customers are enjoying their meal."

She wanted to look away, but my eye contact wouldn't let her. She didn't believe the lie, but we were in a crowded restaurant, and her options were limited.

"Are you visiting San Francisco?" I asked her.

She glanced away, and I took the opportunity to look around the room. I didn't see anyone making eye contact with her, no one who looked like an accomplice, but Earl Zepeda had left the kitchen and saw me talking to this woman. I caught his eye and looked along the far wall, my eyes moving to the central doorway. He understood and sauntered in that direction while keeping his eyes on us.

When I looked back at the woman, she was staring at me. Then she glanced at Earl, panic climbing her throat. She swallowed hard, looking back at me.

"Where are you from?" I said.

She hesitated, doubt playing across her face like a fiddle. "Madrid," she finally managed, repeating the lie she'd told my building manager. She had an accent I couldn't place. Eastern European, maybe.

"*Me encanta Madrid*," I exclaimed, smiling broadly, "*sobre todo en verano.*" *I love Madrid, especially in the summer.* "*Entonces es caluroso y seco, muy diferente de San Francisco.*" *It is hot and dry then, so different from San Francisco.*

Her face was blank, which confirmed what I suspected: she didn't speak Spanish. Claiming to be from Spain was a poor choice, but she couldn't acknowledge she'd come from Azerbaijan. Behind her blank face, she simmered with indecision. A large black purse sat on the empty chair beside her. Should she pull the gun she'd concealed in it or tolerate me until I left?

I glanced at Earl. Her eyes followed mine and were wider when she looked back at me. "*Es mucho más peligroso que yo*, y él sabe quién eres," I said. *He is much more dangerous than me and knows who you are.* Then I smiled at her, playing the gracious assistant manager again, and said, "Thank you for choosing D'ellaria's."

I half-turned away, keeping her in my peripheral vision, and stopped at other tables, thanked them for eating there, and finally made my way back toward the kitchen. Earl remained standing halfway between the kitchen and the main door. He stared at her, and that stare drove her from the table. She made her way to the door, keeping her distance from Earl, and then quickly left. I went to Earl and whispered, "*Creo que es una asesina Azerí. Mira a dónde va y díselo a Padre, pero no la sigas demasiado de cerca. Un hombre con cabello oscuro y pómulos altos podría unirse a ella. También es un asesino.*" *I think she is an Azeri assassin. Watch where she goes and tell John, but don't follow too closely. A man with dark hair and high cheekbones could join her. He's also an assassin.*

In hindsight, I shouldn't have confronted her. I should have eased back into the kitchen and told John and Ari what I saw. I thought we'd see the whole crew arriving, not just her. John's surveillance team had reported nothing unusual—until they did moments later. I thought the Azeris would be wary of attacking us in a confined space they hadn't seen, that they'd wait until we left and ambush us in the area outside. If I'd been them,

I would have created a diversion, maybe set fire to another building. Divert people's attention from the kill zone. I would have hijacked some big trucks and blocked the entrance and exit to Fort Mason—a natural chokepoint that would keep first responders out and trap us in the parking lot, where multiple shooters could have fired on us from every side. I forgot that the Russian way of combat heavily influenced the Azeris, and the Russians attacked straight ahead with blunt force. They aren't subtle.

By talking to the woman, I may have screwed up their timing, but I didn't change their plan.

When I returned to the private dining room, I saw John hustling a startled Ari away from the table while Davros and Hovig pulled their weapons and took firing positions toward the outside door. "They're coming," John yelled, ordering me to cover the entry through the kitchen. I turned and ran back toward the restaurant. I heard screams from the main dining room and didn't understand what was happening. At the entrance to the dining room, I ran into a black-haired devil with high cheekbones. He filled the doorway with his large frame and rushed toward me like a linebacker. He had sharp ears and eyes so dark they lacked depth. I barely had time to see the dark handgun he was raising when he barreled into me and knocked me back into the kitchen, where I slammed into a tall cabinet above the end of a counter.

I grabbed his gun hand and tried to leverage the gun toward the floor, but he was a strong son of a bitch and kept raising it toward my gut. I saw him pull back his head and knew a headbutt was coming. When he jerked his forehead toward my face, I quickly threw my head to one side, and his forehead struck the cabinet so hard it shook. If that hurt, he didn't show it. I was losing the fight to control the gun, so I reached toward the counter behind me with my free hand and grabbed the first thing I touched. I swung it hard at his face, and it burst with an explosion of glass and a sticky red substance that splattered and clung to his face and chest. He lost the gun, and it clattered to the floor. For a moment, he looked stricken, his face and chest coated with red, and I saw then that some rivulets of red were running down his face where he'd been cut with shards of glass that protruded like angry boils from his flesh. As his eyes searched for his gun, I shot a tight fist into his throat. He gagged and then turned and staggered away, picking up his pace, finally running toward the restaurant's main entrance, running through diners who had clambered away and stood to either side, parting like the Red Sea, their terrified faces agog at this spectacle.

His gun was a type I'd never seen before. John told me later it was a Udav handgun, favored by the Russian military. It was fitted for a silencer but did not have one attached. For this hit, the Azeris wanted noise. Lying a few feet away was a red-splotched, white label from a bottle of Heinz Tomato Ketchup. That's what I'd hit him with. I was thanking God for condiments when I heard shooting from the private dining room. I ran back toward it and eased around the door. I saw Hovig lying in a heap on the floor, but he was holding his head up and checking his torso. He had two hits on his body armor but seemed otherwise all right. Davros stood to my left, his arms held out in the firing position. He was aiming toward a large man who lay slumped against the far wall, his big gut oozing to the floor like hot wax. His head lay to one side as though he hadn't understood a question. In place of his right eye was a dark hole leaking blood. He looked familiar. After staring for a moment, I recognized him as the large man who planted the bomb in the men's room at BiblioTech. In the surveillance video, we'd seen him go into the bathroom in a wheelchair and walk out a minute before the bomb exploded.

The dark-haired woman I'd confronted in the dining room sat crumpled on the other side of the door. There were two dark stains on her sweater—one on her chest, the other on her liver—and they widened as her life force leaked away. A large handgun lay by her side, close to her left hand but unavailable to fingers that had lost their grip. Her eyes implored me for a final moment of human contact, so I went to her, bent down, and took her left hand in mine. It was already cold, and I could feel her shaking as her body deserted her. I wasn't sure what to say to an enemy who would have killed me if she'd had the chance. But as she lay dying, I could only think that she was someone's daughter, maybe a sister or a wife. Maybe she had children and was sent to this country doing what she felt was her duty.

"Are you Muslim?" I said. Most Azeris are Muslim, so it was a fair guess.

She may have nodded, or I may have imagined it, but her head seemed to rock slightly, and I saw confirmation in her eyes.

"There is no god but Allah," I whispered to her. I'm not a Muslim, but I knew that's what you would say to a dying Muslim. It's an affirmation of their faith, an acceptance of God's oneness. Maybe I was being hypocritical, but I didn't care. I was trying to comfort a soul passing beyond this life. I don't know if she heard me, for by then, her eyes had turned to glass, and her chest lay still.

I stood up and went to Hovig, who was now sitting with his back against the wall. I asked if he was all right, and he nodded, though he was clearly in pain. The room smelled of cordite and sour sweat, and a layer of gun smoke hovered over the floor like a thinning fog. The door to the kitchen opened, and John walked in, talking on his cell phone.

"Follow him but not too close. We want to know where he goes," he said. Then he looked at me, his eyes widening. "You okay, partner?"

"Yeah, why?" I said, then, looking down, saw that my jacket and T-shirt were spotted with globs of ketchup. I realized I had it on my face and hands, too. "It's ketchup," I said.

John cracked a smile. "The shit's going down, and you're playing with your food?"

I told him what happened.

"They teach ketchup fighting in Krav Maga?"

"One of our many secret weapons," I told him. John snorted. Then I said, "What about the big guy I hit?"

"Earl caught him outside," John said. "End of story. There was a fourth guy. One of my guys said he was a wiry little prick with a bandaged neck. He took off in a car. Earl's following him."

"That should account for everyone in their crew," I said, "at least the ones in the pickup behind BiblioTech."

"All but their spotter," John said. "We don't know who he is. Or where. Or how many more there might be."

"Shit, John, they sent a squad, not an army."

"Never underestimate the opposition," he replied.

Davros returned from the kitchen, and Ari walked in behind him. When John's spotters told him two assassins were headed for the outside door to the private dining room, he led Ari to the walk-in freezer in the kitchen. Ari looked shaken, but the cool reserve he is known for quickly returned as he surveyed the carnage. He lifted his chin toward John.

"Three of them down," John said. "Our side is okay. Hovig will be sore for a while, but he'll recover. Earl's tailing the one member of their crew that got away, the one hit in the neck when they tried to kill you."

"Civilian casualties?" John shook his head. Ari canted his head toward the two dead assassins. "Any I.D.'s on them?"

John shrugged. "They wouldn't want to be identified." He looked at Davros. "But go check." While Davros did, John added, "Someone's directing this operation. He might have been the spotter in the building behind BiblioTech. The guy who got away could lead Earl to him. Until we cut the head off the snake, we're not finished. But we're closer."

"You'll need to do some damage control with your friend, Chef Louie," I told Ari.

He nodded, glancing around the room. Then he smiled. "Louie was a Marine in the Gulf War. He gets it. The notoriety might even be good for his business, and Sana will have this place spotless by dinnertime tonight. I'll cover the damage. Louie's a stand-up guy."

"Sonny's going to owe him for a bottle of ketchup," John said.

Ari raised his eyebrows and looked at me, growing concerned when he saw the mess on my face and clothes. I explained my adventure with the ketchup bottle, and he laughed. "That'll make a good story," he said. "You might even enjoy telling it in years to come."

Davros returned and said, "Che," the Armenian word for no. John said we'd probably find their IDs at their base. When we located their chief, we'd find their documentation.

Sirens in the distance warned that the police were arriving and we'd have hours of interrogation ahead of us. John said he would handle it, but everyone must give a statement. I went to the men's room while we waited and gazed at myself in the mirror. I used white paper towels on the counter to clean my face, neck, and hands. Some red goo had gotten into my hair. I bent over the sink and ran water over my scalp, brushing my hair back with wet hands when I stood up. My good corduroy jacket had globs and specks of ketchup all over the front. I thought wearing a good jacket to a gun battle was pretty stupid. Trying to clean it off with toilet paper just smeared it into the fabric, so I resigned myself to looking like a frat boy with bad table manners.

I felt my left knee throbbing and wondered if I'd stressed it during the fight. I didn't remember that, but your attention is laser-focused when fighting for your life. With no peripheral vision, you miss most of what else is happening. I had one oxy in my jacket pocket and dry-swallowed it before gazing back in the mirror. The guy staring back at me had been lucky. I collided with the Azeri before he raised his gun. I would have been gut-shot if I'd been one second slower. My hand found a makeshift weapon that shattered his concentration. Planting my fist in his throat was a skill honed through Krav Maga training. Hitting him with a ketchup bottle was luck, and that shook me. You can't rely on luck. So I stared at the guy in the mirror, grateful for another chance.

Mercifully, my police interview was short. I hadn't fired a weapon and was defending myself when the big guy attacked me in the kitchen. The detective questioning me was curious about who killed the big guy outside. He died of multiple stab wounds. I pleaded ignorance. I was inside when it happened, I told him. The kitchen staff corroborated my story, so the interview was over quickly.

When I left the building, the media was converging on Fort Mason. I saw them running toward us, jockeying for position, reporters pulling themselves together, tech crews positioning cameras and audio recorders. I eased into the crowd of curious onlookers and circled to my car. Before leaving, I bent down, plucked the GPS tracker from the undercarriage, and smashed it under my heel before I drove home. Kat was working at her computer when I opened the door.

"How was your lunch with Ari?" she said without looking up.

"Good," I answered.

Then she looked at me, her smile fading as she saw my jacket. "What happened to you?"

"Food fight."

Karmagen

I had a fitful night, staring at the walls, listening to Kat lightly snore until I sank into oblivion, waking, thinking it must be four o'clock when it was only 12:30, closing my eyes, falling into a dream, an emptiness so dark and decomposing I couldn't remember its currents, just a feeling of dread as suffocating as a wetsuit, turning over, seeing Kat silent beside me, drifting again, being chased through a black meadow by something monstrous, bitten on my calf, waking as a charley horse seized my leg, rubbing it away, turning, lying in sweat and throwing off the blanket, drifting into a fog of burnt umber, the room suffused with the scent of a dying campfire, feeling warmth on my nose and cheeks, thinking I was being interrogated under a heat lamp, waking to the spotlight of the sun through the bedroom window, my knee aching, nothing new about that, trying to recall what I was doing today—failing at that, my mind slogging like a dump truck climbing a hill in first gear.

Katrina the Merciful brought me a cup of coffee while I was parked on the side of the bed with my feet planted on a cold floor. A long shower helped. By the time I wrapped a beach towel around me and stared into the mirror, I felt marginally human. But as yesterday's events at Fort Mason replayed in my mind, I was reminded that when you taunt the devil, you risk him responding in kind.

With that thought bouncing around in my brain, I went to my music room. The Storm Lake Blues Band was performing Tuesday night, and I told Kat I had to spend some hours with my sax to keep my edge. I began by running through the band's performance repertoire, the songs on our albums and the unrecorded ones we often played on stage. Le'Andra Kimani had learned the guitar parts on all our songs, so I had to rehearse songs we hadn't played in a while in case they made it on the setlist. While I played, I felt the buzz of that electric moment yesterday when the Azeri team made its move. The tension I'd felt crisscrossed my soul this morning like an echo, and I played with attitude, thinking vocally about each song—the backstory behind its creation and its genesis in the blues spectrum from flaming red hot to moods a deeper blue than black. I laid a guttural growl on some low notes, dragging them along like chains pulled across granite, then bending notes on other musical phrases like the wind whipping through box canyons. I was practicing ascending sixths, a standard interval in blues music, when the door opened, and Kat leaned in, her face awash with discovery.

"They got him," she announced.

I didn't need to ask who. We'd been chasing the same phantom for weeks. But I felt an uptick in my pulse. I set my sax on its stand and stood up.

"Who is it?"

"His name is Dwayne Karmagen."

That name scratched at my memory, but I couldn't place him. I still heard blues in my head and couldn't clear the clutter.

"The guy at Ceres Biosciences," Kat said. "Dom Bernardi's assistant."

Now I remembered him. Medium height. On the thin side. Long brown hair parted in the middle. Scars through one eyebrow. A street tough with a soft voice. He looked away when he spoke to you. A social misfit, maybe? Shy? Evasive? I didn't have a strong impression, but I remembered him hovering while we asked Bernardi about Rapture. When we gave Bernardi the tox reports on the victims of Rapture and Zombie, Karmagen wanted to see them. He fit the profile I'd been building in my mind. He was a biochemist with access to CRISPR technology. Was he married? I'd imagined Raylan Major as a loner, but maybe not. Psychopaths marry, have kids, and look normal. I didn't recall seeing a wedding ring, but I wasn't looking. I wondered if that raven-haired siren, Arachne, could identify him. Thoughts collided in my head like fans crowding the front of a stage at a rock concert.

"John called," Kat said. "He's on his way."

"How did they catch him?"

"He didn't say."

I wiped down my sax and put it away, then joined Kat in the kitchen for more coffee. John knocked moments later. When I opened the door, I was surprised to see someone with John. It was Dom Bernardi with a fallen face, his jowls swollen, his head bowed. Fat rolls stacked from his chin to his chest looked like coils in a heavy spring.

John angled past me and hugged Kat. Dom stood at the threshold as though waiting for permission to enter. I waved him in, and he walked to the dining room table and sank into a chair, his elbows on the table, hands clawing through thick, graying black hair. I looked at John for an explanation, and he silently mouthed, "He can't believe it."

"An anonymous tip came in this morning," John said aloud. Then, "Coffee?" Kat nodded, and John went to the kitchen to pour a cup. "Dom?" he asked, but Bernardi shook his head.

We all sat at the table. I felt the way you do when a long-anticipated race is over and the dark horse wins. All the tension leading up to the race is now spent. You're glad it's over but surprised at the outcome. Nothing you expected to happen did, and the actual result was not one you ever imagined. I was relieved, but as I recalled the guy we met at Ceres, the puzzle pieces didn't fit.

"They're sure it's him?" I said to John.

Dom shook his head. John studied him and said, "Took him into custody at Ceres this morning. Then raided his house and found the drugs."

"Both of them?" Kat said.

John nodded and then said to Dom, "You were right. The same guy made both Rapture and Zombie."

"It wasn't Dwayne," Dom said.

John looked at me and Kat. "He rents a place on Anza in the Outer Richmond. Paul said they found both drugs on the workbench in his garage. Along with source chemicals, surgical gloves with traces on the latex, a handheld pill press, chemistry shit, you know, beakers, whatever else . . . everything the guy needed to make the drugs."

"It wasn't him," Dom mumbled.

"Who else could it have been?" John asked Dom. Then he looked back at us. "The formulas were on his laptop. Lab notes. Results of his experiments. With animals first. Then your guy in Sacramento," he said, looking at Kat. "He had clippings of all the stories. Sacramento, Market Street, the shootout on Ocean Avenue, the warehouses on Custer. He made the drugs in his garage, probably after doing the genetic sequencing at Ceres. It's him. He fits the profile."

"Why don't you think he did it?" Kat asked Dom.

He stared at her for a long moment, trying to gather his thoughts. "I've known Dwayne for fifteen years since he was a grad student. This wouldn't have . . . he wouldn't have done this. I know him. He has a pure scientific mind."

"What does that mean?" she said.

"He does science because he wants to know the answers."

"And someone like that can't kill?"

"No. I mean, they could, but not Dwayne. He's . . . not a murderer. He wouldn't do this."

"I've met murderers who seemed thoughtful and kind. Loving parents who beat and abused their children. Sweet teenage girls who killed a classmate because they didn't like her."

"Parents who do that are not loving," Dom responded.

"They appear to be," Kat said. "That's the point. You don't know what people are capable of in their worst moments. Psychopaths are tricksters. They can be charming, like Ted Bundy, or upstanding people in their church, like the BTK killer. He was president of his Lutheran church council. Appearances can be deceiving."

"Does he have a family?" I asked.

"Karmagen lives alone," John said.

"His wife left him," Dom said.

"Why?" I wondered aloud.

Dom shook his head.

"How long ago?" I asked.

Again, Dom shook his head. "Four, no, five years."

"The evidence is on his home computer," John said. "No one else has access to it. The chemicals are in his garage."

"I can't explain it," Dom said. "I just know it wasn't him."

"What about the Cosplay stuff? His costume?" I said to John.

"They found a hooded cloak in his closet. Dark gray."

Like the one he wore to Arachne's party, I thought. "What about a scarlet cloak?" I asked John. "With some kind of trim?"

He shrugged.

"Major bought one like that at Haight Cosplay."

"If it was Major who bought it. You can't confirm that." When John saw that I wasn't content with that response, he added, "If they found that one, I haven't heard."

"It's early stages," Kat said, referring to the investigation. "There'll be a lot more discovery. He might have a storage unit somewhere. Can I get you something to drink?" she asked Dom.

He shook his head, but she brought him a glass of water. He thanked her, took a long drink, then set the glass on the table and held it in both hands.

"Were his prints on the lab equipment in his garage?" Kat asked John.

"Forensics is there now, dusting everything. But he would have worn surgical gloves when he worked, so they might not find usable prints."

"What does Karmagen say?"

"What you'd expect," John told her. "That he didn't do it. He's being set up. Doesn't know anything about the drugs."

"You were there?" I said to John.

He nodded. "Paul called me after breakfast. I was at Ceres for the arrest. After he was taken away, Dom insisted he couldn't have done it and wanted to talk to us."

"It isn't him," Dom said. But I sensed some hesitation this time, conviction draining from his voice like a slow leak as the idea that Karmagen might be guilty burrowed into his mind.

"Nothing on his work computer?" I asked John.

"Not that I'm aware of. But I don't think he would have risked that."

I asked Dom if Karmagen could have done genome sequencing at Ceres without anyone knowing. He reluctantly agreed that it could be done. The lab has good controls and monitors all work progress, but Karmagen is the assistant lab director. He could have been running a sequencer under the guise of another experiment.

"He had the knowledge," Kat mused. "He had access to the equipment, and he fits the profile. He had a costume like the Cosplay character, but why would he do it?" Dom shook his head. "Was he pissed off at the world? Religious freak trying to bring on the Rapture, the End of Days?" Dom shook his head again. None of it made sense to him. "Political radical? An Anarchist?" Kat said.

Dom had no answers.

"Maybe you did it," I said to Dom.

He laughed softly. "I have everything to lose and nothing to gain," he said. "I'm too boring. And too old and too fat."

"I don't like this," Kat said.

We all looked at her.

After a moment, she said, "We walk into Ceres Biosciences to ask questions of the lab director, and days later, an anonymous tipster leads the police to the perp, who is the lab director's assistant? That's awfully convenient."

"Blind luck," John said. "Our visit was a tipping point. Karmagen knew we were closing in on him. He didn't want to act that quickly, but we forced his hand. So he goes to the gun swap on Ocean Avenue and feeds everyone the Zombie drug. Trying to cause as much chaos as he could. I think the tipster is someone in the illegal gun underground and knew Karmagen was there. He put it together and sent the anonymous tip."

"Did Karmagen have guns in his house?" I asked.

John said, "No. None found. But he might have them elsewhere."

"Or he's innocent," I said. "Are the police looking at anyone else?"

John shook his head.

"The real Raylan Major might not be associated with Ceres at all," I said. "But if we assume our visit caused the mad druggist to panic, then who else could it be? Dom's too old."

"And too fat," Dom said.

"We met a woman there. What was her name?"

"Japanese-American?" Dom said. I nodded. "That's Madison Sato. But I can't believe she could be involved."

"Maybe she has an accomplice," Kat said. "Married? Boyfriend?"

"It can't be Madison," Dom insisted, adding that she had a boyfriend, an Anglo, and a history graduate student at Cal Berkeley. Kat asked what he looked like, and Dom said, "Tall, regular build, long brown hair."

"We have to check him out," Kat said. "How many people work in the lab?"

"Uh, twenty-two, including me," Dom said.

"I'd like all their names," Kat told him. "Can you get me their personnel records?"

Dom shook his head. "Human Resources can't release them. Confidential. But I can tell you about everybody and give you a copy of our lab directory."

"Who else has access to your lab?"

Dom shook his head, a doubtful pout on his lips. "Some Ceres managers, but no one younger or with enough knowledge of biosciences. Plus the custodians, but they wouldn't know the science or how to operate the sequencers."

"What about that technician?" Dom gave me a blank look. "The guy working on the equipment when we were there. Short blond hair. Knew me from the newspapers."

"Oh, Chase. Chase Frye." Dom looked doubtful. "He's not the sharpest knife in the drawer, but he can fix anything. He wouldn't know the science. He maintains the equipment."

"Who does he work for?"

"We contract with a company. Antioch Scientific. They're in Alameda."

"Does Dwayne have any friends outside of work?" Kat asked Dom.

"I can check around," Dom said. "I'm not familiar with anyone, but other people might know."

"You've worked with him for fifteen years, Dom, but you don't seem to know much about him," I said.

Dom looked embarrassed by that. "We—my wife and I—socialized with him and Kim, his wife, but he kept to himself after she left."

Kat said, "We need names."

"Karmegan's guilty," John said. "The evidence is solid and points in only one direction."

Kat shrugged. "But digging around is good old-fashioned police work, and I'm good at it."

After John left, Kat sat at the dining room table with Dom and questioned him about everyone in the lab. We ordered Mediterranean takeout, and after lunch, I returned to my music room to practice while the two of them continued to work. I was going through the motions, letting my fingers remember the key sequences and musical patterns, songs I've played hundreds of times. You can get lazy as a musician and play familiar songs by rote, but it didn't feel like that to me. It felt like half my mind was rehearsing the music while the other half dwelled on the mystery of Dwayne Karmagen, a scientist whose brilliance, seduced by loneliness, could have led him into the darkness. After the atomic bomb was invented, Einstein said that our technology had exceeded our humanity. I wondered if the same had happened to this soft-spoken biochemist.

When I emerged from my sound cave hours later, Dom had taken an Uber back to Ceres. Kat sat at our dining room table, typing on her laptop. The waning light through the kitchen windows created a soft yellow glow on her hair, and I admired her for a long moment before she noticed me watching her.

"This is fun," she said. "I'm doing real police work again."

"Finding anything?"

"Maybe. No candidates screaming, 'It's me, it's me.' But I've found a few possibilities. Something interesting, though."

"What's that?"

"Dwayne Karmagen is a ballroom dancer."

"Fleet on his feet? I wouldn't have guessed that."

"I found him on LinkedIn. He lists ballroom dancing as a hobby. So I looked up the ballroom dancing schools in the City. He joined one after his wife left."

"Looking for single women?"

"Maybe he just enjoys dancing. Anyway, I called them and spoke to their dance instructor. He said Karmagen has been a regular for three years and is very good." She smiled at me. "Have you done any ballroom dancing?"

"Not my groove," I told her. "But if they discover that Johann Strauss wrote jazz compositions, I might take it up."

She laughed and looked back at her laptop. "When did you say Eric got the Rapture drug? It was at that party with the oversexed tapestry queen."

I had to recall what I'd learned from Arachne and then gave Kat the date of the party at her place.

"Well, then," she said. "Eric didn't get the drug from Karmagen at that party. Not on that date. You sure?"

"Positive, why?"

"Because he was at a ballroom dancing competition that night in San Jose. He and his partner took second place."

I sat down opposite her and folded my arms behind my head. "So Dwayne Karmagen is not the mad druggist."

"Probably not," she said. "Unless he has a co-conspirator."

"Unlikely. This guy works alone."

"How did Raylan Major's gray cloak wind up in Dwayne's closet?"

"That's an excellent question, detective."

Suspects

I don't like talking to reporters unless I'm asked about music or the band. They have a ravenous appetite for sound bites, and once one starts running with a story, others follow until it becomes a stampede. News of Dwayne Karmagen's arrest was breaking news on the Saturday evening television news. The story broke so quickly that it forced the Police Chief and District Attorney to hold a press conference late afternoon. They did an admirable job of fence-sitting: "... can confirm that a person of interest has been detained in an ongoing investigation ... does appear that a synthetic drug may have been involved in recent incidents of violence ... can't comment at this time; however, investigators are ... no, the individual in question has no previous criminal record that we have ... can't comment on any possible links with ... still under investigation ... can't speculate on ... will keep you informed as developments occur." And so on. It was 25 minutes of fog, misdirection, and bullshit. Still, Karmagen's name was out there whether or not authorities confirmed it, and reporters had asked questions about the drugs and chemical paraphernalia found in the suspect's garage.

Paul called me after the press conference and said that the People's Palace, San Francisco's City Hall, was incensed about the leaks, and he was warning everyone on the task force to avoid the press like they were a COVID cesspool. I told Paul that's my usual modus operandi. By late Saturday, CNN, Fox News, and scores of other local and national news channels were running with the story like they were competing in an Olympic sprint, and Karmagen's life was under the harsh, glaring spotlight of overheated media coverage. One outraged "man on the street" interviewed by the ABC affiliate said he was sorry the governor had a moratorium on the death penalty because no one deserved it more than Dwayne Karmagen.

In bed that night, I said, "If Karmagen's ass isn't already cooked, he'll be spit-roasted by the time he gets to trial."

She curled up against me and yawned. "I don't think he did it," she managed.

"Maybe another guy with long brown hair and a gray cloak bought Rapture and gave it to Eric at Arachne's party."

"Possible," she said. "But unlikely. The man at the party was Raylan Major."

"Karmagen wasn't at the party."

"Nope," she said. Moments later, she was snoring softly.

Kat was already at the dining table the following day when I limped into the kitchen, my knee still throbbing after I'd taken one oxy. She had her laptop open and stared at the screen. With one hand, she drummed her fingers on the table; with the other, she absently rubbed the outside of her left leg where she'd been shot.

I poured myself a coffee and said, "You're hardly limping anymore. Your leg still sore?"

"Umm." She didn't look up from the screen. "Just a little tender now. Marcie's an angel." Marcie was Kat's visiting nurse and had been here every morning since Kat came to stay.

"Did you get anything from your prepper connections?"

She glanced at me and shook her head. "Too many guys fit the profile description, and nobody had heard of Raylan Major." She looked back at her laptop. "I'm ruling out Madison Sato's boyfriend."

"He's an Eagle Scout?"

"Not exactly. His name is Liam Sivers. Grad student in modern European history. Is obsessed with Nazis. On Facebook, he describes himself as an expert on National Socialism in the 1920s. Published two papers on it."

"So he's a history buff. A lot of people are interested in World War II. Nothing suspicious about that."

"No, but his interest might be more than academic. I searched for him in newspaper files and found an article about a Neo-Nazi rally in Illinois last year. Sivers was there. Arrested for disturbing the peace after fighting with protesters trying to tear down a Nazi flag. And I found him on Craigslist, searching for World War II and Nazi collectibles. He had one arrest in Oakland this year. He approached an undercover cop who was posing as a drug dealer and tried to score some coke. Charges dismissed, but this guy's sketchy."

"Nothing in that picture says Rayland Major."

"Nope. Major is too careful. He wouldn't draw that much attention to himself, and Sivers doesn't know the science. He's not a player here."

"Sato?"

"I couldn't find anything incriminating on her. She has bad taste in men but otherwise looks clean."

"You want anything?" I said, nodding toward the kitchen. She shook her head. She scrolled through pages on her laptop as I poured milk into some granola and added blueberries. Kat was like a fox following a scent. She kept her nose to the ground and thrived by tracing a scent along a path toward her prey. When one scent dried up, she changed direction until she found a more promising scent. She was steadfast and relentless, and I admired her for that.

"Here's one guy we should look at," she said, turning the screen toward me as I sat beside her. The photo on her screen showed a young white man with neck-length brown hair. He had a sensual mouth but cruel eyes and unusually long earlobes. His overall affect was defiant, and I could sense a calculating intelligence in the image he projected.

"Who is he?"

"John Cameron-Smith," she said. "He's a lab tech at Ceres Biosciences. Slender, just under six feet. Single. Lives alone in an apartment in Oakland. Dom said he has a master's in biotechnology from USC and is skilled at using CRISPR."

"I don't remember seeing him when we went there."

"Dom said he keeps to himself. Steady worker who does good science but isn't much of a socializer."

"A loner who knows how to make drugs," I said. "I'm liking this guy more and more."

"Yeah, and he's an Army vet who served in Syria and Iraq. I checked his service record. He was awarded the Army's Distinguished Marksman Badge. I wondered if he was still shooting, so I called around and discovered that he belongs to the Richland Rod & Gun Club."

"He might have connections in the underground gun network."

"What I was thinking," she said. "He could be the guy on Ocean Avenue who fed Zombie to others at the guns swap."

I made a mental note to see if Caroline Kruzik, the woman I took down at the warehouse on Custer, could identify him. She was at the gun swap with her father and was now in police custody in the hospital. They wouldn't give me access to her, but John might be able to show her Cameron-Smith's photo.

I said, "We should also check out the equipment technician. Chase Frye."

"He's on my list."

"Anyone else at Ceres?"

She shook her head. "The others working there don't fit the demographic. They're black, Asian, women, or men too old to be Rayland Major."

"Husbands or boyfriends of the women?"

"Or partners of gay men? I haven't cast the net that wide yet, but I will."

I called John Sebastiani and reached him at police headquarters, where he was observing the interrogation of Dwayne Karmagen. I put him on speakerphone, and we told him about Cameron-Smith.

"You're wasting your time," John said. "Investigators found six vials of liquid Zombie in Karmagen's garage, all with his fingerprints. There's no question that it's him. Sorry, Han. You're solo on this one. You and Princess Leia. I have to get back."

"May the Force be with us," I replied.

After the call, we made a salad for lunch, and I poured two glasses of a nice Argentine Malbec. "If Karmagen's not guilty," I said as we ate, "then he's being framed by someone at Ceres who knows him and knows he fits the profile."

"Someone with access to his house. And knows how to hack computers."

"Or knows his password. Maybe Arachne's wrong about the date of the party."

"She's not a reliable witness," Kat said. I smiled and gave her a "no shit" look.

But she decided to keep digging. She had unanswered questions about Cameron-Smith and couldn't close that door until she was satisfied he couldn't be the psychopathic chemist. Whoever created Zombie and Rapture did not do it at Ceres. The risk of exposure was too great, so he would have a lab elsewhere. She was troubled, too, because nothing in Cameron-Smith's profile indicated that he was involved in Cosplay or saw himself as a wizard. While she worked, I retreated to my music room and took out my sax. I ran through all the songs in our repertoire again, feeding on the energy of our hunt and soothing my misgivings about Karmagen's arrest with the comforting rhythms of the blues. When you've played an instrument as long as I have, you can play it without thinking. You let your fingers run in Western music's well-rehearsed patterns and harmonics and feel the sounds unfolding in familiar and occasionally surprising ways.

While I played, I saw Cameron-Smith's image in my mind and wondered what rivers of innocence or malice ran behind those eyes.

My lips were numb when I emerged hours later. Kat was pacing in the main room, crossing back and forth along the smoke-smudged windows, peering through them to the street below, the buildings across, and San Francisco's skyline visible from our top-floor perch. The air was black from wildfires to the north, whipped into a frenzy by 80-mph winds. She stopped pacing when she saw me watching, her lips pursed in thought.

"You discovered something else about Cameron-Smith?" I asked.

"No. I decided to spend time on Chase Frye but couldn't find anything about him earlier than 2015. He got a California driver's license that year, but I've searched tax records, arrest records, utility bills, newspaper articles, and county assessor offices within a hundred miles. He's worked for Antioch Scientific since 2016. Married a woman named Linda Welch in 2019, and they bought a home in Alameda that year. He pays his utility bills on time, has a good credit rating, and has no arrests or warrants."

I asked her how she managed all that research on a Sunday, and she held up her badge. Being a police detective opens a lot of doors.

"What about social media?" I asked her.

"Nada. I couldn't find him on any of the social media sites."

"Where's he from?"

"Unknown. It looks like he parachuted into California in 2015. I can't find anything on him earlier than that."

"Parents? Family?"

She shook her head.

"How old is he?"

"Thirty-five, according to his driver's license."

"Education?"

She threw up her hands. "As far as I can tell, there are no records of a Chase Frye fitting our guy's description who graduated from the California university system, but he might have gone to a private college. I googled 'Chase Frye' and found plenty around the country, but none match this guy in the Bay Area in California."

"Okay. Don't spend any more time on him. Maybe he moved here from another country, and that's why you can't trace him back any farther. Maybe he changed his name. I'll ask my hacker friend to dive deeper on the Net."

I was referring to Bai Tuo Rong, a fellow Aikido black belt who practices in the same dojo I do. Bai is a high school senior and one of the most brilliant computer geeks I know. He's helped me before, and I was reasonably sure I could reach him on a Sunday afternoon. I called him on his cell, told him what I was working on, and asked him to do a deep search on Frye. I told him what we knew, and he said he could get back to me by tomorrow, maybe sooner.

We ate that night at the Fog Harbor Fish House on Pier 39. It's a little touristy, but most patrons were locals like us in late October. I had seared scallops and crab risotto, and Kat ordered linguine and clams. The food was delicious, and we enjoyed it with a bottle of Frog's Leap Sauvignon Blanc. We walked on the pier afterward. The air was thick with the sea's salty aroma, overlaid by the smell of burnt wood. We thought of going home to a cozy, warm bed, but I received a call from John Sebastiani as we returned to my car. He asked me to meet him at his place in half an hour.

I asked if it was about Dwayne Karmagen, and he answered, "Something else." So I dropped Kat at the condo and headed to John's. He met me on the street and handed me the keys to a black suburban. "You're driving," he said.

Earl Zepeda and Sana Houssian sat in the back seat. Sana had a black revolver in his lap, long-barreled with a swollen tip, a silencer. Both he and Earl wore dark gloves. I nodded to Sana, who tipped his head slightly. Then I said, "*Hombre*," to Earl as a greeting. He looked solemn in the faint light cast by a nearby streetlight.

"*Oy, compa*," he replied. *Hey, partner*.

"Where we going?" I asked John as he slid into the passenger seat.

"South San Francisco," he said. "Avalon Park."

I aimed the suburban in that direction and we rode silently through the city's streets. I didn't need to ask what the mission was. As an unnecessary confirmation, John said, "The Azeri who got away in Fort Mason? Earl followed him to an address near the park."

South San Francisco is adjacent to San Francisco International Airport. It's a city of industry, a bedroom community for commuters to San Francisco, and a hub of biotech research, including giant Genentech. The city has a rich ethnic mix, including Asians, Latinos, and Middle Easterners, an easy place for interlopers to escape notice, and with access via land, sea, or air, it's convenient for those who wish to come and go invisibly. I wasn't surprised that the Azeri hit team had chosen this place for its base.

I took the 101 down the east side of the peninsula, crossing over San Francisco Bay. The sky was overcast, clouds and smoke obscuring the half-moon. Wind buffeted the car, rocking us as we drove silently south. When the clouds parted, crystals shimmered on the dark surface of the sea, but I was alone with my thoughts and took only passing notice. John navigated as we turned into the dark heart of the city. Low buildings and trees lined the downtown streets, and the cars approaching us streamed by like boats on a Disney World water ride. What this place lacked in San Francisco's urban sophistication, it made up for in small-town charm. But secrets are everywhere—at the sharp edges of light between buildings, in the shadows of trees, and in the darkened windows of closed stores. It grew murkier and indistinct as we reached Avalon Park.

John directed me onto the dark street of a neighborhood bordering the park and told me to slow down as we passed rows of medium-priced, cookie-cutter homes with their clapboard siding and frameless windows. We could have been anywhere in suburban America where ordinary lives were cocooned in the sanctity of family homes. But in this suburban sanctuary, we were seeking killers, and my compadres would be dispensing frontier justice to them.

We passed the house in question—a green-and-white two-story structure with a double garage and a fenced backyard. Two garbage containers stood in front of one garage door, and neatly trimmed shrubs softened the outline of a stairway leading to the front door.

I pulled to the curb on the opposite side of the street and turned to Earl. *"¿Estás segura de que esta casa es la correcta?"* Are you sure this house is the right one?

"Aparcó en ese garaje, compa. Sí, es el correcto." He parked in that garage, partner. Yes, it's the right one.

"No Podemos equivocarnos." We can't make a mistake.

"Te preocupas como una anciana." You worry like an old woman.

We sat for fifteen minutes, watching the quiet street and scanning the houses. Two cars passed us as we waited, late-night residents returning home. One kept going. Another pulled into a driveway half a block up. We waited until the darkness and silence swallowed us. The target house had one light on, somewhere toward the back, maybe in the kitchen or den.

"This is a rental, John?"

He nodded. "I checked. Stay here. Be ready to peel out of here if the shit hits the fan." Then they opened the doors and left the car. Earl and Sana moved swiftly to the gate and disappeared into the backyard. John crossed the street, scanning for people on the sidewalks, and then crept up the steps toward the front door. He stood still beside the door, deep in the shadows, but I could see his form like a ghost in the darkness. I saw a man walking a dog up the street, but he was walking away from us. Lights shown in the windows of maybe half the houses along this street; the others lay in darkness.

Nothing happened for fifteen or twenty minutes. Then the front door slowly opened, and I saw John slip inside. They hadn't shared their plan with me, but Earl and Sana had breached the house from the backyard. I heard no sounds from inside but hadn't expected to. I glanced at my watch. It was 10:42. John emerged from the front door twenty minutes later and crossed the street. He opened the passenger door and slid inside. He was holding a bulk of something in his hand. I asked him what it was.

"Passports," he said, holding them up. I guessed he held a half dozen. They weren't the dark blue of U.S. passports, and I didn't recognize the cover design. He also held a thick wad of cash, American bills.

"Two men inside," he said. "The wiry guy from Fort Mason, the one with a bandage on his neck. And an older guy, fifties, balding, gray sidewalls, the spotter behind BiblioTech. He was their team leader."

"That's a shitload of money," I said.

"They won't need it."

Then I saw Earl and Sana edging through the gate to the backyard. They slowly crossed the street and got in the back. Sana was as chill as usual. Nothing fazed him. Earl sat looking out the window, his face as dispassionate as a lion's after a successful hunt.

"If Kat asks, you weren't here," John said as we drove back toward the 101 on our return to San Francisco.

"I just had a nice drive on a quiet evening," I replied. "You going to call Ari?"

"When I get home," he said, smiling. "He and I need to catch up."

As we passed the San Francisco city limits, we came to a dark street where a crowd of homeless were warming their hands over a fire set in a trash barrel.

"Pull over here," John said. "Let's play Secret Santa at an early Christmas." I eased to the curb and saw a row of scraggly faces lit by the yellow glow of the fire. They looked uncertainly at the shiny black suburban as John turned and handed the cash to Earl and Sana. Those two opened their doors and stepped out. They approached the dozen or so denizens of the streets gathered by the trash barrel and began handing out the cash. Then John left the car and dropped the collection of passports into the fire.

When he returned to the car, he said, "A group in Baku ordered the hit."

"Baku?"

"The capital of Azerbaijan. We know who they are and will send them a message."

"Is this the end of it?" I asked.

He raised his hands as if to say, "Who knows?" Then he said, "That part of the world has a history of vendettas. They're long on memory and short on forgiveness."

"They'd say the same of us."

"There is that," John said.

When Earl and Sana returned to the car, an enthusiastic crowd on the street waved goodbye, and I drove back to John's place.

Before returning to my car, I told John, "The police may have the wrong guy."

"And I may be the next Pope."

"Well, Your Holiness," I said, laughing, "we'll keep investigating until the College of Cardinals sends up white smoke. Kat found a mystery man who didn't exist before 2015."

He shrugged. "Mysteries abound, my son. But Karmagen did it. I watched him during the interrogation, and the evidence is unequivocal. He did it."

Dark Ain't Deep Enough

I told Kat the truth. If not all of it.

That I'd driven John and two associates to South San Francisco, that they'd gone looking for the rest of the Azeri hit team, that they'd found them, that I didn't know what happened after that, but that John had returned with the money, and they'd given it to a group of homeless people when we returned to the city.

She was savvy enough to realize that the guardrails of justice exist to protect the innocent and that bad actors use every advantage to escape culpability for their crimes. I reminded her that three men were killed when the Azeris tried to ambush Ari behind BiblioTech and that our law-and-order institutions would never have made the people responsible for those murders accountable in the halls of justice.

If I see someone being harmed, am I a better person for calling the police or for stepping in and preventing further harm? Which is the greater good? Following the rules or following your conscience? Aiding a wounded person who may be dying or calling for an ambulance and waiting for it to arrive? Preventing further harm by stopping evildoers or trusting authorities to stop them when you know the authorities are powerless to act?

You can't be a vigilante, she argued. Vigilantes make mistakes.

So does the law, I responded. How many innocent people have been executed for crimes they didn't commit? Or been imprisoned based on false testimony or prosecutorial misconduct? We all must exercise due care and behave responsibly toward others. I could easily have killed that woman I subdued in the warehouse. I could have shot her or killed her with one blow. I have the skills to do so.

But you didn't, she said. Because you're a good man.

We let it go at that. She was still wrestling with the need to step outside the law but acknowledged that even good, honest cops sometimes do it. Her fidelity to her duty as a police officer would be tested sooner than she thought.

She was surly when I left on Monday morning, less at me, I think, than the moral conundrum I represented. Mine is a world nuanced in shades of gray, and I understood the challenge for someone who prefers the blacks and whites of things. As I drove off to meet with my fellow band members, she was firing up her laptop and returning to the comfort of investigative police work, a role she knew well. I could see the determination on her face and let her be. However, as I turned toward the recording studio, I wondered what journey she would take before I returned. Picking at a sore can make it fester, but we must be true to ourselves wherever that path takes us. I can hope our worlds converge, but I can't make it so.

Studio manager Samantha DeGregoris greeted me inside the foyer with a hug and a sloppy kiss on my cheek. She is old enough to be my mother and often acts like it. I smiled into her luxurious green eyes and kissed her cheek. I asked her what was happening that day. She gave me the lineup and said we were in Studio A this morning, but we had to be finished by one o'clock when Sunset Syndicate, a rock band from Palo Alto, would be in Studio A laying down tracks for their third album.

We didn't need much time today, but I hurried upstairs. Garth was setting up his drums when I entered the studio, his long, mangy, black hair tied back in a ponytail, his trademark blue bandana covering his forehead. We gave each other a fist bump, and then I took out my sax and put it together. The X-Man sat on a stool in one corner, thumbing a riff on his bass. Le'Andra stood beside him, the lovely, soft tones on her face alive as she mouthed the words to a song on a sheet of paper she held in her left hand. She gave me a quick smile and then returned to the music. K.C. Vaughn joined us a few minutes later. He looked like he'd slept in the brown linen suit he wore. You won't find him on the cover of GQ, but he plays the keyboard like it's an extension of his soul.

We warmed up individually, and then Xavier handed out the set list for tomorrow night's gig. It was as familiar as your favorite blanket, but one song jumped out. I hadn't seen it before.

"Is a new one," Xavier said. "Le'Andra wrote it last night. She's callin' it 'Dark Ain't Deep Enough'." He gave us sheets with the lyrics and said, "We're gonna' put music to it. I think y'all gonna love it."

With that, Le'Andra sang the first two stanzas a cappella:

You can't hide from me, baby,
Can't slip my mind.
You ain't find no cover, honey,
After bein' unkind.

You won't see me comin', uh-uh.
Ain't nowhere to go.
Dark ain't deep enough, darlin'.
You can't slip me, no.

Her song was a throwback to the classic blues of Muddy Waters and Albert King, and I immediately loved it. She sang it in a husky voice full of more anger and pain than I'd heard from her before, a new dimension of Le'Andra unfolding before us. She could hear the music in her head. We couldn't, but the melody and tempo immediately suggested musical possibilities. Before I realized he was playing, Xavier backed her voice with his bass. Then Garth was rolling with his snare drum and cymbals, and K.C. was feeling out the chords. She repeated the first two stanzas, and they experimented with the music. She sang the next two stanzas with accompaniment:

Seen both sides of you, baby,
Seen that sleight of hand.
Heard all your lies, tellin'
'Bout a promised land.

Said you'd always love me
From your head down to your toe
Dark ain't deep enough, darlin'
You can't slip me, no.

When Le'Andra finished the fourth stanza, she nodded at me and said, "Now there's an instrumental bridge." She was singing in the key of C, so I opened with a throaty C7 riff that reflected the seething fury I heard in her lyrics. I played with a counterpoint to her melody, not completely happy with where I took it, but I heard ways to improve. When I finished, she sang the last two full stanzas and the coda:

Caught you double-crossin'
Sliding into the night.
Sayin' you're sorry, honey,
Don't make nothing right

Someday soon goan' find you.
It don't matter where you go.
Dark ain't deep enough, darlin'
You can't slip me, no.

No, you can't slip me, no.
Can't slip me, no.
Can't slip me, no.

We worked through it again, everyone feeling their way until it sounded right, and when I'd played variations on the bridge four or five more times, it felt smooth as polished marble and matched the tone and nuance of Le'Andra's voice. Then we mapped out an instrumental intro and outro. Two hours had passed when we finished, but we felt we'd nailed it. We asked the recording engineer to lay it down for us, so we played it again, deep in the groove of this number. Afterward, I noticed that Sammy had slipped into the studio and listened to us.

"That one's going to be a hit," she announced, her arms folded, a smile lifting her cheeks. There's no rush more enduring than collaborating on a new creation. Most of the credit goes to Le'Andra, but the band gave life to her idea and expressed it fully. Even K.C. was impressed.

I checked my cell when I returned to my car. Bai Tuo Rong had left a message to call him before 1:15 when he had another class. I had only a few minutes but was eager to hear what he learned, so I called. "You have time to talk now?" I asked.

"Few minutes, yeah."

I could hear street noise behind his voice. He was walking to class. "Anything on the guy?"

"No, man, dude's a ghost."

How do you find a ghost?

"There must be something on him," I said. "He's thirty-five years old."

"Maybe he changed his name, yeah? No Chase Frye before 2015."

"Other states?"

"Sure, sure. Other guys named Chase Frye. High school wrestler in Oklahoma, guidance counselor, Maine; truck driver, Michigan; lawyer dude in Nevada. Plenty of Chase Fryes, but no dudes like your guy. Not that age. Not here."

"What about the dark web? Did you check it?"

"Yeah, yeah. I tried Haystak, Candle, Torch, Ahmia. Even Duck Duck Go."

I had no idea what those were. His world, not mine. "Nothing?"

"Like I said, dude's a ghost. He changed his name. Trust me."

"Did you access any federal databases?"

"Not to admit on the phone, man. Dunno who's listening, yeah?"

"Gotcha. No Chase Frye's anywhere like the one we're looking for."

"Dude's a fiction."

His words resonated as I sat in my car. *We're all fictions*, I thought, even *to ourselves*. From the moment you start figuring out the world—realize you're an entity in it—you're constantly imagining the person you think you are. You're making choices that create and reinforce a self-image—who you are, who your family is, what rung on the ladder they inhabit, where you live, what you do, who you choose as friends, how you fit in your community, how you dress, who you admire, what interests you, how you present yourself, and who you choose as your Cosplay character if you're into that. It's all about defining yourself, creating the fictional you, the person you pretend to be, the person you want others to believe, and your place in this life.

Susan Smotherman's fiction is a sexpot named Arachne, who dresses in black underwear, weaves beautiful tapestries, and uses horoscope readings to shape her world with predictable fantasies. Le'Andra Kimani's birth name was Williams. She changed it as part of her story, a black woman whose core grew from extended family roots with a Kenyan surname. She's crafting her self-image through an emotional caldron called the blues, where she can express her pain, dislocation, and longing through a socially acceptable medium. And Raylan Major, whoever he really is, imagining himself as a powerful wizard, a god controlling others through magic potions. Behind the fiction of Wraithlan Mager of the *Nekromanti Saga* is a real man named Dwayne Karmagen, Chase Frye, John Cameron-Smith, or some monster we haven't identified yet.

How do you find a ghost? You discover who he was before he became a ghost. You search for the corporeal person behind the phantom. In other words, you do solid investigative work, which Kat was doing now.

I called her, not sure if she was still sitting under a storm cloud of moral complexity, but she sounded fine, like her old self. I told her what I'd learned from Bai—more what I hadn't learned. She said she'd been investigating Cameron-Smith but would turn her attention to Frye. She suggested I call Dom Bernardi to see if he could tell us more about these two men. *Good idea*, I thought. I reached Dom through his assistant at Ceres Biosciences. When he picked up the call, I suggested we meet somewhere for a quick lunch. He recommended a café near the Berkeley campus. Afternoon classes had started, so the place wasn't full. We sat outside under the shade of a large, sun-dappled box elder, a cool breeze raising goosebumps on my arms. After we ordered, I told him we were interested in learning more about two men who worked in the lab.

"What can you tell me about Chase Frye?" I said.

Dom sat back in his chair and laced his fingers over an ample belly. His eyes flew up and to the right as he was thinking. "Chase has been servicing our equipment for, I don't know, I'd have to look, maybe four years. A little more," he responded.

"Your impressions of him?"

"Oh, uh, capable, average, down-to-earth, I suppose. Friendly. He loves to talk if you give him the chance, but he can rattle on about trivia. He's a tinkerer. Can repair anything. The kind of person with practical smarts, but I don't think he's had much higher education. I don't know about his schooling, but that's my impression. He's reliable. I can tell you that. Always on time. Does good work."

"What about his past? Where's he from?"

Dom slowly shook his head. His chins followed a half-step behind. "I never asked."

"We can't find any record of him before 2015."

He gave me a blank look and said, "I wouldn't know. When our previous equipment tech left, the company sent Chase. He was qualified, and he's done a good job for us."

"Okay, what about John Cameron-Smith?"

Dom took a long drink of iced tea while he thought about it. "John is smart and diligent, a good researcher, skilled with DNA sequencers and CRISPR. He prefers to work alone. He wants to return to grad school for a doctorate. He won't be content to stay where he is. He's ambitious. Why are you asking about him? He wouldn't have created those drugs."

"Someone did, Dom, someone we think must be connected with Ceres Biosciences. You're convinced that Dwayne Karmagen couldn't have done it, so we're exploring the idea that Karmagen was framed. If that happened, the bad actor is someone in your lab."

"I know everyone in our lab."

"Sure, and you don't think any of them could have done it. But if Karmagen is innocent, someone framed him, someone who knows how to make Rapture and Zombie, someone who knew he'd make a good suspect, someone who knows the password on his home computer or is a damned good hacker. You know anyone like that?"

He said he didn't. I knew he wouldn't accept that anyone in his lab could be guilty, so I tried a different tack. This started on a Saturday when Bob Duggins went berserk and shot up a flea market in Sacramento. I asked Dom if he knew where Frye was on that date. He raised his hands and gave me an exasperated, "How would I know that?"

"Fair enough," I said. "What about Cameron-Smith?"

"We don't keep track of people on their days off. How could I possibly—no, wait." His eyes shifted, and he went somewhere inside. After a long moment, he snapped his fingers and pointed at me. "He wasn't in town. Is that important? He and Janna Langhorn, she's a biochemist in our lab, were at a genome engineering conference in Toronto. They presented a paper."

"You're sure?" He was. He called his lab and double-checked. Bob Duggins was given a dose of a fast-acting neurological agent that led him to commit mass murder, and Cameron-Smith couldn't have laced Duggins' coffee with Zombie. He was in Canada when it happened.

On my way back to San Francisco, I called Kat and told her what I'd learned about Cameron-Smith. "How soon will you be here?" she responded. I said I'd be there in 25 minutes if traffic wasn't bad. "I have something interesting to show you," she said.

When I opened the door to our condo 22 minutes later, Kat was at her computer. She looked up at me with a broad grin of self-satisfaction and then turned the laptop so I could see the screen. It showed a photo of a young man with long, wavy blond hair. He had a blond brush mustache and a short goatee, wore a blue casual shirt with a Henley collar, and had a look of smug self-confidence.

"Who's this?" I said.

"A guy you mentioned, someone you met at Ceres, maybe with shorter hair."

I sat down and looked closer at the image, finally recognizing the long, narrow face and eyes that looked amused. "Chase Frye," I said. "Younger. The long hair changes the shape of his face. Where did you find him?"

"There are only three ways to change your name legally," she said. "Marriage, divorce, or court order. I searched online for records of someone who changed his name to Chase Frye."

"You can find that on the Internet?"

"Sure. There are federal and state records of legally changed names. Tax and social security records, for one. I discovered that a social security number was issued to Chase Frye of Alameda, California, in 2014. That number was based on a birth certificate for Chase Edward Frye, who was born in Cheyenne, Wyoming, 35 years ago."

"And died in childbirth?" I guessed.

"Eighteen days later. Heart defect."

"So our guy calling himself Chase Frye somehow got the birth certificate."

She nodded. "Probably on his way to California."

"From where?" I stared at his photo again. He looked much younger, possibly in his late teens or early twenties.

She turned the laptop back toward her and clicked that photo away. A newspaper front page replaced it, although I could not see it clearly from my angle. Kat looked back at me.

"What if Rapture and Zombie weren't his first attempt to create a designer drug?"

"He's done it before?"

She nodded. "I wondered about that. I couldn't think of any other way to trace him. The Wyoming birth certificate was a dead end. So I searched the NCIC for previous deaths related to designer drugs. Their database is incomplete, but I got a hit 12 years ago in Boston."

"Frye would have been 23 then."

"Right. Two Harvard students died of complications from an unknown hallucinogenic drug the coroner couldn't identify." She nodded at the screen. "This is the article about the incident from the Boston Globe. The police identified a person of interest, a Harvard PhD candidate in bioinformatics."

"What the hell is that?" I asked.

"It's using computers to analyze biological data. It's a field related to genetics."

"DNA."

"Yep. I contacted The Globe, but they wouldn't release more information on the suspect. However, a sympathetic person in the Harvard Admissions Office was kind enough to email me his photo. When I told her what we were investigating, she was happy to help." She tapped a key on her laptop, and Frye's photo returned.

"So he's Raylan Major."

"We can't prove that yet, but I'm 99 percent sure. He's likely created designer drugs before. He killed two people, then had to flee Boston before finishing his doctorate."

I stared at the photo again. "Is he wanted on a fugitive warrant?"

"No. He was wanted for questioning, but the case has gone cold. He vanished before they could bring him in."

"What's his real name?"

"Arend Magnus Larsen," she replied.

"I think you just found our ghost."

Breaking and Entering

Every song tells a story, whether written in words or the aural language of music.

Le'Andra's new song arose from outrage at a lover's betrayal and told the story of her desire for vengeance. *You can't hide from me, baby,* she wrote. *You won't see me comin, uh-uh. Ain't nowhere to go. Dark ain't deep enough, darlin'. You can't slip me, no.* When I compose music, I begin with a feeling, a mood, an attitude—a note, the *right* note, which blossoms into a musical phrase that begins to tell the story. Sometimes, the key suggests itself; sometimes, I search for it. One phrase leads to another, in counterpoint or harmony, following an expected path or branching in directions that resolve tension or complicate it. When I finish, I have a song that tells an emotional story in the tones and timbres of the saxophone. It may evoke the despair of addiction, a sultry whisper between lovers, or the heartbeat of the city during a summer rain.

I thought about that as I watched Kat work through the afternoon building the story of Arend Magnus Larsen. His student visa application told her he was born in Odense, Denmark, on May 17, thirty-five years ago. His parents were Bente Frederiksen and Christoffer Larsen. He has a BS in biotechnology from the University of Copenhagen and an MSc in biotechnology from the Technical University of Denmark. His transcripts tell the story of a brilliant student with "an unusual aptitude for chemistry" and an "exceptional grasp of technology, particularly computer science."

"Dom Bernardi thinks Frye couldn't find America on a world map," I remarked.

Kat shrugged. "What did Rhoda say about psychopaths?"

"They're deceivers. Good liars, skilled at manipulating others. They know how to adapt so they fit in."

"I think Frye's been projecting the image of himself he wants Dom and others at Ceres to believe."

I leaned back in my chair, laced my fingers behind my head, and thought about Larsen's dilemma. "What if I couldn't play the saxophone?" I mused. "What if I committed murder and had to change my identity, move somewhere far away, work at something that wasn't my dream, and never play music? I'd be miserable."

"You're wrong about him," she laughed. "He is living his dream. He's hiding in plain sight, using advanced technology to create mind-altering drugs. The FDA might not approve them, but you think that's important to a guy who dresses up as an evil wizard?"

I shook my head. "We still have to prove it."

She pored over her laptop, scrolling as she read, and then said, "Omigod, look at this." She pointed at her screen and turned it toward me. The screen showed an almost comical image of an old man with close-set eyes, a bulbous nose, and a long, white beard that seemed to encircle his head. He was bald on top, but wisps of white hair rose from the sides of his head to two little tufts that stood straight up on his crown.

"Who am I looking at?" I asked her.

"Aksel Larsen, a Danish writer of science fiction and fantasy novels. Died in 2021 of COVID. He wrote the five volumes of the *Nekromanti Saga*."

"The books featuring Wraithlan Mager."

"Yep. I found a blurb about him, a short biography. Aksel had three sons, one named Christoffer, who had a son named Arend Magnus."

"So Chase Frye is Aksel Larsen's grandson."

"Probably. There may be more Christoffer Larsen's in Denmark, but it's a hell of a coincidence if Frye didn't fancy himself a character in his grandfather's books."

"See what else you can find. I'm going to call John."

Sebastiani was at his office, and I asked him to stop by when he left work. An hour later, he knocked on the door with a bottle of Krug Grande Cuvée Brut, and we sat at the dining room table with three glasses of champagne. I asked John what we were celebrating.

"Good news," he said. "I got a call from Jerry Kennedy this afternoon."

I was about to ask who he was when Kat said, with a slight tremor, "The president of St. Ignacius." I couldn't tell if she was glad to hear the name. She looked anxious.

John nodded. "My old buddy from priesthood days. I called him last week about Sara. They haven't reviewed all the applications yet, but he read hers and said she'll be admitted."

Kat's brow was scrunched up. "I didn't think we'd know for several months."

"They won't, not officially, Kat, but you know how these things work. Jerry will make sure she gets in."

Kat sat back in her chair. She closed her eyes and covered her mouth with one hand. When she opened her eyes, she wiped away tears and said, "You're sure, John?"

"Done deal," he replied.

"She will be so happy," Kat said.

"You can't tell her. Not yet. Wait for the official notification."

She nodded. "Thank you, John."

He smiled at her, and we raised our glasses in a toast to Sara. I caught Kat's eye while we drank. We had some serious conversations ahead of us in the privacy of our lives. For now, we wanted to talk to John about Arend Larsen. Kat summarized what she'd learned about him. She showed him the clippings from The Boston Globe and his transcripts from the universities he'd attended. I think she laid out the case well.

When she finished, John said, "He'd make a terrific Contestant Number 2, but he's not the drugmaker we've been looking for. The police have that guy already." Kat raised her hands to protest, but John cut her off. "Look. No one had access to Karmagen's home computer except him, which was password protected."

"Frye's a computer expert," I said.

"So are a million other people in this country," John said. "There was no evidence of a break-in. And the guy's garage. It was an unholy mess. Let me paint you the picture. Two walls of shelving covered with dust. Old paint cans, power tools, bins of nails and screws, cardboard boxes full of every kind of stuff—magazines, clothing, dental records. Can't you imagine that? Old dental records! Cleaning supplies ten years old, wadded-up dust rags, wasp spray, plastic garbage cans filled with stuff he probably meant to give to charity, and every other damned thing. Canned goods that expired years ago. It didn't look like Karmagen ever went in there except for the back wall, where he had set up a workbench—the only clean thing in the garage. Everything he'd need was on it for home CRISPR experiments and mixing chemicals. We had an expert from UC Berkeley look at it. He confirmed that Karmagen's home lab was sophisticated enough to produce the drugs we found there—Rapture and Zombie. They were in small vials about three inches long with black caps. He had enough doses for a hundred more attacks."

"His fingerprints were on the vials?" I asked. "And you found the source chemicals?"

John nodded. "Along with a used pill press. The works."

"Where did he park his car?" Kat asked.

"On the street. He couldn't have gotten it into the garage."

"So his whole garage was a dusty, dirty mess except for that one area?" Kat said.

"That's right."

"What about the rest of his house? Was it a dusty, dirty mess?" she said.

John shook his head.

"He lives alone," she said, "and his house is clean? Sounds like he takes care of it. Maybe the garage was a mess because he doesn't use it and hadn't been in it for years." John didn't respond, but he regarded her thoughtfully.

"I have one more thing to share," she said. "I was curious about his new name, so I googled variations of Chase, Frye, Larsen, Arend, and Magnus, and I found a book by Rick Riordan called *Magnus Chase and the Gods of Asgard*. It's a fantasy trilogy. The hero is Magnus Chase, the son of a Norse god named Frey, the god of summer. His mother was a mortal woman named Natalie Chase."

John and I were both speechless momentarily.

"The first book in that trilogy was published in 2015," she added.

"When Larsen got a California driver's license in the name of Chase Frye," I said.

"And Magnus Chase grew up in Boston, where Larsen went to grad school," Kat said. "Don't say this is all coincidence."

I patted John on the back and said, "You can't pile too many coincidences on top of each other before they collapse of their consistency."

John drained the last of his champagne, set his glass on the table, and said, "He's worth a look."

An hour and a half later, we were parked in John's black Suburban on a tree-lined residential street in Alameda. The city sits on an archipelago in the East Bay, south of Oakland. Frye's house was a gray bungalow with a wide veranda and red-trimmed windows. A tall sycamore along the curb blocked much of our view of the house, but we saw lights inside. John called the number listed in the directory, and a woman answered. He asked if she was interested in a subscription to the *East Bay Times*, and she said they already took it.

We'd asked Earl to come with us. He sat in the back seat with Kat. He wore black jeans, a black T-shirt, and a black leather jacket. He was reading something on his cell phone, and Kat advised him to put it away because the light shone on his face, and we were trying to be stealthy. She was anxious because we hadn't discussed what we might do. She'd been on many stakeouts, but the police knew why they were staking out someone's house, and they were looking for. She wasn't comfortable with the ambiguity of our non-mission. We just wanted to see where Frye lived, I explained. People's homes can tell you a lot about them.

When it became dark enough, Earl left the car and walked past the house. A long driveway beside the house led to a matching garage in the back. When he returned, he said a blue Toyota Camry was parked in front of the garage. The neighborhood was a mishmash of single-family homes and apartment buildings, crisscrossed with power lines, the street lined with blue plastic trash containers. Lights were on in every house, and we could hear the faint sound of mariachi music from one of the homes. Earl hummed along with the music, something I'd never heard him do.

"*¿Conoces esta canción?*" I asked him. *Do you know this song?*

"*No. He escuchado canciones como esta. Me gusta el ritmo,*" he said. *No. I've heard songs like it. I like the rhythm.*

We sat there for another half hour, debating whether to stay or go. We hadn't learned anything except that Frye lived in a modest, non-descript house on a quiet street in a typical, medium-sized California town. People passing on the sidewalk beside us ignored us. Then, at 8:15, the lights in Frye's front room went out, followed by the lights toward the back of the house. Minutes later, we saw the blue Camry backing down the driveway. The car backed into the street and turned in our direction. As the car passed us, we slid down in our seats, but John got a quick look.

"Two silhouettes," he said. He turned to Kat. "They have kids?"

"Not that I'm aware of."

He paused, looking at me and Earl. "Let's go."

"Go where?" said Kat.

"Inside."

"You're going to break into his house?"

"We won't break anything."

"Very funny. That's breaking and entering, John. I can't be part of this," she said.

"You won't be," he replied. "You're staying in the car."

"We'll be quick," I assured her. The three of us quickly crossed the street. John walked to the front door and rang the doorbell while Earl and I ran down the driveway to the back. No one appeared to notice us, but I thought we had only five or ten minutes inside.

Wherever Frye and his wife went, they might not be away long. Earl and I pulled on dark gloves and waited by the backdoor.

"*¿Qué buscamos?*" Earl said. *What are we looking for?*

"Equipo de fabricación de medicamentos, productos químicos, un laboratorio." *Drug-making equipment, chemicals, a laboratory.* "Creemos que está fabricando drogas ilegales." *We think he's making illegal drugs.* "Busca también armas," I added. *Look for guns, too.*

John opened the back door a moment later. "Nobody home," he said. We crept inside, and I turned on my cell phone light. We were in a small mudroom behind the kitchen.

"Front door was unlocked?" I said.

John shook his head. "I picked it. There's a basement. I'll check it out. You two split up."

Basements are unusual in older California homes, which might explain why Frye chose to buy this house. If he's making drugs here, that's likely where he's doing it. I said to Earl, "*Busca en la cocina. Iré al frente.*" *Look in the kitchen. I'll go to the front.*

The room in the front of the house was a modest living room—a sofa, two easy chairs, a flat-screen TV mounted on a wall, end tables with lamps and coasters, magazines displayed on a coffee table (*People, Better Homes & Gardens, allrecipes*), and a partially completed jigsaw puzzle on a portable table—the usual stuff. A sideboard along one wall displayed family photos: Frye and his wife at the beach, them standing beneath a giant redwood, them at dinner somewhere; then more of her—with an older couple (her parents?), smiling with another woman (sister?), her as a kid with a dog. No photos of him looked older than 10 years.

While I was searching, my cell phone rang. Kat said she could see intermittent lights behind the living room window curtains. I cupped one hand over the cell phone light to keep it lower and crept into the main bedroom. This room looked like a thousand other main bedrooms in Middle America—bed with a floral rose-colored comforter, dresser, a closet crowded with her clothing, a smaller closet with his, a cedar chest (full of sweaters, pillows, and folded blankets), end tables and lamps, paperbacks with dog-eared pages, shoes lined up against a wall. Then a door to a bathroom. I checked all the drawers in the bedroom and the medicine cabinet in the bathroom. I saw nothing unusual beyond everyday over-the-counter products and a few prescription bottles. When I left the bathroom, Earl passed me, heading into what I thought must be a guest bedroom. He said, "*Ordenador*," as he went by, canting his head toward a room he'd just left. I heard noises from the kitchen, and John entered the dark hallway.

"Earl found a computer in here," I said as I walked through a doorway into a den. John came in behind me. We found a large desk with an equipment rack on one side. A screen that looked three feet wide sat next to a desktop computer. The equipment rack held additional computer gear—what, I'm not sure—but this was more sophisticated than the laptops in most homes.

"We don't have time to get into that," John said. "But take a picture."

I took a half dozen shots of Frye's computer setup with my cell phone and said, "Anything in the basement?"

He shook his head. "Furnace, water heater, ducting, washer, dryer, some boxes filled with crap. No guns. No drugs. No chemicals. If he's making that shit, he's not doing it down there."

"We need to check the garage."

"On our way out," he said. We returned to the hallway, and Earl appeared in the doorway to the guest bedroom. "*Víspera de Todos los Santos*," he said.

"What'd he say?" John asked.

"He said, '*All Hallows Eve*'. Halloween."

We followed Earl back into the bedroom. A single bed was snug against the far wall, stuff piled on it. I guess they didn't have many visitors. A large white vanity sat against another wall, with mirrors behind it and lights on the perimeter. It was the kind of vanity I've seen in green rooms where actors and musicians prepare to go onstage. Earl shined his cell phone light on the wall beside me and John, and we turned to look. Taped to the wall were two poster-size photos of Frye and his wife, each dressed as their Cosplay characters. They looked like souvenirs you'd get in a photo booth at a convention. Frye was dressed in a long black cloak, his long brown hair covered by a hood. He held a long medieval sword in one hand and carried a crystal orb in the other. "Wraithlan Mager" was written across the bottom in bold print. Beneath that, in smaller print, it said, "World Cosplay Convention, Las Vegas, 2023."

His wife's poster showed her in a snow-white wig with white-and-green braids, large pointy ears, and heavy eye makeup. She wore a flowing white, green, and gold robe with sleek golden gloves and boots. Her character was labeled "Crymania." On the vanity were two mannequin heads. One displayed her wig—the prosthetic pointy ears beside it—and the other displayed his, a long-haired brown wig.

"These two like to play dress-up," I said.

"*Están locos*," Earl said. *They are crazy.*

John stared at the posters for a long moment. Then he said, "Well, fuck me. I'm going to check the garage. We need to get out of here. I'll meet you at the car."

I took photos of their Cosplay posters and the vanity while Earl searched the room for evidence of guns or drugs. He found nothing, but the closet revealed his and her cloaks, robes, and other costume accessories. On the "his" side of the closet, we discovered black and dark gray hooded cloaks and a scarlet cloak with elaborate trim on the sleeves and neck. I guessed this was the Jacquard trim the clerk in the costume shop mentioned.

I took pictures of the costumes, and then we walked quickly to the back door. I scanned the room as Earl went outside and saw two large olive-drab backpacks leaning against one wall. I hadn't seen them before because they were nearly hidden by hanging jackets and coats. I knelt quickly beside them and examined them in the cell phone light. One had a large hunting knife strapped on one side and a canteen strapped on the other. I unzipped the second backpack and found an Army first-aid kit, a folded camp stove, freeze-dried food packets, folded clothing, and other camping gear. I zipped it back up and hurried to the back door, worried about the time.

Earl stood in the yard, waiting. We heard John close a side door to the garage. He ran past us and said he hadn't found anything unusual in there. He and Earl ran to the street while I ensured the back door was closed and locked. Then I walked quickly up the driveway and paused by the front of the house. I didn't see anyone on the sidewalks on either side of the street, so I walked to the curb and began crossing. As I did, a car turned the corner at the nearest intersection and caught me in its headlights. I played it cool, crossed the street, walked past the suburban, and went up the block.

John pulled over at the next intersection, and I hopped into the passenger seat. He said, "It was a blue car, but it didn't pull into Frye's driveway."

"It probably wasn't them," I said.

Kat asked what we found inside, and I pulled up the Cosplay photos on my phone and handed it back to her. "It's him," she said. "It's got to be him. But you didn't find the drugs?"

"No," John said. "The place is clean."

"It would be," Kat said. "Unless his wife is in on it, he wouldn't risk her dusting a room and finding contraband. He's making the drugs somewhere else."

"If it's him, he did a damned good job of framing Karmagen. The prosecutor indicted Karmagen today. You'll see it on the news tomorrow."

"I found something unusual as I was leaving," I said. I told them about discovering the stuffed backpacks in the mudroom.

"I'll bet those were Go Bags," Kat said.

Earl understood her, but he said to me, *"¿Qué es una bolsa 'Go'"? What is a Go bag?*

I explained to him in Spanish that Go bags are sometimes called 'Bug-out bags,' and they're put together by people who want to be able to leave home quickly in a natural disaster or emergency.

Kat looked at me and Earl and said, "Can I ask you two something? Why do you always speak to each other in Spanish?"

Earl looked at her quizzically, and I laughed. "Habit," I said. "We just normally do. I don't know why. It's Earl's native language. Maybe that's why."

I looked at Earl and said, *"Hombre. ¿Por qué nos hablamos en español?" Why do we speak to each other in Spanish.*

"Porque somos hermanos," he replied.

"Because we are brothers," I interpreted for her.

Kat gave me one of her loopy grins. I think she learned something about Earl and me that she didn't know before. Looking thoughtfully out the window as John drove, she said, "Who keeps Go bags in their house?"

"Preppers," John said. "Survivalists."

Zombie

The following day, Kat sat at the dining room table, printing the photos I'd taken at Frye's house and organizing them and other papers in Manila folders.

"What are you doing?" I asked.

"Putting the evidence together in a case file. It's not admissible, and I don't know how I'd explain where I got it, but I need to document what we've found."

I grabbed some coffee and sat opposite her. One of the photos she printed was a headshot of Frye as Wraithlan Mager cropped from my photo of his poster. He looked at the camera, proud of his transformation into a powerful wizard as the convention photographer snapped his picture.

"You're going to the orthopedic surgeon this morning," Kat said

"Yeah."

She smiled at me. "Good. I'm eager to hear what they say." She wore gray slacks and a dark brown women's bomber jacket with a sheepskin collar. Her hair flowed over her head like liquid gold.

"You're looking pretty good today, hotshot? What are you up to?" I asked.

"Police work," she said, putting the headshot of Frye in an outside pocket of the jacket. "I will show Arachne and Jaycee Washington this photo to see if they recognize him. Then I'll hitch a ride to Sacramento and pick up my car."

My heart stopped. "You're going to thumb your way to your house?"

She laughed. "One of John's guys is going to drive me. I know you can't. Besides, I need a car here. I'm up and around now. I need wheels. While I'm in Sacramento, I'll show the photo to my prepper contacts and see if they recognize him."

"Did our breaking into Frye's house last night bother you?"

"Not as much as I thought," she admitted. "What bothers me more is that all we have is circumstantial evidence that Larsen/Frye is guilty. All we can prove is that he enjoys Cosplay and works in the same lab as the man charged with the crime."

"He may have killed those two students at Harvard."

"*May* have. We can't prove it."

"He pretends to be less intelligent than he is."

"That's no crime."

I nodded. "We're in that liminal space between suspicion and certainty." For centuries, people thought the Earth was flat, which shows that you can be dead wrong while being dead sure. "We showed up at Ceres asking questions. He knows we're getting closer. Maybe he'll stop. There'll be no more incidents, and we'll never catch him."

She shook her head sadly. "No. He might move on, but he won't stop. He is what he is. Even the smartest addicts can't stop shooting up."

"Some addicts do go straight."

"Not this guy. I'm getting a feel for him. He's enjoying this too much."

I met the orthopedic surgeon at an Ortho center on California Street. His office had me do an X-ray and an MRI before I saw him. He poked and prodded, looked at the diagnostic test results, and recommended a total knee replacement. He said a new knee joint might last 20 years or more, if I'm lucky, but I'd probably have to do it again later in life, although they're constantly improving artificial knee joints. Maybe I'd have to do it only once. We spent the last few minutes in his office talking about the 49ers. He'd done surgeries on some of their players' knees and said he was confident he could repair my knee so I'd have no more pain. That marginally reassured me. I've lived with pain so long it feels like a permanent part of my life.

We were playing that night at The Fillmore, one of San Francisco's classic music venues. Located at the intersection of Geary Boulevard and Fillmore Street, the building is in a busy residential and commercial district with limited parking, so I took an Uber to it. I met Garth in The Balcony for a drink before we went to the green room to prepare for the performance. The Fillmore is a Victorian extravaganza with a coffered ceiling, lush curtains, heavy furniture, and crystal chandeliers—all infused with a deep color palette of red, gold, and violet. Before urban renewal dressed it up, The Fillmore was the funkier center of the psychedelic music scene in the Sixties, with performances by Jefferson Airplane, Jimi Hendrix, Janis Joplin, and The Grateful Dead. In the era before that, the Fillmore hosted Duke Ellington, Ella Fitzgerald, Billie Holiday, Charlie Parker, Miles Davis, Count Basie, and John Coltrane—among other African American blues and jazz icons. So you can imagine how great it was for us, the Storm Lake Blues Band, to perform in this venue. It was like going to Mass at Notre Dame or The Vatican. You can't pay homage any better than that. This was a sacred space; we were the latest high priests to step up to the altar.

We gathered in the green room backstage—Xavier, tuning his bass; K.C., mellow with a Sapphire gin and tonic, his eyes closed, playing an air keyboard as he imagined one riff or another; Le'Andra, limbering her voice and fingers, cradling her Fender Telecaster with long, slender fingers; Garth, thumping his drumsticks on his thighs; and me, soaking my reed in my mouth and loosening the keys on my saxophone while I mentally rehearsed my opening solo.

When we walked onstage, we were greeted by an enthusiastic crowd on the standing-room-only ballroom floor and others seated along the sides or balconies. It was a cool evening just before Halloween, and many of the revelers wore costumes, masks, and garish hair colors and makeup. In short, it was a typical crowd of San Franciscans on a night out on the town. We opened with "Killing Time," a fast-and-furious 20-minute song with a pounding beat and multiple solos from the keyboards, bass, guitar, and sax. The room was rocking when Garth finished with a thunderous snare and cymbal flourish. Then Le'Andra stepped up to the mike, and we played her latest, "Dark Ain't Deep Enough." Slow, sultry, and simmering, she had the crowd hooked when we moved on to one of our latest songs on *Storm Damage*.

When we took our first break, I had sweat running down my temples and into my eyes. I needed an ice-cold glass of club soda with a slice of lime to calm my throat, but Xavier gathered us on the stage before I could leave. He said he was reading the crowd's mood, and he thought we ought to cut some slower soul numbers in our second set and replace them with more West Coast bluesy tunes—a melding of blues and rock—and we settled on three songs from our repertoire. He scribbled them on his setlist and said he would call the next one when we finished a song so we didn't have to remember the revised setlist. That worked for me.

As I was about to leave the stage, a server stepped up to the edge of it and held out a glass to me. I knelt and accepted a glass of sparkling water filled with ice and a lime wedge. "The bartender said you like Perrier and lime," she said. She had a dimpled smile and beautiful teeth, and I thanked her for the drink. I took a sip and was approached by a pair of twenty-something guys who asked me to autograph a CD of *Storm Warning*, our first album. They were followed by a small crowd of others who wanted autographs. I was happy to sign the CDs, but Garth hit his snare drum before I could take a real break, and I had to return for our second set.

We started with "Hang Time," a song from *Storm Warning*. When we finished it, Xavier called for "River Crossing," one of the substitute songs we'd selected at the first break. I was mildly irritated that he'd chosen that song but joined in after Le'Andra played the intro. In the middle of that song, I had more sweat running into my eyes, and I wiped them with a rag I kept on stage to keep my sax dry. My eyes stung after I wiped them, and I felt my head aching behind my forehead. The song felt lurchy to me as we played it—as if the tempo had slowed and sped up again. I glanced at Garth as if to say, "What the hell are you doing?" He saw me and scrunched his eyebrows like he didn't understand my meaning. *How could he not get it*, I thought, but when I looked at the others, they didn't seem to care that he was screwing up the song.

Before the next number, I wiped my face again. The room felt like a sauna, and my clothes were soaked. I looked out at a sea of faces and didn't see enthusiastic smiles; I saw leers. Some people gloated at how bad we were playing, and I felt like jumping off the stage bashing them. The ungrateful bastards didn't realize how hard it was to play perfectly night after night. Okay, we don't play every night, but that doesn't matter. It's hard to be a professional when your audience is hostile, like nothing you can do is right. You're on the stage to entertain them; all they can do is criticize and act like you have no right to be there. *Fuck it*, I thought. *Why am I doing this?*

The band started playing the next song, and it clanged around in my head like a fire engine run amok. Jarring and discordant and way too fucking loud. I stared at Xavier, who attacked the bass strings with his eyes shut, a stupid smile on his lips. K.C. banged on the keyboards with fingers that looked like sausages. Christ, I thought, why is that clumsy bastard here? It grew worse—the noise, the chatter, the endless screeching of some woman's voice, drumbeats like cannon fire, and that cymbal cutting through me like a percussive sword, splashing and crashing in a deafening, jarring assault on my ears. When I could no longer tolerate it, I spun around and blew a high-pitched note on my sax that I hoped would shut them up. I blew it again as they gaped at me, startled and confused, and I kept blowing it—one long, high screech—and they careened to a stop, instruments falling silent, and I heard murmurs from behind me, and I screamed, "Shut the fuck up!"

Xavier put down his bass and started for me. Before he reached me, I threw down my saxophone and ran at him, fists swinging. Le'Andra backed away, her guitar held in front of her like a shield, her face agape in terror. When Xavier and I connected, he wrapped his arms around me, and I pummeled his back and then felt my legs knocked out from under me when someone else tackled me. I lay on the stage, struggling with them as another man, a heavy son of a bitch, fell on my back.

"What the fuck?" I heard Garth scream, and Xavier yelled, "Call 9-1-1."

The crowd noise became a roar, a godawful bellowing that assaulted my ears like a thundering herd of elephants. I flailed against my attackers, lashing out with fists and feet. Had they not pinned me down, I would have killed every fucking one of them. My mind was a blaze of anger and resentment and hatred. My eyes burned like hot coals. I felt more hands restraining me, a vicious crowd that pressed on me and tried to smother me. Spit flew from my mouth, and I lurched forward, trying to bite anyone within reach. Someone shoved a rag in my mouth, and I heard someone else say, "What the fuck's wrong with him?"

I fed on their confusion and tried to do as much damage as possible. Then I lay still for a moment, thinking I could trick them into releasing their grip, but they held tight longer than I had the patience for, and I relaunched my attack, trying to strike anything while a tangle of arms and hands like a fucking octopus held me down. A surge of hatred flooded my brain, a searing rush that pounded and pounded and pounded.

"Jesus Christ," someone said, panic in his voice.

"Fuckin' maniac," someone else said.

I struggled with my subduers, yelling at them to let me go, but they swarmed me, a heavy press of hands and bodies, someone holding my head to the stage, others crushing my legs. They pinned my arms down. After an eternity of confinement, my brain blistering with rage, I saw people parting in front of the stage.

"Something's wrong with him," someone cried. Three people in white uniforms rushed forward, followed by a handful of cops. They hovered over me and held me down while other people moved away and the white uniforms crowded in, and one of them started cutting off my jacket with scissors. I tried to bite her, and then another one shoved something hard and spongy into my mouth. I spit it out, but he pushed it back in.

"Keep your hands clear," I heard one of them cry.

The noise of the crowd was deafening. I couldn't keep it out of my ears. It bore into my brain like a power drill, an agonizing whine that tore my soul to shreds.

Someone wiped my arm with something cool and then jabbed me. I tried to rock away from them, but the pressure of so many arms kept me on the floor. Then, I felt myself slipping, my rage more general, the press of bodies around me evaporating, and I floated into darkness.

I woke with a stinging headache, blood pulsing in my head like a hammer striking concrete. I scrunched my eyes and tried to bite down on my tongue, but the hard rubber in my mouth kept my teeth from coming together.

"He's awake," someone said urgently.

I was lying on my back in a room so bright I couldn't keep my eyes open.

"Get Rhoda," someone else said, a woman, panic in her voice.

I tried to raise my arms, to seize the bitch and shut her up, but something held back my arms. I could raise them only a few inches before their tethers kept them from going farther. I yelled at them to keep their fucking hands off me, and blood surged to a point in the middle of my forehead, and I sank back, my head on fire.

Later, I think it must have been later, I'm not sure, but everything felt disconnected; I heard voices around me from somewhere at the edge of a dream. Fragments.

"—turn him over again—"

"—what's his tempera—"

"—Can you . . . hold him . . . still—no, there—yes—"

Then a voice closer, whispering: *"Vuelve, compa. Eres duro. Puedes luchar contra esto."*

A hand squeezing my shoulder. I wanted to kill the fucker and willed my hands to break free, but they were restrained.

"—convulsions? Is that what—"

"—Jesus Christ, keep him—"

"—heart racing—"

"—crashing. Can you help me—Marcie! Marcie!"

I saw movement around me, shapes resolving into men and women, hushed in shadows, lurking, and I knew they were trying to kill me. While my brain boiled, I thrashed my arms and began kicking my feet. One foot broke free, and I side-kicked at the nearest body. They started shouting and rushed at me, and my leg was wrestled back, people holding it down, and they wrapped something around my ankle, and I couldn't kick anymore. I could only shake and try to break free.

"Vuelve, compa. Eres duro. Puedes luchar contra esto," the voice whispered again. A man's voice, soft, insistent. I understood him this time: *Come back, partner. You're tough. You can fight this.*

'"—more Haldol—"

"can't draw blood while—"

"—cardiac arrest—"

The room spun slowly. I was floating in a giant whirlpool in a lake of fire. I spun as the room spun, down and down, into circles of hell I'd never imagined, the fire consuming me without destroying my flesh, spits of flame scorching my eyes. I wanted to kill them all—those who had imprisoned me and kept hovering.

Later, I think, the voices returned from somewhere at the edge of a dream.

--they're sure it was Zombie—"

"—They think it—"

"–lab tested—"

"—glass on the stage, full of the—"

"—who?—"

"—dunno. Didn't see any—"

"—the server, said she—"

"—What else—"

"—metabolic panel to see—"

"—couldn't have been him, Paul, he's—"

"—unknown. We've never seen this"—

"—electrolytes normal—"

"—rule out sodium—"

"—too early—"

That voice again: *"Vuelve, compa. Vuelve."*

Then I saw a golden angel hovering over me, a wet white cloth wiping my brow, kissing my forehead, which burned like a kiln. I wanted to bite her throat out, but something was blocking my mouth, and I was too exhausted to try.

Later, I think, from somewhere far away, I drifted, felt something pressing the crook of my left elbow, something sharp, and a warmth spread throughout my arm, and I felt myself leaving the red-hot cinders behind, the glow fading, drifting in a fog, until blackness eclipsed the room, and I was left with a pinpoint of awareness until it, too, was lost.

In Hell

I lay in a tomb. Cold. Inert.

I couldn't feel my limbs. Couldn't feel anything. I lay in a blackness so profound I couldn't remember what light looked like.

I might have been in the center of a black hole. A consciousness without substance. Disembodied. Alone. I might linger here for eternity, contemplating the isolation and sadness. I had no point of reference, only this awful black surrounding me as though suspended in nothingness. I didn't know how long I'd been here, wherever "here" was. Worse, I didn't know if there had ever been anywhere else. I had no memories of a past—only memories of fire.

An interminable amount of time passed when I had no thoughts. Then I felt a tingling. It was outside myself, giving me hope that something else existed. The tingling persisted. From tingling to pressure. And warmth.

Then someone whispered, *"Vuelve a nosotros, hermano."* I realized I was thinking in English. I don't know how I knew that, but I also understood that what he said was not English. He said: *Come back to us, brother.*

He? I could not imagine what or who the "he" might be. But there was an "other." I wasn't alone.

"Compa," he said. *Partner.*

My eyes opened. I was in a dimly lit room. In a cocoon of white with silver bars on both sides. My eyes swam through a thick fog. I wanted to close them again and sink back into the gloom.

"Compa," he repeated.

A face appeared above me. A man. Young. Black hair. Thick black eyebrows and brown eyes. A handsome face but a fierceness behind those eyes. He looked familiar.

He turned away and called, "Katrina!"

After a moment, a golden-haired woman rushed in. She had a beautiful face and a broad smile that nearly bisected it. "Thank God," she said. "You're awake!" The smile vanished, and she scrunched her forehead and clenched her eyes. "I thought I was going to lose you. Are you okay? Can you hear me?"

Am I okay? I don't know where I am, much less if I'm okay.

"I don't know," I managed through a thick tongue. *But I know her*, I thought, and memories rushed back like a river plunging over a waterfall, an overwhelming kaleidoscope of thoughts, images, and emotions. Kat.

"He's awake!" she yelled to someone I couldn't see. Another woman walked in and stood on the other side of me. I turned my head to her. She was older and had neat black and silver hair. She wore a white lab coat over a blue shirt, and I recognized her. My neighbor, Rhoda. *What is she doing here?*

I turned back to Kat and had a rush of feelings so intense that tears formed in my eyes and coursed down my cheeks. I wanted to hold her, but my hands wouldn't move. I looked down and realized that they were tied to the bed railings. A boxy device was attached to my right index finger, and I could feel something in my nostrils.

"We had to restrain you," Rhoda said. "You were violent."

Another woman walked up, a black woman with a pleasant face. "You keep that shit up," she said. "I'm gonna whup yo' ass." Marcie Bell. The nurse. *Marcie. They called to her in my dream.*

The young man joined them. Earl. "*Has vuelto, compa,*" he said. *You came back, partner.*

"*¿Dónde estaba?*" *Where was I?*

"*En el infierno.*" *In hell.* "*Llamaré padre,*" he said, walking away. *I will call father.* He meant John, and I remembered John. Then, I recalled intense heat. And rage, an awful rage.

"You gonna behave if I cut you loose?" Marcie said. She stood at the silver railing at my left hand and shook one finger at me. "Cause if you don't . . ." she said as she began untying my hand.

"Just his left," Rhoda warned. She pressed something onto my chest. It was plugged into her ears. A stethoscope. She's a doctor.

"Where are we?" I asked Kat.

"A hospital," Kat said. "UCSF Medical Center. They brought you here after the incident at the club."

We were playing, I remembered. I was happy the band was playing at The Fillmore. Garth and I had a drink. It was a void after that.

My nose itched, and I tried to scratch it, but my left arm was too sore to lift to my face. My right arm was still tied to the bed railing. I flexed it, and it was painful. So were my legs, I realized, and my neck. I squirmed, testing my back; it was sore, too. Everything hurt. Kat held my left hand while Rhoda leaned over me.

"What the hell happened?" I said.

Rhoda said, "You were drugged. The Zombie drug. When they got you sedated enough to draw blood, the lab found it in your system. We've been hydrating you and using a catheter to flush your system. The good news is that the amount of Zombie in your blood has been decreasing. The labs from this morning show no trace of it. We think it's out of your system now. I'm going to ask you some questions."

She did, beginning with, "What's your name?" Where were you born? What year is it? What kind of car do you drive? And which film won the Academy Award for Best Picture in 1935? She's a comedian. When she finished asking questions, she shined a light in my eyes, waving it back and forth, and then clicked it off.

I looked from her to Kat. "Both of my girlfriends in one place," I said. "And you're not fighting over me."

Rhoda gave Kat a sour look. "He's fine," she said. Then she told Marcie to untie my right arm. She raised the back of the bed so I could sit more upright, and I saw that I had an IV attached to the crook of my left arm and I was getting oxygen through a nasal cannula. The boxy thing on my right hand measured my blood oxygen level.

"When can I get out of here?" I asked Rhoda.

"Not for a few days," she said. "Trust me, you won't feel like going anywhere until then. We need to make sure you're not going to start killing people."

"Only those who deserve it," I said.

"You may not want to joke about that with the other doctors. I'm not the only one making the decision."

"Gotcha."

"We need to keep you here for observation for a couple of days, and we'll want more blood work to make sure the Zombie drug is completely out of your system. You're the first person to survive this drug, so no one on the medical team knows what to expect. I'm sure you appreciate the need for caution."

I nodded and closed my eyes, thinking I would rest for a minute. When I woke up, the wall clock read 11:25. I'd slept most of the morning. Kat and Earl sat in chairs on the far side of the room. He was dozing while she worked on her laptop. Earl woke up when John Sebastiani walked through the door and joined him by my bed.

"I had no idea you were a drama queen," John said, smiling broadly.

"Anything for attention," I replied.

"You scared the hell out of your bandmates."

I suddenly recalled the look of terror on Le'Andra's face. I hoped she hadn't quit the band. And I hoped we'd be invited back to The Fillmore.

"I don't remember any of it."

"We found Zombie in the club soda they gave you after your first break. Thank God you hadn't drunk much of it," John said. "A stronger dose might have killed you."

"Where'd it come from?"

"The bartender said a guy asked what you normally drank and ordered it for you. Long brown hair and thick glasses with black frames but no cloak. He handed it to the server and asked her to take it to you at your break."

"Chase Frye."

"Probably. For sure, it wasn't Karmagen. Paul thinks Karmagen has an accomplice, but he's not convinced it's Frye."

"Has to be him.

"What I told him."

"He must have seen me crossing the street in front of his house."

"Yeah. The blue car we saw must have been his. I showed Frye's photo to the bartender and server. Both said it could have been him."

"Not positive?"

"The heavy glasses were enough to confuse them, I think. But they said the general shape of his face was right."

I tried to push myself up in bed and must have grimaced. It hurt to move.

"Hate to say it, partner, but you look like the wrong side of a bar fight."

"That's how I feel," I said, "Run over by a steamroller. I remember burning up and being filled with . . . anger. Not the right word. Worse than that. Rage against everything and everyone. I wanted to make it all stop."

"You damn near did."

"Did I hurt anyone?"

He shook his head. "They got to you quickly enough. Xavier and Garth pinned you down. K.C. sat on you. I'm surprised that didn't kill you. He's a big guy. Some men in the audience helped. It took three paramedics and five cops to restrain you and get you in the ambulance. You're lucky, partner. You lived through it, and so did everyone else."

"They put something in my mouth."

"A bite splint. To keep you from biting anyone."

"Este hombre que te envenenó. ¿Es él el que está en la casa que registramos?" Earl asked me. *This man who poisoned you. Is he the one in the house we searched?*

I nodded, and Earl said, *"Luego vamos a buscarlo." Then we go find him.*

I translated for John, and he said, "That may not be so easy. Frye's gone. I've had guys watching his house since Wednesday morning. No sign of him, and he hasn't shown up for work. His wife filed a missing person's report with the Alameda police yesterday."

"Él no está allí," I told Earl. *He's not there.*

"What about his wife?" I asked John.

"She's clueless. Or a good actor. I questioned her after she filed the report. I don't think she knows anything, but we're watching her. I had one of my guys tap her cell phone. So far, there's no indication that she's conspiring with Frye. I don't think she knows about the drugs. She didn't know that he used to be Arend Larsen."

"His car?"

"Still at their house. He might have had another vehicle stashed somewhere. One she didn't know about. We checked the DMV for other licenses and looked for rental garage receipts. Nada."

"He might have used Larsen or Mager to license another vehicle."

"We checked. Nothing by those names that fit. But he knows how to create aliases. He probably has others."

"He had a Go bag in his house."

"It's still there," John said. "But this guy's a survivor. He was prepared to run no matter what the circumstances were."

"He could have taken an Uber to the airport."

"Could have. The police aren't investigating. They think they have the right man. And my company has limited resources. We couldn't check the airports, bus stations, taxis, boats, and private car companies. All we know is that he vanished."

John had to return to work, but Earl stayed. I don't know if Ari told him to stay or if he stayed because he thought I might be in danger. He checked in on me occasionally but otherwise paced in the hall outside the room or sat quietly in the common waiting area down the hall. Kat said he spent time on his cell phone but mainly watched visitors and the hospital staff. He made the medical staff nervous, but she assured them that he would be harmless unless someone came to injure me. If that happened, they could expect theatrics. So, he's a bodyguard, they asked. Of the best kind, she told them. Then Ari and Catherine arrived, and Ari told them that Earl worked for him and was hired to protect me. If they had any questions, they could speak to the CEO of UCSF Health, one of Ari's friends.

Catherine came to my bedside while Ari spoke to Kat.

"I would hug you," I told Catherine, "but it hurts to lift my arms."

"Don't be silly," she said, bending over to kiss me. Catherine has lush red lips. Being kissed by her was like taking an express elevator to heaven.

"Ari told me," she said, giving me a look of sympathy that I wish I had a photo of. I would keep it in my wallet and stare at it whenever I felt down. "They must find the man who did this."

"We will," I assured her.

"I don't like to see you hurt."

"I do my best to avoid it."

But how do you avoid a bad actor slipping a lethal drug into your drink at a concert? Or anywhere else? Someone like Frye is careful and stealthy. He's one of hundreds of innocuous, average-looking people around us all the time. How do you protect yourself if one of them has evil intentions and you are in their sights—or are just randomly selected, like Bob Duggins and Fernanda Alamilla? Or if you receive an innocent-looking package from some psycho like the Unibomber? Or you're in the wrong place at the wrong time when a terrorist strikes? You can't. Life is a roll of dice. Some of us roll a seven, and some of us roll snake eyes. And there ain't no rhyme or reason to it.

Ari commiserated with me and said he'd be sure I had out-of-sight security until this thing was over. Later that night, my bandmates showed up. I thanked Xavier, Garth, and K.C. for holding me down until the cavalry arrived. I was concerned about Le'Andra's reaction, but she blew it off. She understood why it happened after John told the band about the Zombie drug. I wasn't as unfortunate as Eric. He got Rapture and died; I got Zombie and survived. They hugged me and said the Storm Lake Blues Band would be back as soon as I was healthy. The X-Man was confident that The Fillmore would rebook us when we were ready.

My parents arrived Saturday morning and brought Rachel (formerly Erin Hightower). Rachel was one of the children Kat and I rescued from a compound in New Mexico. My parents were now her foster parents. She was a student at Cal Tech, where my mom worked. I asked her if she was the most brilliant student at the university, and she said, "Of course." I didn't doubt it. She was as sharp as a new razor. While I talked to my parents, Rachel and Kat had a warm reunion. Kat had searched for Erin/Rachel for seven years, and their bond now could not have been stronger.

I forced myself out of bed as soon as I could manage and did my rehab and physical therapy. Kat walked with me often, but Earl and Marcie Bell attended to me while Kat was busy. I walked miles in the hospital corridors with Earl and Marcie until the pain subsided to a manageable level without drugs, including oxy.

The hospital released me on Sunday morning. On the ride home, I turned on my cell phone and saw that I had a text from Kat's daughter, Sara. Her mom had told her I was sick in the hospital, and she hoped that I was over whatever illness I had and was back to playing my saxophone. She also hoped to be admitted to St. Ignacius because she loved the school. I wrote that I was much better and was sure she'd get into the school. How could they not admit someone as smart and talented as she is?

Rhoda checked me over when we arrived home and pronounced me healthy, except for my fantasies about older women. Just one, I reminded her.

After she left, Kat said, "I have something to show you." She opened her laptop, and we sat at the dining room table. She brought up a Google Maps image of six buildings shown from overhead. They were arrayed in a rough circle and were connected by silver lines.

"What are those?" I said, pointing at the lines.

"Fences with concertina wire at the top."

"What are we looking at?"

"A private compound. It's in a forested area about a mile outside Ukiah." Ukiah is two hours north of San Francisco. She zoomed in on the image, and I saw a half-dozen cars and pickups, three off-road vehicles, picnic tables, a water tank, several garden plots, and other stuff, suggesting that many people occupied it.

"Arend Larsen had to flee Boston quickly," she said. "He became Chase Frye on his way to the West Coast. If I were him, I wouldn't want to be caught off-guard like that again. I'd be prepared."

"You think he's there?" I said, nodding toward the image.

She looked thoughtfully at the image. "I think it's possible. He can't stay in this area. He'll go to the Midwest or the South, Chicago, Miami, Dallas, somewhere else, and start again."

"Maybe another country."

"Maybe. But I don't think he left yet. I think he's staging his departure."

"Why do you think he's at that place?"

"This compound is called "Solace." My prepper contacts said it's a survivalist compound. Secretive. But within prepper circles, people know about it, although none I spoke to had been there. I checked county tax records and discovered that 'W. Mager' owns it."

"That could be where he's making Rapture and Zombie."

"We always thought the drug maker would be within driving distance of the Bay Area."

"Have you told anyone else?"

"If I had, they'd already be up there."

"What are you doing tomorrow?" I said.

"Police work," she replied. "You feeling up for a drive?"

"Wouldn't miss it. I'll call John and Earl. And see if Garth can take the day off."

"If we find Larsen, I will arrest him and gather evidence. Nothing more. Our posse needs to understand that."

"They will. But this is a survivalist nest. If Larsen has allies there, they'll be armed and suspicious."

Solace

When Kat and I arrived at John's place early the following day, John's black suburban was parked outside. Earl stood beside it wearing a heavy black leather jacket, the one he often wore when he was concealing. I knew he'd have a shoulder holster under each arm, a knife, and another handgun in his belt. John emerged from his garage carrying two black Pelican Vault long gun cases. He opened the rear hatch and began loading them.

Kat said, "We're not going into combat, John."

He smiled at her. "Not planning on it. But bad things happen to good people like us. If we find ourselves in combat, I'd rather have my hands full than empty. I'm a good Boy Scout. I stay prepared."

She rolled her eyes.

Garth roared up on his Harley a minute later. He was dressed in black leather from head to toe. His long black hair was pulled back in a ponytail, his forehead covered by a blue bandana tied beneath his ponytail. He'd be packing, too, although I couldn't see his armament. Kat explained to our motley crew that we were trying to find Arend Larsen, aka Chase Frye. If we found him, she would question him while John called in California State Troopers to arrest him. I told them what we knew about Frye and passed around Kat's photos of the compound.

"The place is gated," Garth said. "How we gonna get in?"

"We'll ask them politely," John said. "And if they're not obliging, I brought these." He reached into the suburban and pulled out a pair of 36-inch bolt cutters.

The sky to the north glowed with a red blush as we crossed the Golden Gate Bridge into Marin County. Roiling clouds of black and gray from new fires in the Mendocino

National Forest to the northeast tumbled over one another as they raced to the heavens. We met a steady stream of cars and trucks fleeing south as we approached Santa Rosa. John wondered aloud if this was such a good idea. We didn't know what lay ahead, and powerful east winds buffeted our car. He worried that with winds that strong, we could be overtaken by the fire before we reached Solace.

This part of California has low-rolling hills, oak savannas, redwood forests, and coastal prairies. It's a rural area of wine groves and other agriculture populated by people who worked hard, valued their independence, and distrusted authority. Years of drought had left the vegetation here hard and dry. Embers flung miles ahead of their fires could ignite the brush and trees with alarming rapidity. The firefighters' preferred "anchor and flank" tactic was useless when new fires could flare up unpredictably and far beyond current containment zones. We were driving into the heart of the beast, and once we passed Santa Rosa, there were few roads leading west to the coast and the safety of the ocean. Ukiah was in a north-south corridor. If trapped by the fire there, we could be in a race for our lives.

"You want to turn back?" I asked John.

He grinned at me and said, "No. What the hell? If Larsen went to Solace, he might have left already, but we won't know until we turn over every rock there. We're following a wild-ass lead into a firestorm, but I don't have any place better to be."

"That's the spirit," Kat said, but her bravado was shaken the farther north we drove. The sky ahead grew increasingly yellow, and traffic south began moving in fits and starts, frequently slowing to a standstill, then speeding up again when gaps opened between vehicles. We started to see cars and pickups loaded with household goods and distress on people's faces. I was reminded of the news images of distraught people during the fires in Los Angeles. They were grateful to be alive, but nothing feels hollower than losing everything.

A blanket of red and black hung over the yellow landscape. Then we could see the fire itself, yellow fingers licking up into the trees, consuming them like a beast driven mad by hunger, with angry red plumes fanning across the landscape, driven by a maniacal wind that formed vortexes of fire swirling skyward and disappearing when they separated from their burning hosts.

"Maybe we should turn around," Kat said.

"No time," John said. "We'll be okay. The road turns west just ahead."

By then, the smoke had formed a thick mantle hundreds of feet high. It glowed black and red, casting a red pall on everything beneath it. We passed a line of firetrucks parked alongside the road, their crews unloading hoses. A state trooper cautioned us about going farther, but John said we lived a short distance away and would be careful. The road turned west, as John said it would, but we hadn't gone more than a few hundred yards more when it turned east. We saw what looked like fireflies flitting across the road ahead—yellow dots flying straight across like tracers fired by a machine gun, and I realized those were sparks and glowing embers driven by the wind. John accelerated, and the suburban shot through the sparks like a rocket. The wind rocked the car, and we felt the heat of the fire through the trees and brush that would soon be consumed. Mercifully, the road veered west again, and we passed through with our lives intact but not our nerves. No one said anything, but we all felt providence had spared us the worst on our fools' errand to find the ghost.

A half-hour later, we neared Ukiah. Kat told us that Solace was on a dirt road a mile beyond the town. As we drove through Ukiah, we saw hundreds of vehicles parked on the streets, people loading supplies and goods for the evacuation north. The road out of Ukiah was clogged with cars escaping the calamity we'd just driven through. When we reached the turnoff, we turned west and stopped in a clearing. John opened the back, retrieved two AR-15s and full clips from the gun cases, and handed us water bottles. In the tension of our drive through hell, we'd forgotten to drink anything. The water felt like a divine gift.

Solace was another two miles up a narrow dirt road that wound up and around low hills. We were cocooned within thick walls of oaks, willows, and bay laurels. By now, we were many miles from the Mendocino fire, but if this area burned, there'd be no escape for us or the inhabitants of Solace. I changed my mind about Solace when we saw the compound. They had cleared a defensible space around it, a buffer where there was no fuel for the fire and no concealment for anyone attempting to cut through the chain link—so much for our bolt cutters. In front of each post in the fence, we saw sprinklers for fire suppression, and atop every other post was a surveillance camera. The thick chain-link fence around it was topped with concertina razor coils. The only entry to Solace was through a black vertical gate. Surprisingly, the gate was up.

John eased forward. When we arrived at the gate, we were met by one guy—tall, thin, about forty, wearing camouflage pants and a red plaid shirt. He was unarmed. They weren't expecting trouble.

"Are you the plumbers?" he asked when John rolled down his window.

Thinking quickly, John said, "Yeah, We got here as quick as we could."

He peered into the car and saw Kat. "Who's she?"

Kat said, "I'm his boss. Look, do you want our help or not? We've got five other jobs this afternoon. I brought a crew so we can do your job and move on."

"Yeah, okay, sorry. Did you see the fire?"

John said, "It's a ways south, but yeah, we saw it. Tell me the problem again."

"The water tank's leaking. It's a fitting under the tank. We tried tightening it but couldn't stop the leak. I'm glad you folks are here."

"We'll get her fixed. No problem. I'll just park over yonder," John said, pointing at the water tank.

"I'll meet you there," the guy said, and as we came through the gate, I turned and saw him push a button beside it, and the gate began closing.

John turned to Kat. "My boss?"

She smiled at him. "I had to make it credible, John. One look at you and people know you need supervision."

He laughed at that. Then Garth spoke up. "I look more like a plumber than the rest of you, and I've fixed my share of pipes and faucets. I'll get out."

"I'll go with you," John said. He turned to me and Earl. "You guys search."

The compound's interior was more extensive than it looked on Google Maps. Three of the six buildings looked like residences, single-story duplexes, ranch-style homes with gardens and fruit trees, bicycles leaning against garages, and children's toys in the yards. Another building seemed to be a combination mess hall and community center. Picnic tables were arrayed outside, with a sizeable half-barrel grill, trash barrels, and a composting site. A dozen people crowded around a radio on one picnic table, listening to a broadcast about the fire. Two other buildings were set off from the rest. One had trucks parked in front of it. It looked like it might serve as a warehouse or storage facility. One side had a dark green awning attached to the wall, and beneath that shelter were scores of olive-drab boxes stacked on each other—military surplus. I imagined we'd find canned and freeze-dried foods, weapons, ammunition, and other survival supplies inside that building. The building beside the warehouse was long and wide with no discernible purpose, probably the headquarters.

As we neared the water tank, which was perched on a heavy wood platform, John turned the suburban around so it was facing out. Then he and Garth got out and walked toward the platform, where they met the guy from the gate.

The guy looked at them and said, "Where are your tools?"

Garth said, "Let's see what the problem is first, 'kay?"

As they walked away, I said, "I doubt if Larsen is in the crowd by the picnic table or in one of the residences. Let's start with those two buildings back there. I pointed at the warehouse-type building and said to Earl, "*Busca en el almacén. Kat y yo iremos al edificio de al lado.*" *Look in the warehouse. Kat and I will go to the building next door.*

He nodded and slowly opened the door. Before he got out, I added, "*Si lo encuentras, tráenoslo.*" *If you find him, bring him to us.*

Kat and I eased out of the suburban. The guy with Garth and John was under the water tank, pointing at the fittings. Earl was ahead of us, walking toward the warehouse. No one seemed to notice him or us. The crowd on the radio was listening to the broadcast and talking to each other. A gaggle of children burst from one residence and spilled into the yard, but they didn't see us. Earl circled to the left of the green awning and disappeared behind the warehouse. We continued toward the other building, acting like we had every right to be there.

We arrived at the screen door in front of the building and opened it. Kat moved her hand to her waist and touched her handgun. I gave her a "here we go" look and opened the front door. There was a small office inside with two desks. A middle-aged woman wearing a green peasant dress sat at the desk on the left; the other desk was empty. She was busy with paperwork but looked up when we entered.

"Who are you?" she said, frowning.

"Plumbers," I replied. "For the water tank. We need to talk to him. Is he in?"

She gazed at us, concern etched deeply on her face. Then she began edging one hand toward the desk drawer.

Kat quickly drew her gun and pointed it at her. "Keep your hands on the desk."

"You're not plumbers," she said fearfully. "Who are you?"

"Extreme plumbers," Kat said.

I grinned at that and walked to the door behind the desks. I tried the knob, but the door was locked.

"The key?" I said to the woman. She held her hands up, looking warily from me to Kat, and pointed to the desk drawer before her. In the front was a set of keys on a ring. I tried several of them until one turned the knob.

I walked into a long, narrow room. No one was there. Weapons were displayed on the left wall—rifles, shotguns, Uzis, and exotic rifles I'd never seen before, along with an array of handguns. On the right side of the room was a counter filled with chemical apparatus, source chemicals in bins, a pill-making machine, and vials and bottles of drugs. At the end of the room was a large desk with a desktop computer —including a wide monitor and stacks of external drives, all connected by cables. On the wall behind the desk were banks of video monitors and another door. The monitors showed the scenes outside and around the perimeter of the compound. A large, hard-shell suitcase sat beside the desk. I was still surveying the room when the door at the back opened, and a man stepped through. He was tall and thin and had short blond hair. He reached for the suitcase and started to pick it up. Then he saw me.

Startled, he set down the suitcase. "You," he said, suddenly smiling. "I thought I'd have more time."

"Going somewhere?" I said.

"You're supposed to be dead," he said.

"Surprise!" I said as though greeting him at his surprise party.

"Hmmm. Zombie, as you call it, is not as potent as I wished. I'll have to work on that."

"It's potent enough. I didn't drink much."

"That's a shame. Swallowing the whole glass would have killed you. But you would have died spectacularly. I can see the headlines now."

"You're an evil son-of-a-bitch," I said.

He shrugged. "That's a stupid moral judgment. Good-bad, right-wrong, virtu-ous-evil. Pointless dichotomies. Only morons like you care."

"The law cares."

He laughed. "The law is a set of rules created by the weak to protect themselves from the strong."

"And you're the strong?"

He held out his arms as if to encompass the whole world. "I am a god," he said triumphantly. "I created potions that manipulate the weak to prey on each other. With Rapture, I created heaven; with Zombie, hell. Could you do the same? Could anyone besides me?"

He had the smug, self-satisfied grin of a serpent who knows his bite is lethal.

"I was surprised you chose Wraithlan Mager as your doppelganger. I would have thought you'd pick more powerful wizards like Voldemort or Merlin."

"You don't understand," he said, as though talking to a child. "I AM Wraithlan Mager. In the flesh. I am He. Transported by means you couldn't comprehend to a realm where I can use magic to herd fools in whatever direction I wish. I am a genius. I could create a potion to make you love someone, eat until you explode, or walk until you die of exhaustion. I can make people do whatever I want. If that's not a god, what is?"

"You're a lunatic."

He shrugged. "One man's lunatic is another's inspiration. I wouldn't expect you to understand."

"You've been a hard man to find."

"And you found me. Congratu-fucking-lations." He clapped his hands in faux applause. "It was time to move on anyway. I've done good work here, but now it's time to relocate."

"How did you frame Dwayne Karmagen?"

He laughed. "Another moron. He hasn't changed his password in years and uses the same one at home as at the lab. Picking his locks and planting evidence in his home was child's play. Even you could have done it."

"His fingerprints on the vials of drugs in his garage?"

"Empty vials from Ceres. I took them from his desk. The moron didn't even miss them." He inclined his head toward the suitcase beside his desk. "I was expecting to have another day before I disappeared. I'm almost packed, but what I can't take now, I can replicate later."

"You think you're leaving?"

"Oh, I am leaving. I'm going to disappear in the fire."

"Did you set the fire?"

"Oh, no, I'm no arsonist. The fire was a happy coincidence."

"There's a cop outside waiting to arrest you."

"The woman who came with you? She won't live long enough to do that, and you can't stop me. Did you think Zombie was only in liquid form? I can make it as a pill or an aerosol. Whatever pleases me."

It was enough of a hint to make me paranoid. I glanced to each side, looking for devices that could spray the drug. Maybe breathing by itself could re-infect me.

"Ah," he said, looking smug. "You're worried. You should be. Soon—sooner than you think—you and your friends will face dozens of maniacs, all of whom will be armed. I regret that I won't be here to witness the bloodbath."

I must have scrunched my brow. He saw that I was perplexed and held up a small black device. "When I saw your car at the gate, I pushed a button on this remote. It opened a valve that added Zombie to Solace's water supply."

"You poisoned your own people? You are a fucking psychopath."

"Probably," he said with absolute joy, "And you know what they say about psychopaths? We're incapable of caring."

I heard a shot outside. Then more shooting and screaming. I turned toward the door and opened it. Kat looked at me, startled. "What's happening?" she said.

"He's given them all Zombie," I cried, and I turned back and saw Larsen carrying the suitcase through the door behind him. He smiled at me and then pulled the door closed. I rushed to the door, hoping I wouldn't trigger a Zombie spray, but it was locked. I tried the keys I'd taken from the desk, but none fit the lock. By then, the chaos outside had magnified. Before rushing back to the office, I put a vial of the Zombie drug in my jacket pocket.

Kat was at the office door, looking out into the courtyard. The woman at the desk was reaching into the desk drawer and pulling out a black handgun. I stepped quickly to her and hard-slapped the palm of my hand against her ear. I may have ruptured her eardrum; she instantly dropped the gun and fell out of her chair. She cried out, holding one hand to her ear, and writhed on the floor. Ruptured eardrums can cause vertigo. One way or the other, she'd be out of commission. I picked up the handgun and joined Kat at the door.

The courtyard was a scene of bedlam. Bodies lay on the ground by the picnic table, and we saw people in the courtyard firing at each other and the water tower. More gunfire came from the kitchen area behind the picnic table and from the two residences we could see. A man with wild eyes and blood flying from his mouth rushed toward our door. He fired an assault rifle in our direction. Bullets pierced the wood siding and smacked the walls behind us, and Kat reached through the door and fired three or four times before the man fell.

The gunfire continued for five or ten more minutes and then became intermittent. We heard a knock on the side of the wall beside the door. I peeked out. It was Earl. I opened the door and waved him in. He said that he'd surprised two men in the warehouse. They weren't armed, so he tied them up with duct tape. I asked about Garth and John, and Earl said they were okay. They'd taken refuge behind the suburban when the havoc began and returned fire at those who shot at them. The guy who'd met us at the gate was all right, just bewildered. When all the firing stopped for several minutes, I opened the door and yelled, "Don't drink the water. It's poisoned."

A woman holding a child with each hand, rushed toward us from a residence to our left. I opened the door for her, and they flew into the office. The woman whose ear I slapped was cowering in the corner by the desk. "Did you hear me?" I said to the women. "Don't drink the water!"

After a few more minutes, I heard John yell, "I think it's over."

Kat and I cautiously emerged from the office and ran to John and Garth behind the suburban. I said I was going back to the office building and asked Kat to stay with them. When I returned, I told Earl to follow me into Larsen's laboratory. When we arrived at his locked back door, Earl shot out the knob, and we kicked the door until it flew open. We were in a small carport with a path that led to the chain-link fence. A gate along the fence stood open, and the path continued through the defensible space into the brush and trees beyond. We looked at each other and started running down the path. It extended for several hundred yards, winding through dense vegetation, and ended at a golf cart parked in a large, graveled area. A heavy plastic tarp was crumpled to one side, weathered bungee cords still attached to the grommets. Fresh vehicle tracks led toward the road we'd come in on.

When we returned to the compound, four state troopers talked with Kat and John. The gate was up, and two ambulances were parked near it. Nine people were dead, including four shooters—the ones who drank the poisoned water. Five others were injured. The rest had hidden to avoid the insanity. Garth and John were okay, but John's suburban was shot full of holes. Fortunately, it still ran, so when the state police released us, we climbed in and headed for home. The road back to Santa Rosa was closed; the fire had overrun it. So we drove north until we could find a westward highway that took us to the Pacific Coast Highway, where we turned south. Along the way, I told them what happened with Larsen.

Kat shook her head. "I can't believe he escaped."

"It was well thought out," I said. "The golf cart was electric, so it was silent. He had a vehicle stashed where it wouldn't be seen. He'd been planning this exit for a long time. We disrupted his timetable, but his plan still worked."

"Any idea where he's gone?" John said.

"No. Arend Larsen is a ghost once again."

The Ghost

Halloween arrived a few days later. Trick-or-Treaters can't enter our building, so Kat and I dressed as his and her vampires and set up a booth on the street for passing children to score some treats. Earl dressed as himself—which was scary enough—and stood nearby in case Larsen targeted us. I didn't think that was likely. Larsen was long gone, but Earl stood back, watchful and firm, like Horatius Cocles at the Bridge.

In early December, we received notice that Sara had been officially accepted for enrollment in St. Ignacius beginning next September. Kat had an offer from the SFPD but hadn't responded until we found out about Sara's school. She and David shared custody of Sara, but David had already indicated a willingness to let her live with whichever parent she wanted. He and his new wife were preparing for the birth of their twins, and he said he would not object to Sara moving to San Francisco. She mostly lived with her mother anyway, so it would not be a big change.

We decided to have dinner that evening at Dalida, one of the city's finest Mediterranean restaurants. I had grilled oysters and pork sujuk. Kat ate durac pork cheek souvlaki. After the meal, we sat with our champagne and made the decision that would shape the rest of our lives. Kat phoned Sara to give her the good news about St. Ignacius, and it was settled. The next day, she notified Sacramento PD that she was resigning, and she accepted the position as an inspector in SFPD Homicide. We moved her things the following week, and she put her house in Sacramento on the market.

I had my knee replacement surgery just before Christmas. It was less painful or inhibiting than I thought it might be. The surgery went well, and I hired Marcie Bell to help with physical therapy. Rhoda volunteered to monitor my drug use, but I found that I didn't need pain medication beyond the first few days. I toughed it out and walked reasonably well in less than a month. I haven't swallowed an oxy since.

We still had the vial of Zombie I took from Larsen's lab in the Solace compound. Kat kept it on a shelf above her desk in what used to be my den but was now her home office. It was a reminder, she said, of a crucial unsolved case. In the weeks following our return from Solace, John, Kat, and I speculated where Larsen would go. We thought it would be in the Midwest if he remained in America. Alaska and Hawaii are too small for his human drug trials to go unnoticed. He might have gone to Asia, Africa, or South America, but they seemed less likely than him relocating to Europe, where he'd been born and might be fluent in some European languages.

How do you find a ghost? You look in places he's likely to be, following his trail from haunt to haunt, from wisps of nothing to traces vanishing in the deepening gloom of sunset, from a death scarcely mentioned in an evening edition to investigations withering through dead-end leads and frustrations. Larsen had killed in Boston and again in the Bay Area. We reasoned that his narcissism was his Achilles heel. He could not resist playing god with his potions, which fed his ego. Do wizards like Voldemort and Merlin retire? No, their nature compels them to continue performing magic. It is their ring of power, their city of gold, their aphrodisiac, and their siren song.

So we looked for traces of him.

John had contacts in Interpol, Scotland Yard, the Sûreté in France, the Cuerpo Nacional de Policia in Spain, the Carabinieri in Italy, Germany's Federal Police, and the national police forces in Belgium, Denmark, and The Netherlands. We wrote a report on Larsen, Rapture, and Zombie. We sent it to all of them, asking that they inform John if they had any unusual drug-related deaths or incidents of mass murder or violence committed by people who were not usually violent. The FBI circulated a version of our report to other police forces worldwide.

For months, the reports John received were easily dismissed; they lacked Larsen's fingerprints, so to speak, and we saw no patterns of repeated incidents. We thought it would take time for him to establish himself, acquire the chemicals and equipment he needed, and resume his drug-making operation, but as winter turned to spring and spring stretched toward summer, we had no clue where he might have landed. Mass murders did occur throughout the world. People died of drug overdoses, and new designer drugs appeared, but none bore the footprint we were looking for. Along with her SFPD investigations, Kat spent hours looking at Cosplay websites globally but found no evidence of our Wraithlan Mager. People imitating that wizard did appear in other countries at Cosplay gatherings, but photos of them bore no resemblance to Arend Larsen.

Sara graduated from 8th grade in May, and we moved her to Pacific Heights. She wanted to spend the summer getting to know and enjoy the city. Between gigs, rehearsals, and recording sessions, I took her around the city while Kat was working and enrolled her in Krav Maga classes appropriate for her age. I'd worried that living with a young teen would be challenging, but we all adapted, and I discovered that I enjoyed spending time with her.

John came to our place on a Saturday morning in late May. He, Sara, and I were going to a Giants game that afternoon. When he arrived, Kat asked him and me to join her in her office. As we sat, she pulled up a photo on her computer. It showed a rustic, tree-lined street with neat hedges in front of tidy lawns and single-story dwellings.

"What are we looking at?" I said.

"This is Loché," she said. "It's a small village in the Burgundy wine-growing region in France."

"Too rural for me," John said.

Kat smiled. "You're a city guy, John. The population of Loché and the surrounding area is about 6,300. Google Maps shows that the whole town looks pretty much like this, except for the vineyards, and there are miles of those."

John said, "Will there be a quiz after your presentation?"

"Yep," she said. "So take notes. I found a recent article in *The Local*—an English-language newspaper covering Europe. I was looking for mass murders or strange drug deaths. Instead, I found a report of an unusual number of suicides in Loché. They hadn't had a suicide there for eleven years. Then they had four on April 22nd."

"Confirmed suicides?" John said.

She nodded. "Two men. Two women. Different ages. Different parts of the village. Different methods. None had appeared suicidal or depressed before their deaths."

"Suicide notes?" I asked.

She shook her head. "I wondered if the same phenomenon had occurred elsewhere in France, so I searched newspaper archives and found an article a month earlier about an increase in the suicide rate in Paris. Their suicides were mainly among young people, and French authorities were trying to determine why this was happening. I broadened my search and looked for higher-than-normal rates of suicide in other cities. The average suicide rate in France is 13.8% per 100,000 population. But in Marseille, Avignon,

Valence, Lyon, Loché, Montbard, Paris, Lille, and London, the rate has jumped to an average of 24.9% in the last three months."

"You think it's Larsen?" John said.

"It has to be. And get this. When I checked in those cities, I found six suicides in Marseille, three in Avignon, two in Valence, four in Lyon, three in Montbard, eight in Paris, three in Lille, and seven in London—all on April 22nd."

"Holy shit," I said.

"Larsen told Sonny in Solace that he could create drugs that would make people do whatever he wanted. What if he's now created a drug that makes people so depressed they want to kill themselves?"

"Is that possible?" I wondered.

John said, "We can ask Dom Bernardi. Or Dwayne Karmagen. Now that he's been released and is back at Ceres, he might be eager to catch the guy who framed him. But if a drug can make people commit mass murder, I don't see why another drug couldn't make them suicidal."

"Any similar increases in other parts of Europe?" I asked. "Germany, Spain, Italy? Anywhere else?"

"Nope. Just around France and in London."

"Well," John said, "if it is Larsen and he's created a hari-kari drug, this still doesn't help us find him."

"I think it might," Kat said. "You know what's common about the cities I mentioned?" She paused long enough for us to feel stupid. "They're all connected by a railway line from Marseille to London."

I was confused. "But you just said that an unusual number of suicides occurred in, what, seven cities in one day?"

"Eight cities."

"If it was Larsen, how could he reach all eight cities in one day? And have time to spike people's drinks with this new drug? France is about the size of Texas."

"The railroad connecting those eight cities is a high-speed train. It goes all the way from Marseille to London in one day."

"I'm curious," said John. "Were those the only French cities with anomalous suicide rates?"

"No, after I made that connection, I kept looking and found higher rates in Reims, Lorraine, Strasbourg, Belfort-Ville, and Besancon-Viotte."

"On the same rail line?" said John.

"No," Kat said. "They're on a different railway line that loops around eastern France. The suicides occurring in those cities happened only during the first week of each of the last three months. The ones on the north-south suicide route occurred in the second and third weeks of those months."

"Nothing in the fourth week?" I said.

She shook her head. "He's poisoning people on the eastern loop during the first week of the month and those on the north-south route during the next two weeks. We don't know where he's located, but he rides those trains. The SNCF, the French national rail service, operates them."

"He could find victims at every stop," John said. "The suicides are taking place around the breadth of France and in London so that the police wouldn't see a pattern."

I patted Kat on the arm. "They don't have a superhero detective like we do."

Kat shook that off. "Just Investigating 101."

John leaned back in his chair and said, "You know anything about fireworks?"

"Only the basics," I replied. "I enjoy seeing them, like everybody else."

"I had a case once where some guys were stealing professional fireworks from a manufacturer in Texas and making bombs with them. There are different types of fireworks: aerial shells, comets, mines, cakes, Roman candles, rockets, parachutes, and others. In professional shows, they select the right kinds at the right time to create the desired effect. Every show ends with the most spectacular and extended display, so audiences are gasping at the dazzling pyrotechnics. Larsen's now made Rapture, Zombie, and Hari-Kari. Maybe more. He's building his repertoire of dazzling effects. I'll bet he's preparing for a grand finale, a spectacular display of his wizardry, maybe by adding all of them at once to a city's water supply. Imagine the clusterfuck that would cause."

"We need to find him first," I said.

"Anybody for a trip to France?" Kat said. "I've always wanted to ride their trains."

Seven of us boarded a flight to Paris two days later—Kat, me, John, Earl, Sana, and two of Sana's Armenian crew—Hovig Gregorian and Taniel Zakarian. With a long black goatee, a thick black mustache, and a perpetual smile, Hovig looked like a demented game show host. Taniel was a handsome kid with long dark hair swept over his forehead and bedroom eyes. Women did a double take when he passed them. We arrived at the Charles de Gaulle airport the next morning and spent the day recovering from an eleven-hour flight. It was the first week of June, which meant our quarry—if we were right about Larsen—would be on the train that looped around the eastern part of France.

French trains have three classes of service—standard, first, and business—which complicated our search. They don't allow passengers from one class to mingle with passengers in another class. We couldn't search an entire train individually, and 19 trains ran daily on the loop route. So we had to book one person in standard class and another in first or business, and choose from among the many daily trains. We assumed that Larsen was located in Paris and probably took the morning trains from there so we could complete the eastern and north-south routes in one day. But we didn't know which day he traveled. Sana remained in the hotel in Paris as our coordinator. Kat and I took one train, John and Earl took another, and Hovig and Taniel took the final one.

Before we left, I'd had Bao make a book of photos for us. He manipulated Larsen's image, so we had shots of him with short blond hair, long blond hair, long brown hair, short brown hair, and black hair—each with and without facial hair. We'd done our best to memorize these images of him. But with the mass of people on each of the trains, we found it hard to search for Larsen inconspicuously and keep it up for hours every day, knowing we might miss him because he'd be in a different class of service or be traveling on another train. Still, it was the best we could do, and we assumed that Kat was right about him and the hari-kari drug.

John and I were the only ones Larsen might recognize, so we wore disguises, nothing elaborate, just dark glasses and hats. We both let our beards grow and wore different clothing daily. After a few days, we knew the French second-hand stores in our neighborhood very well, and the proprietors knew us. Despite our efforts, we didn't see Larsen during an exhausting week around the loop. Much of the French countryside was charming, and when I could relax—after failing to spot Larsen in my part of the train—I found train travel enjoyable. But the charm faded after ten-to-twelve-hour days, one after the other. Then it became monotonous and discouraging. I worried that we would never find the ghost.

When the second week began, we boarded the train in Paris for London and then took the long trip to Marseille and back. We could cover even fewer of these trains because there were 24 daily. On Wednesday of that week, Sana called me and said that Hovig had spotted Larsen on the 0833 train from Paris to London. He had short blond hair and wore dark blue trousers, a red cardigan sweater, and a charcoal tweed herringbone flat cap. Kat and I had taken the 0714, so we were ahead of him. John and Earl were following Hovig on the 0942 train. We departed our train in London and awaited the arrival of the 0833. We saw several men of Larsen's age wearing red sweaters and flat caps. Then we saw Hovig and Taniel leave the train. They walked toward us on the platform, stopped, and spoke to each other. Soon, the man Hovig described left the train and walked in their direction. He was tall and slender, and his clean-shaven face looked—from a distance—very much like Larsen. After he passed them, Hovig and Taniel stepped out behind him at a discreet distance.

As I watched the man, I became convinced that if it wasn't Larsen, it was his brother. But when he reached the terminal, a young woman and two teens greeted him. *A husband and father arriving home from France*, I thought. I didn't think Larsen could have concocted a small family in so short a time. I had to be sure, so I approached the family, circled until I could see the man's face clearly, and realized it wasn't Larsen. But he was so damned close. The nose was narrower, his skin paler, the eyebrows thicker.

Disheartened, we boarded the next train for Marseille and continued the hunt. We had more close calls like that. We decided to discreetly take cell phone photos of any candidates, if feasible, and share them with others in our team. We could more quickly eliminate possibilities. I realized through that effort how alarmingly ordinary Larsen's appearance was. Hundreds of thirty-something men on those trains resembled him closely enough for us to take notice.

Then, toward the end of that week, while I was on the train from Marseille to Lyon, I sat in a window seat in first class. I'd already scanned the first-class cars and seen no candidates, so I was gazing at the now-familiar scenery outside when the conductor entered my car and began checking tickets. I glanced up at him when he was still four rows ahead, and he leaned over to examine a passenger's ticket on the opposite side of the car. Something about his profile struck me. He had short black hair and a neatly trimmed beard and mustache. He wore the dark blue uniform of SNCF conductors with a white shirt and red tie and a dark blue cap with a red band around the crown. As he turned to my side of the train, still a few rows ahead, I got a better look at his face, particularly his eyes. It was Arend Magnus Larsen, although his name tag read "Clement Faucher."

I wore a baseball cap with the emblem of OGC Nice, their French football team. I pulled it lower over my face, put on my sunglasses, and pretended to be asleep. I held my train ticket in my hand. I'd learned that if your ticket was visible, the conductors were less likely to inspect it. I sensed Larsen passing and stole a glance when he was three rows behind me. I don't know how he managed to get himself hired on the French railway system, but now I knew how he could travel so freely on the trains. I texted Kat and the others.

The others were ahead of us on earlier trains, so they waited at Paris Gare du Nord, the central railway station. Paris was the terminus of this train. We hoped that meant Larsen ending his shift. Sana met us in the terminal. I gave them Larsen's description. He might be leaving the station in uniform or civilian clothes, so we watched for both, and we split up to cover every exit from the station, including the ones reserved for employees. Kat and I positioned ourselves inside the terminal at the entrance to the Paris Métro, their subway system. It was 1735. Thirty minutes later, we saw Larsen crossing the huge lobby in a pair of slacks, a light jacket, and a beret. I turned away and texted the others while Kat watched him, pretending to read a newspaper.

As we suspected, he walked toward the escalator down to the Métro. Kat turned to follow as he descended while I texted the others. They reached the right Métro platform before Larsen's train arrived, and seven of us boarded it. Kat and I were in the car behind, John and Sana and Earl ahead, and Hovig and Taniel were in his car. We sped through the evening, stopping at over a dozen Metro stations. I saw from the route map that we were heading south. Then Taniel texted that Larsen was moving. We all exited at the Alésia station and followed Larsen into a cool evening. John, Kat, and I hung back while the others followed more closely. They did rotating surveillance—one or two walking ahead, anticipating where he might turn, the others hanging behind at staggered distances. When he turned a corner, the one behind him moved ahead, and the others rotated positions so he didn't have the same person behind him. Four streets from the Métro station, he came to a quiet residential street, and they watched him unlock the door to a five-story apartment building.

John, who spoke some French, called Uber. Five minutes later, our car pulled up. It was a dark blue Peugeot with no Taxi sign or other indication that it was for hire. Perfect. We told the driver to park on Larsen's street across from the building he entered and said we'd pay for his patience. Hovig and Taniel walked up the street, turned the corner, and waited. Sana and Earl stayed out of sight behind us. We hadn't talked about what we'd do when we found him. Kat and I were debating that in the backseat while John spoke to the driver. Fifteen minutes later, Larsen left his building, walked back toward a public square, and sat at a small table outside a *terrasse* (French for sidewalk café).

We watched him enjoy his meal and then return to his apartment. Afterward, we gathered at the Café Signes on the Rue d'Alésia and had a nice dinner and several bottles of aromatic French burgundy. It was not a bad way to spend an evening in Paris; we felt good about ourselves.

We'd found our ghost.

Chase

Kat and I were up early the following morning. We walked briskly in the cool morning air near Gare du Nord, bought coffee at a nearby kiosk, and waited. Taniel and Hovig sat in a small café near the Métro in Alésia and texted us when they saw Larsen approach the station. They boarded the car behind his and arrived at Gare du Nord at 0714. John, Earl, and Sana were positioned inside the railway station, and we watched the employee exit until Larsen left in his uniform and boarded the 0822 train for Marseille. The train schedule that day told us we had 9 hours and 14 minutes until he returned.

Sana, Hovig, and Taniel bought tickets on the Marseille train for each travel class. Sana texted us later that Larsen was working in the standard class, where Sana was seated. While our Armenian friends spent the day on the train, John and Earl returned to Alésia to prepare for their part in the drama we had planned. Kat and I spent the morning visiting the Louvre and the Tuileries Garden. We had lunch at the Ritz Paris and then toured Musée d'Orsay before taking the Métro to Alésia late afternoon.

I had arranged to meet Larsen's apartment building manager at 1700. Madame Charpentier was happy to show Kat and me the only *appartement* in the building available for seasonal rent. The owner, she said, was on an extended holiday in Quebec, where he had relatives, and would not return until September. We asked about the other tenants in the building and were assured that they were respectable and kept to themselves. While I spoke to Madame Charpentier, Kat perused the mail kiosk and found that "C. Faucher" had an apartment on the fourth floor. When I told Madame I was a musician and would need to practice my saxophone in the *appartement*, she wrinkled her face in distaste and informed me that we could not be considered. We politely thanked her and left.

When Sana texted that Larsen had returned and boarded the Métro at Gare du Nord, Kat and I were sitting at a small table outside Le Zeyer on Rue d'Alésia, sharing a bottle of Mouton-Cadet Bordeaux. Le Zeyer is located on Place Victor Et Héléne Basch, a large plaza where seven streets converge. It was centrally located three blocks from Larsen's building, so we were well-positioned to follow if he moved.

When Larsen left the Métro, Sana and Taniel followed him discreetly to his apartment. Twenty minutes later, he left, as he had the night before, and returned to the same *terrasse*. We were grateful he was a man of habits because John and Earl knew that café well. They'd spent some hours there earlier in the day. Larsen sat at a table outside. John and Kat took a table nearby, John facing away from Larsen. Taniel and Sana sat alone at tables flanking Larsen's. I watched from across the street as Larsen was served his dinner and a glass of clear liquid, probably sparkling water.

When he'd nearly finished his meal, Larsen raised a finger at the waiter who'd served him, and the waiter went back inside the café and returned with a dark green bottle. John intercepted him and unfolded a map. He told the waiter he was visiting a friend in Alésia and couldn't find his friend's residence. The waiter set down his tray and peered at John's map. Earl walked behind them and gazed around. He then nodded in my direction and walked into the cafe. John thanked the waiter and returned to Kat. I watched as the waiter refilled Larsen's glass. When the waiter returned inside, Earl bumped into his arm, and the bottle fell and broke on the floor, causing a minor disturbance. The waiter apologized to patrons as he cleaned up the broken glass. Earl sat at Sana's table, and I waited another minute before crossing the street.

Larsen was surprised when I sat in the empty chair at his table. A look of recognition crossed his face, followed by alarm, but he tried to disguise it.

"A friend recently wrote a song," I told him. "I can't sing it as well as she does, but it goes like this. You can't hide from me, baby. Can't slip my mind. Someday soon goan' find you. It don't matter where you go. Dark ain't deep enough. You can't slip me, no."

He looked like he'd been caught naked in a room where everyone else is wearing formal attire. I watched him trying to decide how to play it. He said, "*Qui êtes vous?*" he said. "*Que veux vous?*"

John appeared beside us and said, "He's asking who you are."

"He knows who I am," I said, staring into Larsen's eyes. I did not doubt that this man was Larsen, but his eyes confirmed it. The soulless mirth behind those eyes said I was looking at a psychopath.

Larsen looked at John and then back at me. Considering his options. "Veuillez m'excuser," he said. He reached into his pocket and dropped some French francs on the table. Then he started to stand. Sana and Earl immediately stood to his right, and Taniel and Hovig to his left.

"I didn't come alone," I told Larsen. "You're not going anywhere."

He slowly sat back down, but his eyes were working the problem hard. Running was not an option, but he knew we couldn't arrest him or harm him publicly. There were too many witnesses. I wondered what options he thought he had.

"My friends and I debated what to do with you when we found you."

He stared at me with increasing intensity.

"You should return with us. You need to answer for those deaths in Boston and the ones in California. We have enough evidence to put you away forever, and it would give families there closure."

He glanced at my compatriots at nearby tables and then back at me.

"Or we could turn you over to the French police. They'd be intrigued by what they found in your apartment when they searched it. You've been poisoning French and British citizens with a drug that compels them to commit suicide. The authorities would not look favorably upon that."

His lips moved, and I thought he might speak, but he kept silent and looked defiantly at me.

"But you are a master of escape and evasion. If we turn you over to the authorities, we can't guarantee you won't make bail and disappear again. And I'm tired of chasing you, Larsen. Or Frye, or Faucher, or whoever you are this week. No, the only solution we found was to end it here. Tonight."

I reached into my front pocket and removed the vial of Zombie I'd been saving for this moment. I set it on the table. "You left this behind in your getaway from Solace. I brought it for you."

His eyes widened, and he said, "I'm not drinking that."

I leaned toward him and gave him a steely look. "You already have."

Blood drained from his face as he studied his glass of sparkling water.

"Never trust a chef who won't eat his own cooking," I said.

Doubt played across his face—and then panic.

"A friend distracted the waiter while another poured the drug into the water bottle the waiter used to refill your glass. That bottle was broken, so no one else will drink from it."

"You're lying," he said.

"In a moment, your eyes will start to burn. You'll feel irritable and then angry."

"I should have killed you."

"You tried," I said. "The rage will come quickly. You'll try to control it, but you can't. You'll pick up that knife by your plate and slash at everyone around you. You'll be consumed by hatred and uncontrollable violence."

I rose, and John and I backed slowly away. He glared at me with a mouth turning downward, his face growing more flushed. He clenched the tablecloth and fought to maintain control.

"My friend called the police," I told him. "He reported a terrorist at this *terrasse*."

As we heard sirens approaching, we saw Larsen grow increasingly agitated. John shouted to other diners and people on the sidewalk, *"Terroriste. Sors d'ici. Maintenant! Terroriste."* Terrorist. Get out of here. Now!"

People were confounded for only a moment before they rose and scrambled away. Four armed police arrived seconds later, and John pointed at the lone diner still sitting outside. Larsen pounded the table, his angry eyes darting around the crowd, seeking an outlet for his rage. Spit flew from his mouth as he jumped up, grabbed the knife, and plunged toward the crowd. The police drew their guns and ordered Larsen to stop, but he wouldn't stop, couldn't stop, and as he rushed them, knife raised, they fired.

The scene quickly became chaotic as people fled into the public space and disrupted traffic. More police arrived, blue lights flashing on their cars. John called his contact at the *Sûreté Nationale*, and investigators arrived within a quarter-hour while the uniformed police managed the crime scene, covered Larsen's body, and restored order. John told his counterpart in the *Sûreté* about Larsen's apartment and what they'd likely find there. That night, after they obtained a warrant, investigators found Larsen's lab, his CRISPR and chemical apparatus, source chemicals, and 2.7 kilograms of Zombie, Rapture, and Hari-Kari, along with other drug compounds Larsen had numbered and whose functions were unknown. They also found a Wraithlan Mager costume. John copied Larsen's computer files onto a thumb drive before the French police impounded his computer.

The *Sûreté* and Scotland Yard found the elevated suicide patterns suspicious and were able to link them to Larsen's travels on SCNF trains. Most of the victims had been cremated, but seven bodies remained, and five of those had traces of the Hari-Kari drug in their systems. The authorities concluded—but could not prove—that most of the suicide victims had probably received Larsen's drug. Time will tell if the average suicide rates in the affected cities return to normal.

John, Kat, and I spent the following day writing a report on how we located Larsen. We said we weren't sure why Larsen became maniacal at the café, but we believed that, once he knew he was trapped, he'd given himself a dose of Zombie, knowing the police were likely to shoot him. In effect, his death was due to "suicide by cop." John shared that report with *Sûreté* investigators, and we sent it to Paul Fisher in SFPD. Paul conferred with his Paris counterparts and was able to close the case.

Kat and I decided to spend a few more days in Paris. John informed us that he, Earl, and the Armenians were on their way to Baku, the capital of Azerbaijan. He said they had unfinished business there. After they left, Kat and I spent three wonderful days exploring the French capital, doing everything tourists do. We were grateful not to be traveling on trains ten hours a day. Strolling through museums, visiting Notre Dame, and enjoying each other's company was pleasant.

A week after we returned home, John Sebastiani came for dinner at our condo. His left arm was in a cast. He told us he'd broken it in Baku and had to return to France to have the arm properly set. We didn't ask how he'd broken it. He just said that Ari was under no further threat. I asked him what happened to the drugs seized at Solace and in Larsen's apartment in Paris.

"I've been told that all of Larsen's drugs, formulas, and papers have been sent to USAMRICD, that's the U.S. Army Medical Research Institute of Chemical Defense. It's in Aberdeen, Maryland. The worst stuff in the world is stored there."

"What do they do?" Kat asked.

"They study chemical weapons and try to develop countermeasures against them."

"Do they have an offensive role in the use of chemical weapons?" I asked.

"Ostensibly, no."

"There's a treaty against using chemical weapons, right?" Kat asked.

"Sure," John said. "But there are bad actors everywhere, and secrets are hard to keep. Iraq used chemical weapons. We believe Syria, Libya, and North Korea have, too, although we don't have proof. Russia used cluster munitions and vacuum bombs in Ukraine. Imagine a future war where one of the combatants flies drones over enemy territory, spraying Zombie and Hari-Kari in aerosol form over enemy troops. Half of those troops would kill themselves, and the other half would kill each other."

"Easy way to win a war," Kat said.

John nodded. "It would be very tempting to use those drugs if you have them."

"I asked Bai Tuo Rong to search the dark web for any evidence of Larsen's formulas," I told them. "So far, he hasn't found anything."

"That doesn't mean it's not there," Kat said.

I nodded. "Larsen may yet be the architect of enormous human suffering. This genie is out of the bottle. They may not be able to put it back in."

About the Author

Terry R. Bacon is a poet, playwright, and award-winning author of over a dozen books, including *The Elements of Power, Elements of Influence,* and *What People Want. Executive Excellence* named him one of the Top 100 Thinkers on Leadership in the World. He has a Ph.D. in Literary Studies from the American University and a B.S. in Engineering from West Point. A world traveler, he now resides in the mountains of Colorado. He was the sax player in a rock band in his youth and today plays the alto and tenor saxophone, guitar, and baritone ukulele. He studies history and cosmology in his spare time and is an active blogger when he is not working on another writing project. *Storm Warning* was the first in his Sonny Marshall series. Storm Damage is the sequel. He also published a science fiction novel, *The Cerulean Ark*, in 2024.